PURSUIT OF THE HAWK

Book Five in the Pantracia Chronicles

PURSUIT OF THE HAWK

Amanda Muratoff & Kayla Hansen

www.Pantracia.com

This book is a work of fiction. Names, characters, businesses, organizations, places, events and incidents either are the product of the authors' imagination or are used fictitiously. Any resemblance to actual persons, living or dead, events, or locales is entirely coincidental.

Cover design by Andrei Bat.

ISBN: 978-1-990781-06-3

Third Edition: February 2024

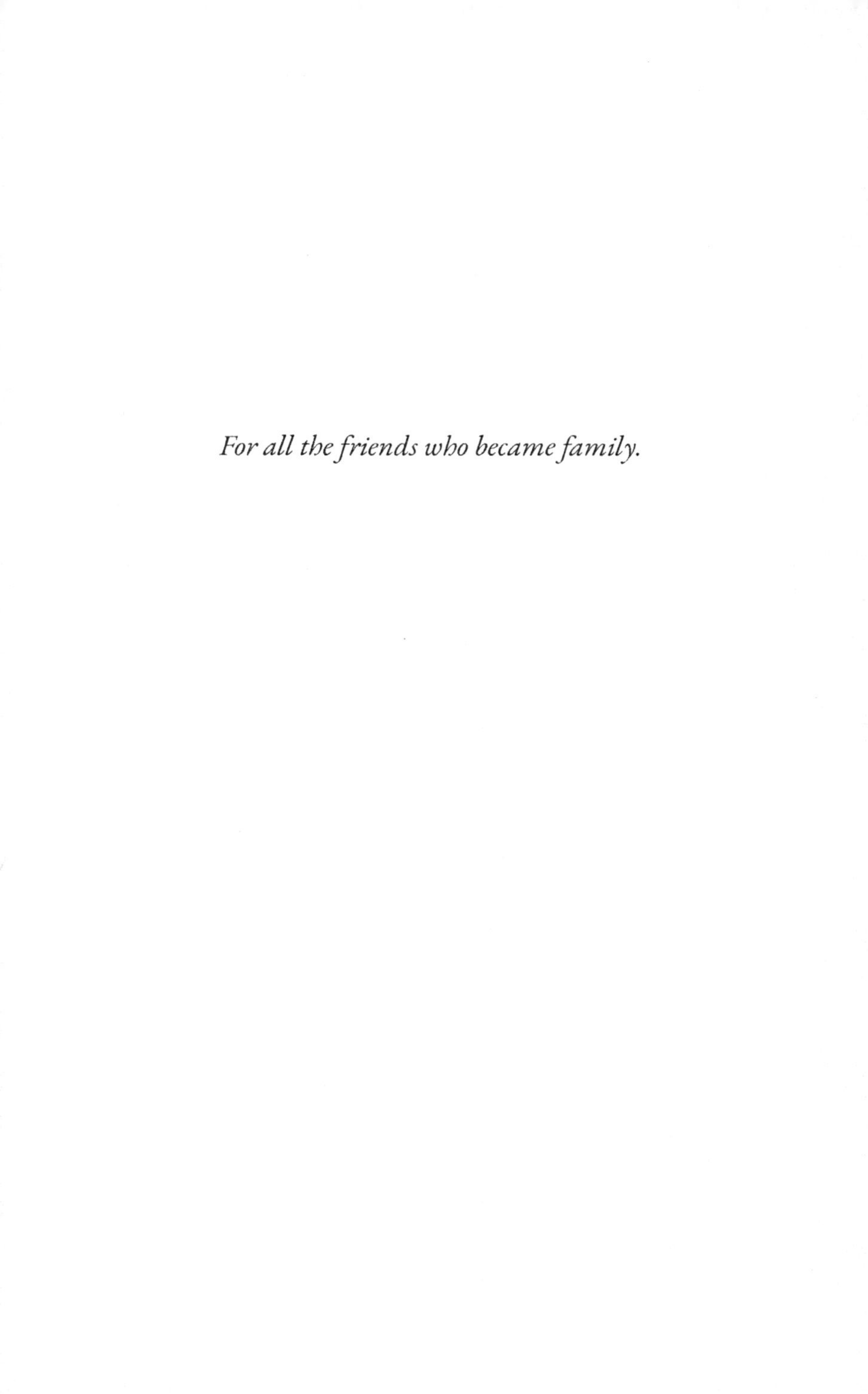

For all the friends who became family.

The Pantracia Chronicles:

Prequel:
Dawn of the Thieves

Part 1: The Berylian Key
Book 1: *Embrace of the Shade*
Book 2: *Blood of the Key*
Book 3: *Unraveling of the Soul*

Part 2: A Rebel's Crucible
Book 4: *Ashes of the Rahn'ka*
Book 5: *Pursuit of the Hawk*
Book 6: *Heart of the Wolf*
Book 7: *Rise of the Renegades*

Part 3: Shadowed Kings
Book 8: *Sisters of the Frozen Veil*
Book 9: *Wings of the Eternal War*
Book 10: *Axiom of the Queen's Arrow*

Part 4: The Vanguard Legacy
Book 11: *Daughter of the Stolen Prince*
Book 12: *Fate of the Dae'Fuirei*
Book 13: *Oath of the Six*

Visit www.Pantracia.com for our pronunciation guide and to discover more.

Chapter 1

Autumn, 2609 R.T. (recorded time)

DAMIEN WOKE, GASPING. HE TOUCHED the bed beside him, but found it empty. Dread built in his stomach, intensified by the voices pressing against his barrier.

Did they wake me?

"Dice?" He looked around the darkened room, streaks of sunlight illuminating the floor through the cracks in the shutters.

Rolling over to the edge of the bed, he cried out as his weight crushed his injured arm. A shudder passed down his body, eliciting goosebumps on his already clammy skin. With clenched teeth, he inspected his burn and the bandage that had yet to be changed.

Sometimes Rae accomplished the feat while he slept.

Where is she?

"Rae?" Damien stood, cool morning air nipping at his exposed body as he tiptoed over to his clothes, still strewn on the floor. Finding his pants, he frowned as he crouched to arrange them to make it easier to pull them on with one arm.

After buckling his belt, he stilled, listening for any noise from downstairs. When he heard no evidence that the Ashen Hawks were in the building, he shook his head.

Maybe she went to get bandages. Or is spending time with Jarrod.

His blood heated while considering the tall, dark-skinned thief spending time with her alone. Chest tight, he eyed the unlocked door before glaring at his boots.

Not worth it.

Pulling his shirt on while barely able to move his arm led to sweat beading on his forehead. He huffed, biting down on his lip to contain his whimpers. He'd been too rough on it the night before, though the time with Rae was well worth the extra discomfort.

I have other ways to sense where she is.

Damien inhaled deeply, closing his eyes, and let his Art seek her ká. Distance hardly mattered and the energies would guide his internal compass. Every ká vibrated at a unique frequency, and he knew Rae's intimately. Especially after a night together.

When he found nothing, his ká echoed hollowly in his chest. Anxiously, he sought confirmation of his power, and blue-white mist flickered between his fingers, brightening the room in a flash.

That's odd. Why can't I feel her?

He tried again.

Rae's ká didn't echo back to him.

Fear wafted through him. In a rush, he tried the next person he thought of. He'd met Jarrod briefly, but remembered the way his energy vibrated. It took longer than he wished to seek it out and when he felt it, his stomach dropped out.

Even from a distance, he recognized Jarrod's soul fighting to free itself from his physical body, seeking to pass into Nymaera's afterlife. Yondé had forced him to memorize the feeling during his intense Rahn'ka training.

Jarrod's dying.

Damien's eyes shot open, panic flooding his veins.

Rae.

Had she died, and he'd been too busy sleeping to notice?

Damien tore the door open, his bare feet thundering down the stairs of the inn as he raced to the exit.

"Hey!" Braka, one of Jarrod's Hawks, stood from his table but made no move to stop him.

The bells on the door clattered as Damien jumped over the stairs of the front porch, squinting in the blinding morning light.

Following the thin thread of Jarrod's life, he sprinted through Porthew. He ran as fast as he could, fear numbing his injuries.

Townsfolk shouted as he whipped past them, dislodging packages in their arms when he pushed them out of his way.

As he exited the city through the open gate, the sickening scent of blood struck him. The metallic odor hung heavily in the air and he skidded to a stop on the quiet dirt road outside the city's wall.

Jarrod lay across the walkway, crimson pooled beneath him.

Damien collapsed beside his body, scanning the area, but the thief was alone. The disturbed dirt around them suggested a struggle, but none of the townsfolk investigated.

He searched wildly with his senses for anything alive in the open meadow beside the lonely path, anyone who might have seen what happened. In his frantic search, he found nothing. Not even Jarrod's soul. He looked down, seeing nothing but the husk of the man he'd decided to hate, staring blankly at the sky.

"No..." Damien shook Jarrod by the collar. "You're not dead."

He choked in a breath, gagging on the acrid scent of death. Setting his jaw, he considered something he'd only read about and thought he'd never attempt.

I can't let him be dead.

Tearing the bandage on his injured hand with his teeth, he ripped it off. Damaged or not, he needed the skin exposed.

Dragging Jarrod's body with a huff, he pulled the man's head into his lap. With a quick glance towards the city gate, he breathed a sigh of relief that no one had followed him.

This won't end well if I'm interrupted.

Wincing, he pushed his burned hand against the side of Jarrod's head, touching his blood-stained temple. He ensured his blistered palm fully contacted the thief's skin, unable to feel it. He placed his good hand on the other side and closed his eyes.

Damien's ká roared to life, adrenaline exciting the power, and it almost ran without him. He didn't hesitate, despite disliking the concept of expelling the entirety of his soul from his body.

Reaching towards where Jarrod's energy should have been, he grabbed the threads still connected to the dead body and dove to follow them.

The world around him blurred and the sensation of falling into perfect darkness left him dizzy.

Just as the ancient texts instructed, he held his breath as icy water surged around him. It tugged on his clothes like a thousand greedy hands as he plummeted through it, still following the wake of Jarrod's departing soul. The pressure built, popping his ears before everything halted.

When Damien opened his eyes, he couldn't tell where he was.

Night enveloped his surroundings, lit by a dim crescent moon. Red brick walls lined a long, wide corridor with pillars on either side. Hunched shadows moved between them, barely visible.

A dirt floor softened Damien's steps, even though an inch of water covered the surface.

As each shadowed figure moved, they made no sound. The water didn't even ripple under their steps.

Damien looked behind him, and a glimmer of light passed over one of their faces. He recognized one of Jarrod's thugs, but the man didn't see him. No soul existed within the Hawk's fathomless black eyes. Energy radiated from everything at the same dull thrum. Like he was looking at a painting rather than an actual person. A replica created by Jarrod's ká as it waited for what came next.

Looking ahead, in the direction the thieves traveled, a feminine hand poked out from under a black cloak. Two fingers motioned forward and everyone moved ahead to the next pillar.

"Sika." Jarrod's voice echoed from somewhere ahead.

The signaling figure crossed the corridor, crouched. "What?" Rae's voice hit Damien like a stone to the stomach. Her face turned into a thin moonbeam, her eyes black like the others'.

"Are you sure this is the right entrance?" Jarrod whispered. "There's no guard."

Without warning, the world swirled around Damien and he crouched to maintain his balance, swallowing the bile rising in his throat.

"He broke my guard." A younger version of Jarrod hefted a lance up under his arm, panting. He sat, clad in silver armor, on a muscled grey stallion much like the ones Damien's family bred.

Damien staggered to his feet, unable to jump out of the way as a squire sprinted through him. The chilling sensation threatened to knock him over again, but he caught himself in time to examine the older nobleman approaching.

"Keep the tip up. Unseat him and finish this."

The squire traded out the lance for a new one, and the adolescent Jarrod grunted as he hoisted it into position beneath his arm.

What made him leave this life to become a thief?

"Jarrod." Damien walked in front of the horse, but no one turned to look at him. The chill of the water covering the dirt crept up his calves, icy against his skin. Looking at the waiting challenger across the arena, the water shimmered like a mirage in the sunlight.

"He's better than me."

"No room for doubt, son."

A trumpet sounded and Jarrod pulled down his helmet's visor.

Jarrod's father backed up, and the young thief spurred his horse forward.

Damien jumped out of the way, spinning to watch the match.

He eyed the water lapping at his knees.

We don't have time for this.

Hooves thundered, and Jarrod kept his lance parallel to the ground. The crowd cheered as the opponents neared each other.

The challenger's lance struck first, hitting Jarrod in the chest, and again the world shifted.

Damien braced himself as the surroundings blurred, holding onto the thread of Jarrod's consciousness to guide him to the next location.

Opening his eyes, he blinked to adjust his eyes to the interior space, daylight filtering through the thin curtains of a glassless window. Surrounding it, fancy, different-colored arrows decorated a wall, with wanted posters beneath them of various faces.

A breeze rippled the fabric at the window, lending Damien a glimpse of the surrounding city.

Mirage.

Damien had served in the desert city within Helgath and his heart leapt, suddenly homesick.

Not real.

He tightened his right hand into a fist, looking down to see his unscathed arm.

How didn't I notice that before?

He turned away from the window, finding two figures in the room with him.

Jarrod stood strong as Rae pushed him in the chest. "Answer me." She breathed hard, grabbing his leather vest. "You can't just tell me it won't work and then fall silent. What do you mean?"

Her blackened eyes stared at Jarrod, her hair done in typical intricate braids, but shorter than he remembered. She wore a tight corset, with a sleeveless shirt beneath it tucked into her pants, cut just below the knee. Sweat beaded on her collarbone.

Damien stood within arm's reach of Jarrod's back and forced himself to look away from Rae. It wasn't really her, but Jarrod's ká manifesting a version of her that felt too personal. The floor tiles rippled beneath the rising water. His feet chilled, like he walked in snow, even though boots protected his feet. The water surged, pushing against his thighs. He couldn't get pulled into the illusion.

I'm in as much danger as Jarrod if I stay.

"Rae, I love you, but I can't keep pretending." Jarrod rubbed the back of his neck.

Rae exhaled a shaky breath. "What are you talking about?" She shoved him again, but it didn't move him. "How can you be so different today, when yesterday..." Her voice trailed off, and Jarrod shook his head. She took a step closer, but he put his hand out and braced it against her collar, stopping her.

"It was a mistake. I can't be with you like this."

"Why?" Rae touched the thief's wrist.

"It's complicated."

Damien winced, familiar with Rae's dislike for the phrase.

Rae backed up, her jaw flexing. "Is that all?"

Jarrod shook his head, stepping after her, but she backed up again. "No, it's not. Can you stay and let me explain?"

The water pulsed against Damien's hips. Urgency rose in his veins, and he gripped the man's shoulder. "Jarrod. Come on, we've got to get you out of here."

The thief spun, dark eyes narrowing on him. "Damien?" He glanced back at where Rae had stood a moment before, but the vision had vanished in the interruption.

"Let's go. This isn't real."

"What are you doing here?" Jarrod backed away from him. The water around him sloshed for the first time and he looked down in confusion.

"I came to get you. And I don't have a lot of time to explain. You'll have to trust me."

"I don't think you should be here. This is Rae's..." Jarrod cupped the liquid in his hands, letting it drain out between his fingers. His eyes hardened as he looked back up at Damien. "I'm dead, aren't I?"

Damien placed his hands firmly on both of Jarrod's shoulders. "Yes. But if you listen to everything I'm about to ask you to do, I can take you back. I need to know what happened to Rae."

Jarrod looked down at his side, where red spread over his clothing. The fabric ripped, showing the stabs in flesh that mirrored the damage to his physical body. Blood dripped to the water, tainting the clear liquid. "Rae... She's pissed. I should have told her sooner."

"That doesn't matter right now." Damien gave him another shake. "Rae won't stay mad, you know that. And if you really love her, then you need to listen and come with me."

The cold nipped at his waist and Damien fought the urge to pull himself out of the water alone.

Jarrod's gaze locked on Damien's. "I'm listening."

"Take my hand. You will feel a tug. It will feel like I'm ripping your arm out of its socket, but you can't let go. Hold on to me. I can't do this by myself, got it?" Damien watched his eyes for understanding. "We're going to pass through some water and it's important that you don't take a single breath. Even if your lungs will explode. You can't breathe any of the water or a part of you will be stuck here."

Jarrod nodded once, taking Damien's hand. "I'm ready."

Damien offered a dry smirk. "You're not, but it's as good as we'll get. Close your eyes. The Inbetween will try to hold on to you."

Seeking the tether he had carefully laid with pieces of his soul during entry to the Inbetween, Damien closed his eyes and gripped Jarrod's hand. He urged the Art to flow through him, snaking up the stream of energy until the cold water barrier between worlds bit his skin.

Jarrod's grip faltered for an instant before locking down.

With a gasp of fresh air, Damien's eyes shot open. Blades of Olsa grass drifted in the autumn breeze, the stench of blood returning to his nose.

The thief wheezed in a breath. Rolling onto his side, he struggled for air, body trembling.

Wisps of steam rose from their bodies.

Sitting up from the pool of blood, Jarrod coughed and gaped at Damien. He touched his side, pulling on the fabric to expose unmarred flesh. "What in the hells *are* you?"

"It's a long story." Forcing himself to his feet left Damien out of breath and he cringed, cradling his injured arm. "And it doesn't matter as much as what the hells happened to you and Rae."

Jarrod looked around, his chest still heaving. Hauling himself to his feet, the thief cursed under his breath. "They have Rae. They took her."

Damien narrowed his eyes. "They who?"

Jarrod ran his hands over his bloody hair, brow knitted. With wide eyes, he turned a fiery gaze on Damien. "But they wanted *you*."

"Helgath? There's no way they would have found me here unless you said something." He took a step towards Jarrod, despite the lethargy in his muscles.

Hand clenched into a fist, Jarrod's jaw worked. "They killed me because I wouldn't tell them where you were. Don't you dare accuse me of bringing the Helgathian scum."

"I brought you back. So that makes us even."

"Even?" Jarrod growled. "I just watched my closest ally take a beating for you. Where were you? Sleeping?" He snatched his dirk up from the ground, sliding it into his belt.

"You're talking about the woman I love. I wish she would have just told them! I'd trade myself for her safety in a heartbeat."

Jarrod laughed. "Then they'd have you, and Rae and I would be permanently dead." Turning, he stalked towards the city gate.

Damien followed. "If they figure out what she's capable of, they won't kill her. They'll take her to the academies."

Under the gate's archway, Jarrod turned to Damien. "What are you talking about?"

Damien might have smirked if he wasn't so damned angry. "I don't understand why Rae didn't just use the Art to get free."

And why I can't feel her if she's alive.

"All right, fine. I'll just *pretend* I know what you're talking about." Jarrod's jaw flexed as he looked back up the dirt path.

"They put cuffs on her almost immediately. She recognized one of them. A guy who looked like he'd had an unfortunate encounter with a lightning bolt. Rynalds, I think."

Damien's heart dropped into his stomach. He couldn't come up with a colorful enough curse and growled, clenching his fists. All he could think about was getting back to the inn, grabbing their things, and chasing after her.

If Rynalds survived...

"That bolt should have killed him." Damien spun to walk past Jarrod into the city. "And Rae caused it. He must have put together that both of us have the Art if he knew to use repression cuffs. And he'd know going after Rae is a good way to get to me."

Jarrod scowled, following. "Seems foolish to let a man like that live."

"His ship is on the bottom of the ocean, so forgive me for thinking that'd do the trick."

As they entered the inn, Braka rose from his seat, a loaf of bread in his hands. "Boss, you all right?" Wide eyed, he crossed the room to his superior.

Jarrod nodded. "Death, apparently, isn't permanent."

Damien stomped towards the stairs. "Don't get used to it."

Chapter 2

"WHAT IS YOUR *PROBLEM*?" JARROD wheeled around on Damien.

I don't care if he brought me back from the dead, I ain't putting up with this shit.

Braka's free hand moved to his hilt, the other pushing the bread further into his mouth.

Damien ignored the big thief, facing Jarrod. "*You're* my problem. I'm going after Rae and you better not get in my way."

Veck entered the tavern, sporting a swollen jaw and a black eye from the night before. He paused in the doorway, narrowing his eyes. "What happened to you? Where's Sika?" He looked sideways at Jarrod. "If she's gone, does that mean the bounty's no longer off-limits?"

Braka's gaze joined Veck's, staring at Jarrod, waiting for a verdict.

Jarrod crossed his arms at Damien's glare, resisting the temptation to take his frustration out on the deserter. "I'm fine, it's not my blood. We need him. Rae's been taken by Helgath and I'm going after her too."

Veck and Braka exchanged looks. "Are we going with you, boss?"

"No," Jarrod and Damien barked in unison.

"Get Melner. Go back to Mirage, report, and send scouts to help find her." Jarrod never turned away from Damien. "Use Lucca if you have to."

Braka shivered. "That woman gives me the creeps."

Jarrod scowled. "Her visions have helped the guild more times than I can possibly count. And she's married to Sarth's brother, so watch yourself."

Braka lifted his palms up in surrender.

"So does this mean you twos are goin' together?" Veck looked back and forth between the opposing men.

"I don't need your help." Damien kept glaring at Jarrod. "I'll find her on my own."

Jarrod's stomach heated with anger and before Damien could pull back, he clamped a hand around the deserter's bandaged bicep.

Damien cried out, grimacing as his knees buckled beneath him. He fell back against a table as he tore from Jarrod's hand. "Asshole."

Jarrod stepped towards him. "I don't get why you're so childish over a little help. Besides, you can't stop me from going after her."

"I think he wants her back," Veck whispered to Braka.

Jarrod shot him a glare. "Why the hells are you still here? I told you to go!"

Braka and Veck exchanged another look before hurrying from the tavern.

"Even your underlings question your motivations for being so damned protective of Rae." Damien heaved himself to his feet. "I don't need your help."

Jarrod sighed. "Is your pride more important than her life?" He tilted his head. "Last I checked, motivations didn't matter. You want to find her alive or not?"

"Of course I do." Damien's tone softened. He touched his arm where Jarrod had squeezed it and winced.

Jarrod withdrew the package of gauze Rae had purchased from a pouch at his belt and threw it at Damien.

He snatched it from the air with his good hand, peering at it with a questioning glance at Jarrod.

"Go on, re-wrap it. If you can do it without help, I won't bother tagging along."

"Fuck that." Damien glowered. "I won't give you the pleasure of watching me try. Fine. I need your help. Does that give you validation?"

"Validation?" Jarrod rolled his eyes. "I wanted to give you the benefit of the doubt, seeing as Rae cares about you, but gods, I can't see why. You want to sit here arguing, wasting time, while she gets farther and farther away."

Damien grumbled under his breath. "We'll need some horses."

Jarrod stalked over to the bar and slung a pack over his shoulder. "Oh really? I thought we'd just walk."

Damien huffed and went up the stairs.

Alone, Jarrod let out a sigh. His knees shook, and he sank onto a chair.

Gods, Rae, what have you gotten yourself into?

Worry wracked through him and he put his face in his hands with his elbows on his knees. Exhaling an unsteady breath, he stood and looked at his blood-soaked attire. "Shit." He dropped his pack again before venturing into the kitchen to find something to clean up with.

Yanking off his black shirt, he tossed it aside. He used a wet rag to wipe his skin before dampening his hair. Leaning against the kitchen counter, he slammed his fist down and squeezed its edge until his muscles burned.

I should have stopped them from taking her.

A lump formed in his throat, and he swallowed.

Looking up, his gaze met Damien's through the doorway into the dining room. He straightened, letting go of the counter, his knuckles aching. Erasing the guilt from his face, he exited the kitchen and returned to his pack. He rubbed the tattoo on his upper arm, three knives with curved feathers weaving between them.

From inside his pack, Jarrod retrieved a spare black shirt and pulled it on. A black leather vest followed, but he left it unlaced at the front to hang open.

"So the tattoo's an Ashen Hawks thing. I've seen Rae's, but she has an—"

"Arrow. Aye, it's a *Hawks* thing." Heat lingered in his tone, and he tried to calm it. "She's skilled with her bow, as I'm sure you've noticed."

"I have." Damien eyed Jarrod, shifting the pack on his shoulder. He'd stuffed the laces of his boots inside, apparently unable to tie them. His shirt was messily tucked, a pouch secured at his side.

Jarrod motioned to Damien's boots and cocked an eyebrow. "You're content to travel like that?"

Damien glanced down and shrugged. "We'll be on horses. I'm not about to ask you to tie my boots for me. It'll be hard enough to ask you to help with the bandage later."

"Suit yourself." Jarrod walked to the front door. "If we can't pick up a trail, we should go to Mirage." He didn't wait for Damien to answer before stepping outside.

"You mean to your guild." Damien caught up, the inn door slamming behind them. "To thieves who'd like to turn me in without a second thought."

"That's the one."

"Forgive my reservations. I can believe *you* would listen to Rae, but would the entire guild be willing to let my reward go? I don't even know what the bounty is anymore."

"Fifty gold crowns," Jarrod said without missing a beat. "That doesn't take into account your new skill in the Art, either."

Damien let out a low whistle. "Gods. Maybe I owe you more credit for saying I'm off-limits to the rest of your crew."

Jarrod stopped, spinning to face Damien. "You may believe that *honor among thieves* is just a bunch of bullshit, but Rae is the closest thing to family I'll ever have and I don't care if they're offering a thousand gold crowns for your capture... I'd *never* do that to *her*."

"Because she says she loves me? That's all it took?"

"That's *all*? I've never heard her say those words about anyone, so yeah, that's all it takes."

Damien hesitated for a moment, pursing his lips. "Other than you, you mean. She's said she loves *you*, too."

Jarrod sighed. "And that threatens you, I suppose?"

"Should it not?"

No, it shouldn't.

The deserter frowned. "Look, I'm trying my damnedest to

overlook your obvious relationship. For Rae."

"Try harder." Jarrod continued towards the stables at the edge of town. "You're so stuck in the leaves, you can't see the forest." He didn't want to explain why he and Rae would never be more than friends. They wouldn't be a couple again, but she meant the world to him. If Damien couldn't understand that, then Jarrod refused to waste his breath explaining something that was none of his business.

Damien followed silently behind. The man may have saved his life, but since he'd 'died' protecting him, Jarrod refused to give him too much credit.

Another thought crossed the thief's mind, but he kept walking. "You said Rae has ability in the Art. Tell me what happened."

"Considering how many times it manifested before she even knew she had it, I'm sure you've seen it too. Have you ever noticed a time when Rae was in danger, or afraid, and something unusual occurred? Like a storm out of nowhere or a fire suddenly growing?"

Jarrod furrowed his brow, remembering how thunder had clapped over the inn when Rae demanded the Hawks break off. "It poured when they hung Theo," he whispered, swallowing back the memory of the young recruit dangling from Helgathian gallows. "I've never seen it rain so hard in the desert. Rivers flooded the streets."

"Based on that, I can tell Rae cared for Theo, though I

haven't heard of him before." He frowned. "Her power manifests in the weather because of her emotions. The Art is linked to them in all practitioners. It must have been dormant because of her auer blood, keeping her safe from Helgathian Reapers."

Jarrod recalled several moments where fire roared or wind howled, and the way one of her eyes had a tendency to shift to a lighter hue.

I'd always assumed that was an auer trait.

"Rynalds knows what she is. He's seen her power. They'll be smart and keep her cuffed. And they'll be cruel."

Clearing the lump in his throat, Jarrod nodded. "Rae is smart. If she gets a chance, they'll all fall, power or no power."

They were silent again as they arrived at the stable.

"Who's Theo?"

Jarrod ignored the question and approached the stable master, busy loading hay off a wagon. "We need to buy two of your best horses."

The man looked up from his pitchfork before stabbing it into the pile and leaning on it. "Best for what? Pulling? Riding?"

"Riding." Jarrod eyed Damien walking towards the fence lining the paddocks. "Fast, calm, and well-trained."

Damien clicked his tongue, holding out his hand, and the horses in the paddock all turned their heads, ears swiveling in his direction.

The stable master watched Damien for a moment before speaking. "I'd recommend Orion, the white gelding over there, and Nestor, the Palomino." He motioned to the two horses.

"What about the pinto?" Damien glanced at them.

The stable master eyed the mentioned horse, whose tail swished anxiously, standing apart from the group. "That's Xyphir. He's fast as hells, but still green. Bucks off my best trainers."

Damien braced his good hand on top of the fence, lifting himself over to plop onto the other side.

"I don't think that's a wise idea..." The stable master straightened, eyes on Damien.

Jarrod waved a hand to assuage the man's concern. "How much?"

Xyphir eyed Damien, shaking his mane and snorting as Damien lifted a hand.

Damien stopped, but kept his palm open, waiting.

Xyphir took a step forward a moment later, giving another snort before he pushed his head into Damien's hand.

Damien stepped closer, rubbing all the way up the pinto's nose, tracing the black patch down the side of his head. Leaning his forehead against the horse's, he patted the horse's neck.

"Well, I'll be." The stable master wiped his forearm over his brow.

After agreeing on a price, Jarrod added tack to the list and paid the man.

When Damien turned to walk across the paddock, Xyphir followed without a lead. The horse stiffened but remained still as Damien lifted the purchased saddle with one arm.

Jarrod hopped over the fence, pausing next to Damien to hold the sliding saddle in place for Damien to cinch it with one hand. Once finished, he let go to tack Orion. "You always such a show-off?" He scoffed. "Let me guess, you talk to horses too?"

"Something like that." Damien grinned, glancing over at Jarrod as he buckled the bridle. "I also grew up around them."

Jarrod laughed. "So did I, but I never learned how to tame a wild one by just standing there. And don't try to convince me that's all there was to it." He eyed Damien, leading Orion out of the paddock.

Damien chuckled, tossing his pack over the saddle before following. "It's complicated."

Jarrod rolled his eyes. "You'd better not use that half-ass explanation with Rae, she'd hate it."

"Oh, she does." Damien smirked. "And I think I know the origin of her distaste now." He cast a sideways glance at Jarrod.

Jarrod frowned, wishing he hadn't relived breaking Rae's heart.

It's even worse that Damien saw it.

Damien pulled himself onto his saddle, settling in while

Xyphir shifted. A gentle pat stilled the horse.

After securing his pack, Jarrod followed suit. With a nod to the stable master, who still gaped at Damien, he nudged Orion forward.

Jarrod rolled his shoulders as they rode side by side through the gate towards the road out of Porthew. "Theo was a Hawk. A recent recruit. He was young, but I don't know his exact age. Too young to be in a noose. Rae led the crew that night and a call she made caused some complications. She blames herself for his capture and subsequent death after we failed to free him before he broke protocol and confessed." He looked over and met Damien's gaze. "It's why she left the Hawks. I didn't hear from her until she wrote to me about you."

"I can't blame her for wanting to learn more about a deserter, especially considering the bounty. I probably seemed like an easy mark when we first met. Hells, she broke me *out* of jail just to turn me in herself." He glanced down at the saddle, fishing into his pack.

Jarrod smiled. "Sounds like her all right. She probably stole your coin while she did it, too. Always showing off."

"Certainly kept me with her at first." Damien pursed his lips as he continued to search, sounding distracted. "Then I think we both got attached. Now it's so much more than that."

"Rae doesn't *get attached*," Jarrod muttered. "She's too fenced off for that. If anything, she loved you from the start."

Damien gave up on whatever he'd been searching for with a

huff. "I need to go back to the inn. I forgot something." Pulling on Xyphir's reins, he turned him around.

The stallion let out a whinny, but obeyed and sped into a fast canter.

Jarrod wheeled around to pursue. "You *forgot* something?" He caught up as Damien dismounted at the inn.

"I have a lot on my mind." Damien tossed Xyphir's reins over the post and jumped up the stairs two at a time. "I'll be right back. Don't worry, I can track Rynalds. We'll catch up quickly." The inn's door chimed as he rushed through it. Distantly, his boots thumped up the stairs.

Jarrod stayed on Orion, pacing the horse back and forth while waiting.

Time flowed by and nerves built in his stomach. "This is ridiculous."

His boots hit the ground, and he looped Orion's reins next to Xyphir's. Jogging inside, he climbed the stairs to the rooms. As he stalked down the hallway, one door stood ajar. "What the hells is taking you so long?" He stopped in the doorway.

The room was empty.

Stepping inside, Jarrod eyed a toppled chair. The hairs on the back of his neck stood straight, and he heaved a breath. "Damn it."

Someone was waiting here to capture him.

He ran from the room to the back stairs of the building.

One of Damien's boots occupied a stair, the other on the landing below.

"Didn't put up much of a fight." Shaking his head, Jarrod descended the stairs. "Who found you?" He picked up one of the man's boots and scowled.

Melner wasn't with Braka and Veck.

Melner's role within the guild was to concoct potions and poisons. He could have downed Damien without much of a struggle.

Jarrod picked up the other boot. His jaw tightened, and he ran a hand over his short black hair.

Fucking Melner making my life more complicated. Rae got captured to keep Damien safe. She'll be pissed if I leave him. Plus, Damien said he can track Rynalds. I need him.

Chapter 3

DAMIEN CRINGED, ROUSING, AND ROLLED onto his side. Dirt and twigs stuck to his face. The familiar sounds of the forest brought some comfort, but something was off.

The invisible barrier he maintained against the voices of his power had vanished. Panicking, he attempted to organize his energies to rebuild it but found nothing. The usual mind-searing annoyance wasn't there. Only the chirp of crickets and the rustle of leaves.

His body weak, he tried to lift his hands but couldn't. His shoulders ached, wrenched into an uncomfortable position with his wrists bound behind him. A headache throbbed at the base of his skull, prickling down his neck like needles. A dull, drunken haze disrupted his vision, but he didn't recall drinking anything. His tongue stuck to the gag wedged within his mouth, muffling his groan.

Opening his eyes, he blinked at the campfire roaring in front of him. He couldn't feel the flames beyond their heat. His stomach twisted as he tried again to reach for his ká and felt nothing.

Two men sat by the fire, the only light other than the moon. One poked the logs and then turned a spit roasting a bird carcass.

The second man looked at him and Damien met the gaze of the Hawk who'd been unaccounted for during Jarrod's instructions to return to Mirage. He struggled to remember his name, squinting through the rising pain in his neck.

Rolling his shoulders, he flopped awkwardly onto his chest, squishing his face into the leaves with a grunt. His arms and legs tingled near his torso, but he couldn't feel anything else.

"It'll wear off." The thief chuckled.

Melner.

"Just a lot slower than it took effect."

"You sure all that rope is necessary?" The other man eyed Melner from his work at the fire. "Burly guy, sure, but seems excessive."

"Can't be too careful, the cuffs only keep his Art at bay. I ain't dealing with chasing the fool if he frees his feet."

Even though he couldn't see them, Damien suspected the growing cold around his wrists to be the Art inhibiting cuffs

Helgathian Reapers traditionally used. Melner must have swiped a pair.

"Shouldn't we just kill him?" The other man's words sent a flood of cold through Damien's veins. "Bounty's good either way."

Melner grunted. "Deadweight is heavier. Plus, he'll stink long before we get him to Helgath. May as well keep him alive until it's not in our best interest."

"What about your buddies?"

"They'll give up looking for me. Maybe they'll assume I'm dead like Lykan or captured with Sika. Doesn't matter. We can have whatever life we want with fifty gold crowns."

Despite the agony resurfacing in his upper arm, Damien shrugged against the ropes binding him. When that failed, he tried to move his legs or twitch a toe. Nothing. The growing terror in his stomach heightened with each failed attempt.

Jarrod won't look for me. Not when he can go straight after Rae.

He wouldn't blame the thief.

I'd have done the same thing.

Bringing Jarrod back had served the purpose of revealing Rynalds's involvement.

Craning his head to the side, something pricked his neck.

The memory of entering the room to retrieve Rae's journal came washing back. He'd shoved the book into the back of his pants. While alone in the room, another ká approached. He'd assumed it to be Jarrod. It was too late when Melner struck him with whatever he had used. Damien had collapsed to the floor, taking a chair with him.

Leaves crunched next to his head as Melner stooped to retrieve the dart from Damien's neck. "Oops. Did I leave that in there?"

Damien mumbled against his gag, trying to prop himself up with an elbow, but it sounded nothing like the curse he tried to fling Melner's way.

The thief chuckled. "I'd think twice about causing too much trouble. There's plenty more darts."

Damien's strength failed and his shoulders collapsed against the ground, crushing his hands behind his back. Fortunately, he couldn't feel much.

"Gonna get more wood." The second man rose.

"Don't be long." Melner settled next to the fire once more.

Damien prodded again for his ká, despite the futility of it.

When the thief's companion's noisy footsteps didn't return after at least half an hour had passed, Melner's glances into the shadowed trees became more frequent and Damien dared to allow some hope to return.

Melner stood, the chirping in the forest quieting. He pulled another small dart from his side satchel with a gloved hand. He twisted the wooden shaft between his fingers, his shoulders tense.

The undergrowth across from Damien rustled and

Melner's grip on his dart tightened when Jarrod emerged from the forest.

Melner stepped back, wide-eyed.

Jarrod's grim gaze lingered on Damien before shifting to his fellow thief. He spun the knife in his hand.

"You're alive," Melner stammered, eyes darting around his camp. "Thank Nymaera. I couldn't—"

"Wait to disobey orders?" Jarrod's arm flexed. "How did you know I was dead?"

Melner opened his mouth and then closed it, still playing with his dart. "I got there too late. You were already gone and so was Sika, so I did what I thought was best."

That's a load of horseshit.

Damien tried to say it out loud, mumbling against the gag. He rolled onto his side, crushing his injured arm, and realized with a cry of pain the numbness had faded.

Jarrod looked at Damien, his expression unreadable. "Is he lying?" His knuckles whitened on the hilt of his blade.

To aid Jarrod back from the Inbetween, Damien had found him only moments after his death. If Melner had been nearby, he'd have sensed him. Melner's knowledge of Jarrod's death was because he had seen the event, not the aftermath.

And the coward did nothing to save Rae or Jarrod.

Damien nodded.

Now uncuff me, you idiot.

The words came out as indiscernible grunts.

Jarrod crossed the camp towards Melner, ignoring Damien. "If you were gone by the time he got there, then you must have watched me die. Watched Rae get taken. And did nothing."

Melner swallowed, stepping back. His left hand went to his belt, closing on the hilt of a dagger, but he didn't withdraw it. "You're a fool for forbidding his capture. *Fifty* gold crowns... None of us would even need the Hawks anymore."

Jarrod advanced until he stood inches from Melner, a full head taller than the subordinate thief. His eyes drifted to Damien once again as he considered Melner's statement.

You can't be serious. He's reconsidering... now?

He met Jarrod's gaze, narrowing his eyes. As much as he hated to admit it, they needed each other to find Rae.

Without warning, Jarrod spun back to Melner, burying his knife into his chest. "This is what it felt like," he hissed, and twisted the hilt as Melner gasped. Yanking his blade free, the other thief collapsed.

Damien's head fell back onto the ground as he relaxed.

Thank the gods.

Jarrod crouched next to Damien, tugging the gag out of his mouth.

Working his jaw and trying to wet his tongue, Damien turned his head towards Jarrod. "Thanks."

"I hope whatever..." Jarrod furrowed his brow, placing a hand on the ground. Closing his eyes, he shook his head.

"You all right?" Damien turned to examine the thief. A wooden dart jutted out of Jarrod's calf, right above his boot cuff. "Quick, before you pass out, you—"

Jarrod slumped, landing on his side on the ground, Melner's dead body behind him.

"Son of a..." Damien sighed, collapsing back in defeat. He growled at the growing pain, and his leg twitched for the first time. He watched the dirt near Jarrod's nose carefully, where it swirled with the flow of his breath.

Just another paralyzing dart.

Damien shifted, trying to find a comfortable position with his bound hands beneath him. He stared up at the dark foliage of the trees above him.

A delay is the last thing we needed. I'm sorry, Dice.

Chapter 4

JARROD GROANED, ROLLING ONTO HIS back as sunlight bored through his eyelids.

"Good morning, sunshine."

Opening his eyes, he twitched in surprise at seeing Damien so close to his face. He scowled and tried to sit up. The trees spun around him. "Why do I feel like I drank a whole keg?" Lifting an arm to rub his face, he scowled. His hands tingled, but he felt nothing in his legs.

"Courtesy of that friend of yours. Guess I was right to be untrusting of your crew. He jabbed you in the leg with one of his little dart things."

Jarrod cringed, looking at Melner's body. He'd hoped he was wrong, and that the thief wasn't capable of such treachery.

"He got what he deserved." Sighing, he rested his head on the ground.

"You think you could do something about these cuffs? Or are you going to fall asleep again?"

Jarrod shot him a glare. "You make it difficult to like you. Last I checked, I just killed my guildmate to keep you alive, so how about a little patience?"

Damien growled. "Forgive me. The excruciating pain makes me a little testy first thing in the morning. My poison wore off hours ago and I can feel everything."

"Lucky you. I still can't feel my legs." He sat up carefully, rubbing his hands together. Using his arms, he maneuvered to Melner, searching his pockets. Finding the small key, he crawled on his stomach back to Damien, but held it out of his reach.

Damien glowered. "Is this the part where you offer me a deal?"

"You're not exactly in a position to negotiate." Jarrod reached for his bloody knife where it had fallen in the dirt.

"What is it you want?" Damien eyed the knife.

"Not to get left behind." Jarrod pulled himself to sit next to Damien and started cutting the rope binding him. "Gods, why did he use so much rope?"

"Never can be too careful." He sat up once the rope loosened, despite his hands still cuffed behind him, and rolled his shoulders. "And I won't leave you behind as long as you keep up. And listen when I say something needs to be done a certain way."

"And how am I supposed to keep up if I can't walk?"

Damien's jaw tightened. "Get these damn things off and I'll fix that problem."

Jarrod narrowed his eyes and huffed. "Turn around so I can reach them, then."

Once the cuffs clattered to the ground, Damien stood, rolling his shoulders again and stretching his neck from side to side. "Never thought I'd be so relieved to hear those again." A glimmer of pale-blue light refracted in his eyes. It faded with a subtle flash, echoing through the tattoos visible along his collarbone.

Never seen the Art do that before.

Damien extended his hand to Jarrod. "Come on."

Jarrod eyed the offering, but took his hand. A wave of heat passed from Damien's palm into his, and his entire body lit ablaze within. He let out a grunt of discomfort as the pain whooshed through his legs, leaving them tingling and sore. As it subsided, Jarrod wriggled his toes inside his boots.

"Sorry, should have warned you it'd probably hurt." Damien grinned and pulled the thief to his feet.

Jarrod glowered at Damien, wiping his hands off on his pants. "Rae has impeccable taste." He stalked into the trees towards where he'd tied the horses.

"I would have to agree. Except for that thief she was with

for two years." The deserter walked in a strange pattern, his silent footfalls uneven as if avoiding stepping on something.

Jarrod rolled his eyes, but took pleasure in goading while untying Orion's reins from a tree. "Two *fantastic* years." Pulling Damien's boots from his pack, he tossed them at him.

Damien caught them and approached Xyphir, who seemed relieved to see him. The horse butted his head into the man's chest while he scratched near his ears.

"If they were so fantastic, why didn't it work out?"

Jarrod glanced at him. "Who says it hasn't?"

"You did. As I recall, you said it was a mistake and that you couldn't be with her like... that. And something about it being complicated." Damien smirked and stuffed his feet into his boots. "Or did you already forget how I yanked you out of the Inbetween and I saw that conversation?"

Jarrod fell silent, thinking about the look on Rae's face as he'd ended their relationship. His heart weighed in his chest.

Things got much better after that, though.

"I guess it is pretty complicated if you're willing to let go of fifty gold crowns and chase after her."

Meeting Damien's gaze, Jarrod swallowed. "I will *always* chase after her if she's in trouble. You will never be rid of me so long as she wants me around." He mounted Orion. "And she will *always* love me back, even if you don't understand our relationship."

Damien pursed his lips and turned towards his horse. He hesitated a moment before he pulled himself onto the saddle using his good arm. “You’re right, I don’t understand it. But I know what we have is real. So I will do the same. You won’t be getting rid of me either.”

Jarrod smiled. “Good. Rae doesn’t deserve any less.”

Damien furrowed his brow, picking up Xyphir’s reins. “We’ll need to take a quick detour. I can’t go another day without these bandages getting changed and there’s a stream nearby.” He gestured with his head to the east. “I’ve already picked up on Rynalds, they’re traveling by land. We can catch up.”

Jarrod shook his head, letting out a breath. “Lead the way. You give a whole new meaning to the word *complicated*.”

Chapter 5

TEARS RAN DOWN RAE'S FACE to the uneven wood beneath her. Her mind replayed the scene of Jarrod getting stabbed. Twice, the long knife sank into his body under his ribs. Blood flooded the ground and as much as she'd screamed, he hadn't opened his eyes.

Her closest friend. Her brother. The only man she loved besides Damien, dead on the ground. All because of her.

The steel-walled wagon she rode within bounced, jarring her position and causing her body to throb. A barred door dominated the back, giving her a view of the road behind them.

Where are you, Damien?

Days had passed, but she wasn't sure how many.

The shackles binding her wrists in front of her blocked her access to the Art and likely Damien's ability to feel her. Rae couldn't think of another explanation to justify why he hadn't come for her yet. But with Jarrod dead and her gone, nothing would stop Veck from trying to capture Damien. Melner wouldn't stop him, but Braka might.

The carriage ground to a halt and Rae cringed. Every stop meant more interrogation.

I'll kill you all as soon as you make a mistake.

The barred door screeched open, swinging wide on its rusty hinges.

The only indication of how much time had passed were the wounds on Rynalds's face as it appeared in the doorway. The redness around the lightning strike scar had faded, the burnt skin healing with wicked deformations around his eyepatch.

"Out." Rynalds tone remained aggravatingly calm.

Rae rolled onto her back and pushed herself away from the door. She narrowed her eyes. "I'm fine right here."

Rynalds grunted, gesturing into the carriage with a tilt of his head. He'd learned not to go in after her himself, and two of his goons piled in instead. One was the man who'd killed Jarrod.

Gritting her teeth, Rae sat calmly while he got closer and took her arm. With a huff, she pulled him down and locked her knees around his neck while the other leapt to his defense.

When prying her knees apart failed, he lunged for her throat. His big hands clamped down, blocking her breath.

Rae held on as long as she could until her lungs burned and

the carriage spun around her. Dipping into the pools of unconsciousness, her legs relaxed. Soon after, breath flowed, and she sputtered alert.

The scum who'd killed Jarrod lay still, and she smirked before the other man punched her in the stomach. Buckling forward, she coughed, watching the blacked-out man's chest rise with breath.

One day, death would come, and not just for him.

When Damien catches up...

Her body crumpled to the dirt outside the carriage, shocking her existing bruises back to life. Moaning, she rolled onto her knees and lifted her torso from the ground. Before she could speak, Rynalds slapped her, sending her into the dirt again.

"When will you learn?" He kicked her ribs in the same spot as the day before and she cried out.

A hand tangled with her hair, ripping her body upward. Someone grabbed her elbow, lifting her to her feet, while Rynalds kept a tight grip on the roots of her failing braids.

He leaned into her, close enough that his hot breath wrinkled her nose. "Tell me."

She knew the question. He'd asked so many times already.

"Lanoret didn't have the Art before. How did he get it?"

Rae came up with a different answer each time. "He ate pigeon shit, maybe you should try it."

Rynalds rewarded her creativity with another punch to her

side and she choked, blood splattering from her mouth.

His frigid hand clamped down on her jaw, twisting her head towards him again. "You think you're funny?"

"A little... Mostly, I just think you're pathetic enough to try it."

His chest rumbled. "Why do you protect him? It'd be so much easier to give him up."

Rae scoffed. "For what? So you'll let me go? You think I'm stupid enough to believe you'll ever do that after what you saw?"

"I may be more easily persuaded than you think," Rynalds whispered. "Especially because Lanoret is more of a prize with that power of his."

Rae leaned towards him, maintaining eye contact. "You really want me to tell you how he got his power?"

"I do." The hand in her hair released, caressing down her cheek.

Rae turned her face into the touch, closing her eyes as his finger traced her skin. Jerking her head to the side, she caught his index finger in her mouth. Without hesitation, she bit through his flesh, blood rolling onto her tongue.

Rynalds screamed, yanking back, but couldn't free his hand. He brought his other fist up, slamming it into Rae's jaw.

Her head spun, but she clenched down with the strike to break through the joint, tearing his finger off.

Cursing, Rynalds drew his hand against his chest, eyeing

the stump of his index finger, his face flushed red. "I should kill you, bitch."

Rae spat the finger and his blood into the dirt. "Go ahead, asshole. Touch me again and I'll take another one."

Rynalds punched her, following it up with a back-handed slap before she could straighten. Her body sagged in the arms of whoever held her from behind. He said something, but the words garbled beneath the ringing in her ears.

She yearned to lie down, feel the cold dirt against her bruises and aching muscles.

Blood dripped from her lips onto the ground at her feet, a mix of hers and Rynalds's. She tried to count the drops to help her focus and understand the words exchanging around her.

"...better equipped in Lazuli, sir." A man held out a white handkerchief to Rynalds.

The one-eyed sergeant snatched the cloth, pushing it to his hand. Crimson blood soaked into the linen, spreading like the pools beneath Jarrod's body.

Her heart ached, and she closed her eyes.

"Let them deal with her." Rynalds grimaced as he squeezed the cloth. "Lock her back up. No food for a week." He glared at Rae before stomping off around the carriage, out of her vision.

Forced towards the carriage door, the guards heaved her inside. Air expelled from her lungs as she hit the floor. The door clattered shut behind her, keys jangling against iron to lock it.

Rae crawled to the door, using the bars to help pull herself upright. Sitting in front of it, she watched the tall grass move away from her again.

Damien. Please hurry.

Night fell and Rae hadn't moved from her spot at the door. Rain pattered off the roof of the carriage, bringing a certain calm with it.

Staring into the bleak night, a spot of light reflected at her.

Sitting up straighter, she narrowed her eyes and focused on where she'd seen it.

It happened again, but two spots moving in unison.

Eyes.

At first, dread leapt into her chest, but as their pursuer got closer, Rae recognized the dark features of the huge valley wolf. Grabbing the bars in front of her, she bit her lip. "Neco."

Chapter 6

FOLLOWING RYNALDS WITH HIS SENSES proved easier than Damien first expected. He'd known Rynalds before becoming a Rahn'ka, but the memories alone wouldn't have assisted in tracking him. They did help in sorting the recollection of the battle on the Herald. During the fight, pieces of Rynalds's ká separated to adhere to Damien's, like any physical contact, enabling him to recall the right vibrations to track.

Jarrod, fortunately, didn't ask many questions, trusting that Damien was doing all he could to find Rae. They'd resolved to long periods of silence, leaving Damien to his thoughts.

He couldn't decide how he felt about Jarrod, even if the thief had rescued him from Melner. He admired the man for his dedication to Rae but questioned his motives.

With Jarrod's surprisingly gentle assistance, the burn on Damien's arm continued to heal. But the ragged, grotesque scar forming limited his movement.

"If I'm going to be any good in a fight when we reach Helgath, we need to make a temporary stop." Damien slowed Xyphir to a trot at the base of the craggy mountains east of Terg. "I need to heal my arm."

Jarrod eased Orion to ride next to Damien. "A stop?" He shook his head. "If we have a chance of catching up before they reach Helgath, we should take it."

Damien gritted his jaw and shook his head. "I won't get another chance after this one. There aren't any sanctums farther east. Backtracking in the event we don't catch up would take even more time."

Jarrod looked around over the open meadows to the south. "And you say there's a... sanctum, nearby?"

Damien gestured with his head towards the crags as he brought Xyphir to a stop, the horse snorting. "In the hills just north. I can feel it." He raised an eyebrow as Jarrod dismounted. "What are you doing?"

Jarrod stepped a few paces ahead and knelt in the dirt. "Blood." He touched the ground. "Maybe a day old." This wasn't the first patch they'd come across while following Rynalds and Rae.

Spinning Xyphir around, Damien slid off during the turn and stepped towards the discolored soil. The dirt had absorbed most of the blood, but an ominous stain remained. With a breath, he let his power trickle out to find what he suspected. "Some of it's Rae's." He furrowed his brow. "But not all of it."

His senses directed him to search for a pinprick of Rynalds's energies still clinging to something. Damien stooped down into a clump of grass and picked up a man's severed finger. He eyed the torn flesh at the base and couldn't help the brief smile.

Jarrod came to stand beside him, eyeing his findings. "Are those...?"

"Teeth marks."

"Atta girl."

Damien glanced up at Jarrod, surprised by their shared pride. He flicked the finger back into the brush, wiping his hand on his breeches. He stood up and looked down the road in the direction he could still feel Rynalds's ká traveling.

"He'll leave her alone for a few days at least. Maybe finally give up on whatever torture he's been attempting." His eyes traveled along the ground to search for any other sign of what might have occurred. The energies of the animals around hummed, still agitated from the disruptions in their quiet meadow. And it hadn't been just the passage of a Helgathian prison carriage that'd riled them up.

On the other side of the road, in fine silt, Damien spotted the culprit. A print, the size of his hand. A valley wolf had passed through and, by the looks of it, not long after Rynalds and his soldiers.

"Neco." Damien touched the print. It echoed with the familiar presence and relief sagged his shoulders, a tingle of fear filling his stomach. Neco would defend Rae if he saw her being mistreated, but he'd likely die in the process. Damien prayed the creature was smart enough to just follow.

"A wolf print?"

"A very particular wolf. Neco. Rae rescued him around when we first met. We had to leave him in Ashdale because he couldn't get on the Herald. It's good to see he understood my request for him to travel to Porthew on his own. He's probably been following Rae the entire time."

Jarrod scoffed. "Trust her to *rescue* a valley wolf."

"He was smaller at the time." Damien stood. "I think we can spare the day, knowing Neco is following and Rynalds is likely to keep his hands off her for a few days."

Jarrod sighed but offered no protest.

A hawk screeched overhead, drawing Damien's attention skyward.

It soared above in circles, having followed them since leaving Porthew. Even though the brown bird disappeared for extended chunks of time, it always returned.

"Yours, right?" Damien swung himself onto Xyphir.

Jarrod followed suit. "Aye. Liala."

"So is getting your own hawk like a rite of passage in your guild then?"

"Something like that." Jarrod mimicked the vague answer Damien gave while befriending Xyphir. "It's *complicated*."

Damien rolled his eyes and encouraged his horse off the north edge of the road. The grass grew so high it brushed against his thighs as they wove through them towards the craggy mountainside. He didn't bother looking behind him to see if Jarrod followed, Orion's hooves thumping on the hard ground.

"So in this kind of situation, where's Din? Is he following Rae?"

"I sent him to Mirage. Letting him follow her wouldn't do anyone any good. Helgath might realize more about who she is."

The thrum of the sanctum's energies already fed Damien's ká, pressing against the barrier he used to keep the voices out. "You're not part auer, are you?"

"Actually..." Jarrod started, receiving a glare. He huffed a laugh. "No, I'm not, why?"

"The spirits don't take kindly to auer. So I guess we'll find out either way. If you feel a charge like a lightning storm, you'll want to turn around." Damien turned Xyphir towards a jut of the mountain. The crags split into a gorge, a pair of pillars pushed against the rock side, partially consumed by the dense grass and plant life attempting to grow on the cliff.

"Can't imagine how you learned that," Jarrod grumbled.

Xyphir stopped and Damien hopped off, finding his footing on the solid stone hidden beneath a layer of sand. He knelt to tug the laces of his boots free from where he'd tucked them as Xyphir backed up.

The pillars hummed with power and Damien watched the hint of the blue ká energy all the sanctums contained. He glanced at Jarrod as he pulled off his first boot. "You curious enough to follow me?"

Jarrod slid off Orion, looping his reins over Xyphir's saddle. "Do I need to take my boots off?" He quirked an eyebrow.

Damien shrugged. "If you want to." He tucked the boots into one of Xyphir's saddlebags. "I don't even know what the place will look like to you. Probably just old ruins."

"And what does it look like to *you*?" Jarrod stepped forward, eyeing the stone entry pillars.

"Like old ruins." Damien smirked. "But I can see the energy of the place too, so it gives it another layer." He closed his eyes as power coursed through the stones at his feet.

"At least *something* isn't complicated." Jarrod shuffled across the stone, prompting Damien to open his eyes and watch as he walked into the ruins.

Sighing, Damien followed.

As Jarrod passed between the pillars, their clouds of energy rippled in acknowledgment, but no more.

With Damien's entrance, they flared to life. Thin wreaths

of pale energy wrapped like snakes around the pillar's surface, licking over the runes. The hum in the Rahn'ka's mind doubled, the pressure mounting in an excited flurry. A quick glance at Jarrod confirmed the thief saw and felt none of it.

Inside the sanctum, the crumbled rocks formed a circle of collapsed monoliths. Only two cracked stones still stood. The swirl of stone meant to lead towards the altar was covered in the same sand as the outside walkway.

Jarrod stopped near one of the fallen monoliths, looking at the half-collapsed structure on the edge of the altar circle. "What does Rae think of your mysterious power?"

"She asked a lot of questions and didn't trust it at first. But she's the reason it didn't drive me insane."

Ká coalesced in the stones, trying to form the shape of their guardian spirit.

The sand disrupted the flow, and Damien eyed the altar. "Shield your eyes." A surge of his power built with his will. He brushed the sand away with his toes, finding the cool surface of the rock beneath. He knelt, touching the stone and pushing his energy into it.

Jarrod lifted an arm to shield his face.

The sand in front of them shifted like a beast moved beneath it. A burst of air followed the stream of energy Damien summoned upward, dispersing the thin layer disguising the surface of the ruins. It hovered in the air like mist, before a gesture sent it into the rock side. The plants nestled between the stones shivered in gratitude, uncurling to greet the sun pouring down from the open sky.

Beyond the altar, a hulking scaled form rose in a pale shimmer of the energies assembling into the guardian. A reptilian head lifted from the stones, tail lashing towards a monolith only for it to pass straight through. The figure rocked back onto their hind-legs, navy blue claws tapping the stone surface.

"Nymaera's breath." Jarrod stepped back. "What the hells is that?" His wide eyes took in the creature Damien had been convinced the thief wouldn't be able to see.

Hissing laughter echoed between the sharp white teeth of the spirit, head swiveling as they took a step forward.

"You can see them?" Damien narrowed his eyes at Jarrod. "How?"

"Because I allow him to." The spirit's voice vibrated off the stones in a giddy tone. "It's been too long since a mortal came to visit."

"Is it..." Jarrod straightened, eyes locked on the spirit reptile. "...Friendly?"

Damien had to give Jarrod credit for not turning and running.

The hissing chuckle came again and the spirit's body, bird-like in posture, stepped forward and shook with the glee. "I won't eat you. Probably."

"I apologize for disturbing you. I came to use your ká to

help me heal." Damien approached the spirit. "May I?"

"You aren't disturbing me, Rahn'ka." The guardian rotated their head back towards him. They stepped in a wide circle, eyeing Jarrod. "But I'm curious about your companion. He is human?"

Jarrod studied the serpent but stood his ground.

Damien couldn't decide if the thief was brave or foolish.

"Aye." Jarrod nodded. "As far as I know."

"It's a shame Sindré already chose you, Rahn'ka. Or *he* might have made an interesting alternative." The guardian approached, pushing his head close to Jarrod.

A wave of heat passed through Damien at the suggestion. "Too bad." He narrowed his eyes. "Yondé approved of Sindré's choice, do you not?"

"Yondé is too trusting of Sindré's decisions. We, Jalescé, are a little more reflective before making such choices. Perhaps there could be two chosen?"

Jarrod still hadn't moved a muscle beyond flexing his jaw.

Jalescé's scaled snout nearly touched his face, their slitted navy blue eyes blinking. The spirit's head tilted to the side, like a bird. Their jaw opened to reveal razor teeth inches from Jarrod's face.

Damien took a step forward, pulling the thief back with a hand on his shoulder. "You know that can't happen. To create a second Rahn'ka would probably kill me, so I'd rather we not."

Jarrod shrugged. "Might be fun to try." He smirked at Damien but a shadow lingered in his gaze.

"You don't even know what he's suggesting." Damien stood between Jalescé and Jarrod.

Jalescé gave another hissing giggle, recoiling. "Does he not, Rahn'ka? You bring a companion to my sanctum who doesn't know? And such a worthy vessel, too."

"Jalescé." Damien forced his tone to remain respectful. "I'm sorry but we're in a bit of a hurry. I need to heal, then we will leave and not bother you again."

The reptile's body sagged, as if disappointed. He peered at Damien's injuries. "Perhaps we *should* consider this human if you are so eager to damage your vessel. So careless already?"

Damien growled, but Jarrod spoke first. "The damage wasn't his fault. Caused by an auer."

"Auer?" Jalescé hissed. "Disgusting beings, who still relish in violence." The spirit's tail lashed across the grass while they looked at Damien.

Damien wasn't about to correct Jarrod's lie.

"You may use my ká, Rahn'ka. With the assurance you will dispatch your attacker without mercy."

Damien didn't have a problem with that. Rynalds would die for his actions. He gave a solid nod to the guardian, who hummed with pleasure.

"And visit." Jalescé cocked his head. "Bring your human companion. I enjoy the turmoil in his ká."

Damien furrowed his brow, but bowed his head. "Thank you, Jalescé. I'm happy to agree to your terms."

The serpentine head swayed towards the failing structure on the east side of the ruins. "Go. I'll keep the human company while you do." His gaze turned again towards Jarrod. "I promise not to *eat* him."

Damien looked at Jarrod.

Jarrod made eye contact with him and nodded, much to Damien's surprise.

Brave idiot, then...

Damien wound through the ruins, familiar with the layout because it matched Yondé's sanctum where he trained for months.

Fortunately, no Shade hid in the shadows here.

The three-tiered fountain mirrored the one he and Yondé had sat beside, though the base had crumbled. Embedded in the wall, actual water didn't flow, but a stream of energy took its place. It bubbled out of the mouth of the fountain, falling into the large basin at the bottom that would have caught it before trickling down the cracks to seep into the ground.

He didn't linger on the subtle differences between Jalescé's power and Yondé's, taking it into his ká like a wanderer in the desert. He lifted pools to his lips, inviting it to mingle with his energy.

Focusing the power on his arm came easily at first. As the skin rushed through the healing process, the pain spiked and he had to slow to let it subside before continuing. The process took longer than he wanted, the sun disappearing as great rain clouds swarmed across the night sky to hide the stars and moon.

Jalescé's sanctum didn't grow dark, the runes on the stones glimmering with the power of the Rahn'ka filling the ruins with a faint illumination.

When Damien finally ran his left hand over the unmarred flesh, his entire body shook with exhaustion. Stretching his arm, he ushered in another swell of Jalescé's power to ease the lingering discomfort. He flexed his knuckles, standing to return to the altar circle where he'd left Jalescé and Jarrod.

Did the guardian tell Jarrod about the Rahn'ka?

It had been naïve to allow Jarrod to follow. Perhaps Jalescé trusted Jarrod because of his companionship with Damien. It made Damien's gut roil to consider Jarrod would know his secrets.

"How did Yondé capture the Shade in the first place?" Jarrod leaned forward from where he rested against a monolith.

Jalescé had curled up, dog-like, near the thief's feet, their head raised to answer. "Ailiena captured it before her death. She'd sworn she would perform the same process she'd done on her lover but didn't make it back to Yondé's sanctum before the other Shades caught up to her."

"It's a shame, what happened to her."

Jalescé heaved a sigh, vibrating the surrounding stones. "It was. But her sacrifice was necessary to preserve the Rahn'ka. Even though she never came to visit me..."

Damien furrowed his brow as he approached them. "Sacrifice? Didn't the Shades kill her?"

Jalescé's head swiveled towards Damien. "Yondé left that bit out, I see."

"What bit?" Damien frowned.

Jarrod stood, nodding at the reptilian spirit. "It was enlightening to speak with you, but if Damien is finished, we need to get moving." His gaze met Damien's again, silently urging his haste.

Jalescé gave a grievous sigh and shuffled to their feet. "Very well, but you will uphold your promise to visit." It wasn't a question as he turned his head to look at Damien. "I don't want the sands blocking my ability to take physical shape again."

"When all this is over, I'll come back." Damien nodded. He'd have to ask Jarrod later about the sacrifice the spirit implied. Stepping towards the exit, he glanced back to see Jalescé watching them as they walked away.

"Don't damage your vessel again," Jalescé called after them. "Auer are not to be trusted."

Damien and Jarrod didn't speak as they walked past the pillars that still glowed with the power of ká at the entrance.

Xyphir and Orion munched on grass near where they emerged from the gorge.

When Jarrod reached Orion, he pulled the reins free from Xyphir's saddle and shook his head. "You sure took your time." He pulled himself onto his horse.

Damien glowered, retrieving his boots and thrusting them onto his feet. He tied the laces for the first time in far too long. "I did it as fast as I could. You try growing back all the skin on your arm and let me know how that goes for you."

Jarrod scowled, jaw flexing. "We will never catch them before they reach Helgath now." He gazed in the direction the men had taken Rae. "If they kill her..."

"They won't kill her." Damien tried to convince himself as much as Jarrod. He grumbled, looking at the other man as rain fell. "We'll catch up, but not if we exhaust ourselves and our horses trying to navigate through a storm like this at night. We should make camp." He didn't like it either but, close to the ruins, they were more likely to find shelter and get a good night's rest.

"Camp?" Jarrod gaped at Damien. "We sat here all day and now you want to make *camp*?" Rain dripped off his chin and his horse sidestepped.

Damien frowned. "I didn't think the time would come that I would be the more sensible between us."

Thunder rumbled in the distance, and rain poured down.

"If you want to sit on your ass, you go right ahead, but I'm going after her. I lost her when she left the Hawks and I won't let it happen again."

Damien stepped away from his horse, grabbing Orion's bridle to keep the horse still. "That won't happen. We'll find her."

Jarrod turned his fiery gaze on Damien. "If we find her dead, I swear, I'll..."

"You'll what?" Anger rose in his chest. "Trust me, if that happened I'd do it to myself. But it won't."

"Not you. Me. I'll never forgive myself if something happens to her."

"Quit acting like this is your fault. We both know they were after me."

"And I could have given you to them!" Jarrod slid off Orion's back. For a moment, Damien thought Jarrod meant to take a swing at him, but he turned and walked the other way while running a hand over his short black hair.

"You're right, you could have." Damien squinted at him through the rain. "So why didn't you? You care so damn much about her. Which is what I still don't get." He stomped after Jarrod, mud squishing under his boots. "If you love Rae, why did you break her heart?"

Jarrod whirled around, eyes darker than usual as his hands balled into fists. "That's none of your damn business."

"Oh, I think it *is* my business. You think you can get her back if you save her, don't you?"

"I don't want her like that." Jarrod shook his head. "Just because I love her, doesn't mean I want to be with her."

"Bullshit. Why not? She's beautiful, quick-witted, a talented thief... Just your type, I'm sure."

Jarrod's chest heaved as he glared at Damien. "She is all those things and so much more, you don't even know. But you're wrong, she's not my type."

"Why not?"

With a growl, Jarrod threw his arms up in the air. "Because she's a woman! Men are my type, all right? Men. Are you happy now?"

Damien's eyes widened, his mouth already prepared to retort the answer he thought Jarrod would say. But the surprise left it hanging open. He forced his jaw closed, taking a moment to comprehend the emotions suddenly rushing through him. His shoulders fell as he averted his gaze to the splashes of rain hitting the puddles.

In the silence, Jarrod grabbed Orion's reins and pulled the horse towards a high outcropping of rock near the road.

Damien got his legs working again, jogging after Jarrod.

Xyphir followed behind, discontent to be left in the rain.

"Jarrod." Damien huffed as he stepped under the overhang. He ran his hand back to push the water out of his hair. "I... owe you... I'm sorry."

Jarrod shook his head. "Don't bother." His tone lacked the anger it'd held before. "I know how it looks, that I care for her, but it's not like that."

"It makes a lot more sense now. I couldn't comprehend

why, knowing the person Rae is. But you pretended when you were with her, didn't you?"

"I tried." Jarrod watched Damien. "I wanted to like women, so I tried to. It worked for a while, and when I admitted the truth... She agreed to help me keep up the charade, but it got exhausting."

"Why didn't you just tell me? Why didn't *she* tell me? It's not like I'd have judged you." Damien imagined all the angst he would have been spared with the knowledge.

"Because it's no one's business. No one knows, and I'd rather keep it that way. Is that so hard to understand?"

"I guess not. It's your choice, but I don't think it's anything to be ashamed of. I know plenty of good men who feel the same way. There's more in the military than you'd think." He paused for a moment, trying to catch Jarrod's gaze. "I won't tell anyone."

Jarrod huffed an exhale, but didn't reply at first, unfastening his pack from his saddle. "Just don't get weird, all right?"

Damien chuckled. "I don't think it'd work out between us, anyway."

Jarrod scowled, but the hint of a smile threatened the corner of his mouth. "You're also not my type."

"I could always set you up with my—"

"Gods. Please, no." Jarrod groaned. "Don't even go there."

JARROD WISHED HE HADN'T TOLD Damien, despite his understanding. He always kept his private life private. Whenever he neared telling anyone, his mother's voice crept into his head to tell him he could never be who he wanted to be.

Luckily, he'd never met a man who held his attention longer than a night.

Riding Orion at a canter next to Damien and Xyphir the next morning, Jarrod was so lost in thought he hadn't realized Damien spoke to him. "Sorry, say that again?"

"Gods, you sure are in a different place, aren't you? We're almost to the Belden River. We won't see another water source for a while, so we should stop and stock up."

Jarrod nodded. "Good call."

Ever since their heated conversation outside the strange ruins, a new respect between them had emerged. All tension dissipated, replaced by the potential for camaraderie.

"The horses need a break too. Orion is a little sluggish today. I think the travel is getting hard on him." Jarrod patted his horse's neck as the sound of a rushing river touched his senses. "How did you know the river was so close?" He looked over at Damien, who gave him a grin.

"Same way I know Orion has been sluggish because there's a burr wedged in his shoe. He doesn't like complaining though and is patient enough to wait until we stop at the river to remove it." Damien gave Jarrod a look, daring him to ask more.

Jarrod avoided the topic of Rahn'ka after his encounter with Jalescé. Curiosity tended to lead him down paths he had no business on. And the words the reptile had said still bothered him.

"And apparently it could have been me." Jarrod scoffed. "Talking to horses and rivers."

"Apparently." Damien shrugged. "Jalescé liked you. But I don't think you would have liked Yondé much. They were much more round-about with how they talked and you would have been too bull-headed to train with them."

Jarrod raised a brow. "And you're the epitome of patience."

Damien frowned. "In the right circumstances. I was a soldier. I can take orders from time to time. You don't strike me as having the same blind loyalty... And I mean that as a compliment."

Jarrod looked down at his right hand, where his middle finger donned a once-gaudy gold ring. The filed-down top left little evidence of the initials and crest engraved there originally. "No, I suppose not *blind* loyalty." He swiveled the ring before looking ahead of them. "I was never a soldier, either. But why did you train with Yondé so blindly? After what happened to the previous Rahn'ka, I would have been more than a little reluctant to become the next one."

Damien hesitated, staring ahead. "I didn't want it and I tried to say no. But Sindré threatened Rae and left me no choice. I didn't realize my choice to protect her meant I'd become the Rahn'ka."

Jarrod stared at Damien with a furrowed brow. "How long had you known Rae by then?"

"Only a day. But she'd already saved me from a jail cell in Jacoby. I tried to ignore the call towards Sindré, but the guardians can be persistent."

"So you felt like you owed her."

Why else would he protect her after only a day?

"It was more than that. It didn't feel right that I had the power over such a life-changing decision for her." Damien sighed, rubbing the back of his neck. "Her auer heritage made the guardian determined to end her bloodline, one way or another. But I drank the vial instead."

Jarrod watched Damien, trying to decipher exactly what he meant. "You're saying the guardian wished to make Rae barren. And you put that on yourself instead. Does that mean you can't...?"

"I have no idea."

Jarrod blew out a breath. "Wow. So you save her from that only to fall in love with her, probably now fearing you'll never be able to give her the children you tried to preserve the choice of. Cruelly ironic."

"I didn't realize at the time how much I'd come to love her. But yes. I don't know if I'll be able to give her children."

Jarrod studied the Rahn'ka's face. "Does she know you did this for her?"

Damien hesitated again, glancing at Jarrod before shaking his head slowly. "I haven't told her. Not yet. I don't even know how to begin."

Sighing, Jarrod shrugged. "The only thing you might have working for you is that I don't think she wants a family. As long as I've known, she's hated everything about marriage."

"And that hasn't changed. Which is why I haven't really thought it pertinent to bring up my possible infertility."

"With Rae not with you, why do you still have... *most* of your sanity?"

"Yondé trained me in how to control ká. He taught me how to stop the headaches and wield the power."

"And Rae was there for that?"

"No. We separated while I trained with Yondé. It wasn't the most peaceful separation either. I wasn't in control of myself when Yondé made it clear Rae wasn't welcome in the ruins."

Jarrod narrowed his eyes. "She never mentioned being apart from you in her letters. What happened?" He couldn't help the protective tone.

How long was Rae on her own?

She could handle herself, but something like Jalescé being unhappy with his friend made his insides curdle.

Damien explained Yondé's spiritual attack on Rae, commenting on the surge of her power he witnessed. When he mentioned the grygurr following and attacking Rae, Jarrod yanked Orion to a halt.

Working his jaw, Jarrod did his best not to lash out without thinking his words through. "So you're telling me that after trusting you during your first grygurr encounter, she ended up nearly *dying* trying to get *away* from you?" How Rae forgave Damien was beyond him. "I sure hope you felt like shit for that."

"Far worse." Damien circled Xyphir around Orion, his horse resistant to stopping.

Jarrod tried to lessen the anger in his tone. Rae survived the incident. "I still don't understand." He lowered his voice. "You aren't worried the same fate that befell Ailiena will happen to you? How can you subject Rae to the risk?"

"I can handle Shades." Damien's lips flattened into a line.

"And the risk is Rae's choice, don't you think?"

Jarrod furrowed his brow. "I'm not talking about Shades. I'm talking about what would happen to Rae if you *chose* to leave her."

Xyphir whinnied as Damien pulled him to a stop beside Jarrod. "What are you talking about?"

Understanding shook Jarrod's insides. "You don't know."

"Know what?" Damien's voice grew strained.

"Ailiena killed herself."

The color drained from Damien's face. "She what? Yondé told me that Shades killed—"

"Yondé, the straightforward one?"

Damien's eyes dropped to the ground, his hands twisting Xyphir's reins.

"Ailiena killed herself to avoid being captured by Shades. And those spirits are crazy enough to call such a thing her duty. Of all the things you should have been privy to, I'd have thought that would be one of them."

"Me too." Damien's knuckles whitened. With a deep inhale, he released the reins, rubbing his palms. "What else did Jalescé tell you, since they seem far more forthcoming than my other instructors."

"They were angry that Sindré didn't help Ailiena. Apparently whatever binds Shades to their Art can be altered and Sindré knows how."

"Sounds like I need to pay a visit to Sindré rather than trust what Yondé told me." He shook his head. "I can't believe you're taking all this information Jalescé threw at you so casually. My head was spinning when I realized Shades were real and not just bedtime stories. And you have a guardian tell you how it would have chosen you as an ancient power and you're acting like it's just a regular day."

Jarrod shifted in his saddle, unsure how the conversation got turned around on him. "I may not have any access to the Art, but I'm not inexperienced. Plus, losing my head wouldn't help anything. I've met a Shade before, so I already knew they were real. Serpentine spirits don't seem like much of a stretch after you've seen what I have."

"I'm interested to hear that story when we have more time. And more about what Jalescé told you. Yondé insisted the only way to deal with a Shade was to kill them, but if there's another way, I'd like to know it."

Jarrod nodded. "I'll tell you my entire conversation with your reptile ghost if you'd like to hear it, but that's as much as I can offer. Honestly, I've already said too much. It's best not to speak of Shades, especially those who were once friends." He nudged Orion to walk around Xyphir.

Damien hesitated, but they rode in silence the rest of the way to the river.

No one manned the stone bridge, leaving them free to maneuver down to the riverbank. They followed the grooves of an old road to the water, where wagons had stopped to accomplish the same thing they planned. The dirt pathway turned to a rocky shore, great boulders worn smooth in times the river flowed higher after the winter snows.

Damien dismounted, slipping out of his saddle before Xyphir came to a full stop. He unfastened the ties of his packs while the horse rocked anxiously.

Jarrod trotted Orion farther downstream to peer around the tall grass, wanting to ensure they were alone. Once satisfied, he returned and joined Damien on foot.

Running his hand down Orion's front left leg, he lifted the hoof.

"Other side." Damien walked down to the river with the waterskins for the horses.

Jarrod clenched his jaw and put the hoof down after a quick inspection. "Rae ever tell you that comes off as condescending?" Finding the burr in Orion's front right shoe, he dug it out and flicked it into the water.

Damien chuckled. "I don't think she's told me that." He loosened the neck of the second waterskin bag and dunked it into the water.

"Well it does," Jarrod muttered. "Might wanna keep that in check once we get to Mirage, I know a few of the Hawks won't take kindly to it."

"Trust me, I have no intention of letting your *Hawks* know that I have any kind of Art."

"I suppose I'm just *lucky* then." Jarrod knelt, refilling his own waterskin.

"Uh huh." Damien's voice sounded distant.

Jarrod's gaze wandered past him, landing on a stone near the water, a short way upstream, with a brown stain on it. Advancing, he crouched next to the stone and narrowed his eyes.

A handprint, or at least half of one, marred the rock. Browned from age, his heart hitched. Female in size and created by blood.

"Damien." He turned to see the Rahn'ka crouched in the grass and stood. "I think they may have stopped here."

Damien didn't respond immediately, picking up something from the ground, which he turned in his palm. "They did." His hand closed to a fist around whatever he'd found. His shoulders shook as he stood up.

Jarrod narrowed his eyes and stepped over the rocky ground towards Damien. "What did you find? There's blood over there..."

"Her necklace." Damien glared across the river towards the road they would be taking. He sucked in a shaky breath. "How fresh is the blood?"

"Not fresh. Couple days, give or take. They must be driving the carriage in shifts to avoid stopping and make better time." His hopes of catching up to Rae dimmed. "She hasn't worn a necklace in years."

"I gave it to her." Damien turned to look at the other shore. "We won't catch up before they reach Helgath. We shouldn't have stopped at the sanctum." His jaw grew tight as he stomped over to the waterskins, snatching them off the ground.

Xyphir flinched away from Damien. Even Jarrod felt the anger. Instead of the usual comforting touch Damien would give Xyphir when he became anxious, he growled beneath his breath and roughly tossed the straps of the waterskins over the saddle.

Jarrod clamped a hand down on Damien's shoulder. "This isn't your fault. You were right to stop. Showing up half-injured would have given them the upper hand to arrest you as well."

Damien twisted his shoulder out of Jarrod's grip, spinning to face him. "This is completely my fault. They took her because of me and you damn well know that. Rynalds wants *me*. He's hurting Rae to get to *me*. If I offer to trade myself, maybe—"

Jarrod set his jaw and grabbed Damien's shirt collar, yanking hard enough to make the Rahn'ka stumble half a step forward. "Damien. You know as well as I do that if you do something that *stupid*, Helgath will get both of you." Several inches taller, he looked down at Damien while doing his best to control his own fear. "I love that girl too and we will get her back. But we'll fail if you can't get your head straight." He pushed Damien back, releasing his shirt at the same time.

Damien narrowed his eyes, tugging his shirt to straighten it. "So what are we supposed to do if they get over the border? Every soldier and guard will know my face. You've seen the posters and know the price. Even the common folk will be clambering to turn me over. Unless your Hawks can somehow change my face."

Sighing, Jarrod shook his head. "Aye, I know the price on your head, how could I forget? But you underestimate us. We can change enough, don't worry. You think there are any posters with my face on them? There aren't. You know why? Because I'm *never* seen. And you won't be either. You're going to have to trust me."

"Trust a thief." Damien scoffed. "You know, before Rae, I don't think I could have. Not with what I've heard of your guild. But I don't have much of a choice, do I?"

Jarrod frowned. "Sure you do. You can stay right here and I'll go without you." He turned around and walked back to Orion, anger rising in his chest. Spinning around, he glowered at Damien. "You have some nerve questioning my loyalty. I didn't defect from my position in the Hawks. I didn't run away. I traveled all the way here for *Rae*. My *friend*. Only to *die* after failing to protect her. Tell me, *Damien*, what have you heard of my guild? That no one has ever turned on each other? That Helgath has never successfully forced one of us to talk? That we actively try to avoid hurting those who don't deserve it? I don't know, man, but I'd say we've got a cleaner record than the military." Jarrod huffed. "Melner excluded."

Damien stiffened, clenching his fists as he glared at the ground. For a split second, Jarrod thought he saw a flare of light against his collar, where his tattoo peeked out from his shirt. But it promptly stopped, and Damien's shoulders slouched. "I won't deny that. And I suppose I deserve your anger. I'm really not in a place to be questioning you. I'm sorry. It's just..." Lacing his fingers behind his head, he pulled his chin down as he stormed away. "Sometimes I wonder how it all got so crazy."

Jarrod let out a breath, worry replacing his frustration. "Look, even if you feel you can't trust me, you can trust Rae, right?"

Damien nodded.

"And you already know *she* trusts me, so how about you let that be enough? Besides, I'm in the same spot you are, as she's the only reason I trust you." Jarrod laughed. "You think I don't realize you could probably kill me with little more than a thought?" He took a drink from his waterskin before tying it to his saddle.

"I'm not that kind of man. And it's not all about trust. Even if I trust you completely, it might not help if Helgath finds me."

Jarrod sighed. "You'll be right under their nose, but I promise they won't find you."

"And *everyone* in your guild will go for that? I'm all for believing in honor among thieves, but we're talking about a lot of money. Melner already proved that it can be a great enough temptation for betrayal. Understand my hesitation. Just a few weeks ago, before you knew me, you would have turned me in yourself. What would stop any of your other guildmates?"

"I understand." Jarrod nodded. "But I never told the guild master we were after you. Just that we left to get Rae. No one knows about you, and we'll make sure that only essential members are aware of you now. They won't betray the guild, or turn you in, because everyone will be focused on efforts to find Rae. This may come as a shock to you, but she's rather high ranking for someone so young and I won't be the only one royally pissed off at her capture."

Looking up at the sky, Jarrod narrowed his eyes on the horizon before meeting Damien's gaze with a stern look. "You restored my life. And I will lay it back on the line if that's what's required to keep you safe. I swear it."

Damien watched Jarrod, his eyes narrowed ever so slightly. He huffed a quick breath, then took a step forward, offering his hand. "Thank you."

Jarrod gripped Damien's hand and shook it once before trying to release it.

Damien didn't let him, turning their hands over while staring at the back of Jarrod's. As if coming back to himself, he released Jarrod and took a step back.

"Didn't notice that before." Damien gestured with his chin towards the broad gold band on Jarrod's right hand. "Looks like a proxiet ring. Didn't think one would ever let it out of their sight."

Jarrod controlled the flinch but closed his hand into a fist.

In Helgath, the reigning Dannet house led the monarchy, but bloodline alone didn't decide next in line for the throne. Four other Dannet families assisted in the ruling of Helgath, with their sons each being proxiets. Only a proxiet could challenge for the throne once of age, though a power shift hadn't occurred in centuries. None of the current families expressed a desire for a change from the individual rule they practiced over their jurisdiction.

The last thing Jarrod needed was someone recognizing the ring, even with its surface filed off. His pulse hammered harder. "Not sure. I found it in the guild coffers and it fit, so..." He shrugged.

Damien studied him. "Perhaps it was a prize for winning a jousting tournament?"

Jarrod clenched his jaw, turning away.

You had it with the first guess.

Damien checked on Xyphir, who responded calmly to the gentler approach. He refastened the ties around the extra waterskins, securing them to the saddle. "Are you ready to keep going? I'd love to make our entire argument invalid by catching up to Rae before the Helgathian border."

Chapter 8

MOONLIGHT SHONE THROUGH THE BARS of the prison carriage door, casting long shadows across the wooden base. An owl hooted somewhere in the distant forest, rousing Rae from her half-conscious state.

Her eyes struggled to focus, her throat parched. The last time they'd let her drink had been at the river. Which river, she had no idea, but she'd left her necklace behind in the hopes Damien might find it.

Is he even looking for me?

A headache throbbed in her temples. She couldn't remember the last time she'd eaten.

They hadn't beaten her for a few days, but her body ached anyway. Her ribs were cracked and bruised, a gash on the side of her head leaving a patch of matted blood in her hair.

The carriage lurched to a stop, bouncing as the driver hopped down from his bench.

"What's the holdup?"

"I need to take a shit."

Someone groaned. "Hurry up."

A horse snorted as a twig snapped somewhere outside behind the carriage, but the driver had walked the opposite direction.

Rae scuffled closer to the barred door and peered into the darkness. "Neco?" she whispered, her voice hoarse. She hadn't seen the wolf for days, but something told her he still followed. Soon, he wouldn't be able to.

Something chuffed, and the black wolf padded from the underbrush.

Rae sighed. He was her only chance to relay a message to Damien.

Neco's ears twitched as he approached, his big head close enough for her to reach through the bars and touch. His fur warmed her dirty fingers and his amber eyes bored into her.

"You can't follow me anymore." She retracted her hand. She'd overheard the plan the previous day. "Find Damien. Tell him we're going to Lazuli by sea from Serityme. Damien, Neco. Find Damien." She closed her welling eyes and composed herself before opening them again. "Go. Go now."

Neco took a step back from the carriage and whined with a tilt of his head.

She nodded. "Please go, boy. Find Damien."

The wolf turned, giving her one last look before loping into the darkness.

In Serityme, Rae resisted Rynalds with all her feeble strength as he hauled her by her shackled wrists aboard a large transport vessel. The weather had turned, and her chin dripped with rainwater.

Her boot caught on an uneven plank when Rynalds shoved her into her cell. Crashing into the wall, she gasped and slid to the damp floor.

Curling up in the corner of her cell, Rae closed her eyes for an indiscernible amount of time. Her bones ached, wrists cut and raw from the cuffs still locking away her access to the Art.

When will it end?

Rae pulled her feet closer, delirium threatening her with hallucinations of Damien next to her. "Are you here?" Her voice caught in her throat.

"I'm here if you want me to be."

She leaned on his shoulder and closed her eyes. The scent of his skin lulled her into relaxation. "Please don't leave me," she whispered as she fell asleep.

When her eyes found the strength to open again, Rae lifted a hand to touch where Damien had sat, only to find herself leaning against the cell wall. Sighing, she sat up straighter and forced her vision to focus. "Well, that's cruel." The back of her head hit the wall with a gentle thunk. "I miss you."

"Miss who?"

A female voice straightened Rae's spine. Squinting in the dim light, she crawled to peer into the cell across from her.

Chains scraped across the wooden deck.

Sitting with her back against a wall, arms over her chest, was a blond woman a few years older than Rae.

"Who are you?" Rae's heart soared at having someone to talk to.

"Paita." She ran a hand through her shoulder-length, dirty hair. "I saw them bring you in yesterday. What's your name?"

Rae's shoulders slumped.

How has it already been a day?

She must have slept longer than she realized. "Rae."

Paita's hazel eyes reminded her of Damien's, her tone sad. "Who is it you miss?"

Regardless of who asked, Rae couldn't say Damien's name aloud. So she focused on Jarrod. "My friend." Her throat tightened. "He was killed during my capture." She whispered the last part, avoiding the raw grief. Jarrod died defending Damien's secret. Before the rush of agony could overtake her again, she stacked walls around her heart and hardened herself.

"I'm sorry." Paita pressed her hand to her heart.

"Why are you here?" Mirroring Paita, Rae leaned against the wall.

"They think I have information." She shook her head. "My husband… They say he abandoned his military posting. They say he deserted and isn't coming back. He left me and our daughter to fend for ourselves…" Her voice trailed off and Rae's brow furrowed. Paita's eyes became distant, and she looked at her hands before burying her face in them. "The soldiers took Siefa and won't tell me if she's all right."

Rae's heart twisted for the sobbing woman, confusion muddling her mind. There'd only been one successful deserter.

The memories of Damien's hesitation with her in the beginning scalded her mind. She'd even accused him of being married, but he'd sworn he wasn't. He'd claimed he'd never been with a woman before her. The coil of suspicion in her gut made her nauseous.

"What was his name?" Rae leaned against the bars.

"D-Damien." Paita didn't lift her head. "I don't know how he could abandon us. He was everything to me."

Rae's mind whirled and her breath came faster.

It can't be possible.

Somewhere within the ship, a child screamed.

Paita's eyes flew wide open, and she threw herself at the bars. "Stop it! Don't hurt her!"

Rae rose onto her knees, gripping the bars.

A guard stomped down their hallway, and keys jangled. "Are you ready to talk?"

Paita kept screaming her pleas and Rae closed her eyes,

backing away from the bars until her back hit the far wall. She watched as the guard hit Paita, again and again, and then dragged her struggling form from the cell and out of sight.

Paita's yells mixed with the child's screams and Rae held her hands over her ears.

This can't be real.

She shook, knocking her forehead against her knees as she curled into a ball.

It's a lie. It's a lie.

The noise quieted, but didn't disappear. Rae struggled to catch her breath.

Someone snuffed out the lamp, extinguishing the only faint light illuminating the cells in the bowels of the ship.

What if a child really suffered at the hands of the Helgathian soldiers? The sobs continued, ragged and desperate with an occasional high-pitched shriek of renewal. Paita's wails echoed each call of the child, who eventually grew hauntingly quiet.

Is she really Damien's daughter?

Shaking, Rae pulled her knees to her chest and prayed for it all to stop. She had the information they sought from Paita, but she couldn't give it to them. Rae cried out in the darkness, willing her voice to drown out the screams of the others still resounding through her mind.

Eventually, the only sobs were her own, vibrating within the cell.

When Rae opened her eyes, she was lying on the floor of her cell. Someone had relit the lantern and dim light flickered in the corridor once again.

Rising on quivering arms, Rae focused on the cell across from her, unaware of how much time had passed.

A figure slept in the other cell, curled up and facing away from the bars. The back of her plain dress was bloodied and ragged.

Rae tried to swallow, but her tongue stuck to the roof of her mouth and she coughed.

Paita lifted her head, her movement weary. Rolling over to face Rae, her dirty face was streaked with trails from tears. Her sunken eyes met Rae's.

Crawling to the bars again, Rae rested her forehead against them. She couldn't bring herself to speak, drowning in uncertainty.

"They're going to kill me," Paita whispered, voice devoid of emotion.

Rae closed her eyes. "Tell me about your husband."

"I don't want to talk about him right now."

"I know a Damien... I can't imagine him being your Damien, though."

Paita's head lifted from her thin cot. "You do?" Hope rose in her voice. "What does he look like?"

Rae rolled her lips together, her head spinning. This would be a tricky conversation to balance. "Blond hair, hazel eyes. He had a tattoo on his arm, numbers and stars…" She pretended to think. "He had a scar on his back near his shoulder blade. Like a crescent moon. I don't know exactly how he got it though." Rae held her breath.

"That's my Damien." Paita gasped, taking the bait. She shuffled to the bars again and gripped them until her knuckles turned white. "Please, if you know where he is, tell them. They'll kill me if you don't. They'll kill my Siefa."

Rae's stomach sank, but her heart lifted at catching Pieta in a lie. While Damien had scars, none were like the one she described, and his supposed *wife* would have known that. "How did he get that scar? He mentioned a horse."

"His… his horse kicked him when he was a kid. He grew up on an equestrian ranch."

Meeting Paita's gaze, Rae backed up again as far as she could. Her breathing came in unsteady gasps, unknowing of what would happen if she gave away that the ruse was over.

Damien had never been married. He had no wife, no daughter.

Tears escaped her eyes, and she closed them.

Paita's next words fell on deaf ears as Rae mentally shut out her surroundings. Her body shuddered. Losing her mind to a sea of torment, she heard the distant scrape of a blade on a whetstone and screamed.

Chapter 9

THEY PUSHED THE HORSES HARDER than they should have to catch up with Rae.

Xyphir, already in a foul mood because of the long ride, slid to a frantic stop from a full gallop.

With only a moment to react, Damien tightened his grip on Xyphir's reins to keep himself from being thrown off while the horse reared. He locked his grip on the top of the saddle, leaning forward as he tried to calm Xyphir both aloud and through his Art.

Manic, Xyphir whinnied and stomped, uneasy about a scent he'd picked up.

"Whoa, boy." Jarrod circled Orion around as his horse also revolted, though not nearly as violently. "What's got them so spooked?"

Damien sought the surrounding energies, trying to find the source of the horse's agitation. Plenty of life thrived in the dense meadows to sort through. He continued to shush Xyphir, patting his neck as he dismounted.

Before he found the source, Damien heard a whimper from within the tall grass to the south. It gave him direction, and he recognized the tone of the voice he allowed through the barrier protecting his mind. His stomach dropped, and he released Xyphir's reins as he hurried into the dense grass without offering Jarrod a response.

The ocean of grass in front of Damien rustled as something within rushed towards him. He knelt, opening his arms.

Neco hurtled his massive body into Damien, tackling him onto the dirt. A whoosh of air left his lungs and a wet tongue assaulted his face.

"Damien!"

"It's all right," Damien shouted through the shower of kisses. He grabbed Neco's ruff, scratching and pushing him back so he could sit up.

The wolf whined and Damien doubted he could have gotten him off without Neco's compliance.

"Gods, you've grown again." Damien ruffled the hair on top of the black wolf's head.

Neco's pink tongue lolled out the side of his mouth before he quizzically tilted his head towards Jarrod. Both sitting, Neco was taller than Damien.

"The hells." Jarrod stood with his knife in his hand at the edge of the road.

Neco lowered his muzzle and snarled. Razor sharp fangs Damien would never want aimed at himself bared at Jarrod. The wolf stepped forward.

"Whoa, Neco." Damien grabbed hold of his thick ruff again. "He's a friend." The language wasn't enough, and he fought to remember the way he'd communicated with Neco before. He found the emotions, the feelings to express to him, and pushed the surges of power from his ká to Neco's.

The wolf calmed, the vibrating growl in his chest subsiding. Neco tilted his head at Jarrod before meeting Damien's gaze.

"Put that away." Damien glowered at Jarrod before refocusing on the wolf, tangling his fingers in Neco's fur. "Where's Rae?"

Neco whined and laid down, pushing his head into Damien's lap.

Jarrod sheathed his dirk and knelt beside them.

Glints of dried blood clung to the fur around Neco's face, a muddy brown-red that made Damien feel sick. It wasn't from hunting. It was Rae's. He touched Neco's head, running his hand down his neck.

"He's upset," Damien explained aloud for Jarrod's benefit, but it also helped him process Neco's ká attempting to communicate. It was jumbled, a collection of images and sounds Damien had to sort through.

Neco scrambled to his feet and nudged Damien's hand before he lifted his muzzle to the dawning sky. A sorrowful howl broke from his throat.

"You couldn't have done anything, boy." Damien scratched the wolf's ear.

Neco whined and barked with a tone mimicking a voice, talking in a wolfish language.

Jarrod scoffed. "Seriously? He's not actually talking, is he? Can you understand that?"

Damien snorted. "Of course I can't. Who could possibly understand wolf?" He shot Jarrod a smirk.

Jarrod shoved him sideways.

Neco growled and snapped at Jarrod, making the thief recoil and stand.

"Nymaera. Would you tell him to lighten up?"

Damien rubbed Neco's pinned back ears. "He's just being protective. Maybe you shouldn't be so rude while I figure out what he's trying to tell me."

Jarrod rolled his eyes but fell silent.

Neco pushed his forehead into Damien's face, almost sprawling him backward again.

He held onto the wolf's neck to help keep him sitting up straight. "All right, buddy. We will try something different. I just need you to let me."

Guiding Neco's head up, Damien leaned into him, pushing his forehead against the wolf's. His fur tickled his eyelashes as he closed them. Like many things he'd done recently, he tapped into the memories of what he'd read about with Yondé. Recalling the techniques necessary to find what he needed within Neco's memories, his skin heated as he asked for help from the grass. The energies coursed up his spine into his hands, still buried in Neco's fur. His forehead throbbed as his ká extended to bind with the wolf's.

Instincts came first.

The rumble in Neco's belly made Damien want to hunt at his side, but other anxieties prompted uncharacteristic behaviors, overshadowing instinct. Grief surrounded his thoughts of Rae, enabling Damien to find the right focus.

Find Damien.

The first two words prodded against his concentration, but he didn't recognize the voice. It came again, and he realized the voice belonged to the wolf. He sucked in a deep breath, straining to make the connection stronger.

Find Damien.

This time, Damien nearly fell out of his concentration when the words came with Rae's voice. Broken and hoarse, but he'd recognize her tone anywhere.

His vision shifted from the black of his eyelids to a misty collection of images and shapes. He could make out Rae's face, but it was so much more than that. It was her scent, the sound of her voice, and the way her hands felt touching his fur.

She was on her side, behind a barred door, and Damien

could feel Neco's frustration at not being able to free her.

"You can't follow me anymore." Rae retracted her hand from his fur. "Find Damien." The image flickered to show Damien's face as if Neco was recalling it in the moment, his scent. Then it shifted back to Rae. "Tell him we're going to Lazuli by sea from Serityme. *Damien*, Neco. Find Damien." She closed her eyes briefly. Scrapes and blood marred her face. Footsteps in the meadow drew the wolf's attention, prompting the inclination to hunt, but not for food. He imagined stalking the wandering soldier and tearing out his throat. He could taste the blood.

"Go." Rae tore him from the instinct. Attacking the soldiers wouldn't work. There were too many. "Go now."

Neco took a step back from the carriage and whined. He didn't want to leave her, but wanted so badly to do what she asked. His mind flickered to Damien again.

She nodded. "Please go, boy. Find Damien."

Damien heaved in a breath that helped draw his ká back to himself. It separated from Neco's with a snap that left his head buzzing like he'd had too much to drink.

Neco whined, pulling away to lick the tip of Damien's nose.

Jarrod stood patiently behind him, and his boots shuffled. "Anything?"

"She's alive. They're taking her to Lazuli." Damien drew away from Neco. "By ship. She sent Neco with the message."

Ultimately, the transport to Lazuli wasn't a surprise. It was home to Helgath's most notorious prison, which Damien had served at. But the shift of going by ship was distressing.

Jarrod started pacing. "Shit. They're probably halfway there already."

"Are they still searching ships? Can we follow?"

Jarrod sighed. "Every single one ever since you deserted. We can't. They'll find you, without a doubt. We have to go by land."

"Damn it." Damien rubbed the growing sore spot on his forehead.

"Could Neco tell how she was?"

His gut wrenched as he thought of how Neco had seen her. Her condition was horrendous. He didn't know what he'd expected, knowing Helgath's typical treatment of their prisoners. But seeing it made everything in him numb.

How had he ever doubted her loyalty to him? She looked the way she did because of him and he hated himself for it. He had to free her, no matter the cost.

Neco licked his hand, nudging it.

"Not good." Damien scratched behind Neco's ears.

"Then let's not waste time." Jarrod rose and stomped back to the horses. "We need to get to Mirage."

Damien forced himself to his feet, his headache mounting. "Go hunt," he told Neco. "It'll give me some time to get the horses ready for you to come back."

Neco whimpered but rose to his feet.

Damien patted the wolf's head, not needing to lean over to do it. "We'll get her back."

Returning to the horses, Xyphir didn't seem keen on the unfamiliar scent his rider had picked up. It took some reassuring, but Damien purposely rubbed his palms over Xyphir's nose to put the wolf's scent on him.

"I can see why you didn't try to get Neco on Andi's ship, she would've had a fit. No passing that creature off as a dog." Jarrod shook his head. "Not that a dog would've been welcome, either."

Damien scoffed. "I wouldn't take Captain Trace to be much of a dog person. She and Rae became close, but that was just as unexpected."

Jarrod raised a brow and pinned his eyes on Damien. "Andi became close with Rae?"

"Despite locking me up in the brig for most of our journey, yes. Judging by your tone, that isn't exactly common for the captain, is it?"

By the time Damien asked his question, Jarrod had dismounted Orion again. "No." He rifled through his pack. "It's not at all and I wish you'd mentioned it sooner." Pulling out a stick of graphite, he wrote on a piece of parchment. Once finished, he folded it and lifted his gaze. He whistled lowly, then rose the pitch higher.

The sharp response of his hawk, Liala, drew Damien's eyes to the lingering rain clouds. The umber bird swooped down, landing with a wide flap of wings on Jarrod's well-placed bracer.

"I wouldn't waste your time if you're doing what I think you're doing. The captain made it clear she never wanted to see me again."

"This isn't about you." Jarrod wrapped the note around the hawk's leg. "If Andi cares for Rae, she'll want to know that she is being taken *by ship* to Lazuli. The Herald might be near enough to reach them." Looking at Liala, he stroked her head. "Andi." The one-word command made the hawk coo before Jarrod launched her back into the sky.

Damien frowned. He wasn't eager to involve the privateer, regardless of how logical it was. He opened his mouth to protest again, hand closing on Xyphir's saddle horn when the horse shuddered and sidestepped. A sigh escaped his mouth instead of words, and he shifted his attention to comfort the horse yet again. He tapped into the swells of the fabric, bringing an awareness of their surroundings. His gaze shot down the road, where it curved around a bank of tall grass.

He couldn't see them yet, but at least two mounted men were about to come into view.

"Someone's coming." Grabbing Xyphir's reins, Damien urged him into the grass to hide from the oncoming strangers.

Jarrod followed, leading Orion off the road with Damien. Obscured by the grass, the thief shoved his horse's reins into Damien's hand. "Stay here." He drew a dagger before crouching and stalking back towards the road.

"Sure," Damien whispered after Jarrod was out of earshot. "I'll just stay here and paint my nails."

The sound of two horses trotting along the road quieted his tongue. To his dread, the hooves slowed and stopped near the place he and Jarrod had left the road.

"Those tracks look fresh to you?" The consonants of a young man's speech were harsh, an accent Damien recognized from the streets of Veralian, Helgath's capital.

A slight parting of the foliage in front of him granted a glance at the pair of soldiers. They wore light-weight armor, steel buckled tight to their arms and legs. The chest piece, a series of steel plates laced together with dyed leather, allowed them freer movement than the heavy pieces Damien had absconded with when he deserted.

Loose, short cloaks draped over their shoulders, layers of crimson material like a scarf around their necks. The golden crest of Helgath's monarchy latched the cloaks at the scouts' shoulders.

"Looks like." The other scout glanced towards the grass and Damien leaned back, letting the grass fall back into place. Something about the voice of the second scout nudged distant memories.

"Should we check it out, Captain?"

The captain gave no answer, but his saddle creaked as he dismounted.

Damien felt with his power for Jarrod, trying to get a sense of the potential fighting field without needing to look with his eyes.

Jarrod crept near the edge of the road, the surrounding wildlife hardly noticing his silent passage. He'd circled around to come up behind the two scouts, both off their horses now. The scout reached to his side, touching the hilt of his sword.

"No reason to assume whoever it is is hostile." The captain put a hand on his hip next to his sword, but made no move to withdraw it.

The familiarity of his voice rammed into Damien's mind again. He couldn't see his face and didn't recognize his energy. Of course, all that meant was he hadn't seen him since he'd acquired his powers as a Rahn'ka, which left almost all of his old comrades.

Jarrod took a step forward, directly behind the higher-ranking soldier while the younger ventured towards where Damien hid.

Crouching, Damien touched the grass at his feet to help harness his energy. He funneled it towards the tattoos on his arms and back, narrowing his eyes where the scout would soon appear.

"Velok," the captain snapped. "Ease down. You're jumpier than a field mouse."

Damien's heart leapt at the phrase, his throat catching as the familiarity hit home. Not only the voice of the captain, but also the name of the younger soldier. He knew them both.

Jarrod rose to his full height behind the captain, reaching around with his blade towards the man's throat.

"Stop!" Damien rushed to his feet and burst from the tall grass.

As Velok jumped back, Jarrod wrapped his other arm around the captain's torso, yanking him against him. The thief maintained his raised blade, his grip tight on his target. His dark eyes locked on Damien and, for a moment, Damien thought he would slice the man's throat regardless of his protest.

The captain stood rigid in Jarrod's grasp, his hand moving towards a dagger at his side. When his warm brown eyes met Damien's, they widened. "Stand down, Velok." He remained still, eyes darting down to the knife at his throat, but he didn't struggle.

Jarrod's knuckles whitened, but his steady hand kept the blade off the man's skin.

Velok took a nervous step back again, his eyes shooting from Damien towards his commanding officer. "Sir?"

"I said *stand down*." The captain's voice rang with authority, anger buried within it.

Damien heaved a deep breath as he tried to comprehend the ramifications of who stood before him and what it might lead to. "Jarrod. Let him go."

"Are you crazy?"

"Please."

The thief hesitated, then exhaled and stepped back, lowering his weapon but keeping it ready. "This better be good since you gave them my name." He shifted his gaze between the Helgathian scouts.

The captain relaxed, his shoulders slumping, and he removed his leather gloves. He took a step towards Damien, whose stomach tightened until the captain lifted a hand, extended in greeting. "Didn't think I'd see you here." They traded grips, and Damien was pulled into a rough hug. "Little brother."

"Corin." Damien sighed against him, returning the embrace. "Gods, am I glad to see you."

Jarrod stomped off the road, passing Damien with a shaking head. "Cut it a little close, don't you think?" He entered the grass to retrieve the horses.

Corin chuckled, taking a step back. "Just like Damien. He's always cutting it a little close."

Damien studied his brother's face. He hadn't seen him in several years, but their similarities were strong. The locks of his golden blond hair were hidden beneath the Helgathian helmet and he had the clean-shaven face Damien used to prefer, along with the strong Lanoret jawline.

"Where the hells have you..." Corin trailed off as Jarrod emerged with their mounts, his gaze locking on the thief, studying him.

Jarrod paused next to Damien when the captain stopped speaking. "Problem?"

Corin blinked, his body stiffening. He opened his mouth to speak, but Velok interrupted.

"Captain Lancet?" The scout gaped, shaking his head in confusion. "What are you—"

"Lancet?" Damien quirked an eyebrow.

"My inconsiderate brother made it necessary to adopt an alternate surname from time to time." Corin turned towards his fellow scout. "What is it Velok?"

"Damien Lanoret is your brother?" He shook his head again, grip tightening on his sword. "But he's a deserter. We need to..."

Jarrod pushed the reins into Damien's hand and when he met the thief's eyes, he saw fire within them. The thief slowly circled on the road, coming to stand on the other side of Velok.

Corin gave Damien's shoulder a squeeze before he stepped past him towards his scout. "Perhaps I misjudged then. I had hopes for you."

Velok backed up directly into Jarrod's waiting grip.

Jarrod looped an arm around the shorter soldier's neck, holding him in place. His other hand grabbed Velok's wrist and twisted it, wrenching the sword from his hand.

Corin withdrew the dagger he'd started for when Jarrod had entrapped him, the steel scraping against the sheath.

"You seem to have brought a problem with you." Jarrod raised an eyebrow at Corin.

Corin paused as he glanced at Jarrod's face, his jaw tightening. "I didn't think he would be. But I think it's up to Velok whether he remains a problem, and how we solve it if he does."

"Whoa." Damien stepped between his brother and the young soldier he used to command. "Aren't we getting ahead of ourselves here?"

"If you tell me to let him go too..." Jarrod glowered at Damien. "I swear to the gods, it ain't happening."

"Captain?" Velok squeaked as Jarrod twisted the scout's arm behind his back.

Corin ignored Damien, using the tip of his dagger to lift the brim of Velok's helmet, flicking it to the side and onto the ground. "Since you served under my brother, I thought you might have a different reaction if you saw him. You said you respected him."

"I did." Velok choked. "But we serve King Iedrus. He betrayed our country and our honorable king. We should treat him like the traitor he is."

Damien grabbed hold of his brother's wrist, twisting the blade away from Velok. "He's just a kid."

"A kid who will get us all killed," Jarrod growled.

"Looks like you finally got smart about the company you keep, little brother." Corin gave a half-smile towards Jarrod.

"He's not my biggest fan." The thief shrugged.

"He never was the best judge of character." Corin's mouth curled into a full grin. "And he's always been a little squeamish."

Chapter 10

"HEY, CAN WE STOP TALKING about me like I'm not here?" Damien frowned. "I'm the one who's the traitor—"

"And I'm, what, a law-abiding citizen?" Jarrod's anger deepened. "He knows my name. This isn't solely your decision."

"And he knows that I faked my name to get this scouting post."

"You can't just kill him!"

"You're right." Jarrod looked at Corin. "We should get off the road first."

Corin gave a nod and Damien cursed colorfully.

"You're all traitors!" Velok struggled against the thief.

Jarrod tightened his hold, cutting off anything else the young man intended on saying. He stepped into the grass while Corin held it aside to make space for him.

"Stop!" Damien followed them.

Jarrod paused, looking at Damien and tilting his head. "This isn't your call. Try to think of the bigger picture." He didn't enjoy killing, but would when necessary.

Like now.

"He's right, Damien. You always had a bleeding heart, but this isn't the time. You don't know everything that's at stake." Corin lifted his knife toward Velok.

"Then explain it to me." Damien caught his brother's hand, but he yanked free.

Velok bucked, stomping his foot down on Jarrod's. In the moment of distraction, the scout's hand slipped a glint of steel from his side and plunged the blade into Jarrod's exposed forearm.

Jarrod yelled as Velok twisted the blade, forcing his arm away.

Dropping his weight, Velok fell to the dirt at his feet, scrambling to get away.

Blood poured down Jarrod's right arm, and he grabbed the wound, gritting his teeth. "I'm so fucking sick of being stabbed."

Corin's armored boot caught Velok in the gut, splaying him onto his back with an exhale of surprise. Pinning his arm with one knee, Corin attempted to secure the flailing scout's other arm. Another flash of metal in Velok's hand caught the sunlight, plunging towards Corin's exposed chest.

A pale wisp of mist appeared from nowhere, encircling the soldier's wrist and stopping it before he struck Corin.

Damien's power ripped the blade away, and Velok's eyes widened in horror.

Corin rocked back, away from the power.

With his uninjured arm, Jarrod yanked his blade from his belt. Velok scrambled to his knees, trying to crawl away, but the thief caught up. He brought his knife under the soldier's chin, slicing it across his throat. The edge of the blade caught on Velok's spine and it took an extra grunt of effort to finish the motion before Velok collapsed face first into the dirt.

Blood gurgled as Velok choked, the ground beneath him flooding with crimson.

Blood dripped from Jarrod's injured arm, mingling with the pools on the ground. His stomach churned.

Corin rose, nudging Velok's limp arm with his boot.

"Gods." Damien huffed, his voice raw. "Just a kid." His eyes locked on Velok and Jarrod wondered what Damien could see as he died.

"Don't even think about it," Jarrod said to Damien through a clenched jaw.

Bringing the man back would only cause him to suffer his death twice.

Damien ran his hands through his hair, closed his eyes, and dropped to a crouch.

"Don't think about what?" Corin's brow furrowed.

"He can bring him back."

"Fuck, Jarrod." Damien glared at him. "And you get mad at me for just saying your name!"

"What?" Corin stared at his brother.

"Oh, so you're allowed to make choices and share whatever information you want, but something as crucial as this, I'm supposed to keep to myself?" Jarrod's face heated. "How about you take a walk?"

Damien's fists clenched, his knuckles turning white. Standing, he glared behind Jarrod as if contemplating something, but then spun on his heels. "You're an asshole." He stomped deeper into the meadow, disappearing amidst the growth.

Jarrod threw his hands up in the air, which sent blood spraying onto the grass. "Don't worry about me, I'll just bleed out! Again..."

The rich sound of Corin's laugh came from behind him. The captain stepped forward, pulling off his helmet. His hair, the same shade as Damien's golden blond, was cut short. The helmet left it messy and made Jarrod's jaw flex.

"I'll wrap it for you." Corin gave a low pulsing whistle identical to Damien's usual call for the horses. His sauntered forward and Xyphir looked thoroughly confused.

Jarrod pulled his gaze from Corin to look at the body of the soldier with a sigh. "What are we going to do about him?"

"Burn him, I suppose. But I don't see you being much good at that while you're *bleeding out*."

Jarrod laughed, looking at the seeping gash on his arm. "No, I suppose not. I guess Damien doesn't feel like healing me this time." If he'd been using his other arm, his bracer may have helped protect him. But he only wore the bracer for Liala to land on. He rolled up his sleeve to get a better look.

Corin dug a small pouch out of one of his saddlebags and waved Jarrod towards him. He encouraged the horse another step sideways, blocking their view of Velok's body. "I'm sorry, but you're going to have to run that one by me again." He met Jarrod's eyes with a curious look. "Damien? Heal? He's never had a lick of Art in him."

"I'm not sure it's my place to tell you." Jarrod lifted his injured arm between them. "But seeing as he stopped me from killing you, I think he'll just need to get over it. I don't know details, but after deserting, he... came into some form of the Art. He can heal, but there's a lot more to it than that."

Corin lifted a hand, waving off the need to continue. "He'll tell me when he's ready then. I won't bother with stitches if Damien can do something about this." He pulled a thick roll of gauze from the pouch, then tucked the sack under his arm. He held the edge of the gauze between his lips while rolling Jarrod's sleeve further out of the way.

"Depends how much of a grudge he holds." Jarrod smirked. "Though it seems you've let the attempt on your life go?"

Corin couldn't answer right away with the medical supplies still held in his mouth. But the corners of his lips turned up. Taking the gauze out, it evolved into a full, attractive smile. "Never had time for grudges. You stopped and I'm grateful. You could've ignored him. So how I see it, I owe you my gratitude."

Jarrod shook his head. "No need."

"You know, with the way you two go back and forth at each other... If I didn't know for certain Damien is as straight as an arrow, I'd say you make a cute couple." Corin's voice lowered with the teasing tone.

Jarrod coughed, clearing his throat. "He's not my type. I happen to be good friends with his woman, too."

"Woman?" Corin glanced up from wrapping the wound. "Sounds like deserting was exactly what my little brother needed. Course, I told him not to enlist in the first place."

"Rae," Jarrod whispered, his mind drawn to what a delay could cost her. "She's why he's returning to Helgath."

"Leave it to a woman to make Damien lose all sense." Corin sighed. "Helgath knows he's coming, that's why I'm out here. I volunteered for the scouting troops and hoped I'd find him before anyone else did. Do you think we can convince him to turn around?"

Jarrod furrowed his brow. "She was captured because of him. I don't think he'd ever let her pay for his crimes and I'm not about to turn around either."

Corin scowled a little. "What Damien has done isn't a crime. At least it shouldn't be."

Jarrod shook his head again. "I couldn't agree with you more, but that changes nothing."

"So now the two of you are on a mission to save this girl, Rae? Do you even know where they're taking her?" He finished wrapping Jarrod's wound, but his hand lingered at the edge of the bandage.

"Lazuli." Jarrod muttered the word, eyes fixated on Corin's hand. He lowered his arm, stretching his hand, and Corin slowly withdrew. Returning his gaze to Corin's face, he realized the man was staring at his right hand.

"Can't imagine you're looking forward to being there." Corin lifted his chin, meeting Jarrod's eyes. "All things considered."

"What are you talking about?"

"You're a Martox. Damien was too young to remember, but I do. You visited my family's ranch when we were kids."

Jarrod stiffened, finding the air suddenly thin. He took a slow, deliberate step back. No one in the guild even knew his surname. His lineage. Not even Rae.

Corin lifted his hands, exposing his palms to Jarrod. "I won't say anything. I just didn't think I should pretend not to recognize you."

Jarrod sucked in a breath. "Damien doesn't know. No one does, and I'd prefer it stay that way."

"No problem." Corin lowered his hands. The charming smile returned. "I'm better at keeping secrets than my brother. But the word is that you're dead."

Jarrod smirked, glancing away before turning back to Corin. "I'm not surprised. Saves face rather than admitting their son left."

"I suppose that's true. I doubt they'd approve of your apparent chosen lifestyle." Corin touched the collar of his shirt as if plucking something from it.

"No less than they approved of anything else I did. Besides. Jarrod Martox *is* dead."

"Looks pretty alive to me."

Jarrod smiled. "Aye. But you're looking at someone else, not the boy you saw at your ranch... When we were kids, huh? How come I don't remember you, because I feel like I should."

Corin shrugged. He tucked the pouch of medical supplies back into his saddlebags as he took a step towards Jarrod. "We didn't actually... meet. I kind of just creepily watched you from the hayloft while you picked out that dapple grey stallion."

"Titian... He was an exceptional horse."

"Of course he was. He was Lanoret bred." Corin grinned. His gaze broke away for a moment, dropping to follow Jarrod's body up as if studying him.

Jarrod straightened under the scrutiny.

"So, you say Damien isn't your type? What *is* your type?"

Raising an eyebrow, Jarrod smiled. "Someone a little more direct, perhaps."

"How direct?" Corin took another step closer. His right hand reached up, running a thumb down Jarrod's bicep.

Jarrod's blood heated and he forced his feet to be still. Openly portraying his sexuality wasn't something he'd done before and he wasn't sure if his feet would draw him closer to Corin or farther away. "You should have introduced yourself."

"I'm not as shy as I used to be." Corin's hand trailed down his arm before his fingers touched Jarrod's palm. "You could say I've been waiting for this opportunity for a while."

Finding courage beneath his pounding pulse, Jarrod closed his hand over Corin's. Their fingers entwined, sending a shiver down his spine.

When he heard footsteps somewhere within the grass, Jarrod stiffened again and pulled his hand back.

He turned, pacing a few feet away and running his hand over his hair.

What am I doing?

The horses shifted uneasily, Xyphir in particular, as Damien emerged into the little grass clearing with Neco at his heels.

The wolf snarled and Corin reached for his sword.

Jarrod clamped a hand down on Corin's wrist. "No." He let go as Corin relaxed and looked at Damien.

Damien ran his fingers through Neco's coat at the back of his head, silencing the growls. "I know, buddy. I'm tired of people pulling blades out too."

Jarrod frowned. "I'm the one with the stab wound again."

Neco calmed, approaching Corin with a twitching nose.

Damien rolled his eyes and took a step towards Jarrod. "Sorry," he murmured under his breath. "Looks like Corin stopped the bleeding at least."

Jarrod's posture relaxed, and he rolled his shoulders, attempting to recover from the lingering tremble in his stomach. He struggled to keep his gaze away from the source. "So you're not pissed at me anymore?"

"You were right, I just needed a walk to clear my head." Damien cast a wary eye towards Velok's body. "I'm not mad at you. Just this entire situation."

"Does that mean you'll heal my arm now?"

Nodding, Damien gripped Jarrod's elbow where his skin was still exposed. His touch was entirely different from Corin's, but as his skin heated, Jarrod's gaze ventured to the captain.

"This will hurt a little."

"Thanks for the warning this time."

Corin's warm eyes met Jarrod's. His chin tilted ever so slightly to the side in a curious quirk.

Maybe a little pain will help bring my mind back to reality.

The heat of Damien's hands turned to a roaring shock that ripped across his skin and he hissed.

Yup. Definitely helps.

Where the blade had penetrated his flesh seared with invisible fire, like it was tearing all over again. Then it faded, leaving the area aching like an itch he couldn't reach.

Damien promptly let go as Corin approached.

Jarrod untucked the gauze Corin had wrapped, peeling it away from where the blood still stuck it to his skin. While the crimson marked what had been there, his skin was perfectly smooth.

"What'd you do?" Corin looked from Jarrod's arm to his brother.

"What does it look like I did?"

"Come on. What happened to you?"

Jarrod sighed. "Can we talk about this later, once we're moving again? Rae isn't getting any closer and we still need to burn a body. The sooner we get to Mirage, the sooner we can secure passage to Lazuli." He grimaced at the next question surely to come from Corin.

"Mirage?" Corin sounded surprised. "Not a lot of good can come from that place unless you've got an in with the guilds." He glanced at Jarrod, who set his jaw at his own stupidity.

"We've got one." Damien gestured towards Jarrod nonchalantly. "Or was I not supposed to say that either?"

Apparently he hasn't completely forgiven me.

Jarrod scowled at Damien, his chest tightening. His upper lip twitched. "Careful, Rahn'ka, there's always more I can say."

It was Corin's turn to frown as Jarrod and Damien stared at each other, each challenging the other to say more.

Neco growled, stepping forward from Damien's side.

"Look." Corin moved between them and placed a solid hand on their chests to bring the attention onto him. "Jarrod's right that we should get going. Another scout team shouldn't be far behind us and we need to take care of Velok's body."

Jarrod watched Damien. "Can you manage burning it, or do I need to do it for you?" Anger still tainted his words, fear edging its way into his senses. Corin knew too much about him already.

Corin shoved Jarrod's chest, drawing his gaze. "Not helping."

Damien took a step back, still glaring at Jarrod. "I've got it. I'm more likely to show his body some respect." He turned to walk towards the corpse, kneeling beside it.

Jarrod turned from them, eager to get some space from Damien. The space he sought from Corin was for entirely different reasons. He ran his hand over his face, thick with stubble.

I will not let a soldier get to me. Especially not a Lanoret.

Neco laid in the grass, huffing out a breath before closing his eyes.

Jarrod walked to Orion, trying to center his thoughts.

"How were you planning on getting past the border?" Corin's voice behind him made him tense.

Without turning around, Jarrod shrugged. "We were kind of playing that one by ear. I have some connections, but not specifically at the border."

Corin groaned. "I don't think *by ear* is how you're going to want to approach that one."

Jarrod heard him shift to the side, boots scuffling in the dirt. His nerves grated until his gaze met Corin's as the captain purposely made it difficult for Jarrod to avoid him.

"Did I piss you off?" Corin had tugged the scarf of his cloak from his neck, exposing his richly tanned skin still several shades lighter than Jarrod's. "Or is it still my nitwit brother?"

"You didn't do anything." Jarrod's voice sounded gruffer than he meant it to. "Your brother gets under my skin. Plus, it seems you have me at a disadvantage with sensitive information." Admitting it out loud seemed foolish, but something about Corin's expression compelled him to.

Corin offered a wide grin. "You're usually quite the private one, aren't you? I know we barely know each other, but I swear I won't tell anyone."

Jarrod wanted to believe him, but couldn't help wondering if his inclinations were getting the better of him and his judgment. Looking over Corin's uniform, with one hand on Orion's saddle horn, Jarrod shook his head. He'd never have considered any Helgathian soldier an ally, yet here he was, with two.

He rubbed his short beard again.

Time for a subject change.

"Can you help us get across the border?"

"Sure." Corin shrugged as if Jarrod made a simple request. "I definitely have more connections than you do there." He shifted closer, leaning with a hand on Orion's saddle behind Jarrod's shoulder. "Do you realize how attractive you look when you're angry? It doesn't give me much motivation to avoid pushing your buttons."

Jarrod clenched his jaw, his heart picking up speed.

Why does he have such an effect on me?

His gaze flickered in Damien's direction, but the Rahn'ka was still busy dealing with the dead soldier. "Do you realize how difficult you're making it to focus?"

"Good." Corin smirked. "Then at least the feeling is mutual."

Jarrod sucked in a breath through his teeth and narrowed his eyes.

"I'm not usually this forthright, but with you..." Corin drew in a slow breath. "There's something about you."

This is a terrible idea.

A slow grin spread across Jarrod's face as his tongue disagreed with his thoughts. "It'd have been a real shame if I'd killed you. *Something about me...* Something about *you*. You might just make putting up with your brother all this time worth it."

Shut up, Jarrod. Stop talking. Use your head. He is not your ally.

Corin's smile sent another rush of heat through Jarrod's body. The captain stepped forward, his eyes following his index finger as it teasingly traced the silver buckle securing the top of Jarrod's vest. "So a Martox turned thief? Dare I ask which guild?"

A flurry of ways Corin could use the information against him weighed on Jarrod's shoulders. Doing his best to think logically, he took a step sideways. Gulping, he averted his gaze. "You don't want to know. I should see if Damien is almost finished."

Without waiting for a response, Jarrod walked away. Corin's presence suffocated him with conflicting feelings, and he needed to be smarter. Following the direction Damien had gone, he shook his head.

Now you're an asshole and an idiot.

The acrid scent of smoke wafted into his nostrils, and he cringed. He entered a clearing, one that hadn't been there before, and his eyes fell on Damien standing by a short pyre.

The flames swirled in against themselves, concentrated away from the dry grass of the meadow. Faint flickers of pale light surrounded the fire, creating a dense barrier in the air. The smoke swirled within, escaping only at the top like an invisible chimney.

Neco sat beside Damien, leaning against his leg. His ears perked up at Jarrod's approach.

Damien tilted his head partially in Jarrod's direction. "We need to get going."

"Aye." Jarrod walked closer. "But I need to talk to you."

Damien's jaw flexed, but he turned to face him. "About what? There isn't any more to talk about regarding this business." He waved agitatedly towards the burning body.

"Look, would you? I'm sorry about how everything happened. It's a shit situation and I shouldn't have said what I did about your ability." Jarrod stuffed his hands in his pockets. "I just assumed you trusted him."

"I do." Damien sighed, looking in the direction his brother was. "I think."

Doubt seared in the back of Jarrod's mind.

"He's my brother. Family. I trust him. But I know what serving Iedrus can do to a person and I'm not sure he's the man I remember anymore."

Jarrod forced himself to keep breathing steadily. "I know you're probably still pissed at me, but I need you to keep my allegiances private." If Corin learned he was a Hawk... the man already had too much to hold over his head.

"Right." Damien nodded. "I shouldn't have said anything. My emotions aren't the clearest right now and I overreacted. I apologize."

Jarrod nodded. "No more information and I'll do the same."

"Sounds fair to me." Damien crossed his arms. He glanced at the burning pyre, then turned his back on it. "The fire won't spread, I've made sure of it."

Jarrod extended a hand. "Are we good?"

Damien eyed the offer for a moment and then took it. "Good."

Chapter 11

"You can't be serious." Jarrod gawked, leaning forward in his saddle, and pointed at Damien. "Him?"

A horrible shadow of dread rumbled through the Rahn'ka. Gripping Xyphir's reins tightly, he tried not to tug on them. The horse had finally accepted Neco running beside him and didn't need his tension. They kept a steady pace, riding side by side on the wide caravan roads toward Quar.

Jarrod and Corin rode ahead, refusing to slow even while they talked, shouting over the pounding hooves.

The clouds had thickened overhead, but rain had yet to come down. The overcast sky mirrored the feelings in Damien's gut. Only one night had passed since reuniting with his brother and he was already being bombarded with unsettling news.

Corin laughed. "I'm serious. Damien only added more fire to something that's been boiling under the surface for a long time."

Damien wanted to wrap his dense cloak tighter and find a hole to hide in until it all passed. They were on a major road, which Jarrod and Damien had been avoiding until Corin came and insisted they needed to go through one of the major border crossings rather than a small secluded one. He justified that the soldiers tasked with getting many people in and out wouldn't be paying as much attention.

"Well, I don't want it." Damien glowered at the back of his brother's head.

"Too bad, little brother. You got it. You're the inspiration for an entire uprising. You proved it's possible to defy military rule. And there are plenty interested in sowing more distrust in the king. You're a convenient figurehead. Your picture is everywhere."

"How are we going to get him across the border, then?" Jarrod held his horse's reins with one hand, the extended riding apparently comfortable for him.

I saw him jousting in the Inbetween, so it makes sense. And the big gold ring he wears... Guild coffers, my ass. He used to be a noble and ran away to become a thief?

Corin shrugged in his usual casual way, which made Damien grit his teeth. "Leave it to me. I'll get him across. Just one more way to thumb our noses at the monarchy."

Jarrod glanced at Damien so briefly that if Damien hadn't already been looking at him, he would have missed it. The thief didn't like the plan either.

No time to focus on Jarrod. Could Corin be lying?

Damien hated that he was questioning his brother. The irony of trusting a secretive Ashen Hawk more than his own blood only grew with each hoofbeat closer to the border. "I'd like more details about this plan, if you don't mind."

"Aye."

"Fine." Corin sighed, sounding almost irritated, but explained.

Quar sat on the border between Helgath and Olsa, its sprawling walls serving as the barrier between countries. The city stretched along the border, where the Olsan meadows turned to rough patches of sagebrush and creosote.

The desert storm brought cool temperatures that made Damien's thick cloak a bit more believable.

He tucked a scarf up around his face, like Corin had instructed both him and Jarrod to do, and rode in the back.

Damien sent Neco another way, assuring him they would meet again on the other side of the city. A valley wolf wouldn't gain attention running across the wild parts of the border alone.

They'd fortuitously timed their entrance through the grand

arching tunnel built into the wall. They followed behind a large group crossing into Helgath and a caravan of tobacco traders rolled in behind them.

The big wooden gate opened only on one side, creating a bottleneck no wider than ten yards. The sun couldn't penetrate the deep passageway. A combination of torches and Art-created lanterns aided in providing light.

When firelight glinted off the top of the guards' helmets, Damien's heart leapt into his throat. There were at least fifteen.

So much for Corin's theory about the way being sparsely guarded.

The only comfort was the guards hardly paid attention to the people going through, more interested in chatting with each other or picking out the occasional unlucky traveler to harass.

Corin urged his horse ahead, dismounting in a swift motion as he drew close to the large doorway. He pulled the scarf of his cloak down, but the din of voices bouncing off the stone archway made it impossible for Damien to hear what his brother said to the guard.

The man with a dark, long mustache grinned and exchanged a handshake with Corin. He tipped the wide brim of his metal helmet back, and they continued talking.

Damien tore his gaze away to look at the gate, focusing on it alone as he urged Xyphir to remain calm in the tight space.

Without the sky above him, he couldn't breathe, the cloak covering his nose and mouth suffocating him.

Jarrod glanced over his shoulder at him and pulled his hood over his head. He'd told Damien earlier how he hadn't liked the sound of the plan and Damien hoped his reassurance that they could trust Corin would prove true.

A sleepy guard, leaning heavily on his halberd, controlled the traffic through the gate. He would shift which direction people were allowed to move in large groups and cut off the flow into the city just in front of Jarrod.

Lurching Xyphir to a stop, Damien felt light-headed. He forced himself to slump in his saddle instead of straightening. He could use his power to kill all the soldiers without much of a thought, but that wouldn't be right. Regardless, his Art remained locked tightly behind a hiding aura in case another Artisan was present. It wasn't uncommon for the military to engage their services at the border.

Orion shuffled his hooves beneath Jarrod, showing the anxiety of his rider.

In his peripheral vision, Corin grabbed the guard he'd been talking to, forcing his attention towards Damien and Jarrod. He pointed wildly and being so close behind Jarrod, for a brief horrible moment, Damien thought his brother was pointing at him.

The plan had been for Corin to cause a distraction and potentially use a poor innocent bystander to accomplish it.

Judging by the direction Corin pointed, that poor bystander was now Jarrod.

Two guards playing a dice game by the door bounded to their feet. With no room to turn or run, Jarrod could do little as guards surged towards him.

Orion backed up, bumping into Xyphir, and whinnied.

Damien urged Xyphir to the side, nearly crushing his leg against the stone wall as the sleepy guard startled to life. The mustached man blew a whistle, its shrill tones echoing through the tunnel.

The guards grabbed Orion's reins, tugging him towards the open space beside the main gate.

Jarrod shouted at them, apparently attempting to play the part, even if he hadn't been prepared for it. A guard and Corin pulled him right off his saddle, and they all collapsed to the ground with a cacophony of clattering.

Cries of panic rose among the crowds and the mustached man shouted at the poor sleepy guard to clear the travelers out.

Reminding himself of his purpose, Damien nudged Xyphir through the cleared opening and into the crowds of the busy Helgathian city.

Jarrod will be fine.

As long as they all stuck to the plan.

Damien didn't dare glance back as he steered Xyphir onto a southern road wedged between the dense buildings of Quar.

The condition of the homes worsened the farther south he

went, and the commoners crowding the streets grew more ragged. The infamous Brigg's Hollow tavern had been their agreed meeting place.

Damien never would have considered entering such a place before he became an outlaw. He'd almost automatically vetoed Corin's suggestion to use it. The usual patrons were not exactly those Damien would associate with. But that was before he became a traitor and friends with thieves.

Not to mention loving one.

No guards patrolled the area, the city's security lackadaisical because they believed the border crossing would stop crime from entering their city. But criminals already infested it along the southern wall.

Damien dismounted Xyphir and secured his reins to a railing outside the establishment. No other horses waited, and a whisper of power sealed the leather reins together. It guaranteed Xyphir would still be there when he came back out, even if the horse would probably kick anyone else.

Slinging his pack over his shoulder, he climbed the creaky half-set of stairs to the front door. It dragged along the ground as he pushed it open, making an awful grinding sound.

Already busy, despite it being early afternoon, the patrons of the establishment quieted and glared in his direction.

His breath, still trapped amidst the material of his scarf, dampened his beard as he made his way to a shadowy corner away from the fireplace. Plopping his pack as deep as he could in the corner, he settled onto a chair. Relief flooded through him when the crowds returned to whatever conversation or business they were conducting before he'd entered.

He sat there, alone, far longer than he hoped. He kept his senses tightly secured, resisting all temptation to seek Jarrod or Corin with his Art. It was too dangerous to risk. He knew how to hide his power, but was not practiced enough to do it while actively using the Art.

Finally giving in to the persistent barmaid who kept checking in on him, Damien ordered a second ale.

Maybe it will help calm my nerves.

Tugging his scarf low enough to allow the drink to reach his lips, the tavern's door burst open and his eyes settled on Jarrod's furious face. His scowl caused anyone in his way to step out of his path.

Jarrod's gaze found Damien and his shoulders relaxed, even if only partially. He moved through the crowded space, not looking back as Corin entered behind him.

Taking a seat at Damien's small table, Jarrod snatched the mug straight from Damien's hand and lifted it to his mouth, downing the ale. A bruise and scuff marred his jawline. A series of cuts on his forehead and chin.

"Have fun?" Damien received a death glare from his friend that would have silenced most. "You got a little somethin'..." He pointed to his own chin.

Corin laughed from somewhere within the crowd.

"Thanks, Ollie. You're a sweetheart." He gave the barmaid a wide grin as she pushed two overflowing mugs across the bar top to him. No one seemed to even give him a second glance

Jarrod huffed, but said nothing, running a hand over his hair. His wrists were raw from bindings and Damien winced.

Whatever he suffered, he did it for me.

"Oh gods, little brother!" Corin placed the two mugs down on the table, one in front of Jarrod. "You should have seen his face. Though I am sorry they had to muck it up." He settled in a chair. It screeched as he dragged it a little closer to Jarrod. "They didn't do anything permanent, did they?" A glint of mischievousness that Damien recognized from when they were kids surfaced in his brother's eyes, but something else tangled with it when he looked at Jarrod.

Instead of answering, the thief lifted the fresh mug and took a long drink. Once it emptied too, he slammed it down in front of Corin. He grabbed the captain's mug, already at his lips, and pulled it away. Frothy liquid spilled out onto Corin's shirt.

"This would have gone smoother without him." Jarrod tilted his head at Corin.

"Got him in, didn't I?" The soldier frowned, brushing the froth from his chest. He lifted a hand to gesture for three more to Ollie, who gave him a cheerful reply. "Besides, I thought it went pretty smooth. Convenient that Jarrod looks just like an

Olsan spy Helgath has been looking for. I thought it was better that the surprise on your face be genuine…"

Jarrod grumbled. "Racist bastards, thinking all black men look the same." He took a smaller drink of ale.

"What'd they do to you?" Damien ignored Corin, leaning on the table towards Jarrod.

Jarrod looked at Corin finally, quirking his eyebrows in a prompt to answer.

Corin heaved a sigh. "They may have interrogated him a little."

Damien pursed his lips, familiar with Helgathian interrogation techniques. "What kind of interrogation?"

Corin rolled his eyes and gestured to Damien's face. "You can take that thing off. No one in here cares. Hells, most of them have a poster up somewhere in the city for their own bounties."

Damien hesitated and Corin reached across to tug the cloth down himself. The cool air of the tavern struck his face and felt wonderful. Ollie didn't even glance at him as she put the three full mugs on the table between them.

"The fun kind of interrogation." Jarrod pulled a mug towards him despite still having the half-full one he'd taken from Corin.

"I wouldn't have let them get too far." Corin frowned, lifting his drink. "I like your face the way it is."

Jarrod gave Corin a sideways glance and Damien swore he saw the corner of the thief's mouth twitch.

"So we're in the clear then? What's next?" Damien settled back into his chair, eyeing the busy tavern.

"Mirage, ain't it?" Corin drained his mug.

"Aye." Jarrod narrowed his eyes at Corin. "And what about you?"

"Well, there are certain benefits to being a captain. And moderately skilled at forgery. I just need a little time tonight and I'll be transferring to the Lazuli peace force. They're in need of my skills." Corin smirked as his hands slipped under the table.

A brief pause lingered between them before Jarrod tensed. He stood up with a screech of his chair. "I need some air." He turned and wove through people towards the exit.

Damien's mouth hung open, stuck with unvoiced protests. He looked at his brother, who had a smug smile on his face, leaning back with both hands laced behind his head. "Why did you do that?"

"Do what?" The front feet of Corin's chair lifted off the floor as he rocked himself with his boot on the lip of the table.

"Bring all that attention to Jarrod. You were supposed to use a bystander."

"No one else around looked anything like a wanted criminal." Corin shrugged. "He was the easiest solution. I just feel bad about messing up his cute face."

Damien frowned. "You can't be serious."

"Why not? I can be quite serious, little brother."

"Corin."

Corin's chair clunked back to the ground, and he leaned over the table. "Do you doubt my intentions?"

"Yes." Damien met his brother's glare. "You're tormenting him, aren't you?"

"Depends on your definition. I don't think you're in much of a position to judge what's right and wrong here. We haven't seen each other in years."

"Right, we hardly know each other. So how can you possibly expect unconditional obedience out of me? I'm not just your little brother anymore."

"No, you've gone and made sure you elevated from that position. Now you're a leader, whether or not you like it. I sure hope you aren't the Damien I used to know, because if that's true, we're fucked."

Damien growled. "And I sure hope you're not the Corin I used to know, because Jarrod deserves better."

Corin's face hardened, and they stared at each other, both refusing to break the steely silence.

"Look..." Corin sighed in defeat. "I haven't lied to you. And I haven't lied to Jarrod either. There's a lot at stake here. Hells of a lot more than you could comprehend right now. And your part doesn't give you the right to assume what I may or may not be feeling."

"You could've picked a better time to start *feeling* whatever it is."

"I think I could probably say the same about you. Course, you haven't even mentioned the girl to me. I had to hear about her from Jarrod."

Damien winced, lowering his gaze to stare at the table.

"*And* you haven't said a word about whatever this new power you have is. I'm your *brother*, Damien."

"You're also a Helgathian soldier."

Corin leaned back and gestured to the room. "You think I'm just a soldier if I can sit here, in full uniform, and no one is even giving me a second glance? It's far beyond that now and it's because of decisions *you* made."

"I didn't make the decision for you, or for anyone else. I did it for me."

"Well, you have to deal with it now. Unless someone else steps forward to lead this rebellion... I see a potential candidate to replace you, but that needs a lot more time."

"So what *are* your intentions?"

Corin's brow furrowed. "About what?"

"Jarrod."

Corin paused, scratching the back of his head. "I'm not sure yet. But I won't lie to him or to myself."

"I guess that's all I can ask." Damien sighed.

"So tell me about Rae."

As Damien recounted to his brother how he'd met her in Jacoby, his heart swelled and broke at the same time. Telling Corin the story also led to him inevitably admitting his new powers. It pleased him when his brother remained quiet through the retelling, refraining from asking questions.

Recalling the time apart from Rae while he trained with Yondé made the wounds he'd tried to hide open up again.

He missed her desperately. Everything in him ached to run to Lazuli, taking from the energies of the lands on the way and not stop until he found her. He imagined the feeling of her breath on his collarbone while they slept in each other's arms, the quirk of her lip when he said something stupid. It all made his head hurt worse than the migraines of the Rahn'ka.

How could I let Helgath take her the way they did?

Visions of Rynalds's face made him sick to his stomach. He'd kill him if he saw him again. Rynalds deserved no mercy, exempt from the redemption Damien often believed in.

"I thought Jarrod was crazy when he said you could have brought Velok back." Corin's face looked pale after Damien concluded the story of reviving the thief.

Damien shook his head, sighing. "No, and I have this feeling that so many more awful things will happen because people are trying to protect me. It happened again today when Jarrod took a beating for me at the border. It will probably happen again. I can't stand it. I never wanted this for anyone. But especially not Rae."

Corin's hand clapped down on top of Damien's wrist from across the table. He squeezed tight enough that Damien flinched. "Stop it. All of us know who you are. Hells, sounds like Rae knew from the beginning. Our choices aren't your fault."

Damien looked up and met his brother's eyes. He suddenly wished he could be a child again and look up to his older brother to rescue him from whatever situation he got himself into. Like when he'd fallen into the reservoir and Corin had fished him out, nearly drowning himself. They'd kept the adventure a secret from their parents and Corin had been the one to counsel him on the way to do so.

"What if protecting me gets you killed?"

"Isn't that what big brothers are supposed to do? But I don't plan on dying anytime soon. I have too much to do." Corin grinned, releasing Damien's hand. "Starting with getting Jarrod to forgive me and you to trust me again."

Chapter 12

FOREGOING HIS MILITARY UNIFORM MADE Corin's stomach turn, but he couldn't afford to be stopped in the streets even if it felt like he left a piece of himself behind. Unsettling news, whispered in the halls of Quar's military barracks, urged him to return to Damien and Jarrod as quickly as possible.

He tugged his hood lower over his face while passing by a posting of soldiers on a street corner.

Walking up the creaking staircase of the inn he'd arranged for his brother, Corin debated which room to go to first. He stood in the hall, considering the two doors across from each other.

Stop being a child.

Turning to the left, he knocked before he lost his nerve. Despite years of training as a soldier, his body tensed in anticipation.

This is the chance you've been waiting for your entire adult life. Don't fuck it up.

Jarrod jerked the door open, his eyes dark and shirt gloriously absent. He straightened, the shift of his muscles making Corin's mouth dry. "What are you doing here so early?" Clearing his throat, he left the door ajar and stepped towards his shirt.

Corin eyed Jarrod's tattooed back and the bruises along his ribcage. He cringed, knowing they came from his beating at the border.

Above them, black ink depicted a wolf staring at him, half its face fur, the other half formed with plate armor.

Corin averted his gaze. "Sorry. Didn't wake you, did I?"

Jarrod faced him again, pulling on and buttoning his black shirt. "That's what you're sorry for? Waking me?"

"Not only." He cleared his throat and leaned awkwardly against the doorframe, still refusing to look up. "I'm sorry for other things too." He dared a slight smile with a shrug. "I guess I knew you could handle it and I freed you as soon as I could."

Jarrod slid a single bracer onto his left arm, cinching it. "And if they'd recognized me?"

"They wouldn't have. Not this far from Lazuli. It's been too long since you left. I only recognize you because..." He pursed his lips, stopping himself before he said too much. "Why didn't you have Damien heal you?"

"Because I can handle it." Jarrod's tone lowered, eliciting a chuckle from Corin.

"See, I was right." Corin gestured towards him. "Though, I'd rather see you without all those bruises." He hesitated but took a slow step into the room. "Think you can forgive me?"

Jarrod's gaze traveled down Corin to his boots before returning to his face. "Close the door."

Corin's heart jumped. "Uh, with me inside, or outside?"

"Inside."

Corin obeyed, closing the door, the latch sliding into place.

"I can forgive you for getting me detained and questioned." Jarrod walked closer. "Bruises heal. But next time I'd appreciate being in the loop, rather than out of it. I don't like surprises."

"Really? It didn't seem like you minded them the other day. Though perhaps my forwardness wasn't entirely welcome." Corin watched as Jarrod took another step forward, the tension in his stomach boiling. "But it's good to know you don't like surprises. I'll try to keep you better informed of my intentions in the future." With Jarrod close enough now, the temptation to reach out and touch him raged through his mind.

Jarrod's jaw worked and something tumultuous filled his gaze before the thief turned away. Walking towards the window, he ran a hand over his hair. "I'm not used to this."

The pit of Corin's stomach dropped out, additional questions flooding through him. "To what?" He denied himself the step forward he wanted. Old desires, now mingled with new, surfaced unbidden and he yearned to massage away the tension in Jarrod's shoulders.

Jarrod turned around and motioned to Corin. "This, this... whatever *this* is. What are you doing, in my room, first thing in the morning?"

Corin swallowed. "I have something I need to tell you and Damien, but I came to you first, gods know why. But it's important for me to know you can forgive me, that perhaps this..." He gestured between them like Jarrod had. "Could be something. Unless I mightily misjudged and you're not—"

"Interested?" Jarrod tilted his head.

"Yes." Corin sighed. "I know it's horrible timing, all things considered, but—"

"Aye." Jarrod whispered the interruption. "I'm interested." He crossed his arms, the hint of a smile playing at his lips. "It's probably the root of my inability to be angry at you for the stunt you pulled."

Corin couldn't help but return it, his entire being humming. "So you don't hate me?"

Jarrod quirked an eyebrow. "Hate? Now that you're out of that uniform, I can't even hold that against you. Nah, I don't hate you."

Looking down at himself, Corin toyed with the loose hem of his cotton shirt. "It feels strange to not have it on, honestly." He looked up and met Jarrod's eyes. "Does the uniform bother you? I suppose I can understand why it might, but I see it another way."

"It doesn't bother me, but it serves as a reminder that we stand on two *very* different sides of Helgath, with only your brother in common."

"The only side I'm on is Helgath's."

"Precisely." Jarrod walked to a chair where his vest hung and pulled it on. Silver hilts gleamed within, but the border guards had confiscated his dirk.

"No, I don't think you understand what I'm saying. I support my country, not its king. That's what this rebellion is for. House Iedrus needs to be removed from power, and I have relinquished all loyalty to him. I serve to save the people, not the crown."

Jarrod strode closer, stopping only a foot away, and lowered his voice. "Iedrus has hanged people for saying much less than that. We can't afford to draw attention while heading to Lazuli."

Corin furrowed his brow. "I have no intention of drawing attention. As far as the military knows, I'm still a loyal servant who's been properly transferred to the Lazuli peace force. They won't be able to hang all of us at the rate this rebellion is spreading."

The thief's eyes narrowed, trailing down Corin and then back up. "You haven't answered my question."

Corin's body heated with the passage of Jarrod's gaze, taking a step back to help himself remain in control, and he bumped into the door. "What question?"

Jarrod put a hand on the door next to Corin's head. "Why are you in my room?"

Corin's breath caught, and he tried to remember how to draw it in again. He glanced at Jarrod's wrist, then followed the muscles of his arm back to his handsome face. "Uh..."

Huffing an exhale, Jarrod stood straight again and crossed his arms. "Don't remember?"

Trying to...

Corin's eyes traveled down to Jarrod's shirt, and he chewed his bottom lip, trying to organize his thoughts. Watching the gentle rise of the thief's chest with his breath didn't help. He shut his eyes, forcing a slow inhale.

"Maybe you'll remember on our way to Lazuli." Jarrod's whisper came right next to Corin's ear before the thief's footsteps echoed away from him.

A shiver passed through him, but he remained vigilant in keeping his eyes closed.

I was in the barracks... something I heard...

"Rynalds." Corin blurted as the memory came flashing back and he opened his eyes. He'd recognized the name after hearing Damien say it the night before. "He's in town."

Jarrod whirled around, breath coming faster. "What? He's here?" His voice dropped an octave, laced with a deadly tone.

"Just arrived last night from Serityme..." Corin took a cautious step from the door. "You all right?"

"I need to fulfill a promise. Where is he?" Jarrod brushed past him, reaching for the doorknob.

Corin caught his hand, turning to face him. "Hold up. You need to be smart about this. Sergeant Rynalds is staying in the barracks, he'll be inside for debriefings all day. You and Damien can't just go storming in looking for vengeance."

Jarrod looked down at his captured hand. "I didn't say anything about inviting your brother."

"Doesn't this have to do with Rae? I'd think Damien should be involved if that's the case..."

"Aye." Jarrod nodded. "But I warned Rynalds to kill me good. I need to return the favor."

The knot in Corin's stomach twisted into a hatred for the man he'd never met. If Damien hadn't been there... It still felt odd to consider his brother's power. Bringing someone back from death shook the foundation of all Corin understood about the Art.

He tightened his grip on Jarrod. "You really died, didn't you?"

Something flickered across the thief's expression, banishing the anger with an unsettling appearance of calm. "Tell me how to get to Rynalds. I think he should experience it too."

"He's probably still asleep this early."

A humorless laugh escaped Jarrod's throat. "Then direct me to his quarters."

Corin stared into his deep brown eyes, fighting the instinct to pull Jarrod into his arms. He wanted to comfort him from all the suffering he'd faced, protect him so it might not happen again.

He doesn't need my protection.

Corin released his hand. "I had the sense when you slit Velok's throat that it wasn't your first time, but would you really do it while someone slept?"

Jarrod stepped closer, the loose front of his vest touching Corin's chest. "I don't grant honor to those who have none. Does that bother you?"

"Yes." Corin maintained his footing. "But I'm trying to understand."

Jarrod shook his head slowly. "Unless you've experienced what I have, you can't understand. A week ago, I was laying in the dirt in a pool of my blood and I feel the same cold *every* time I shut my eyes." Grasping Corin's hand, he lifted it within his vest and pressed the soldier's palm to the bottom of his ribs. "I understand better now what I inflict with my knife, since one was buried here, twice."

Looking down to where they touched, Corin couldn't help but imagine the blood and flinched. He pressed harder against the spot Jarrod indicated, feeling nothing but smooth skin beneath the shirt. The anger for Rynalds deepened as he imagined Jarrod dead once more. "So what's the plan?"

Jarrod pushed Corin's hand away from his ribs. "You tell me how to get to his quarters and I'll kill him. Damien doesn't need to know until it's done."

Corin sighed and stepped back, leaning against the door. "Damien would never forgive either of us if we didn't tell him. He needs to be involved and you know it."

Jarrod's jaw flexed, and he motioned towards the door with his chin. "Then let's go get him."

Corin sidestepped, pulling the latch as he did.

As they walked into the hall, Jarrod didn't even pause at Damien's door. He only pounded on it three times with the base of his fist as he passed it.

Corin watched him walk away, waiting for his brother. He took a moment to admire Jarrod's swagger down the hall.

Damn.

The door to Damien's room opened, and his brother yawned. "What's going on?"

"Jarrod's going after Rynalds." Corin clapped his hand on Damien's shoulder. "Rise and shine."

Damien's eyes widened, and he muttered under his breath as he disappeared back into his room, thumping around to gather his things.

Corin didn't wait, hustling down the hall after Jarrod. When he emerged outside, sunlight nearly blinded him and he lifted a hand to shield his eyes.

Jarrod walked north, towards the barracks.

"It's too early to run," Corin grumbled, but urged his muscles into action. He caught up, Jarrod casting a glance over his shoulder at the sound of pounding feet, a hand inside his vest. Catching Jarrod's shoulder, Corin stomped to a stop and forcefully turned Jarrod towards him, gasping for breath. "Hold up. We need to stop and think for a moment."

Jarrod swatted Corin's hand away. "Just tell me where to find Rynalds."

Corin frowned and replaced his hand on Jarrod's shoulder, watching the thief's face.

Furrowing his brow, Jarrod shirked away from Corin's touch. "Will you stop it? That's not helping."

Shaking his head, Corin took a step back. "You can't just go sneaking up into that barracks. You won't even make it into the officer quarters."

"You don't know who I am as much as you think you do." Jarrod scoffed.

"Well, then stop being such a mysterious asshole. I know that barracks a whole hell of a lot better than you do."

Sighing, Jarrod ran his hands over his face. He closed his eyes, rolling his shoulders as more pounding footsteps ran up behind them. "You're right. What are you thinking?"

Damien came up beside them, looking far too relaxed to have just run the distance that winded Corin. He breathed as if he'd just taken a leisurely stroll and Corin glared.

"All right. Here's what we'll do..."

Corin did a final check of the gaudy emblem securing his cloak and scarf in place. Besides showing off the crest of Helgath, it displayed the name he'd taken on to avoid the negative connotations with Lanoret and a duplicate carving of the tattoo on his arm.

S. 2600

✯✯☆☆

Damien had supplied his old officer's morning routine, leading to Corin locating Rynalds in the mess hall of the barracks after most had already reported for duty.

The man's silver hair was cropped unevenly on the left side, ragged with pink puckered scars in the shape of a lightning bolt. He held a cup of coffee, one of his hands wrapped in thick bandages with a strip running over his missing index finger.

"Sergeant Rynalds." Corin tapped into the tones he reserved for command.

Rynalds glanced up, one eye hidden beneath a leather eyepatch. He scowled, opening his mouth like he was about to chastise Corin for interrupting him, but then his gaze locked on the emblem and he straightened. "Captain." He put down his mug to push back his chair and offer a salute to his superior with his fist to his chest. “Sir.”

Corin waved a hand and Rynalds relaxed before he even had to say the command. “I come seeking your assistance, Sergeant. I heard you’re familiar with the deserter Damien Lanoret.” He pushed as much disdain as he could into his brother’s name.

Something sparked in Rynalds’s face, his jaw tightening. He leaned his uninjured fist down on the table, knuckles white. “I am. Unfortunately.”

A creeping feeling entered Corin’s stomach, eyeing the hand of the man who had beaten Rae and ordered Jarrod’s death. He swallowed the inclination to punch Rynalds in the jaw right then. “Well, it is rather fortunate in this case. We have detained a man attempting to cross the border and suspect him to be the deserter. We’d appreciate your help in verifying his identity. Our usual methods are... proving less than effective.”

Rynalds grunted. “Hope you’ve got him cuffed.”

Corin didn’t respond, narrowing his eyes to imply the stupidity of the statement.

“Right. Apologies, Sir. Happy to help.”

“Good. Come with me, Sergeant.” He spun on his heels and marched out of the mess hall, the man following.

Rynalds didn’t question when they strode through the front gates of the barracks into the city, sparing Corin the need for the excuse he’d invented. There were plenty of outposts closer to the border crossing that could hold a temporary prisoner.

Like where they questioned Jarrod.

Corin glanced at Rynalds's hand as he nursed it near his chest. "What happened to your hand, Sergeant?"

Rynalds growled. "Lanoret's whore we detained in Porthew. Stupid bitch bit my finger off. She's on her way to Lazuli now."

Corin hid his smile.

I like Rae already. And now I know for sure she's still headed for Lazuli.

"You seem familiar with the fact that Lanoret has ability in the Art." Corin spoke over his shoulder once he'd walked past the agreed upon number of alleyways.

"I am. Had a bit of my own private showing of it, you could say."

"Have you told anyone else about it?" Corin stopped and turned to face Rynalds.

The sergeant narrowed his eyes, meeting Corin's. "If you'll pardon my forwardness, why do you ask, Sir?"

Corin gritted his jaw. "As you can imagine, that's information best shared sparingly. We don't want the entire country finding out that not only did we lose a soldier, but were grossly incompetent in identifying his ability at a younger age. Wouldn't you agree?"

Rynalds flinched at his sharp tone. "Yessir. Of course. None of my men know, as I didn't see it necessary. It was more important for them to know about the woman we captured in his stead."

"Another failure." Corin sighed. "What a shame you couldn't get a woman to confess his whereabouts, but instead sustained an injury." He tutted, shrugging as he walked away. "But I suppose it no longer matters."

When Rynalds didn't resume his pace, Corin turned. Eyeing the paling face of the sergeant, he followed where his gaze fixated on the alleyway entrance to their left. In the shadows, Corin could barely make out Jarrod, his hood pushed back enough to show his face.

Corin fought the grin, tightening his mouth. "Problem, Sergeant?"

Rynalds blinked, turning towards Corin, then back to the alleyway.

Jarrod hadn't moved, standing perfectly still, ignored by the bustle of the busy streets.

"Do you see that man?" Rynalds's voice turned gruff. "Over there?" He pointed, and Corin followed it to Jarrod.

Squinting, he focused on a spot to the side of the thief. "What man?"

"That one." Rynalds pointed more frantically. "The one standing in the alley there, with the hood over his head."

Corin furrowed his brow, turning to Rynalds. "Sergeant, have you been drinking?"

"Nymaera's breath." Rynalds gaped. "He's here. But he's dead."

Jarrod turned around, walking deeper into the alley and disappearing among the shadows.

Rynalds shifted uncomfortably, rubbing the scars on his jaw.

Corin sighed. "Sergeant, I—"

Before he could finish, Rynalds rocked forward, hurrying towards the alleyway.

Corin paused, his part of the plan completed. He gave a half-hearted call. "Sergeant!"

Rynalds continued, and Corin followed him towards the alley, destined to be his place of death.

Rynalds's murder is more than vengeance.

It protected Damien from Helgath finding out about his abilities. The secret needed to die with the Sergeant.

This murder is justified. No honor for the honorless.

He urged himself to believe what Jarrod had proposed, but his stomach soured.

Jarrod had vanished into the blackness, his clothing serving the purpose for which it was designed.

The alley curved, a bulk of crates blocking the dead end from the view of the townsfolk. The hem of Jarrod's short cloak wisped around the corner, disappearing as Rynalds jogged to catch up.

When Rynalds rounded the corner, he stopped, staring at the empty space.

Next to Corin, Jarrod stepped out of the shadows, casting him a sidelong glance.

Boots thudded behind the stunned Rynalds as Damien jumped down off stacked crates, landing behind him. Before the sergeant could react, Damien's arms wrapped around him, his right bicep locking around his throat, his other hand secured against the back of the man's neck. He squeezed, and Rynalds let out a choking gasp.

Jarrod pulled his hood the rest of the way back, his chest swelling with each quick breath.

The sergeant yanked a sword from his belt, but Jarrod caught the blade with his thickly gloved hand, using his other to pry it from his fingers and fling it to the ground.

"I warned you." Jarrod withdrew the long dagger Corin had lent him from his vest. Jaw working, he plunged the blade up under Rynalds's ribs. The thief growled, twisting the hilt as the man gasped. Yanking it free, he buried it again. "Meet Nymaera."

Chapter 13

SKIRTING THE SOUTHERN BORDER OF the Gilgas desert a week after leaving Quar, Damien broke his quiet demeanor to request setting up camp for the night in the middle of nowhere. Halfway to Mirage, sandstone monoliths dotted the horizon to their left, jutting defiantly towards the sky. Damien's gaze lingered on them, and Jarrod recognized the look.

Something Rahn'ka.

"What are they?" Corin nodded towards the distant ruins as he pulled the saddle from his horse. It dropped with a thud, sending a thin cloud of red dirt into the air.

The terrain ran rugged and full of strangely shaped rust-colored cliffs carved by wind and rain.

"I'm not sure yet." Damien shrugged. "But I can feel the Rahn'ka energies gathered there. They're just faded." He removed Xyphir's bridle, ushering the horse towards Jarrod. "I probably won't be back until morning."

Neco trotted over to Damien and whined, tilting his head.

Damien scratched behind his ears and nodded. "Sure, boy."

Until morning?

Jarrod hid his displeasure by rubbing Orion's nose after removing most of his tack.

Filling water buckets for the horses provided another distraction, even though they'd just passed a stream.

"Should we come with you?"

Damien shook his head at his brother. "I need some time. I better visit these ruins alone. Neco can come, but only because he asked first."

"You're just worried another guardian will tell you he would've preferred me." Jarrod rose from his crouch.

His joke earned a half-smile from Damien. "Maybe."

"If you're staying out, take some blankets."

With the approaching winter, nights grew bitter cold, even though the days remained warm enough to travel without a cloak. It made for heavy packing, with woolen blankets occupying several saddlebags. Before Corin could retrieve one, Damien waved his hand.

"I'll be fine. Just..." He eyed Corin. "You know."

Corin glowered.

Jarrod's gaze darted between the brothers.

The captain shrugged. "See you in the morning." He knelt to his packs to set up their campsite.

Once Damien left earshot, with Neco in tow, Jarrod looked at Corin. "What was that about? *You know?*"

"Just something we talked about in Quar." Corin arranged rocks in a circle for a fire pit, keeping his gaze on his task. "Don't worry about it."

Jarrod rolled his eyes and ran a hand over his clean-shaven face. He'd run a blade over it that morning, but with the oncoming chill, he wondered if he'd made a mistake.

A screech drew his gaze to the sky where a large red hawk circled high above them.

Shit.

Corin squinted at the dimming sky, but turned his attention back to the fire pit.

Pulling a bone whistle from an inner vest pocket, the thief blew on it, drawing Corin's gaze.

The predatory bird, nearly twice the size of Liala, swooped down in utter silence, pushing his arm to the side as it landed on his bracer. A beat of his wings caused a burst of wind, displacing Corin's pile of kindling.

Eyes wide, the captain fell onto his backside, blinking. "Friend of yours?"

Jarrod ignored the inquiry and removed a piece of

parchment from the hawk's leg. With a huff, he sent the bird back into the sky.

"You know. You've been giving me this silent treatment and I'm not entirely sure why."

"His name is Red." Jarrod glanced at Corin before unrolling the parchment.

"That's original." Corin paused and chuckled, rearranging the scattered kindling. "Should have guessed."

"Guessed what?" Jarrod slowly decoded the written message in his head.

"That you're a Hawk. An Ashen one, to be precise. Far more than just a thief."

Jarrod's gaze shot back to Corin, and he gritted his teeth.

Corin lifted a surrendering hand. "I can't help it when the clues fall right in my lap. It explains a lot, actually."

"If you have something to say, then say it." Nerves boiled in Jarrod's stomach.

"What is there to say? I don't know you, right?"

Jarrod sighed, falling silent as he composed his thoughts. "No. But maybe I want to change that." He walked to the fire pit and crouched on the other side to face Corin. "There's something unspoken whenever you look at me, so why not just let it out? What are you afraid of?"

Corin's brow furrowed before he looked up. When his brown irises softened, he let out a sigh. "Do you feel better? Having your vengeance? Did killing Rynalds help?"

Jarrod swallowed when Corin found the question that had nagged at his insides since Quar. He stood, resisting the inclination to walk away. "No." He looked at the sky with a deep breath. "Not even a little."

"So, what's next then? What *will* help?"

"I don't know. But you knowing all my secrets doesn't."

Corin gave a brief laugh. "I told you before. I'm not going to tell anyone."

"Why not?" Jarrod looked at the soldier again. "I get why you wouldn't turn your brother over, I mean... he's your *brother*. But you have no loyalty to me, so why not reap the reward of uncovering the runaway Martox lurking within the ranks of the Ashen Hawks? You'd be a general in no time."

Corin stopped fiddling with the kindling and looked up, meeting Jarrod's gaze. "I can't do that to you. Not to mention, Damien would kill me. Nor is there much benefit. I'm a rebel, remember?"

Can't do that to me? We hardly know each other.

Jarrod lowered his arms and stuffed the note into his pocket. "No desire for riches?"

"Not particularly." Corin stood, brushing his hands on his pants. "You don't seem to have a need for them, either. Otherwise, why would you have left a wealthy family to become a thief?"

Jarrod studied him, evaluating what the captain wasn't saying.

"I understand why you're so secretive." Corin took a small step around the pit, but stopped, breaking his gaze by looking at his feet. "But you don't need to be with me. I don't know how to further prove my trustworthiness to you."

"I don't know how either." Jarrod shook his head. "I want to believe you, but I can't shake the feeling that there's more to the story than you're telling me."

Corin dug his boot into the ground and rubbed the back of his head in a boyish fashion. "Well, I guess I do have a confession. I wasn't completely honest when I said we hadn't met before. We have."

Jarrod's back straightened, mind hurrying to recall where.

I'd remember him, wouldn't I?

"The first time I saw you, we were just kids and there was something about you. Maybe the beginning of this." He gestured between them. "Whatever *this* is exactly. I didn't understand it then, but I couldn't stop thinking about you. From what my older brother was saying, I should have been thinking about the girls in the village, but I couldn't care less about them. So when I heard about the jousting tournament in Degura and that the Martox house would be represented, I couldn't stay away."

The memory of the only tournament he'd participated in Degura dawned in Jarrod's mind. He'd re-lived it only weeks ago in the Inbetween. "You were at that tournament?"

Why, of all the tournaments, did I experience that particular one again?

He remembered how his back had struck the ground after being unseated in his last match. All the air had been knocked from his lungs, but through his blurry vision and the narrow opening of his helmet, he'd seen a blond-haired boy race over to him.

It couldn't have been Corin...

Corin's face showed a hint of a smile, the faintest color rising in his cheeks. "Pretty sure you smacked your head on a rock when you hit the ground. I thought you were dead, and I panicked and leapt the fence to the list field. I didn't want to believe you could be dead, not after what I'd begun to understand by watching you. The way you looked perched atop Titian, your helmet under your arm before you took up your lance, and the..." He motioned to his chest. "Fire you evoked."

"I lost that match," Jarrod whispered, gaping.

"But you won a blubbering fourteen-year-old who was convinced the only person he'd ever love was dead at his feet. I don't know how I could possibly explain the relief that washed over me when your perfect dark eyes fluttered open, even if just for a second. Gods, your parents were furious. Not to mention the beating I got from my old man when I was brought home by a pair of your family's guards."

Jarrod's mother had berated him that night because coming

in second place wasn't worth traveling to Degura.

Finding his ability to breathe, Jarrod swallowed. He opened his mouth to speak, but couldn't put the words he wanted to say in the right order and promptly closed it again.

Corin huffed a laugh, shaking his head. "Kind of pathetic."

"No." Jarrod breathed out the word. "I remember you. I asked my father later who you were, but he didn't know."

"We were from two different worlds. I never dreamed you'd remember me, let alone that I'd see you again. I accepted who I was and joined the military. When I heard about the death of the Martox proxiet..." He shook his head, jaw flexing. "I tried to move on with my life. Or thought I did."

"Until I came back from the dead and almost killed you," Jarrod mumbled, finding himself more grateful than ever that Damien had stopped him.

"Kind of a lucky day for me, if you think about it. I almost didn't recognize you at first. That beard covered the scar you got that day in Degura." He reached up and touched his own chin to mirror where Jarrod's scar was. "But when I saw your eyes after hearing Damien say your name..." He took a step forward, slowly reaching to touch Jarrod's jaw where the scar marred his skin. His thumb felt impossibly hot as it glided over the imperfection. "I never thought I'd get to do this and not have you push me away."

Jarrod's heart thundered in his ears and only Corin's voice broke through the deafening noise. Gripping Corin by the shoulders, he pulled him closer and banished the space between them with a hard kiss.

Corin stepped into him, his arm encircling Jarrod's waist as the entire world spun. His lips were as hot as his skin and they sank into a hungry rhythm.

As Jarrod broke away, he contemplated the repercussions of his actions with distinct ambivalence. He'd never felt so strongly for someone, and the idea was both terrifying and invigorating. "I don't think I'll ever push you away."

Corin touched his forehead to Jarrod's and closed his eyes. A slow, content sigh escaped him, making Jarrod's body ache for more. "This feels too perfect. I'd protest now that you've properly enthralled me."

Questions of the future filled Jarrod's mind, but only for a moment before he pushed them away. He didn't need to worry about who might find out or what his guildmates would think. None of it mattered yet.

Jarrod took a deep breath and smirked. "I think you found your way to prove I can trust you." He dipped his head slightly with the potential of another kiss.

Corin sought his lips, but smiled when it passed without forming, a frustrated breath tickling Jarrod's lower lip. "My master plan all along." He tightened his grip against Jarrod's back, their hips pressing together. "You've been my fantasy for over a decade. I don't think I'd survive screwing up now."

Seeking to reassure him, Jarrod kissed him again, but

slower. He let his mouth linger, enjoying the sensation for an extra breath before pulling back.

"I could never betray you," Corin whispered, caressing Jarrod's jaw. "And now you know why."

Jarrod nodded once. "I'm not sure I'm deserving, but I understand." Taking Corin's hand, he kissed his knuckles and then lowered it while entwining their fingers. Awe floated through him at the revelation of their history he'd forgotten until then.

Red screeched from the sky and it shook Jarrod from his trance enough to look up. Sighing, he released Corin's hand. "Do you mind if I read the rest of this?" Shoving his hand into his pocket, he retrieved the letter.

Groaning, Corin leaned in for a brief kiss at Jarrod's neck near his ear, eliciting a sharp inhale. "Fine. I suppose I should finish making the fire so we don't freeze to death tonight."

Jarrod raised an eyebrow. "I don't think freezing will be a problem." He unrolled the parchment again, trying to decode the rest of the message. He squinted in the twilight, the sun having vanished without them noticing.

His guild leader, Sarth, had the worst penmanship. Add that it needed to be translated, and it became more than tedious. Finally finishing reading, he sighed.

"Good news then?" Corin struck a piece of flint against his knife. He leaned over to blow on the flame, encouraging it to life.

Instead of bristling at the inquiry, Jarrod chuckled. For once, he didn't doubt his ability to be open. "I have some explaining to do, it would seem. Guild master wasn't pleased with my vague reasons for leaving in the first place and now Sarth is calling me home. Good thing we're already on our way."

"Will it be a problem with Damien? I know the Hawks rarely cash in on bounties... but it's seventy gold crowns for his capture. Ashen Hawks could buy their own city with that."

"It's seventy now? Good thing they already practically own Mirage." Jarrod groaned. "Sarth will respect Rae's call that Damien is off-limits. This doesn't bode well though. I sent word about what's happening with Rae."

"You sure it's wise to follow through and go to Mirage? Shouldn't we just press through to Lazuli?"

The fire took to the wood he placed on it, sending crackling embers dancing into the air.

Jarrod shook his head. "When my leader calls, I need to answer. The Hawks might have information we need about Rae. Sarth cares about her almost as much as I do, so it'll just take some explaining. No one will touch Damien."

"Uh oh." Corin donned a charming smirk. "Should I be jealous?"

Jarrod grinned. "Damien was when we first met. Rae and I were together for a time, but I hadn't figured myself out yet and after I did... She stuck around awhile to keep anyone from asking questions. She's a good woman, you'd like her."

"So we're headed to Mirage to meet with the leader of the Ashen Hawks?" Corin turned his attention back to the fire, placing another log onto it. "Another thing I never thought I'd do. This is turning into an interesting month."

Jarrod crouched next to him after retrieving a piece of graphite from his bag. "Aye. But you'll be safe too. If you'd rather not come, though—"

"You're kidding, right?" Corin turned towards him.

"I don't mean with us, I mean into the headquarters. You could wait for us in town if it makes you uncomfortable." Jarrod scrawled a simple acceptance and signature on the back of the paper.

"Not uncomfortable." Corin sat cross-legged. "Just unexpected. I'll come along. Just so I can give that leader of yours a piece of my mind, especially if you get too much shit."

Jarrod laughed. "That'll go over well. Just don't offer a bribe, all right?"

"Aw, but bribes are what we Helgathian soldiers do best." Corin leaned closer. "What about you? Do bribes work on you? Because I can think of a few things..."

A rumble reverberated from Jarrod's chest. "Depends what you're after, I suppose, *Helgathian soldier.*" He scoffed. "And I thought Rae was crazy."

"It's that Lanoret breeding." Corin smirked. He touched

teasingly at Jarrod's abdomen before running his hand up over his chest. "I'd like to kiss those wonderful lips of yours again, if I may be so bold. Though it seems hardly appropriate for me to be propositioning a proxiet."

The term rang through Jarrod's head, disrupting the blissful chaos Corin caused. Trying to ignore it, he leaned with a hand on the ground as he met Corin's mouth. The kiss filled his soul, satisfying a part of him dormant and forgotten for too long.

Jarrod broke away and touched Corin's chest. "Stop distracting me. I'm no proxiet." He stood, looking up at Red.

I gave up that title happily. I don't want the responsibility.

Lifting the whistle to his lips, he let out a short blast and the hawk responded with a screech. Red plummeted towards him and Jarrod muttered a curse as Red landed with a solid grip on his outstretched forearm. Talons nearly bit through his bracer and would have drawn blood if he hadn't been wearing it.

"Are you sure you're not an eagle?" Jarrod tucked the parchment into the metal cuff on the bird's leg. "Go home." Pushing Red back into the air, he watched the animal take to the sky and soar towards Mirage.

Turning back to Corin, he watched the soldier shake out a bedroll and layer blankets on it. Standing again, he removed his uniform's cloak, revealing his military regalia.

The armor is growing on me.

Walking to Orion, Jarrod retrieved his own bedroll, still considering what Corin had said.

Proxiet.

It wasn't a word he'd been associated with in nearly a decade. The monarchy was none of his concern and certainly not his responsibility.

Jarrod shook out his bedroll, dropping a thick blanket onto it. Watching Corin remove the carapaced steel from his arms, he caught a glance of the tattoo on his left shoulder through the thin material of his undershirt. He wondered how a man destined to become a rebel would ascend so far in the ranks of Helgath's military. Corin's admitted ability to move himself around to different parts of the country probably allowed him to dodge growing suspicion.

"So, when you tire of a place, you just forge documents to transfer to somewhere else?"

Corin leaned to slough off his leg guards, glancing back at Jarrod at his question. "It's the most elegant solution." Rising, he shrugged off his chest piece and the thin, damp shirt beneath clung to his toned torso. "You know, you claiming not to be a Martox is like that hawk claiming he's a pigeon. It doesn't suit the hawk any better than you."

Jarrod frowned. "I never said I wasn't a Martox."

Why are we talking about this again?

He sat on his bedroll, watching Corin. "I just said I wasn't a proxiet. Because I'm not. In case you didn't notice, I'm a thief, not a noble. When I said Jarrod Martox is dead, I meant the title, not my name." He stretched his legs out in front of him, relaxing his arms on his bent knees.

Corin knelt to unlace his boots, then laid his armor out beside his bedroll. "Just like I'm a rebel, not a blind soldier?" He gestured with his head towards the armor and its careful positioning. "Yet, I can't seem to let all the soldier go..."

Jarrod furrowed his brow. "And that's *your* choice. I've made mine. I belong in the monarchy about as much as anyone else in the Ashen Hawks."

"Well, maybe that's the change this country needs." Corin turned towards Jarrod, finally meeting his eyes. "I can think of a lot of worse candidates closer to the throne than you."

A weight pressed down on Jarrod's chest. "If I didn't know any better, I'd think you might have a lot to say on the matter. Why are you concerned about my status?"

Corin sighed and rubbed the back of his neck. "That's not it." He paced to the other side of the fire and knelt on the bedroll beside Jarrod. "It's not the status I'm concerned about. It's *you.* All these secrets have to be wearing you thin."

They weren't until you brought them up.

He shook his head, trying not to notice how the orange flames reflected in Corin's brown eyes. "You don't need to worry about me. I've had more peace being with the Hawks than I ever did in Lazuli."

"But we're headed to Lazuli." Corin put his hand over

Jarrod's. "And things have gotten a lot more complicated with the rebellion. It might be quiet for now, but it *will* reach a boiling point." He sighed, looking down and shaking his head. "We don't need to talk about this now. I'll drop it." Rocking back onto his heels, he moved to stand.

Jarrod grasped his hand, urging him with a tug to sit back down. "Don't do that."

"Do what?" Corin's jaw tensed as he settled onto the bedroll beside Jarrod.

"Don't shut down. You want me to talk to you and I'm trying to be more open, which isn't easy for me. You've always been straightforward with me, sometimes more than I'm prepared for, so don't stop now."

Corin's grip tightened on Jarrod's and he gave a curt nod. "It's the rebellion. I don't know how to share with you how important it's become. To me and to others I've recruited. Very little of what I feel relates to my brother being the one who unintentionally started it. When the breaking point comes, that will be the moment when it either fails or succeeds. I don't want to fathom a Helgath where this tyranny continues. But a rebellion can't survive without someone to rally around..."

Jarrod's stomach knotted. "They have Damien. It makes sense. He started it, they all know his face and name."

"He's the catalyst that started it, true. But what's a lieutenant going to do when the corruption runs deeper than the military? Sure, a coup might do the trick, but the loyalty to the Dannet families runs too deep in our heritage to ignore them. The people would never follow a horse-hand from Degura. Besides, can you imagine Damien on the throne?"

"No. But that doesn't mean *I'm* the better choice. I don't want to rule." The idea sent a shiver down his spine and he squeezed Corin's hand. Pulling the soldier closer, he tried to calm his nerves. "I don't want to be a king."

Corin followed Jarrod's pull, wrapping his arm around his shoulders. He leaned in to Jarrod, kissing his temple. "That's why you'd be so damn good at it." Corin rested his forehead against the side of Jarrod's head.

Jarrod's mouth twitched in a smile. "You just want to be with a king."

"That's assuming you'd keep me. And I survive all this." Corin caressed Jarrod's chin, encouraging his face closer.

A rock formed in Jarrod's chest. "Are you planning on otherwise?"

"At this particular moment?" Corin brought Jarrod's mouth to his own. The tender kiss lingered, deepening before he pulled away. "My only plans are to indulge in what I've been dreaming about for far too long."

Chapter 14

THE BUZZING RAHN'KA ENERGIES HELPED calm Damien. They pressed against his soul, urging his mind to quiet all the thoughts of guilt and shame. His anger towards Rynalds and Helgath faded into a weighty sorrow. No matter how fast they chased, Rae had to already be in Lazuli and the suffering she would endure under the prison's wardens made him nauseous.

The pale glow of the monoliths beckoned Damien into the center of the ruins, where the red rocks curled into a corkscrew canyon. The runes of the Rahn'ka ran along the walls, pulsing with power. Damien traced them with his fingers, feeling the rough-hewn surface of the sandstone.

Neco crept silently behind him, ears forward as if he could sense the voices of the stones.

Energy seeped from his bare feet, boots abandoned at the mouth of the canyon. Wisps of power blew sand away from the carved walkway.

One hundred yards into the narrow passage, the canyon walls widened, curving archways draped with hearty desert plants clinging to their tops. The altar lay in crumbles, a mound of weathered stone surrendered to the elements hundreds of years ago. But the power still trickled from the walls, where underground rivers fed the wild.

It wasn't a sanctum. Damien couldn't sense a guardian. But the ruins had a purpose he struggled to decipher.

Crossing to one arch, he ran his fingers over the runes carved into the stone, nearly worn smooth. Summoning his ká, it danced from his fingertips into the symbols, lighting them in pale blue.

Reading the ancient language, his heart thudded as he concluded how he could use the power this place offered. The walls spoke of dreams and sleep, but it was more than that. The power of the soul to wander, to leave the host body, and explore beyond.

"Rae." Damien turned towards the altar.

Neco's head lifted from where he had settled for a nap, watching Damien as he stepped towards the mound of sandstone at the center of the ruins.

Sitting on it, Damien brought his legs beneath him. "Sorry, buddy. Can't take you with me this time."

Neco whined but plopped his head back onto his paws.

Meditation had become a standard practice for him. It didn't fully replace the physical exercise his body craved, but he had little time for either while chasing Rae. It didn't feel right to give himself those things while she suffered. He relished the moments of quiet each night and sometimes even while riding, allowing himself to forgo his barrier and listen, practicing sorting the ká around him.

Connecting with the strands of power in these ruins came slowly. When he rushed, they recoiled, and he had to start again. By the time he finally got his mind to settle and take the steadying breaths to do it properly, the moon was bright in the sky.

Like all of his Art, he hardly knew what to expect when his ká connected. The tether to the ká of the land yanked, threatening to tear him apart if he struggled. Suddenly light-headed, the dizziness resolved into a distinct disconnection of mind from body.

His consciousness floated far above his physical body, peering down into the canyon. The terrain looked unfamiliar, outlined with the blues and whites his vision shifted to when he allowed himself to visualize the ká of those around him. A line anchored him to the ground, where it connected with the great grid of power that blanketed all of Pantracia.

The weaves tangled in perfect design and he focused on the thread he wanted to follow.

He teased the power with memories of Rae and the way her ká felt when they were close. The Art within him sought it out like a bloodhound. No longer constrained to the speed of physical travel, he'd have grown nauseous if he had a stomach when the strings of his power jolted him forward.

When the light stopped spinning, darkness overtook the room he was in. The sky was no longer above and the stone walls glowed with the faintest flickers of power. Life was hard to find, and that which existed felt broken. Like the pieces of their ká didn't fit together right.

His feet connected with the ground, yet it seemed far away. He looked down at his toes, but saw Rae instead.

She was curled in on herself, her dark clothing dirty and tattered. Wrists near her chest, she faced the wall with her eyes closed. He couldn't tell if she was asleep, unconscious, or dead. Except her energy lingered, assuring him the last option wasn't the accurate one.

They had cut her hair, the once long strands shortened to just below her ears with uneven strokes. A wide copper cuff, with tiny designs etched into the metal, pierced the cartilage of her right ear, which had previously only donned one hoop at her lobe.

He suspected the use of Art-obstructing cuffs, a common tool of Helgath, but this was different. The compact earrings were specific to Lazuli Prison, designed for imprisoning practitioners.

Long, thin cuts marred the bottoms of Rae's bare feet. Some fresher than others, and some already fading to pink scars. Bruises covered her arms and legs in various states of healing.

The sight nearly shook Damien from the concentration it took to maintain his form, his hand reaching towards her flickering like torchlight. He steeled himself with a deep breath, forcing the energies back into place.

He took a step forward, reminding his ká it should remain above the ground even though it wasn't there for him. He felt sick despite it all and his eyes burned as he knelt behind her. "Rae?" He choked out her name.

She flinched and lifted her hands to cover her ears. Her knuckles were bloodied. "Go away," she whispered, her voice rough. "It's not real."

A shudder passed through him, but he swallowed to keep his spinning head in place. "It's me." He touched her hip. While his hand would have passed through, the warmth of his ká touched hers, the familiar pulse sending another shiver down his spine. "Oh, Dice. I'm so sorry."

Rae's hands lifted from her ears, but only slightly. Her head turned, revealing her gaunt face and sunken, tired eyes. Her breathing quickened when her gaze met his. "You're not real." Wheezing in a deeper breath, she sat up against the stone wall.

Damien closed his eyes, but he could still see through the power of his Art. He wanted to sob, but it would crack his control. "It's me, mostly anyway. I don't know how to explain it, but I'm projecting my ká to where you are."

Her eyes narrowed, but after a moment of hesitation, she reached for him. Once her hand touched him, it passed through, but the tingle of their ká mingling during the touch caused a warm wave similar to physical touch.

"I'm coming. We'll be there soon. I'm so sorry," Damien whispered, his voice quivering.

Tears sprang from her eyes, and she shook her head. "Don't come here. I'll be dead before you reach me, then they'll have you."

"I won't let that happen." Damien pulled himself towards her again, his incorporeal hand stretching towards her cheek. He wanted to brush away the tears, but his hand did nothing as it touched them.

Rae's eyes closed, and she sucked in a deep breath. When her eyes opened again, they were brighter.

"You will survive this."

"Rae." Someone spoke through the solid stone wall of the cell next to her and she turned her head. "Who are you talking to? Are you all right?"

"Bell." Rae looked from Damien to her side. "Bellamy, it's him."

"It's not real." Bellamy's tone was comforting. "Remember?"

Rae nodded. "I remember, but this time it is. He's actually here."

Damien glanced up, able to see the faint outline of the man on the other side of the wall. Something stood out about his ká. He struggled to understand the familiarity until he saw the way the man's soul was tethered in his body.

Damien's gut twisted, and he shook his head. "Leave it to you to befriend a Shade." His thumb caressed her cheek.

Rae managed a smile. "I know. But he *is* my friend."

"Speaking of friends... Neco misses you."

Her shoulders relaxed, but her expression looked pained. "He found you."

"Yes. And Jarrod's driving me crazy."

Her smile vanished, and a sudden sob shook her shoulders. "You're *not* real. Jarrod's dead. I watched him die."

Damien cursed silently for not thinking the thought through. It'd been so long he'd nearly forgotten the trip he'd made to the Inbetween to rescue Jarrod.

What does that say about the last few weeks, if I can forget a trip to the Afterlife?

The distraction threatened his focus and his hand flickered.

Steeling himself, he regained control and reached for Rae again, touching her chin. "No, he's not dead. I brought him back. He's alive. I found him in time." He looked up towards the wall and pushed a bit of his energy out to carry his voice through it. "Bellamy, tell her you hear me too. I'm really here."

Bellamy paused. "How in the... Rae?" His voice held a tone of awe. "I think it's really him."

Rae's expression contorted with a mix of grief and joy, and she buried her face in her hands as she cried. "Jarrod's alive?" She looked up and reached for Damien again, this time rising to her knees. When she still couldn't make physical contact, she curled back in on herself. A pained grin spread over her face, as if she'd received the bit of information that would grant her peace within the darkness she faced. "It's all right. They're getting rather sick of me here and I know what that means. You shouldn't come."

Damien's heart tore. "Tone it down a little? We're almost to Mirage. Then I'll be coming to Lazuli to get you." He reached to touch her again, wishing he could pull her into his arms and never let go.

Rae's eyes widened. "You're in Helgath?" Tears ran down her cheeks. "No, Damien. Please. Don't come here."

"I'm with Jarrod. We're going to the Hawks for help." Heat built behind his eyes, making him feel even more light-headed. "I'm coming, Dice. No matter what."

A sad smile crossed her lips. "Please listen to what Sarth tells you. This is where my story ends."

"I won't let you die for me." Damien tilted his head to meet her eyes.

Her jaw flexed, and she tilted her head to match his. "What better reason is there?"

The instinct to kiss her overcame him and he leaned into her. The sensation felt like an electrical storm as their mouths met.

She whimpered, hands hovering on the sides of his face, barely touching his ká.

Painfully, he drew away and touched the back of her hand. "I love you. If you die, I won't want to keep living without you." He touched her cheek. "Don't give up, please."

Rae nodded. "I won't. I'll stay alive. But you better do the same, because if I survive, I'm going to need you."

He gave a choking smile and nodded. "I will."

"I love you, my non-Helgathian, non-soldier."

He laughed, but his throat felt raw. "Just Damien will do."

Rae smiled but it looked haunted. "I love you, Damien."

Chapter 15

WHEN THE MORNING SUN PENETRATED Corin's eyelids, he groaned and buried his face into the savory scent of Jarrod's shirt. He inhaled deeply, questioning for a moment if he was merely dreaming again. But when Jarrod's arms shifted around his shoulders, he couldn't help the smile crossing his lips.

Their legs tangled pleasantly together amidst the thick woolen blankets that kept them warm. The fire had fallen to neglect in the night, but their shared body warmth had rendered it unnecessary.

Corin took another breath, allowing himself the contentment of the moment. His hand slid up Jarrod's back, nestling his head at the thief's collarbone. His mouth found the opening of his shirt and kissed his skin.

Jarrod's chest rumbled, his embrace tightening. He dipped his chin and their mouths met in a fiery kiss Corin keenly encouraged.

Speaking so candidly to Jarrod left him raw and more vulnerable than he'd ever experienced. Even more so than the ridiculous hazing the military put him through. The exchange with the thief led to something unimaginable, and he lost himself in arms he never thought he'd feel.

Touching Jarrod's jaw, Corin rose on his elbow, continuing the kiss as he rolled the thief onto his back. Nibbling on Jarrod's lower lip, he pressed his body against him. His lips wandered down his jaw, trailing onto the salty sweetness of his neck.

Jarrod moaned. "You're setting a new standard for how I wake up in the morning." His bass tone vibrated through his throat.

It elicited a hum of pleasure from Corin, tickling his lips and tongue as he slowly broke away. "Are you complaining?"

"Absolutely not." Jarrod twisted his legs with Corin's, pushing firmly on his shoulder. Before Corin could shift his balance, Jarrod had him on his back, hovering above him. "Though I imagine your brother may return soon and ruin it." He met his mouth again, kissing harder than before but drawing away too quickly.

Corin sought to follow and maintain the rising heat, but Jarrod pushed him back down.

"Better get in all we can then?" Corin traced a hand up over Jarrod's abdomen, feeling the muscles beneath his shirt.

Jarrod laughed, a deep sound that sent a shiver down Corin's spine. "As much as I'd like that, I feel for the guy. I'd rather not rub it in when he's already down." Removing Corin's hand from his stomach, he kissed his knuckles before standing, using the grip to help Corin to his feet.

The morning air nipped through his thin shirt, meant merely to keep his armor from rubbing against his skin. Losing the heat of Jarrod against him only made it worse, but Corin nodded. He squeezed Jarrod's hand before releasing it, stepping towards their packs on the other side of the dead firepit. "Should we get breakfast going then?"

"Probably a good idea, I'm starving." Jarrod gave him a wry smile.

"Well, we forgot dinner."

"You are a rather effective distraction. Keep that in mind before you use your powers for evil."

Corin grinned, starting his work on the fire. He pushed the old ashes away, building a fresh pile of kindling. He already wanted to abandon all attempts at civility. He cleared his throat and forced his eyes to remain focused on the task in front of him, muttering quietly to himself. "Damien is going to kill me..."

Jarrod had started walking to Orion, but paused and looked back. "Why?"

Corin winced, not realizing he'd spoken aloud. He rubbed the back of his head as he fished for his flint in his cloak pocket. "He might have questioned my intentions towards you, back in Quar. But he doesn't know the whole story. I've never told anyone what I told you yesterday."

Jarrod raised an eyebrow. "Damien questioned my intentions too, once. I think it's just what he does. Though it's cute he cares." His tone laced with humor as he continued to his horse.

"He's damn untrusting for someone who acts as righteous as he does. If he wasn't my little brother, I'd punch him."

Jarrod laughed. "I don't know how I've staved off the inclination myself. Probably because he saved my life." He added the second part with a slightly more somber tone as he returned with a saddlebag of cooking supplies.

Corin frowned, unable to prevent his mind from imagining what Jarrod had looked like bleeding out.

As Jarrod crouched beside him, Corin touched his wrist. "And for that reason, I can continue to stave off mine too." If Jarrod had died, he wouldn't be able to experience the bliss of knowing that being with him was possible. The electricity that raged invisibly between them left Corin pleasantly dizzy. He'd have to seize control of it at some point, or he'd be useless to everyone around him.

"What are you thinking?"

"Just... the chances. Of all of it. Leading to this..." Corin closed his hand over Jarrod's, entwining their fingers. They felt perfect together. "I didn't think I'd ever have this."

Jarrod's deep brown eyes swirled with emotion. "I could say the same thing." He squeezed his hand. "I feel lucky, too, you know."

Corin laughed, shaking his head. "I don't know why. Don't I complicate things for you?"

"Oh, definitely." Jarrod chuckled, kissing Corin's knuckles before releasing his hand. "A worthy complication, though."

The sound of panting drew Corin's attention behind him, expecting to see Damien accompanying Neco, but the wolf approached alone.

"Checking to make sure the coast is clear?" Corin asked the animal, and Neco huffed and licked Jarrod's shoulder.

The two had grown close during the travel through the desert, mostly because Jarrod would always give Neco scraps of food. Since they were sitting, Neco stood taller than them both and Corin couldn't help but consider the damage the creature could do if he reverted to his wild instincts.

The sound of rocks bouncing down the incline beside their camp signaled Damien's approach and Corin withdrew from Jarrod.

"Welcome back." Corin stood and turned to face his brother. He wasn't used to the beard yet, which Damien let grow thick and didn't keep in any kind of shape other than the occasional trim. The tattoos running down one arm poked out where his sleeves were rolled up. He walked barefoot, his boots clutched in one hand. His face looked hollow, eyes distant.

Jarrod eyed Damien. "What happened?"

"I saw Rae."

Corin opened his mouth to question, but Jarrod beat him to it.

"What? What do you mean, *you saw* Rae?"

"A Rahn'ka thing." Damien waved a hand as if it explained everything. "But I saw her."

"Is she alive?"

"Yes, but I don't know how much longer." Damien rubbed his face. His tears had mingled with red dust from the stone, staining his cheeks. "She looks bad, Jarrod. We have to hurry." His voice cracked.

Corin stiffened, casting a glance at Jarrod.

His face hardened, all evidence of his previous pleasant mood long gone. The thief snatched up the pack of supplies. "We'll eat on the way."

They reached Mirage in three days, pushing the horses to their limits on the rocky, dry terrain. The red rock turned into sand dunes which butted up against the Gilgas mountains behind the city. Craggy grey stones jutted up on the horizon like a sudden eruption had put them there.

The tall sandstone and mud structures of Mirage stood out against the dark background of the mountains. Towering walls surrounded the city, but they were not meant for a military purpose. They were made of long carved wooden poles laced with cascading fabrics that danced in the wind. Clouds of sand brushed up against them, then slid to the high-piled dunes at their base. The large gate sat open, red and orange cloth hanging loosely across the beams.

Beyond, the buildings ranged in size, including some still surrounded by scaffolding supporting their half-conceived structures. Based on the wear of some boards, it was likely the buildings had been like that for a while.

The streets were busy, merchants shouting over each other to sell their wares for cheaper than their neighbor.

Corin grew distinctly uncomfortable. He was the center of attention in their small group since he'd decided not to disguise his military attire.

Jarrod walked opposite him, a dangerous-looking dagger at his hip. He'd acquired it while entering Mirage, a split blade with a sword break in the center. The previous owner had taken none too kindly to Corin's blatant entrance to the guild-controlled portion of the city, but Jarrod had encouraged a change of opinion.

No one dared approach them, not with the escort of the Hawk, but eyes and sinister smiles stayed locked on Corin.

Jarrod had abandoned wearing a shirt, despite the tepid weather, and left his leather vest loose at the front. The attire exposed the large black tattoo on the back of his right arm. A staggered row of three daggers woven with feathers, displaying his position within the Ashen Hawks.

The fleeting exchanges with Jarrod had diminished, leaving Corin feeling hollow. He understood, but it didn't make Jarrod's withdrawal any less painful. When Damien spoke of Rae, Corin saw a change in the thief each time. But he wasn't jealous. Jarrod's care for Rae was something different. Instead, Corin felt a twinge of pain in his chest, hoping desperately they would get to her in time. It felt like he already knew Rae and missed her too.

Jarrod didn't need to say it out loud for Corin to understand that he felt guilty for having happiness amidst the dire circumstances.

Damien walked in front of them, drawing shockingly less attention than Corin expected. Wearing a new long leather tunic, he pulled the hood over his eyes. The tunic left his arms uncovered, fully exposing his Rahn'ka tattoos, which completely hid the old military tattoo marking his years of service.

Corin wondered if Damien could rid him of his own, eventually. But for now, it was more important he stay deeply seated within the military. There, he could do the most good for the rebellion. The need fueled his refusal to remove his armor, despite Jarrod's insistence. If a fellow soldier caught him out of it, it would have been more complicated than dealing with the stares of some criminals.

Neco trotted between Jarrod and Damien, catching his fair share of glances. His tail was stoically still, ears pricked forward. Occasionally, Damien would stroke his ruff and the wolf would calm until the next loud city sound made him tense again.

Jarrod guided them through the streets until he reached an alleyway, taking the lead down it.

Shadows engulfed them from the tall buildings on either side, an unmarked lone door at the end. An unlit lantern hung beside it.

He rapped on the door and a small trapdoor at eye level opened, revealing a partial face.

"Do you have something to light the lantern?"

Jarrod nodded. "Aye. But I'd rather walk blind."

Something thunked, and the door stuttered open.

Right. Because that ain't creepy.

"Stay behind me," Jarrod whispered to the two of them before entering first.

Damien and Corin exchanged a brief look, while Neco chuffed and followed Jarrod. Damien entered next while Corin fiddled with the hilt of his sword before he stepped through the doorway.

The room housed a rocking chair, a half-eaten plate of food, and several bookshelves laden with texts.

Jarrod ignored the man who'd opened the door and strode to the bookshelf on the far left. He pulled three books partially out and pushed on the left side of the shelf. The whole thing moved much easier than it should have, sliding inward before rotating.

The thief entered first again, Neco at his heels. Once Corin and Damien stepped through, the bookcase rotated shut and sealed them in complete darkness.

Corin let out a sharp breath as he blinked. "A little literal, isn't it?" He lifted his hand in front of his vision, but couldn't even make out the shape in the utter blackness.

Neco growled.

"Easy, boy." Jarrod's voice sounded close. "That's kind of the point. It's a maze. Everyone must return this way after being gone for a while."

"Great."

Damien hissed. "Damn it!"

Corin reached for his sword. "What? What is it?"

"Ringing! You don't hear that?"

"It's warded. Stop using the Art, you idiot."

Damien let out a sigh. "Well, then I can't see either."

Jarrod's footsteps fell flat on the air, confirming the narrow corridor. "I hope you're fine with confined spaces."

Damien cursed, but shuffled forward.

Corin tried to take a step, but his shin hit Neco.

The wolf growled again, snapping a warning, and Corin recoiled. "So how are we supposed to follow you?"

Neco's nails clicked on the hard floor, but it was unclear what motivated him to walk.

Jarrod's hand closed around Corin's. "Like this, I suppose. Take Damien's hand."

The heat of Jarrod's hand in his and the way they fit together made Corin miss the night when they'd first kissed.

As if Jarrod could read his mind, while Corin reached for Damien's hand, his hand lifted higher. The gentle touch of breath and lips grazed his knuckles, making his knees weak before Jarrod lowered it again.

"Ready?" Jarrod squeezed Corin's hand.

"Almost." Corin grinned and ceased his search for Damien. Before the thief could protest, he pulled him into his arms, touching his neck with his free hand. He found his lips in the darkness, hungry to express the need for him while Damien couldn't see.

"What's the hold-up?" Damien tugged on Corin's cloak, pulling his mouth from Jarrod's before he could properly sink into it. The captain let out a choking sound and swatted at his brother while Jarrod cleared his throat.

"You can hold on to that. Just don't... strangle me or anything." Corin slid his touch down Jarrod's body to take his hand again.

"Then don't tempt me to," Damien growled. "We're ready, Jarrod."

"Finally." Jarrod scoffed. "Keep a hand on the wall as we walk."

"Just needed to remind you," Corin whispered to Jarrod, extending his hand as instructed. The wall was closer than he thought it was, his elbow not reaching the full extension before he touched the dry stone.

"Like I'd forget." Jarrod lowered his voice to match, leading them ahead. His steps held no hesitation, turning at one place, then another. Each turn came without reaching the end of a hallway.

"How do you know where you're going?" Damien yanked on his brother's cloak, making him choke again.

"Gods, stop that."

Jarrod turned another corner and Neco's clicking nails brought up their rear.

"They use this maze as part of the initiation process. If you can't get through it in a certain time frame, you fail. You run it until you can run it flawlessly." His last words echoed off the stone, indicating they'd entered a larger space than the hallways. He walked a few more yards before stopping.

"Is there a rule against light? Warded or not—"

"Shut up," Jarrod hissed and let go of Corin's hand.

Neco's growl rumbled across the stones behind them.

Jarrod's steps slowly ventured farther. "Lykan! Reporting home."

Silence followed, and Corin heard Jarrod take a step closer.

"Is something supposed to be happening?"

Damien pulled hard on Corin's cloak, nearly tearing him off his feet. "Shut up."

Corin clawed at the wrapping around his neck, freeing himself to take a deep breath. He listened, trying to sense whatever the other two were waiting for, but he couldn't hear anything. Just the distant drip of water, which seemed odd for a desert city.

Jarrod gasped. "Down!"

Corin didn't question, he just dropped, grabbing his brother's collar and dragging him down with him.

Bowstrings twanged and something whistled through the air next to Corin's head.

Damien fell on top of his brother, knocking the wind out of his chest.

"Break off!" Jarrod's order rang clear, but no one answered.

Wood and sinew creaked as arrows were nocked, followed by silence.

Fire erupted in a brazier in front of them, blinding him. Corin blinked, watching Jarrod's blurry shape stomp over to the closest archer and rip the bow from his hands, throwing it to the side.

"Lykan!" A voice erupted from the far end of the room and Jarrod spun around, chest heaving.

Corin groaned, pushing Damien off him, but his brother's weight vanished. Someone pinned Corin's wrists behind his back and lifted him to his feet before he could fight.

Neco's growl grew louder, his teeth gnashing, but Corin couldn't see the wolf. Chains rattled in the shadows as the wolf snarled.

A hooded figure stood behind the brazier, the amber light dancing on their black attire. They stood perfectly still, features impossible to interpret. "Are you telling me that *my* Lykan, *my* own recruit, not only broke the rules, but brought a Helgathian Captain and his infamous, *valuable*, brother into *my* home?" The voice of the figure came out rough but had a feminine lilt.

The thieves holding Corin wrapped his wrists with rope, tying them together. A glance revealed the same happening to Damien, who looked too calm.

Jarrod made eye contact with Corin, but his stern expression didn't change before he looked back at the one scolding him. "I can explain."

A flash of doubt ruptured through Corin. Looking at Jarrod, he realized just how much trust he had put in the man. Not only his own life, but his brother's. These were the Ashen Hawks, the most notorious criminal guild in all of Helgath, and they'd walked right into their hands. Both Damien and

Corin were valuable, especially with what Jarrod knew of the rebellion.

He shook away the doubt as promptly as it had appeared.

It can't all be lies.

Turning his back on Corin, Jarrod walked towards the hooded woman. They talked in hushed tones and it took longer than Corin thought it should.

Eventually, the woman picked up the torch from within the brazier, lighting the bottom half of her face. Her jaw sported a thick white scar running the length of it, turning up at the cheek. "Bring them."

Jarrod didn't turn around as he followed the shrouded woman through the door.

The goons holding Damien and Corin shoved them forward, while two men struggled with chains to restrain Neco.

Damien's attention shifted to the wolf, who quieted. "Hush, buddy. Save your strength."

Neco whined, snapping at a chain, but ceased his struggling. He sauntered forward to keep up with Damien, held back by the chains of the two men now being dragged forward.

"You got a backup plan?" Corin whispered over his shoulder as the thief behind him kicked his heels forward.

Damien's voice darkened. "Sure. I've got a plan."

They emerged through the doorway, and the architecture immediately changed. Tall ceilings boasted intricate chandeliers, casting abundant light. They entered a great hall, with tall pillars surrounding a level lower by four stairs. Rib vaulting supported the ceiling, with long banners hanging from the stone walls.

Jarrod walked next to the woman, who had now lowered her hood, and no longer carried a torch. She limped, setting the pace a little slower. They still talked, but specific words were inaudible.

The man pushing Corin shoved him harder, causing him to fall hard on one knee.

His armor clanged against the stone, the vibration radiating through the padding. "Careful, asshole. Armor's worth more than you."

The man lifted him by the collar. "Don't tempt me. I'll knock your teeth in."

"Nyphis!" Jarrod barked from the front and the man lifted his gaze with a frown.

"Lucky for you, you have a wolf on your side and I don't mean the furry kind. But as soon as he ain't looking, try that smart mouth again."

Wolf? And hold on, isn't Nyphis a breed of snake?

"Don't worry, Nyphis. I'm looking forward to you trying."

"You military dolts are all the same."

"You might wanna cut it out." Damien glowered at Corin.

Where's the fun in that?

Reaching the end of the massive room, they went through another doorway, down a hallway, and entered a chamber with two large banquet tables and a throne-like chair at the far end. Bench seats flanked the tables, capable of seating ten people per table. The meeting room stood empty.

The woman Jarrod walked with sat in the ornate leather chair, elevated on a small platform, keeping her right leg straight in front of her. Her long red hair wove into a low braid that draped over her shoulder, streaked with grey. Dull green eyes studied Corin and Damien before looking at Jarrod. "Where's Sika?"

Jarrod's jaw flexed. "Lazuli."

The woman seemed to contemplate that bit of information. "She's probably dead." Her tone was softer than Corin expected. "You'll go anyway, I figure?"

"Aye."

"And these two?" The woman motioned to Corin and Damien.

"They'll come—"

She silenced him with a lifted hand. "The Lanoret brothers. Sparking and leading a rebellion from what I understand."

The few thieves in the room exchanged glances, and Corin's mouth dried. "And he gives *you* shit for saying too much?" he whispered behind him to his brother.

Damien grunted.

"Leave us." The woman waved a hand at the unoccupied men standing around.

They turned and exited, leaving only the two holding Neco and the two holding Damien and Corin.

"All of you."

Corin's wrists slacked behind him.

"Take the rope, too."

The pressure of the rope vanished, and Corin rolled his shoulders.

The woman looked at Jarrod. "And the *dog*?"

Jarrod nodded and the men tentatively unlatched the collar around the wolf's neck.

Free, Corin rubbed at the burns the ropes had left and glared at Nyphis as the belligerent thief left the room.

Neco made eye contact with Damien and remained silent while the rest of the Hawks exited. The door at the back of the room slammed shut, leaving them alone with the woman.

She sucked in a deep breath and rubbed her leg. "I'm Sarth. Lykan seems to think you two are allies of the Hawks, but all I see is a rebel and a deserter. Both worth more than their weight in gold."

Of course Sarth is a woman. That explains why Helgath hasn't been able to pin-point the Hawks' leader.

"It's definitely more complicated than that." Corin drew her skeptical gaze.

"Enlighten me." Calm authority echoed in her tone.

"We don't have a lot of time." Damien stepped forward, Neco close on his heels. "Rae doesn't."

Sarth frowned. "Jarrod, why don't you go to Lazuli, then. I'll keep these two here, I think."

Corin sighed. "I'm not sure that's in your best interest."

Jarrod shot Corin a look. "You mind?" He turned back to Sarth. "It's true, though, they'd make getting Sika back a lot easier."

"Hear me out." Corin ignored Jarrod's request. "I'm willing to bet Jarrod didn't tell you about the rebellion. You already knew because of how connected the Hawks are throughout the country." He watched her face for any kind of reaction, but got nothing more than a quirked brow.

Jarrod ran a hand over his face.

"I hear a lot of things. This isn't the first time discontentment has stirred in the streets." Sarth shifted her right leg, her jaw twitching.

"It's never gotten this far before. You must know how fragile it is right now. Can you imagine the blow the movement would take if Damien was turned in and executed? He might become a martyr, but that's not enough to keep this going. And we both know a rebellion is good for the Ashen Hawks."

Turning to Jarrod, Sarth tilted her head with a smirk. "This one talks a lot."

Jarrod sighed. "Aye. You definitely don't need that in our prison." He smiled. "Time *is* of the essence though, Si—"

Sarth raised a hand, cutting him off with the motion for the second time. "I want her back as much as you do and I know she ended the call for Damien's head, but the rebellious captain... as far as I know, is still fair game."

"He's not." Jarrod's words came out clipped. "By my word, he's not an option either."

Sarth snorted and stood, putting her weight on her left leg. "This is a substantial loss of potential income for the guild."

Jarrod rolled his eyes. "The guild doesn't need it, we both know that."

Sarth shrugged with a smirk. "More coin never hurts. But I suppose I can see things your way." She turned to Damien and Corin. "Try not to hold the dramatic greeting against me, I put the lives of my Hawks above others, even when they've broken the *rules*." She sent Jarrod a sideways look.

"Will you help us?" Damien took a step forward.

The leader of the Hawks eyed him. "Damien Lanoret... You caused this uprising, and yet, reluctant to lead it. I don't blame you. Leadership is rather tedious."

Damien shifted, his spine straightening, but didn't open his mouth.

"You may mean a lot to *my* Sika, but you mean nothing to me, especially if you refuse to aid the rebellion." Sarth turned to Corin, and he straightened too under her hard stare. "And you, a captain, with little to offer in leadership. No one will rally around a captain, even if he *is* the brother of the face of the rebellion. You ask me to help, but the Ashen Hawks won't side with a losing battle. It's not... good for business. So tell me, Captain, who will lead your little rebellion? Convince me it has a chance at success and you will have the full support of the Hawks behind you."

The answer stood beside her. Corin knew it and the look on Jarrod's face showed he did too. Corin forced himself not to look directly at him as the thief stood stone still. Corin gritted his teeth and locked eyes with Sarth.

His breath caught as he tried to make his tongue work, to form any words, but it felt stuck.

Tell her it doesn't matter. The rebellion will survive until the right person steps forward.

But it wasn't true. The rebellion stood on the edge of a precipice, and even the slightest breeze might crumble it. The support of the Hawks would cement its footing, with or without a clear leader.

Corin's jaw locked, and he stared at Sarth until she spoke again.

"Lucky for you, I don't expect an answer at this moment. Recovering Sika, in whatever condition you find her, is a more pressing matter. You two..." She motioned to the brothers. "Are welcome here as long as you have an escort. The valley wolf may also join you, unless he causes trouble." Sarth met Corin's gaze, her eyes narrowing, which deepened the lines at their corners. "Next time I see you, you'll have a name for me."

And Gods, am I looking forward to the look on your face when I give it to you.

Corin offered a tight nod.

Sarth turned a breath later and limped back to her chair to sit. "If you're determined to go to Lazuli, I'd suggest you do something about your face." She stared at Damien. "I got word of your arrival moments after you set foot in Mirage. A beard and some tattoos are not enough to hide who you are." Her gaze slid to Jarrod. "Lykan will assist you with that."

"That's it?" Damien gaped. "Letting us stay the night and suggesting I do something about my face? And you dare to claim you care for her..."

Unflinching, Sarth stared at him. "And if you were in my position, what would you do?"

"Use your contacts to organize a jailbreak. Bribe the guards. At least send more of your thieves with us to help. Anything other than what we were going to do, anyway." Damien took a step towards her, but Corin caught his shoulder. "You're the most notorious guild in all of Helgath and the most you can do is say good luck?"

To his surprise, Sarth lowered her gaze to the floor and for a fleeting moment, her eyes flashed with glassy emotion. When she lifted them, her expression had hardened again. "Yes. It is the most I can do. Because Sika... Rae gave me very specific instructions if a circumstance such as this were to arise. I would risk no one to save her life."

Jarrod dropped his gaze and closed his eyes with a cringe.

"She never could have predicted these circumstances. You didn't see her." Damien's voice darkened and threatened to crack, causing his brother to turn to him in surprise.

Corin tightened his grip on Damien's shoulder.

Sarth looked at Jarrod, who wearily met her gaze. "Do you remember the mission to free Dunn when we lost three Hawks in the process?" He nodded. "It was after that. She told me her wishes, and thus my wrists are bound by my word. Yours are not." Leaning back in her chair, she pursed her lips. "Take *anything* you think may help you. You may now leave."

Neco looked up at Damien, pushing his nose into his hand, which fell limply against his head. With another nudge, his fingers started to idly scratch.

Corin gave his brother another tight squeeze before he looked at Jarrod, silently asking what was next. He sure wouldn't be able to find his way back out the maze and hoped there was another way out.

Perhaps one with better lighting.

When Jarrod walked past them to the door without another word, Corin put his hands on his brother's shoulders, encouraging him to walk in front.

Jarrod opened the door, holding it for them.

"And Lykan. Next time, follow the rules."

Chapter 16

WITHOUT SPEAKING, JARROD GUIDED THEM through the expansive corridors to his private dorm on the second floor. His elevated rank within the guild meant he no longer had to cohabitate with anyone. His room wasn't overly large, with a window overlooking a combat arena.

A tidy single bed occupied one wall, his desk positioned under the window. On it sat an ink well and a short stack of blank parchment. A quarter-inch thick gold chain necklace lay strewn next to the parchment, which he picked up and stuffed in his pocket.

No sense prompting unnecessary questions.

Neco's mottled black form took up most of the floor space.

Corin paused in the doorway while Damien sauntered halfheartedly towards the bed. The captain leaned against the frame with one hand just above his head, eyeing the pocket Jarrod had stuffed the necklace into, but said nothing before he met his eyes. "Well, *that* was interesting."

Jarrod sighed. "I'm sure it was."

"So should I call you Lykan now? I was feeling pretty left out."

"I'd hate to see what you'd consider as *involved.* You guys were supposed to let me handle it." Jarrod scoffed.

Corin shrugged with a charming smile. "I've never been good at keeping my mouth shut, Lykan." He said the name with a seductive emphasis and Jarrod crossed his arms.

Now is not the time.

"There are supplies in another room to help disguise you." Jarrod turned to Damien, ignoring Corin as best as he could.

Damien looked over his shoulder. "Why would she do that? Why would Rae stipulate that the guild couldn't help her in a time like this?"

Jarrod frowned. "She didn't want anyone dying to save her. She felt her life wasn't more important than anyone else's. I remember how upset she was after we recovered Dunn, but I didn't realize she'd spoken to Sarth."

Damien ran his hands into the long sides of his hair, pulling it back from his face. "Gods, she can be so stupid sometimes." He groaned. "She's so much more important to me. To us."

Jarrod took a deep breath. "While I agree with you, dwelling on her choice won't help. We need to get stuff together and get moving."

Damien nodded, and Neco lowered his big head into his lap. He scratched his ears as the wolf whined.

"Well, while you two do that, I better go check in at the barracks." Corin jerked his thumb over his shoulder. "Will you get me out of here?"

Jarrod opened his mouth to protest, but closed it. He didn't like Corin in Mirage alone, wearing his uniform. "Aye." He looked at Damien. "I'll escort him out, are you all right here in the meantime?"

"I'll survive. And I promise not to do anything rash."

He's changed since visiting Rae.

Before Jarrod allowed himself to think about it for too long, he walked to the doorway, only to be blocked by Corin, who hadn't moved from his leaned position. Planting a hand on Corin's chest, he pushed. "Let's go, Captain."

Corin grinned, resisting his push for a moment before he backed into the hallway. He waited for Jarrod to close the door before he spoke. "I think I like it when you call me captain."

Jarrod laughed. "You always have such incredible timing. But I'll remember that for a more opportune moment."

Corin glanced down the empty hallway, then leaned back against the doorframe. "I don't see anyone around. And I've felt fairly neglected these past few days. That was quite the tease you gave down in those tunnels."

On this side of his door, Jarrod couldn't have felt more

exposed, regardless of the vacant halls. "Not here," he whispered, even though his body yearned to give in to the inclination to be close to Corin.

The soldier frowned but dropped his arm to his side. "Really?" His voice lowered. "Will you always be looking over your shoulder to make sure no one sees?"

Taking a deep inhale, Jarrod stepped back. "This is my life. It's been three days. I think you can spare more time for me to acclimate to letting anyone know."

"You've been hiding this much longer than three days."

"Because I've never had a good reason *not* to."

Corin quirked an eyebrow. "And I suppose that question Sarth asked me wasn't a good reason either? You're the one with the power here, Jarrod. How am I supposed to believe any of this is real if only we know about it? For all I know, you're humoring me to keep me quiet. Gods know I made it easy for you."

Jarrod scowled, Corin's words stinging. "If that's truly what you think of me, then why don't you march right back to Sarth and spill it all."

"Don't think I'm not tempted." Corin took a step closer, a rumble in his chest. "But forgive me for having a bit of hope that I mean enough to you."

"Whether no one knew, or everyone did, wouldn't change how I feel. And if you're so easily tempted to break your word, then perhaps you should think twice before you give it again."

He stepped sideways, starting down the hallway. "I'll show you the way out."

Corin caught Jarrod's wrist, yanking him back. "I haven't broken a damn thing." He promptly let go, tossing Jarrod's hand away.

"I'm not doing this here," Jarrod hissed through a clenched jaw.

"So when are we going to do it then? Or is that just going to wait until it *feels right* too?"

Jarrod growled. "Pressuring me into something won't have your desired result. Try all you want, but I do things when I *want* to, and if you're not all right with that, then just say it."

"Things can't always be the way we want them to be. We don't all have that luxury."

"If you don't feel your efforts here are paying off, feel free to find another proxiet to seduce," Jarrod whispered. "These issues are one in the same for you, aren't they?"

Corin's jaw tightened, lips pursing as he gripped his fist in front of him like he was contemplating throwing a punch. "You know that's not—"

A door slammed down the hallway and Jarrod's gaze darted to the noise.

Corin lowered his hand and turned, running his hands up through his hair.

Braka stood twenty yards away, looking at them. "Hey, boss. Everything all right? Melner sure caused a stir here with the news you sent."

"Aye. Melner got what he deserved. Still looking for Sika, though."

Braka nodded. "You'll get that woman of yours back, boss."

Corin's shoulders tensed, and he put a hand against the wall, leaning on it.

Jarrod gritted his teeth. "Aye. We'll get her back. But she's still not my woman."

Braka shrugged. "Either way. I know you's close."

Corin turned, a tight smile on his face. "Hey, Lykan has enough on his plate. You mind showing me the way out of this place, big guy? I wouldn't want to be a *burden* on him any longer." He shot a glare at Jarrod before pushing past his shoulder to walk towards Braka.

Braka eyed them both before holding up his hands. "I ain't getting involved." He cast a wary glance at Jarrod, jutting his thumb at him. "My ol' lady used to look at me like that when she was pissed. Sorry. Nope." He stepped backwards into the room he shared with two others and shut the door.

Jarrod quirked his head at Corin. "Really?" He turned and stalked down the other hallway, back the way they'd come. "Let's go, *Captain*."

When they finally reached the exit to the city, Jarrod threw the wooden door open with enough force that it struck the stone wall outside, sending a group of chickens clucking and fluttering to get away.

Corin walked past, shoving him on the way. He turned back to Jarrod after stepping onto the dusty street. "Difference between us is I pretend to be something for the good of my country and to fight for a day I don't have to lie anymore. But you pretend because you're scared."

Jarrod glanced down the other side of the alley, finding it empty. He slammed the door behind him and stepped towards Corin, hands balled into fists. "I will *not* be a pawn in the game you're playing. This is how I want my life and if you want to be part of it, you need to respect that."

"I don't want you to be my pawn. I want you to be my partner."

"Partners don't force the other into something they aren't ready for." Jarrod's blood heated. The pulse in his ear nearly deafened him.

"Partners don't act ashamed of each other, either."

"It's been *three days*." Jarrod gestured with his hand. "Gods, could you be any more impatient? I need more time and you being an ass isn't helping."

"Fine, take another day without me around to muck it all up." Corin spun on his heels and stomped down the alleyway, sending the chickens squawking again.

Jarrod growled, striking the bottom of his fist against the stone wall. He wanted to say more, tell Corin to be careful. Tell him to watch his back and to come back. But he remained silent while Corin rounded a corner and exited the alley.

I knew this was a terrible idea.

As he relaxed his arm, he stuffed his hands into his pockets and closed his eyes when his fingers touched the cold necklace he'd hidden. The flat gold chain tangled in his grip as he pulled it free.

Why do I keep this?

Sighing, he shoved it back and walked inside. Letting the door swing shut on its own accord, he made his way to one of the Hawks' stash rooms to gather supplies to change Damien's appearance.

He busied his mind by thinking of a cover story. They both needed to be someone else in Lazuli.

Arriving back at his room after passing Braka, who gave an empathetic, yet knowing look, he shut the door and looked at Damien.

The Rahn'ka sat perfectly still on the edge of the bed, his hands on his knees and eyes closed in meditation.

Neco opened one eye to check who'd entered before his tail thumped on the wooden floor.

Jarrod knelt and scratched the wolf behind the ears, trying not to disturb Damien. Once he sat cross-legged on the floor, Neco put his furry head in his lap and whined for more attention.

"I'm an idiot," Jarrod whispered to the wolf, stroking his long dark muzzle.

"Won't catch me arguing." Damien's shoulders relaxed, and he opened his eyes, letting out a long slow breath.

Can people just give me a damn break?

Jarrod sighed. "You too?"

"Well, I was joking... But sounds like someone else isn't?"

"It doesn't matter." Jarrod ran his fingers through Neco's thick ruff. "You Lanorets can be infuriating."

Damien gave a wry smile. "We're particularly talented at it." He stood and walked towards the desk where Jarrod had put the supplies. He eyed the bottles, picking them up to examine. "If it counts for anything, Neco thinks you're swell."

Jarrod chuckled. "That's because I can't resist his whines for scraps." Looking at Damien, he wanted to ask how he was feeling with everything, but decided bringing up Rae was probably a terrible idea. "I think we should go to Lazuli under the guise that we're brothers. By marriage. I'm from there, originally, and I don't need anyone recognizing me either."

Damien quirked an eyebrow. "So am I married to your sister? Or are you married to my brother?"

Clearing his throat, Jarrod huffed. "It's you. You're married. Congratulations."

Damien frowned and rolled his eyes. "I'll let you explain that to your *sister*. Rae's close enough, isn't she? She's made it clear she's against marriage. But it'll be easy enough to pretend for a little while."

"More than close enough. I imagined it would be easy for you since you'd probably leap mountains to marry her."

"And more. Which is why I'm willing to do anything, say anything to make this work." He looked back at the bottle in his hands, turning it over. "What's this for?"

Jarrod gazed out the window at the sky. "It's dye."

He uncorked the top of the bottle and grimaced, leaning away from it as he caught a whiff of the contents. "This has to go on my face, doesn't it?"

Neco sneezed, and Damien laughed. "I know, buddy."

"What'd he say?"

"He said it smells like horse piss."

Jarrod smirked, and the Rahn'ka pulled out the chair, spinning it to face the room.

"You're helping, right? I have no clue how this works."

Jarrod reluctantly moved Neco's head off his lap and stood. "You get used to the smell."

Once again, Neco sneezed, and Damien laughed.

"What now?"

"He mocked our noses. Suggested that we might get used to it because of our inferiority. But that he won't."

Jarrod smiled. "Or perhaps we're just tougher."

Neco took a moment, then growled at Jarrod, his tail wagging.

"He doesn't approve of that statement. Nor do I approve of playing constant messenger between you."

Jarrod couldn't resist the ability to communicate with his animal namesake through his friend. "Well, he should learn to speak to me, then."

"I ain't telling him that," Damien grumbled. "Or he'll start bugging me to make it happen."

Jarrod laughed and bent over to ruffle Neco's fur. "Sorry, bud, I don't think your pal is quite that talented."

Damien pursed his lips. "Seriously? Is that a challenge?"

Using a mocking, child-like tone, Jarrod kept speaking to Neco. "See boy? Now he's all upset."

Neco yipped and gave Jarrod's chin a slobbery kiss.

"Don't *you* start." Damien glowered at the animal. "Or we'll dye you too."

Jarrod rolled his eyes, retrieving the bottles from the desk as Neco scooted away. "Ready?"

"As I'll ever be, I suppose. Have you done this before? Better be gentle, it's my first time."

Jarrod smirked and nodded, remembering when Rae had asked him to lighten her hair. "Oh, I'll be gentle, Might sting your scalp a little." He held up two bottles. "Brown or black?"

Damien wrinkled his nose, looking at the two. "Well, it's got to look real. So which do you think would be better?"

Jarrod put the black dye down, pulling on thick leather gloves and uncorking the other. "Brown it is. Plus, it washes out better later. Just don't get this shit in your eyes."

Damien squirmed in the chair. "The things I'll do for that woman." Gritting his jaw, he nodded. "Let's get started."

Jarrod grinned, but his heart sank.

So why can't I make myself uncomfortable for Corin?

He shoved the thoughts away with a roll of his shoulders and poured the dye into the palm of his gloved hand. Walking in front of Damien, he rubbed his hands together before spreading it over the Rahn'ka's blond hair.

Damien frowned, but the expression seemed exaggerated.

Careful to cover as much as he could without getting too much dye on Damien's skin, Jarrod saturated his hair. They both grew quiet while Jarrod worked to check all the sections of his roots.

"Do you think she'll ever change her mind?"

Jarrod paused, looking down at Damien's head. "About what?"

"Marriage." Damien tensed, shifting slightly under Jarrod's hands. "I shouldn't be thinking about it now, all things considered, but..."

Do I give him hope or answer honestly? Better yet, avoid the question.

"Why is it important to you?"

"It's just one of those things, isn't it? Something always looming and making you wonder about the future. Will I ever be able to have that kind of thing now? A family... Especially if I can't give her children."

Jarrod paused. "Who says you can't have that *kind of thing* without being wed? Just because she doesn't want a husband, doesn't mean she doesn't want you."

"But what if I want a wife?"

"I can't speak for Rae." Jarrod shook his head. "But it sounds like you're putting that cart before the horse."

Damien quieted, working his jaw. "Probably. We need to save her first."

Jarrod nodded and amused himself by forming the sticky clumps of hair into interesting shapes as he went. Unable to stifle it, he laughed.

"Having fun?" Damien's tone sounded dry.

"Aye." Jarrod chuckled. Using one finger, he swiped dye over Damien's eyebrows. "You're gonna be so handsome." He mimicked a tone a mother might use for her child.

"Oh good. You sure you wouldn't rather play the part of lovers then? All the girls will be jealous of you, having a good-looking man like me." The humor returned to his voice, but it sounded strained.

Jarrod shook his head, crouching to dye Damien's beard. "Better stop talking. This stuff doesn't taste good. And to be honest, I think I can do better." He raised one eyebrow as he slathered goop over Damien's face.

Damien pursed his lips, keeping them sealed while Jarrod worked on his mustache. His nose wrinkled at the scent and his body convulsed with a cough he held in. When Jarrod focused on his chin, Damien parted his lips enough to talk in a breathless tone. "Like Corin then?"

Jarrod frowned, running his hands a final time over Damien's hair. "Your brother isn't thrilled with me, so I'm not sure about that."

"But I'm not wrong?"

"Depends what you think you're right about."

"I know his looks, I've seen them since I was born. And I might be distracted, but I'm not blind. Something happened when I went to those ruins."

Jarrod fell silent, remembering waking up that morning with his arms around Corin. He'd never felt more at home, even in the middle of nowhere. "*Something* sounds about right." He walked behind Damien. "Not sure if he'd still be interested if I wasn't in the position that I am."

"Corin's about as good at hiding his emotions as I am. And he's a lot more blunt. But I've never known him to stick around after the chase ends."

Jarrod wrinkled his nose, glad Damien couldn't see him. Doubt warred within him. Falling silent again, he focused on the dye. Satisfied he'd covered everything, he pulled off the gloves. "Done."

Damien stood awkwardly, like he was afraid to tilt his head in any one direction.

Jarrod gave him a droll look. "You can relax, it won't drip."

"So, we'll be brothers? Will you go by Lykan?"

"No. It's an alias as a Hawk. Not a good idea."

"And Sika is Rae's?"

"Aye." Jarrod returned to the desk, corking the bottle.

"Fitting that you get along with Neco so well then, if they named you after a wolf."

Neco's head popped up, his tongue lolling out to the side.

"With that logic, Rae should fit right in with Feyorian lionesses." Jarrod smirked.

Damien chuckled. "Oh, she would."

Silence fell as Damien crossed towards the window next to Jarrod, glancing out at the uncovered training arena below. A pair of thieves sparred, another watching and giving instruction to the less experienced.

"You told Sarth I'm reluctant to lead the rebellion." He turned slightly towards the thief. "Do you think I should feel differently?"

Jarrod shook his head. "No. I don't blame you at all. I don't want to lead it, either." Damien furrowed his brow at the slip, and Jarrod rushed to continue. "Or, at least, I wouldn't want to." He closed his eyes briefly, damning his own stupidity.

Damien reached up as if to smooth his hair, but stopped himself with a sigh. "I never dreamed something like this would happen. Of course, I didn't really think through the whole desertion thing either. I just did it and didn't look back. I figured I'd live as long as I could, to spite Helgath. I'm a soldier, I don't have any noble blood. My family isn't one of the Dannets. And Corin makes it sound like he wants me to step up and dethrone King Iedrus."

Jarrod forced his expression to remain the same. "Maybe the rebellion doesn't need a proxiet."

Damien shrugged, then plopped onto the bed facing Jarrod. "I think it does, especially if this turns into a full-scale war, like Corin makes it sound. I know you didn't serve, so you don't know the corruption and how deep it runs. Fixing the military would be a feat in itself, but it'd be pointless if we didn't cut off the head of the snake. And only a Dannet family could do it. The old ways are too ingrained and Helgath would crumble if anyone else tried a coup. So, here's hoping the rebellion can find a proxiet to make it possible."

Oh, Corin would love to hear this.

Jarrod patted his knee and Neco rose to accept more ear scratches.

"He wants you to get his chin," Damien leaned back on his arms. "What now? How long do I have to sit here?"

Redirecting his hand to scratch Neco's chin, Jarrod shrugged. "It needs to dry, then you brush it out. It will survive a little dampness after, but if you venture out in a downpour, the dye will bleed."

Damien nodded, then pursed his lips. "All right, now he wants you to scratch his ears again. That's the last message, boy."

Jarrod laughed and used both hands to scratch Neco's ears and ruff, digging deep through the thick undercoat. "Don't worry," he whispered to the wolf. "I'll get all the scratches for you."

Neco gave a happy chuff, licking Jarrod's fingers.

"I'm pretty sure that wolf likes you a lot better than me, now. Probably best since he'll need someone if something happens to me. This rebellion means Helgath won't forget me anytime soon."

Jarrod frowned. "You'll be fine. You and Rae both."

Why are Lanorets so obsessed with preparing for their own deaths?

"I'm tired of running." Damien sighed. "That's the life I'm offering Rae, and it doesn't seem fair. Maybe I should stop and fight like Corin wants me to. *Lead.*" The word sounded sour on his tongue. "What do you think?"

Jarrod stared at Neco's face, trying to find some source of wisdom in the wolf's eyes. His spirit kin, according to the Ashen Hawks, and supported by the tattoo on his back. "I don't think leading Helgath is in your future. You have a history in the military, but it takes more than that, like you said. I think you have a different purpose. Someone else will lead, it's just not clear who yet. But it's clear this country needs someone to forge a new path."

"But do you think a rebellion is what it needs? A civil war?"

Jarrod sighed, wondering if Corin put Damien up to the conversation. "Probably. Helgath is as corrupt as it gets. Couldn't make it any worse."

"I remember being so proud of our country, proud to serve when I enlisted. It's strange to look back and realize how blind I was."

Scowling, Jarrod gave a sardonic laugh. "I never felt proud. I was ashamed to be born here. Ashamed to partake in outdated and crude traditions. Becoming a Hawk was the closest I could come to feeling redeemed from my blood."

Should I tell him?

Damien tilted his head as if about to ask a question, but then shrugged. "I don't know, I find some charm in the old traditions. But it sounds like you might have experienced different ones than I did growing up on a ranch. You said your family's from Lazuli?"

"Aye. And them learning I'm a Hawk is the last thing I need. Our traditions were far from ideal."

"I'm glad I don't have that problem. I thought I'd need to avoid my family too, but Corin is a pleasant surprise. I wouldn't be able trust Andros, though. He's probably a general now."

"Gods, more Lanorets." Jarrod exhaled. "The two of you are plenty, I'd think."

Damien huffed a laugh, shaking his head. "What can I say? My da loved my ma very much. Just three of us boys, though. My sister died when I was a kid. So that's all you have to worry about."

Jarrod's shoulders slumped. "Sorry. My parents had a troublesome time having children and were *blessed* only with me." They'd only had him because they were pressured to by the other Dannet families.

Lifting a hand, Jarrod tested Damien's hair. "Dry." Standing, he fetched a thick linen drape and a comb from a cabinet at the far side of his room. He offered Damien the comb and laid out the drape.

Damien ran his fingers and the comb through his hair and beard, the dried clumps of dye dropping onto the linen. He did a thorough check before turning towards the shaving mirror Jarrod kept on the wall behind the door. Examining himself, he turned his head back and forth and frowned. "I look better blond." The dark beard made his face look hollower. "Do you have some shears? I should probably do something about how ratty this beard is getting."

"Are you sure? Looks a far cry from any military man I've ever met."

"I look like a beggar."

A sharp rap came at Jarrod's door, followed by Braka's voice. "Boss?"

Jarrod crossed the room to open the door. He tensed at Braka's wide eyes.

"The local peace officers just uncovered a rebel hiding in their ranks. They're aiming to make an example of him to quash the rebellion."

Jarrod's gaze shot to Damien's and his heart leapt in his chest.

"When did this happen?" Damien found his voice quicker than Jarrod.

"Not more than an hour ago."

Corin.

Jarrod pushed past Braka and sprinted down the hallway, keen to reach the captain before anything permanent happened. Neco yipped and Damien cursed behind him, but he didn't look back to see if they followed. His boots pounded as he rushed down the narrow stairs he'd led the soldier down on their way out.

Their heated disagreement echoed in his head, tormenting him with being the final words spoken between them.

Regret tainted each breath as he reached the door and burst through. It ricocheted off the wall, bouncing back, but Jarrod was already past.

Sunlight blinded him as he ran in the direction Corin had disappeared. He lifted a hand to shield his eyes, a dim shape coming into focus right in front of him. He halted, skidding to a stop on the sand-coated street.

"Whoa. Where's the fire?"

Jarrod's eyes adjusted and when Corin's face became clear, his knees just about gave way. Shaking his head, he ran forward again, not bothering with words as he wrapped his arms around Corin and pulled him into a tight embrace.

The captain's solid arms closed around his shoulders and he pressed his cheek against Jarrod's temple. "It's all right. It wasn't me."

Without letting himself overthink it, Jarrod pulled back from the hug. He claimed Corin's mouth with his and the soldier responded eagerly.

In the distance, Braka muttered between panting breaths. "Maybe if I'd ended fights like that with my ol' lady, she wouldn't have left me."

Damien chuckled. "Mhmm."

Chapter 17

NECO TROTTED NEXT TO THE open cart hitched to Xyphir and Orion, having expressed his fervent displeasure for the bouncy ride in the back with the Rahn'ka.

Jarrod sat up front, driving, suiting the pretense they'd agreed on. He was taking his sick brother to Lazuli for the care of a known apothecary.

After the arrest of a rebel, Mirage became too dangerous for them to linger. Damien regretted pointing out that Corin needed to travel separately to maintain their aliases. Jarrod and the captain probably had plenty to say to each other, considering the reunion between them, but it needed to wait.

Damien propped his chin against his arm on the panel behind the driver's bench, watching the growing shadows on the grey craggy mountains ahead. The sun approached the horizon, changing the rows of desert clouds to fields of orange and pink. Ahead, the stone dropped into a tight gorge, framing a narrow road.

"Shit." Jarrod pulled up on the reins briefly but then loosened them.

A man-made structure blocked the road into the pass.

Too late to turn around.

The local battalion had cut and hauled pine trees to create a barricade, connecting two boulders on either side of the road. The Helgathian flag drifted in the breeze, dying daylight glittering on the gold-stitched emblems.

Damien's heart plummeted. He'd suspected the possibility of a blockade, part of the reason Corin rode ahead, but it didn't make the reality any less daunting. The pass didn't offer crowds to hide within like the border in Quar. Instead, the soldiers sat bored, eager to entertain themselves with an unfortunate traveler.

"Get down," Jarrod whispered. "You're sick, remember?"

"I remember..." Damien pulled the hood of his ragged cloak tighter over his head. He didn't like laying like an invalid when he would've preferred to fight his way through.

But killing soldiers would tell Helgath we're coming, and those men probably have families.

He curled up on his side, hiding his eyes as best he could while avoiding jostling his head against the bottom of the cart. Being unable to see what was happening didn't help.

An eternity passed.

"Hold."

Damien mustered a cough to add to his act, letting it rock his body. Their cart ground to a halt and he silently told Neco to remain docile and play his part too.

"Evening." Jarrod sounded calm, at least.

Boots clunked around the cart and Damien dared a glance around his hood to see the military regalia of the blockade soldiers rounding towards the back.

Neco flitted a worried thought into Damien's mind as the guards peered at the cart.

"Destination?"

"Lazuli."

"And your purpose there?"

"I'm seeking an apothecary to heal my brother. He's unwell. Healer at home suspects it might be Cerquel's plague."

The soldiers hesitated, armor rattling as they stiffened. Whoever had pulled at the gate at the back of the cart stopped and Damien let out another harsh series of coughs.

There was a lengthy pause, likely the guards debating silently who would have to inspect him.

"I'll check it out." One guard spoke softly to another, and the cart rocked backward as he stepped up. He kicked at a clump of hay, serving as padding to make Damien's ride more comfortable.

Maybe it would if it didn't get under my shirt and make me itch.

The man knelt, lifting the edge of Damien's hood with a tentative finger and Damien readied his powers in a hasty precaution. The teenage soldier's jet-black hair poked out from under his leather helmet and his dark eyes met Damien's.

Damien tensed as a sense of knowing filled the boy's eyes, and he prepared himself for the fight he craved.

Then the boy winked.

The barest hint of a smile curled on the soldier's lips. "Gods, he looks awful." He dropped Damien's hood back into place.

Damien started coughing again, but more out of surprise, suppressing the building power within him.

The soldier hopped off the back of the cart, and it settled after a drunken sway.

Damien peeked out from his hood.

The boy gave the barest nod to the man who had stopped Jarrod.

"Good to go then."

Damien buried his head in his hands, a mixture of confusion and relief washing over him.

"Appreciate your cooperation."

"No problem, Sir." Jarrod flicked the reins.

The cart bounced into motion, the soldiers' voices fading.

Damien dared a glance out the back of the cart, between the sideboards, but they'd rounded a curve in the gorge and the blockade was no longer visible. Huffing a sigh, he pushed himself up.

He leaned against the front of the cart, removing his hood and regaining his ability to breathe. "Well, that was easier than I thought it'd be." The rumble of the cart's wheels forced him to speak louder.

Jarrod nodded. "I thought for sure he'd recognize you."

"Pretty sure he did." Damien rubbed the back of his head. "He winked at me."

Jarrod fell silent for a moment before he chuckled. "Must be your brother's doing."

"Damn, I hate to admit it when he's actually helpful."

The sky dimmed, fading to darkness before they found the marker Corin left beside the road. A pair of sticks crossed over each other pointed the way towards their camp for the night.

Jarrod pulled to the side and unhitched the horses while Damien gathered foliage to cover the cart.

Go find the guys some dinner, Damien mentally instructed Neco, who gave a joyous bark before disappearing into the woods.

Leading the horses through the trees, they found Corin sitting next to an empty fire pit, sharpening his sword. "Figured you could do something about the fire, little brother. To keep it more discreet?"

Damien nodded, letting Xyphir's reins loose and crouching near the prepared pit. He'd been careful with hiding his power since entering Helgath and the chance to use it came as a relief. He urged the ká still clinging to the gathered wood to expel any retained water. He looked up at Corin's low warning whistle and caught the piece of flint thrown at his head.

Jarrod dropped his pack next to the fire, sitting several feet away.

Corin looked up at him. "You made it through all right, I see."

Jarrod nodded, meeting the soldier's gaze with a solemn expression. "We figured you had something to do with that."

Damien lowered his head as he lit the fire, encouraging the flames to dance with the help of his energy. The smoke rose, but with a bubble of his will, he created a pocket in the air to catch it. It spun like a little cloud, gathering anything rising from the fire until Damien could change the way the fire ate at the wood to reduce the smoke.

Corin cleared his throat, drawing his attention before motioning his head at something behind him. His eyes darted at Jarrod as if trying to silently communicate something about him.

Damien looked in the direction Corin motioned but saw nothing. He frowned and looked back at his brother. "What?"

"Do you think you could go find more wood?"

"You have plenty of wood already."

Corin's face tightened.

"You could just ask me to give you space, you know." Damien stood.

Before he reached the edge of their camp, laughter echoed from the trees, and footsteps approached. He cursed internally for not listening to the ká of the woods to get an earlier warning. Tensing his arm, he channeled the focus of his ká into his tattoos. They pulsed with light as his power coalesced, his spear erupting from his fist.

"Whoa!" Corin grabbed Damien's forearm, forcing his spear lower. "First, I invited them. Second, what in the hells is that?" He gaped at the conjured weapon.

Jarrod rose to his feet, eyeing the direction of the voices. "Invited who?"

"People who could benefit from seeing Damien right now." Corin still focused on the spear. He reached out to touch it, as if expecting his hand to pass through.

Damien's jaw tightened. "What do you mean seeing me? The whole point is for people *not* to see me." He yanked the spear away from his brother, shoving his shoulder just before the soldiers the voices belonged to broke through the tree line.

The boy who had winked at Damien at the blockade led the trio. He had his arm slung around the neck of a shorter, stockier man, who carried a pack under his arm. Their laughter rang out through the clearing, making Damien flinch.

A third soldier, a woman with short black hair, held a cask. "Gods, could you two be any louder?"

The noise stopped when they spotted Damien standing there, spear in hand.

"Damien Lanoret," the woman whispered under her breath, shoving the cask into the boy's arms. "My wife will never believe this. It's an honor to meet you, Sir."

Damien shot a glare at his brother, who stepped forward to take the pack of food from the older man.

Jarrod exchanged an uncomfortable glance with Damien. "You should warn Neco."

Damien had forgotten about the wolf in the wave of frustration with his brother. He grumbled beneath his breath, turning without offering a response to the enthusiastic woman. Reaching out to Neco, he cringed when he interrupted the wolf's efforts to seize a rabbit.

"Was it something I said?"

"Nah, he's just shy. He'll warm up."

Damien shot a glare at Corin, but resisted growling. Stepping to be behind the newcomers, he flexed his grip on his spear.

It gave way to the power as it drew back into his skin, darkening his tattoos.

No one seemed to notice in the flurry of interest over what the three rebels had brought with them.

"Thanks for getting them through, Remmy." Corin nudged the black-haired boy.

"Course. Just about shit myself when you said Damien Lanoret would be coming through. Glad I was there."

"Me too."

Damien centered himself with a deep breath and turned towards the fire. All eyes returned to him, except for the shorter man, who watched Jarrod, a quizzical expression on his face.

"Sorry." Damien turned towards the woman. "I'm still… getting used to this whole… being *known* thing."

Corin urged Damien forward to meet the other rebels. The woman, Willow, shook his hand harder than Remmy or Ermel.

"I didn't think my desertion would cause something like this." Damien rubbed the tingling sensation of their ká lingering on his hand.

"That's what I've been trying to tell you since Olsa." Corin ushered everyone to take a seat. "It's getting bigger every day."

"It's damn good of you to come back." Willow nodded. "The rebellion needs all the help it can get right now."

Damien fought the temptation to cringe. "That's not—"

Remmy thrust a tin cup of aromatic bourbon into Damien's hand and offered one to Jarrod. "You ex-military too? Haven't seen any posters looking like you though."

Jarrod shook his head, accepting the cup. "Nope." Instead of elaborating, he took a drink, and the group fell silent.

"But you're fighting for the rebellion?" Willow studied Jarrod.

The Ashen Hawk lowered his cup. "I'm fighting to get my friend back. It's complicated."

Damien snorted, taking a slow drink. "And getting more complicated by the second."

Ermel bobbed his cup in Jarrod's direction. "You look familiar, but I can't quite put my finger on it. We met before?"

Jarrod shook his head. "No. You must be mistaken."

"I don't think so. Where are you from?"

"Mirage," Jarrod said through clenched teeth.

Ermel shook his head. "Nah, that's not it. You ever been to Lazuli?"

"We're headed there now." Damien furrowed his brow at the stocky man's insistence.

Jarrod is from Lazuli.

The thief stood, leaving his cup on the forest floor. "I'd better go check on Neco."

Corin's hand shot up to catch his wrist. "Oh, come on, Jarro—" He clamped his mouth shut, but Ermel gasped.

"Jarrod!" Ermel pointed at the thief. "That's it! You're Jarrod Martox."

Damien choked on his drink, pressing his lips together to stop from sputtering it all over the fire.

Willow elbowed Ermel. "What you talkin' bout, old man? The Martox boy died almost ten years ago."

"Your eyes aren't what they used to be, Ermel." Corin's tone was tense, something Damien recognized from when they were kids. "He ain't a Martox."

The passing of the only heir of a Dannet family had shaken the country, leaving a void of power. Damien never knew the boy's full name but remembered the event clearly as Corin had taken a leave from the military shortly after. His brother had been distraught, and Damien hadn't understood why. But the young soldier locked himself in his room, avoiding all contact until he returned to service two weeks later.

I thought it was a coincidence with the timing, but...

He turned his gaze from Corin to Jarrod's stony face.

Jarrod stared at Ermel for a long moment before glaring at Corin, who withdrew his hand and lowered his eyes to the ground.

"Nah, I don't forget faces. Especially one like this one." Ermel pointed at Jarrod again. "This is great!" He sloshed his bourbon, stretching across the clearing to pound Corin in the shoulder. "Why didn't you say we had a proxiet on the side of the rebellion, Cap! This changes everything." He started smacking Remmy's chest. "Do you know what this means, boy?"

"Fuck." Corin covered his face with his hands.

"I sure as hells don't..." Damien muttered, watching Jarrod.

The thief twisted the gold ring on his hand.

He lied to me.

The realization stung more than he expected.

"You know, I think you were right, Corin. We do need more firewood." Damien set his cup down by his pack and stepped towards Jarrod. "Feel like stooping to help the common folk with the task?"

Jarrod glared at him but nodded once. "Most definitely." He followed Damien as he slipped into the trees, the light of the fire behind them vanishing. Once they were deeper, he caught Damien's forearm. "It's not a big deal."

Damien stopped, forcing himself not to pull his arm away, though every fiber in him wanted to. "It kind of is. Why didn't you tell me?"

"I wanted to, but I've never told anyone and I didn't know how. I'm not *him* anymore. The guild doesn't even know."

"Does Rae know?"

"No."

Well, that's a surprise.

"Then how in Nymaera's name does Corin know? He did a piss-poor job of covering it up, that's for sure."

Jarrod's jaw flexed. "He recognized me the day we met."

So Corin kept it from me too. They knew each other before.

His own brother, keeping secrets. Considering the budding relationship between the two men, he tried to understand.

Maybe this means Corin is serious about Jarrod.

"I honestly didn't believe it mattered." Jarrod interrupted Damien's rampant thoughts. "Until Corin kept bringing it up, talking about leading the rebellion. I didn't know how I could tell you without ruining the trust between us."

"Well, it wouldn't have mattered before, but now it matters a whole hell of a lot." Damien pulled his arm from the man he thought of as a friend. "My brother's wasting his time pressuring me to lead when there's a much more obvious answer right in front of him."

Jarrod narrowed his eyes. "You can't possibly agree with him on this, can you? You think I should lead this shit show?"

"Doesn't have to be one. You said it yourself that Helgath is fucked up right now. It needs this rebellion, and the rebellion needs a leader. We both know that it can't be me."

"I'm a bloody thief." Jarrod threw his hands up in the air. "Not a king. Not even close. I'm dead, didn't you hear her? And it's for the best."

"I don't want to argue with you about this." Damien sighed. "Not now, anyway. We both have a much bigger problem we're more worried about than a rebellion and that's Rae."

"Agreed. How about we worry about her first? Then if we must, we can circle back to this later so I can remind everyone that I'm no leader."

"Good luck with that." Damien huffed. "You don't know how stubborn us Lanorets can be."

Jarrod smirked. "I'm getting a bit of an idea."

Damien took a step forward, holding out his hand towards the thief. "You could have told me, but I understand why you didn't. No more secrets between us though. We might only be pretending to be brothers, but I think we really could be."

With a firm grip, Jarrod took his hand. "All right, Brother. But there are no more secrets to tell."

Damien nodded. "Well, I doubt anything could top that one, anyway." He grinned. "Your Highness."

Jarrod frowned, but a smirk lingered. "You're an asshole."

Chapter 18

WHEN THE TIME CAME FOR the rebels to return to their military camp, the moon high in the sky, all were feeling the effects of the bourbon. Particularly Corin, who'd downed several cups while Jarrod and Damien disappeared to gather more firewood.

Ermel was the last shoved out of their camp by Corin, shouting a final farewell to Jarrod, embellishing it with a drunken bow.

Corin couldn't determine who out of the two men and wolf looked the most relieved about the rebels finally leaving, though settled on Neco.

The wolf emerged from the woods, where he'd been watching and gnawing on his catch. He lumbered towards Jarrod with a huff, shoving his big, furry head under the thief's arm. Once Jarrod started scratching through his thick fur, Neco sat and leaned against his legs.

Damien pushed up from the ground with a grunt, eyeing his brother and then Jarrod. "I'm going for a walk."

The captain gave his brother a curt nod, grateful he hadn't had to ask for the time alone with Jarrod. They needed it now more than before. His body tensed despite the effects of liquor, preparing for the inevitable fight.

Jarrod gently pushed Neco. "Better go with him, boy."

The wolf rose with a huff and padded off after Damien, both disappearing into the shadows.

Corin heaved a sigh of relief for the quiet. He'd partially removed his armor during their drinking, but finished taking off his chest piece before he turned to Jarrod. "I'm sorry." He pushed every ounce of his shame into it. He never imagined Ermel would recognize Jarrod, having invited the rebels to distract and taunt Damien. It'd gone horribly wrong. "Leave it to me to fuck everything up... again."

Jarrod ran a hand over his black hair and stood. "You couldn't have known he'd recognize me."

He's not angry?

Corin held his ground, even though he wanted to walk up to Jarrod and make sure he understood how sorry he was. Not just for this, but for the panic he must have felt in Mirage.

The way the thief had burst through the door in the alley, having heard the news about the rebel arrested in the city, made

Corin's chest ache. But the tension turned into a whirlwind of joy when Jarrod took him in his arms, kissing him. Neither of them had thought about who was there to see. Corin hardly deserved it with the way he'd been pressuring him. It hadn't been fair.

Who am I to show up and turn his life upside down? I just want him to be himself. Especially with me.

"I'm sorry for everything else too." Corin glared at the ground where he dug his boots into the dirt. "I was being an asshole. And an idiot."

Jarrod's soft footsteps came closer, and he touched Corin's chin to lift his gaze. "I'm not ashamed of you. I never want you to think that. I just needed more time and maybe courage."

Corin's heart twisted, and he smiled. "I know." He brought his hand up to touch the back of Jarrod's.

"When I thought they'd arrested you..." Jarrod closed his eyes.

Corin kissed Jarrod's palm, causing his eyes to open.

"I panicked. If it'd been you, I'd have broken all the rules to get you back. Anything. Even if I had to use my old name, I would have."

Corin shook his head, cradling Jarrod's hand against his cheek. "Why would you do that for me?"

"Because if something happened to you that I could have prevented, I'd never forgive myself. Anonymity be damned if I don't have you."

Corin smiled. "Getting a little ahead of yourself for four days, aren't you?" He drew the back of Jarrod's hand towards his mouth, kissing his knuckles.

Jarrod frowned. "Do you always have to be a jackass?"

"Don't lie, you like it." Corin's left arm encircled Jarrod's waist, encouraging him closer.

Jarrod's chest rumbled. "Perhaps next time I'll use your tactics of jackassery instead of giving you a serious response." He quirked an eyebrow.

Corin hummed against the back of his hand and frowned. "That wouldn't be very becoming of a proxiet." He lowered Jarrod's hand and traced the bottom of his jaw, sobering his tone. "I don't want to make you do something you don't want to. Especially because of me."

"If your life was on the line, what I'd *want* is for you to stay alive and safe. Even if your own loud mouth landed you there."

Corin laughed, and it felt wonderful. "So does this mean you forgive my loud mouth? And I can use it to kiss you again?"

"Your brother will be back soon," Jarrod whispered, leaning in closer to Corin.

"He'll just have to deal with it."

Jarrod's mouth closed on his, and he tasted like bourbon. After one slow kiss, he drew away enough to speak. "Did you purposely wait until I'd had enough to drink before bringing this up?"

"I did rank top in my class for strategy at the military academies." Corin hovered teasingly close to his lips.

"And let me guess, last in your class for general observation skills." Damien's voice broke the air.

Jarrod didn't even flinch. "Your fault for returning so soon." His gaze lingered as he pulled away, his hand finding Corin's.

"Oh, don't stop on my account."

Jarrod smirked and shrugged. "It appears he insists." He pulled Corin to him for another kiss and drew it out, making Corin's heart thud harder.

It'll be nice not to hide anymore. Gods, I missed him.

Chapter 19

HUDDLED IN THE CORNER OF her cell, Rae yearned to see Damien again. Now that he'd visited, it made the hallucinations crueler. She resorted to making him speak to Bellamy, but never again could Bellamy hear him. Her hope shattered each time.

Why did he only come to me once? Has he given up?

Rae closed her eyes.

I told him to give up. But he won't.

He'd come with Jarrod. Her heart soared knowing her friend lived, even after she'd seen the life drain from his eyes. Damien saved him. He'd done it for her. The two men hadn't exactly gotten off on the right foot, so it was the only explanation.

Helgath left her alone after Damien's visit, the days impossible to track. The physical reprieve added to the emotional strength she'd gained from seeing him and it gave her determination to continue breathing.

"Bell, you there?" Even without seeing his face, her cell neighbor had helped her in ways beyond imagining.

It was quiet for a moment, but then his weakened voice came. "I'm here. You seeing him again?"

"No... Just wanted to hear your voice."

He gave a raspy laugh. "I understand."

"Are you all right?" Turning, she leaned her cheek against the cold stone wall.

"Just sick. Can't keep anything down. A side effect, I think. It'll pass." He didn't sound convinced.

Rae closed her eyes, imagining the face of the only person who'd been kind to her in months, but she'd never seen him. "Are you sure he can't find you here?"

"Pretty sure he would've by now if he could. But I think the guards are onto me. I might not be here much longer."

Rae's heart sank.

I don't want to be alone in here and Bell isn't safe out there.

"I hope not. Did they give you an ear cuff too?"

He laughed, and it turned into a ragged cough. He hissed in another breath as if he was shivering. "Only because I wouldn't stop begging for it until they did. Easier to shut me up. That's what's keeping him from finding me. Blocks the connection. Damn, it's cold in here."

"Maybe you can keep it after they release you." She touched the wide cuff they'd pierced through her ear near the top. It sent a shock through her fingertips, and she withdrew her hand. She'd tried to rip it out several times, but the pain always increased enough to steal her consciousness before she could.

"It's a nice thought. I'd be willing to deal with accidentally shocking myself every time I brush my hair to stay hidden from him."

"Who is he, anyway?" Rae pulled her knees to her chest.

Bellamy didn't answer right away, the silence drawing out to the point where she wondered if he was even still there. "His name is Uriel, but I wouldn't say that anywhere outside of here. He might hear it and it'll bring him down on you. I wouldn't want that to happen to you."

A rock formed in Rae's stomach and she nodded. "I understand." She ran a hand through her cropped hair. It didn't even touch her shoulders anymore. "Do you know anything about him?"

"He's the most powerful Art user I've ever seen or heard of." Bellamy's voice grew stronger. "Other than that, not a lot. By the way he dresses, he's got to be rich. He looks plain enough, except his eyes..." He trailed off and even though she couldn't see him, Rae imagined Bellamy shuddering. "You can't tell anyone what I've told you, Rae. If he found you..."

"He won't. I won't tell anyone, I promise."

"Shhh, someone's coming."

Rae fell silent, dread filling her chest as she shuffled back into the corner of her cell as far as she could go.

New sounds echoed through the hallway. The gentle swish of a cloak, footsteps so soft she could barely make them out.

No chains. No grunts or threats. No torment.

The unknown made her dread worse.

The clicking of the lock on the solid oak door of her cell reverberated so quietly she thought it was someone else's door at first. Blinding light spilled into the darkness, rushing from the doorway towards her.

Lifting her arms, Rae shielded her face. As her eyes adjusted, she lowered her arms and squinted at the silhouette standing in her doorway. "I'm still not talking."

Whoever they were, they didn't speak before stepping into the cell. The visitor glanced back, and light illuminated his face. His features were hard and sharp, with pure white hair cropped close to his scalp, long bangs styled back from his face. His eyes gleamed a topaz yellow, like her right one when she used her Art. She couldn't make out his pupils, the dark dot disappearing among the gem-like irises.

"You're auer." Rae spoke loud enough for Bellamy to hear. "Helgath run out of local torturers?"

"I'm not here to harm you, Raeynna." His voice sounded sugary sweet, pitched in a way surely meant to calm her. "My name is Kynis'cairn. And I'm here to assess you. Would you come with me, please?" He reached towards her, exposing the length of his uncovered arm, his skin a dark olive tone like hers.

Rae stared at his offering, struggling to comprehend a kind touch. Doubt and distrust ran rampant as she glanced back and forth to his face. Swallowing hard, she placed her hand in his with a shaky grip.

His cool fingers closed around hers. He drew her up to her sore feet, and she only stood as tall as his shoulder. The silver stitching on his black, sleeveless tunic, shimmered in the torchlight.

When she took a step towards the door, pain shocked through the wounds still healing on the soles of her feet and she stumbled.

Kynis'cairn caught her, one hand supporting her elbow while the other wrapped around her waist. He was gentle enough that her bruised ribs hardly reacted to his touch.

Leaning on him, she closed her eyes. "Where are you taking me?"

"Somewhere far more hospitable. For a little while, at least. Hopefully longer."

"Am I not coming back to this cell?" She forced herself to straighten partially.

Kynis looked down at her with a puzzled expression. "It remains to be seen. Why do you ask, child?"

Tears welled in her eyes and she looked at Bellamy's cell. "My friend. I'd like to say goodbye if I can..."

"This friend is another prisoner?"

Rae nodded, placing her palm on the stone wall she shared with Bellamy. "I've never even seen his face."

Kynis glanced at her hand, but gave a small nod. He encouraged Rae to put more of her weight on him as he carried her out of her cell the rest of the way. "Give me your keys." He looked towards the far wall, where Rae hadn't even noticed the guard.

He stood far back, as if unsure of the auer. The look on his face at the demand would have made Rae laugh if not for the pain.

He thrust the keys forward, holding them at the full extent of his arm, and Kynis snatched them. Settling Rae against the wall beside Bellamy's cell door, he patiently sorted through the keys until he found the proper one to open it.

"Would you like my assistance?" Kynis turned the key, but paused before pushing it open.

"Rae?" Bellamy's voice came from behind the door. "What's going on?"

"They might take me somewhere and I asked to say goodbye to you. Is that all right?" She watched Kynis, silently asking him to wait for an answer.

The noise that came through the door sounded like a half sob, but it was quickly swallowed. "I'd like that."

"Don't open the door much, please," Rae whispered to Kynis. "I'll be fine on my own."

Kynis nodded, twisting the handle with a raspy click. He didn't open the door, though, stepping aside for Rae. "I'll give you a few moments, but I believe the patience of our escort may wear out quickly. Please don't be long."

"Thank you." Rae pushed the door open just enough to slip through. Ignoring the stabbing pain in her feet, she closed the door most of the way before approaching Bellamy.

He huddled against the wall, his face buried against his knees to avoid any contact with the light that came into the room. Blood marred his forearm, lines of a tattoo barely visible beneath the scratches.

Rae fell to her knees beside him, and he lifted his face. "Bell." She frowned at how young he looked, stroking dark hair from his damp forehead before pulling him into a tight embrace.

His body felt frail in her arms, dangerously weak from days of uncontrollable sickness. But through all his suffering, he'd continued to talk to her.

Bellamy returned the embrace. "Don't give up," he whispered in her ear. "Neither of us can."

Rae squeezed her eyes shut as tears rolled down her cheeks. "I won't if you don't."

"I'll fight the entire way. But I refuse to touch the power again. No matter what."

Rae smiled. "You're strong. I'm proud of you. Thank you, Bell, for everything you did for me."

With surprising strength, considering how much he trembled in her arms, Bellamy pulled back on her shoulders and met her eyes. "You're far stronger." His dull brown eyes boasted shadowed bags, the surrounding skin sunken. "Maybe we'll meet again? When we're both older and wiser."

Rae nodded, studying him. "We'll meet again. Just remember that for all you desire redemption for, in my eyes, you're redeemed." Swallowing back the lump in her throat, she sighed. "I'll miss you."

"And I, you," Bellamy squeezed her shoulder. With a gentle shove, he encouraged her away.

"Maybe they'll change their mind and I'll be back soon." Rae wasn't sure which to hope for. The evil she knew, or the potential of the one she didn't. She rose to her feet, cringing as she backed towards the cracked cell door. "If you see Damien..."

"I know." He offered her a weak smile. "I'll tell him."

Rae nodded, grateful for his understanding. "Close your eyes." She wanted to spare him from the pain the light would bring. Once he had, she slipped out through the door, coming face to face with Kynis. "Can't you take him, too?"

Kynis pursed his lips and shook his head. "He isn't auer, nor an interest to the council. He must remain."

Rae dropped her gaze, falling silent as the auer locked Bellamy's cell once more. She put her hand on the wooden door. "Bye, Bell."

This time, Kynis didn't wait for her to stumble before supporting her around her waist, lifting some of her weight off her damaged feet. He led her down a series of halls and stairs she was painfully familiar with and her heart rate increased with each step.

Kynis stopped at the bottom of a spiral staircase, holding Rae just out of the hallway she'd been dragged to on more than one occasion.

Remnants of sunlight fought its way through grates in the ceiling, illuminating the wide area. Trails stained the ground where bodies had been dragged, barely visible in the dim light.

"Where are you taking me?"

"As harsh as this place is, there is a quiet location we can talk under the sky just beyond this hallway."

Rae flinched at the shouts of a poor prisoner suffering at the hands of an interrogator.

Under the sky?

Rae tried not to get her hopes up. She hadn't seen the sky in far too long and buildings shrouded the little glimpses through the grates.

"First..." Kynis waved a hand towards the guard who still followed them. The man nervously stepped forward. "I'd like to remove this, if I may?" He gestured to the side of her head, and it took a moment for Rae to realize what he talked about.

She resisted touching the earring again. "You'll remove it?"

I'll have access to my power?

The guard gave Kynis an incredulous look, but the auer's expression remained stern.

"I will warn you that I am a skilled practitioner of the Art and must encourage you not to try anything once it's removed. I'd hate to use my power against you, but will, if necessary, to remain in good faith with our Helgathian hosts."

Rae gaped, but nodded. He could have asked her anything and she would've agreed if it meant removing the block to her power. In her current state, her promise of compliance meant nothing.

The guard reached into a pocket at his thigh and withdrew a tiny copper key that he offered to Kynis. "With permission, Sir. I won't be sticking around. No offense meant to your ability to control her."

"None taken." Kynis grabbed the key. "My companions will see to the coming negotiations."

The guard nodded, then hurried up the stairs behind them.

Kynis guided Rae to a wall so she could support herself while he gingerly tended to the cuff on her ear. His fingers felt like ice where they touched and the click of the mechanism releasing echoed in her ear.

Rae's body flushed with energy and she gasped a deep inhale. Her connection to her own aura reignited, and she abruptly felt more alive than she had in months, even if everything still ached.

Kynis tucked the earring and the key into a pocket of his grey breeches.

Hyper aware of the surrounding energy, Rae tried to calm her heart. "Thank you."

"Come." Kynis offered his arm again. "It'll feel even better beyond these stone walls."

Taking his arm, she leaned on him as he led her down the hallway. The tortured sounds still emanated from a room ahead, making her want to stop and run the other way.

I'm safe. I have my power.

As they passed by the open door, Rae couldn't help her eyes from straying inside.

An older man sat shirtless in a chair, blood and dirt caking his skin. A guard struck him with a hand whip each time he failed to answer a question, ragged cries thundering in her ears. The orange glow of a brazier heated the room beyond a comfortable temperature.

As her pulse rose in her ears, she couldn't hear the words being asked of the prisoner, just the crack of the whip that had once been used on the bottoms of her feet.

Her steps halted at the doorway, and Kynis didn't force her to keep moving.

Turning, Rae faced the two men inside the room, emotion raging through her.

The torturer stood straight, following the gaze of his prisoner to Rae. The firelight glowed on his face, making him look more like a monster than a human. His lips curled into a sneer at her, his face peppered with dark specks.

Rae had seen that man's face more times than she wished to remember. She didn't know his name and didn't want to.

She let go of Kynis's arm and took a solid step into the room, no longer feeling the stone under her feet. The brazier danced in the corner of her vision, daring her to use it for her own interests.

This man had cut her feet, her hair, and snapped her ribs with his kicks.

"Come for more, girly?" The torturer stepped from behind the old man. He fiddled with the whip in his hands, strolling towards her. He neared the brazier, reaching for a heated iron rod within it.

"Yes." Rae's fingers twitched, the Art within her forging its own path at her command. The smoldering rage within her fed it.

Fire leapt from the brazier, curling up the iron rod.

The torturer barked in surprise, dropping the iron, but the fire had already engulfed his arm. He beat at it with the hand still holding the whip, but it did nothing to calm the flames.

Rae's veins lit ablaze, letting the power loose.

Burn.

The fire spread over his body in merciless heat. Unblinking, she watched as he screamed and fought his invisible foe. Her ears roared with noise, deafening her against any semblance of forgiveness.

He fell to his knees, flames licking and charring the ceiling above him. Finally, his struggles ceased, body crumpled on the ground as the scent of burning hair and flesh overtook the room.

Rae stood silently, staring at his charred remains as the flames continued to devour, turning his flesh black. She heard a footfall behind her as Kynis stepped forward.

The flames snuffed out against each other as if a great wind blew them away. The flesh of the torturer still smoked, burnt beyond recognition.

Feeling no remorse, she turned and looked at Kynis.

Why didn't he stop me like he said he would?

Kynis met her eyes, the sharp definition of his face impossible for her to read. She couldn't tell if he was upset or satisfied.

"We have much to talk about, after all, Raeynna." Kynis offered his hand. "Let us leave this place."

Chapter 20

"YOU SENT YOUR HAWK TO *WHO*?"

Jarrod sighed. "It's not a big deal, she's a friend of mine and Rae's."

Even though I thought those two would butt heads the whole time.

"Captain Andirindia Trace is your *friend*?" Corin dismounted from his horse.

Jarrod scratched Liala behind the head and she ruffled her feathers with an affectionate coo. "Aye."

"She's not as bad as everyone makes her out to be." Damien stayed on Xyphir as the horse shuffled, wary of the hawk on Jarrod's arm.

Jarrod laughed. "She kept you in the brig your whole trip. And she and Rae got drunk, quite often based on what you told me."

"She could have killed me." Damien shrugged. "Considering our family history."

Corin huffed, rubbing the back of his head. "Gyrin was kind of an ass anyway. He probably deserved it."

"And I'm sure Rae would have protested if she tried to kill you." Jarrod rolled his eyes. "She's an honorable person, really. Will be a good ally to get Rae back, should we need her. I wouldn't be surprised if she's docked nearby. Could also end up being our escape route once we find Rae."

"Because bringing pirates into this whole mess is clearly the most logical answer." Corin stepped closer to Jarrod, but eyed Liala.

Jarrod moved his hawk closer to the captain. "Unlike Rae's savage creature, she's friendly if you want to give her a scratch."

"Din likes *me*." Damien's attention shifted down the road towards Lazuli.

Only because you use your weird animal connection.

Corin glanced at Jarrod with a smile and slid his glove off before stroking Liala's chest with the back of his fingers.

Liala chirped, tilting her head to the side as she examined the captain.

Smirking, Jarrod bounced his arm and Liala hopped onto Corin's armored forearm.

Corin jumped but recovered when the hawk settled. He hoisted his arm up, showering Liala with more attention while making his own cooing noises at her.

"She likes you." Jarrod quirked one eyebrow at Corin.

"She's got good sense."

Neco whined as he pushed up against the back of Jarrod's legs, nearly knocking him over.

"Jeez, boy. No need to be jealous." Jarrod stroked the wolf as he turned towards the smoke rising on the horizon.

Lazuli was just over the next hill crest, and Jarrod looked at Damien. "Should we wait for nightfall?"

"Probably best." Damien dismounted, whispering to his horse while scratching his nose. "You'll need to check in at the barracks, right?" He turned towards his brother.

Corin nodded once, his smile for Liala turning into a frown. "To receive my post after the assignment officer finishes questioning why they transferred me. But I might be able to find out what happened to Rae."

Damien nodded. "We'll meet in the Hedge after that." He referenced a part of the city they were all familiar with. Home to the poorest citizens of the region, they could blend in like they had in Quar.

Jarrod kept his distaste to himself about Corin heading to the barracks.

It's protocol. Nothing will happen.

After the scare in Mirage, he'd been on edge. Being in Lazuli didn't help his nerves since he'd have to be more careful about who saw him. Hopefully sticking to the seedy part of town would prevent running into old acquaintances.

Regardless, the anxiety swirling in his stomach prevented him from sleeping the night before or eating that morning. Being open with the Lanoret brothers about his tension helped, bringing unexpected comfort with the kinship.

As if sensing it, Corin touched Jarrod's bicep, drawing his gaze. "You all right?" He lowered his voice so Damien might not hear.

"Just nervous. I don't need anyone else recognizing me. And the idea of you being on your own again..."

Corin's lips spread into a charming smile. "You don't need to worry about me. I'll be back before you know it. Don't get too sappy or I'll start thinking you really care or something." He touched the scar on Jarrod's chin with his free hand, a new habitual show of affection.

Jarrod kissed his knuckles. "Being an ass won't make me worry less. Just be careful."

Corin opened his mouth to respond but before he could, Xyphir let out a whinny as Damien mounted again.

"We've got to go now."

Jarrod pressed his forearm into Liala, prompting her to step onto it. "What's wrong?" He shoved his hawk up to launch her into the sky.

Neco huffed, bounding towards Damien, which further irritated Xyphir.

Damien leaned forward to comfort the prancing horse. "It's Rae. Something's changed. I can feel her ká. She's still here." His cheeks beneath his dark beard looked pale, his eyes wilder than Jarrod had seen in a long time.

"What happened to waiting for nightfall?" Jarrod's blood rushed at Rae being so close.

Damien is right, this is our chance.

He clamped a hand down on Corin's shoulder and squeezed before swinging himself onto Orion.

Corin cursed and moved to follow Jarrod. "Go ahead, better we enter separately. I'll find you later."

Damien pushed Xyphir into a gallop, Neco following with a yip.

Jarrod looked at Corin and shook his head. "One day we'll have to stop parting like this."

"That's exactly what I'm fighting for." Corin smiled back. "Be safe." He gave Jarrod a final pat on the leg before stepping back.

Jarrod nodded. "You too." Nudging Orion into a fast chase to catch up to Damien, he didn't look back. Orion's hooves pounded to join Xyphir. "Can you tell exactly where she is?"

"Definitely the prison. I can sense her tapping into her Art and how angry she is..." The Rahn'ka's brow furrowed and his jaw twitched in the way he did when focusing his powers on something specific.

"The prison?" Jarrod hoped to get something logical out of Damien. "You want to charge straight there, like this?"

Quieting again, Damien continued their race towards Lazuli until they'd nearly reached the top of the hill. He slowed Xyphir, allowing Jarrod to catch up.

"No." Damien huffed as if out of breath. "That won't work. But she's here." His eyes begged Jarrod to have the perfect answer for what to do. "She's so close."

"I get it, man, I want her back too, but let's be smart." Jarrod walked Orion beside Damien. "We're only an hour off nightfall, so put your hood up, and let's get closer. Maybe we can find out what's going on. They wouldn't have accidentally let her power loose."

Lazuli sat nestled among the hills of Helgath's coastline. The walls rose and fell with the natural curve of the land, stone monstrosities separating nature from the population. They approached from the northwest, the road dipping low to enter the city close to the Hedge before the neighborhoods spread like squares of a quilt across the land. Glittering ocean rimmed the southern horizon, masts of ships barely visible through the clouds of smoke clinging to the city's silhouette.

To the east, stretching like a black scab across the land, the spires of the prison dominated the skyline. Even where they stood, Jarrod could see the fluttering flags atop the towers and the pacing Helgathian guards.

Beyond it, if he could have seen through the smoke and stone, stood the behemoth of his old life, separated from the city enough to claim to be clean of its corruption. He had no desire to go anywhere near the Martox castle and hoped that with the coming winter his family would be locked up tight within its walls, no longer interested in visiting the city.

Still, his stomach flopped.

"You're right. We will have to sneak into the prison somehow." Damien heaved in a breath and his face turned grim. "I can't feel her anymore." The tone of his voice shifted from the panic to something far more harrowing.

Jarrod's eyes widened, his pulse rising. "What does that mean?"

"It could mean a lot of things." Damien kept his eyes ahead. "Some possibilities are much better than others. But I can't think about that now. We need to find a way in." Pulling his hood up, he didn't wait before he urged Xyphir down the hill.

Jarrod nodded, pulling his hood up, and Neco hurried ahead of the horses.

As they approached the open gates of Lazuli, Jarrod breathed a sigh of relief that their assumptions had been correct and no guards manned the entrance. They'd abandoned the cart and their story of Damien's illness because the likelihood of continued heightened security deep within Helgath was low.

Most of the populous had disappeared into their homes in the twilight. A boy ran past them with a lantern to ignite the street lights, jumping and scrambling away at the sight of Neco, who trotted beside the walking horses.

Arriving near the prison's main entrance, Jarrod guided Orion into an alley between a pair of two-story buildings with narrow openings allowing them to view the prison gates without exposing themselves to the guards.

The drawbridge leading into the prison creaked as it lowered, stretching across a trench of stagnant water. Walls made of dark lava stone reached higher than the city walls. Narrow torch-lit windows looked out over the city.

Stopping within the shadows of the alley, Jarrod looked at Damien. "Breaking into that prison is a tall order. We wouldn't even know where to look for her."

The drawbridge thudded as it struck the ground, revealing eight soldiers stationed at its entrance. Beyond was a narrow courtyard with rough-hewn floors and an additional set of squat buildings surrounding the gallows. A noose swayed in the evening breeze, and Jarrod shuddered.

Sweet Nymaera, let her be alive.

Two more soldiers appeared, carrying a man between them.

The man's feet dragged along the ground as if he'd rather stay in the prison. Shrouded by a ragged black cloak, his body looked sickly thin. He landed on the cobblestone road with a huff after the two soldiers threw him. The drawbridge lifted before the guards even finished walking clear of it.

"Gods," Damien whispered as Neco growled. "It's so much worse than I imagined... I've been here before, but never realized..." He swallowed, closing his eyes and turning his head to the side. "I can't go in there. I wouldn't be able to control my power. There's too much lingering energy from the dead."

Jarrod eyed him. "If it comes to that, I'll go alone. Can you manage being this close?"

Damien nodded. "They're not as bad out here. Less angry."

The released prisoner remained on his knees until the bridge thunked closed. He struggled to his feet, stumbling away from the prison, and wove a crooked path as if drunk.

"We should follow him." Jarrod wheeled Orion around within the narrow alley to go back the way they came. "A fresh release will be easy to bribe. He could know something."

Hooves clattered behind him as Damien turned his horse, followed by the sound of Neco's nails scratching on the street. Jarrod stopped at the mouth of the alley again, watching the prisoner stagger.

The lean man didn't dodge the occasional oncoming cart or pedestrian, forcing them to go around his hunched form. It earned him glares and shouts of annoyance.

Jarrod stayed several yards behind.

Be patient.

A soldier in military uniform caught his eye and his gaze shot to the side, expecting to see Corin. Instead, the soldier was a man he didn't recognize, busy talking with a distraught woman.

Jarrod released a breath, shaking his head.

Damien encouraged Xyphir ahead towards the open mouth of a narrow covered alley.

Neco pushed past a startled baker carrying the day's leftovers out the back door of his shop. The goods would have gone sputtering across the street if Damien hadn't hopped from Xyphir and caught the man's shoulder, righting him.

The baker rambled off his appreciation before disappearing inside his shop, the lock clicking into place.

Jarrod sat on Orion, looking from Damien to the alley.

The man they'd followed sat on a crate at the end, leaning against the stone wall. The hood had fallen, exposing pale and sunken skin. He looked like a ghost, his head disembodied because of how his cloak blended into the shadows.

An arch marked the entrance into the alleyway, too short for them to ride the horses through. The alley widened farther in but ended with a crumbling brick wall and forgotten storage containers.

Jarrod dismounted, looping Orion's reins around a nearby hitch post as Damien did the same. "You want to approach him together? Don't wanna scare him off."

"I'll go first. You and Neco stay here, in case he runs. I can defend myself without a weapon."

Nodding, Jarrod ruffled the top of Neco's head and leaned against the stone wall. "Do you have something to bribe him with?"

Damien gave him a vague nod, then stepped into the alley, keeping his hood up.

Chapter 21

DAMIEN TRIED TO KEEP HIS gait as unthreatening as possible.

The man sat with his knees pulled to his chest, leaning his head against the cool stone. Dark bags circled his eyes as if he hadn't slept in weeks. A thin beard grew in uneven patches on his otherwise youthful face.

"Evening." Damien softened his tone, changing his usual cadence to disguise his voice. He'd locked down his barrier completely, eliminating any sense of the man's ká and leaving him uneasy. But remaining in control of his power was necessary.

Last thing I need is to repeat the events from Ashdale.

Though, a riot of ghosts would be a worthy distraction to get Rae out.

The man startled belatedly, as if he hadn't heard at first and only noticed when Damien stepped within view of his lowered eyes. He straightened and pushed himself against the wall. "Leave me alone. I have nothing to steal, I swear."

Something about his voice sounded familiar but Damien couldn't place it. He maintained his approach, keeping to the opposite side of the alley. A chase would draw too much attention.

"I'd actually like to give you something in exchange for some information."

The man glanced down the alleyway towards where Jarrod and Neco waited, their bodies faintly outlined by the street lamps beyond. A wracking shudder rocked the prisoner's shoulders, his body falling into a tremble that he sucked in a ragged breath to stop. He plopped a leg off the edge of the crate he sat on, but the tremble vibrated up and down his limbs as if he had no control over it. He rose a shaky hand to his forehead and hissed.

"Headache?" Damien thought of Rae and the way she'd helped him combat his raging migraines before he learned to control the voices of the Rahn'ka. The nostalgia distracted him from maintaining his false timbre. "I might be able to help with that if you'll help me."

The man's eyes shot open and pierced right through him. "You're Damien." His body convulsed with a cough.

Damien's stomach dropped out, but he waved his hand to dismiss the idea. "Who?" He reinstated his disguised voice. "I think you might be confused."

The man's expression softened, and he lowered his voice. "Rae said you'd come."

Surprise rushed through Damien as he looked at the man. "Bellamy?" Emotion heated his cheeks as he stepped closer.

Nodding, the Shade coughed again. "It's nice to meet you in person." Bellamy motioned towards the mouth of the alley. "Jarrod and Neco?"

Damien grinned, taking another step, and held a hand out to Bellamy. "Want some help with that headache? Then you can tell me about Rae. Please tell me she's still alive?"

"She's alive. At least the last time I saw her." He accepted the offered hand.

Hope sprouted but Damien forced himself to focus on helping before asking more questions. He glanced at Neco and sent a thought to encourage him to come, assuming the thief would follow.

Damien focused on the Shade's hand and how clammy it felt. He kept a close hold of his power so it wouldn't extend beyond the alley and his ká tangled with the Shade's. It buzzed differently than a normal human's, slivers of his master's taint seeping through every sinew of his spirit. He wove around them as he sought the muscles in Bellamy's head, urging them to release their strain. Avoiding the corruption made the process more tedious than it should have been and Damien's ears rang.

Jarrod approached. "What's going on?"

Bellamy's shoulders sagged with relief, looking at Jarrod. "Rae will be so relieved to see you alive."

Jarrod stopped in his tracks and looked from Damien to Bellamy and back again. "Is this a joke?"

"No." Lightheadedness threatened Damien, and he steadied himself on the alley wall. "This is Bellamy, we... kind of met when I visited Rae. He was in the cell next to hers."

Jarrod visibly relaxed. "Is she alive?"

Bellamy shuffled his feet, straightening. "I don't outright know. They took her just before they released me."

"Taken?" Damien's head spun. "By who? Torturers?"

"No." Bellamy shook his head. "An auer showed up today. He seemed kind, even let her say goodbye to me." As he spoke, his gaze dropped to the ground. Knitting his brow, he looked at Damien with clearer eyes. "It wasn't long ago. If he intended on taking her from here, it'd be by ship. You could catch her if you go now."

Damien's heart leapt into his throat. It hadn't been long since he'd felt her power, but the auer complicated things.

Why would the auer care about a quarter-blood?

Yondé's prejudice slipped to the forefront of his mind, prompting him to feel it too.

"Let's go." Jarrod motioned towards the horses.

Damien drew away from Bellamy as another shivering fit took over his body. Glancing at Jarrod, his mind battled against itself. "Just a moment. I need to help him first." He put his hands on Bellamy's shaking shoulders.

Focusing his power, Damien urged his ká to guide the Shade's. Despite the healing, Bellamy's shivers continued. The Rahn'ka furrowed his brow, giving the man more. Searching Bellamy's ká, he found no remnants of what he'd already given. The corruption within the Shade gobbled all he gave.

"I don't understand. You're not sick. This is something else."

Bellamy shook his head, his body responding vaguely to Damien's silent prodding. "I haven't used my connection to my master in weeks. My body is craving it and it's so hard to keep saying no when I can feel it right there. Tempting me."

Neco let out a blood-curdling snarl and Jarrod spun around.

Damien's gaze darted to the end of the alley, following Neco and Jarrod's, but nothing was there. Mist, dark in the encroaching night, drifted towards the archway while a flicker of a shadow shifted at the ground.

Neco gnashed his teeth, lips curled.

Bellamy grabbed Damien's hand, his nails biting into his skin. "Run!"

The shadows of the alley swirled, seething unnaturally forward, making Damien's skin crawl. He secretly feared the day he'd encounter another hostile Shade.

Jarrod cursed as he drew his wicked split dagger, eyes locked on the moving shadow. "Shades have such perfect timing. I don't much feel like running, how about you?" He glanced at Damien.

"Nope." Damien pushed the last pulse he could into Bellamy before releasing him and facing the alley's entrance. He thinned his barrier to activate his awareness of the surrounding energy. The ká of the few living creatures nearby screamed in fear, flooding his mind. The Shade devoured their energies to feed his own.

Damien flexed his forearm and spread his stance. He channeled his ká into his leg as he ground a foot on the street. His vision flashed as a pulse of light whispered out from his boot, surging forward to where the Shade's shadows curled. When the two forces met, they slammed into each other with a crackle like splintering ice.

Everything snapped to a stop, the shadow wriggling up as if crawling over a glass bubble only feet ahead of Jarrod and Neco.

The shadow rolled back onto itself when it attempted to climb too high. It continued for only a few breaths before it recoiled, coalescing into a mound of black tar at the center of the alley. The collection rose, building on itself until it was the size of a man with broad shoulders, similar to Jarrod in height.

The shadows flaked away like ash, revealing the lightly tanned skin of the one who controlled them.

Neco snarled louder, but Jarrod kept a hand on his ruff, stopping the wolf from lunging.

The Shade's pale blue eyes looked nearly white in the moonlight penetrating the alley. With neatly cut chestnut hair and clean-shaven, he looked noble in his fine attire. Far different from the one-eyed vagrant Shade Yondé had imprisoned.

"There's no need for your deaths." The Shade's calm baritone voice filled the alley. "I only came for my friend there. The rest of you are inconsequential."

A sword glinted under the layers of the man's cloak, but Damien decided against an honorable fight.

Not with a Shade.

The low rumble of Neco's growl still echoed through the alley while the wolf glared at the Shade.

"Jarrod. Could you come here?"

As they all stood in contemplation, the occasional whip of a shadow tentacle struck the surface of Damien's shield, only to withdraw and try again. The Shade stood still, his arms crossed beneath his cloak, a lopsided smile on his lips.

Cocky bastard.

The thief cast Damien a sidelong glance before stepping closer.

The Rahn'ka lowered his voice. "I'm a little drained. There's not enough around for me to use, and I wanted to ask before—"

Jarrod lifted his arm in offering, and Damien grasped his wrist to draw on his ká. The physical contact made it easier to control the amount he took, and he ended the connection as Jarrod slumped.

The thief caught himself before he fell, leaning on a pile of crates with closed eyes.

Able to breathe again, Damien rolled his shoulders. His ká buzzed with the extra power, relieving him of all previous weariness. The Rahn'ka drew the invisible energies together within him and turned back to his target.

The Shade's steely eyes narrowed. He took a step closer to the shield and pulled the sword from his belt. The arrogant patience he'd shown vanished, and he lifted his blade to slash through the Art with physical force.

Damien hurried to find the proper weaves holding his shield in place. He outstretched his hands in a rush. Fingers taut, he condensed the shield down like balling a scrap of paper, its fine blue sheen flickering through the air. He fed the energy he'd taken from Jarrod into it as he clasped his hands together to form the flickering lights into a malleable sphere. With a thrust, the white energy shot forward.

The Shade summoned a wall of shadow, dark tentacles of power soaring upward to protect him.

It took only a thought for Damien to split through the energy and swirl his around both sides of the shadow defenses to strike his opponent's chest. The Shade's eyes widened as Damien latched his power onto his ká and pulled as hard as he could.

The light colors of the man's ká erupted from his skin. Tangles of black held tight, like the roots of a weed trying to keep hold of the soil while being plucked.

The Shade fell to his knees, the shadows around him dissolving into the ground. A war ensued between the Shade's master and Damien regarding the proper placement of the man's soul.

Damien's muscles screamed as if he pulled on an unmovable object, but he refused to stop until the Shade collapsed into a heap on the alley floor. Even then, he held it a breath longer, just to be sure. When Damien released his hold on the man's ká, it ricocheted back into place.

Letting out a sigh, Damien let go of his power. His shoulders drooped, an influx of exhaustion dropping him to a knee as he tried to make the world stop spinning.

Neco still growled, but licked Damien's face before inspecting the fallen Shade.

Jarrod coughed, leaning against the stone wall with his head back. "Is he dead?"

"No. Just unconscious. The nature of their bond doesn't allow me to kill them that way."

Bellamy rose to his feet, steadier than before. He approached the man who'd been hunting him.

Jarrod spun his dagger. "But we can kill him another way."

Damien glowered. "You'd kill him while he's unconscious?"

The thief sighed. "Don't be so righteous. He'd kill all of us without a second thought. I thought you said you'd met a Shade before? They don't deserve mercy. With rare exceptions." He glanced at Bellamy before frowning at Damien. "If you're not intent on finishing this, then we should go after Rae. We might still catch her."

Bellamy pulled his cloak tighter on his shoulders. "You should go. Hurry. I'll be fine. Go get Rae before they get her out of Helgath."

A growl formed in Damien's chest. He didn't want to argue with Jarrod and hardly had the energy to spare. He forced himself to his feet and clapped a hand on Bellamy's shoulder. "This is your decision then." He gestured towards the unconscious Shade. "And thank you."

Bellamy's eyes looked distant, but he nodded. "Go."

Damien glanced at Jarrod as he replaced his dagger in its leather sleeve, shaking his head. "You up to running?"

"I'd run all night to find her, but let's take the horses. It's faster." Jarrod strode around the limp man towards Orion.

"Always the practical one." Damien looked at Neco. "Let's go find her, buddy."

Neco yipped as they all rushed to the horses, leaving Bellamy standing over the Shade who found him.

Damien stopped and turned at the end of the alley. "I'll come back. I think I can do more to break your bond."

Bellamy looked up, meeting his gaze. "I won't be here. And hopefully neither you nor Shades will find me." He glanced down at the collapsed Shade, then turned away towards the mouth of the alley.

Orion's hooves thundered as Jarrod took off down the wide street towards the docks without him. Neco bolted after the thief, leaving Damien to kick Xyphir to catch up.

With the sun set, they no longer feared being recognized and pushed the horses into a gallop through the city. Luckily, pedestrians were scarce, leaving few obstacles in their haste. Their hoods flew back as the salty breeze rushed past them.

Jarrod leapt off Orion's back at the start of the wooden docks and they both found the energy to sprint over the planks above the water.

Damien searched for anything remotely auer in appearance, but too many ships blocked their view of the horizon. None matched what he expected to see, and they ran to the end before finally getting a clear line of sight east.

An auer ship, dimly lit against the dark backdrop of the sky, sailed away. Its single translucent sail showed the stars beyond.

It couldn't have left more than an hour ago.

His chest pounded as he slid to a stop beside Jarrod.

The thief ran both hands over his hair as Neco lifted his muzzle and let out a heartbroken howl.

A roar of anger escaped Damien's lungs as he spun on his heels and paced down the dock. His exhaustion forgotten, he turned back to the torturous sight confirming how close they'd come.

Jarrod sank to his knees, hands still on his head as he watched the ship grow farther away. "She's right there."

Damien opened his mouth to respond, but the sound of armored boots rushing down the dock behind him stole his attention.

"Just what we need," Jarrod growled, rising to his feet.

"You there!" A voice bellowed, eliciting another snarl from the wolf. "Halt!" Two uniformed soldiers hurried down the docks.

"Shit." Damien sought the aid of the energies of the ocean. He drew the pulse of the waves, and the energy it created, into his ká, readying himself as the soldiers approached.

One soldier suddenly sprawled forward, face first on the docks. He slid across the moist planks, shouting as he dropped off the side and splashed into the water.

The other soldier skidded to a stop. "You clumsy dolt." He peered over the side of the dock. "Get your ass to shore. I'll hold them until you get back."

Damien had been called a dolt in the same tone too many times to not recognize his brother.

Corin grinned at them as he tipped his helmet back from his face, shaking his head as he walked towards them.

Neco quieted, tail wagging back and forth.

Jarrod's entire demeanor shifted, and he let out a sigh.

"In the name of the king, I command you to come peacefully!" Corin put on a show for the man swimming to shore out of sight.

Damien's body protested amidst his release of gathered energy, but he forced his legs to stop shaking.

"I heard about two men running their horses through the city streets like madmen, with a massive black wolf in tow... Oh, I wonder who that could be. Sounds a lot like something my dumb ass little brother and the man I've foolishly fallen in love with would be doing right about now." Corin's face sobered as he looked back and forth between Damien and Jarrod. "What happened?"

"Rae." Damien huffed. "I don't know why, but they have given her to the auer. We just missed her." He gestured towards the horizon.

Corin's eyes followed his hand, and his frown deepened. "I'll find out what port in Eralas they're sailing for. But you two need to make it look like you gave me trouble and got away. Then lie low until we figure out a way to get you out of the city. Neco needs to stay completely hidden."

Damien nodded, looking down at the wolf, who gave him a baleful look. "I'm sure Jarrod can help with giving you trouble.

I'll get Neco out of here." He stepped away, but not out of earshot from Jarrod and Corin. He scratched Neco while keeping them in the corner of his vision.

The couple often denied each other affection for his sake, but the misplaced pity made him feel worse.

If they can find something good in this mess, I'm happy for them.

Jarrod groaned and stalked towards Corin. "I'll give you trouble, all right," he muttered, kissing him quickly before pulling away. "See you in the Hedge." He grabbed hold of the front of the soldier's light armor, pulling him closer as if for another kiss. Before their mouths met, Jarrod shoved Corin's chest. The captain stumbled backward, unable to catch his balance before he fell off the dock with a shout.

Jarrod met Damien's gaze as Corin splashed into the ocean below. "Does that work?" His tone held a mixture of play and frustration, mirroring how Damien felt.

"Works for me." Damien smirked as Corin sputtered curses from below. "Lets go."

Jarrod jogged next to him. "You go try to find Bellamy? I'll get us a place in the Hedge. Probably best to split up, anyway."

"Agreed. Take the horses. Neco and I will go on foot."

Chapter 22

CORIN'S CLOTHES DRIPPED AS HE walked out of the city sheriff's office, dislodging another pocket of seawater in the regalia. He and his comrade had been reprimanded for an hour after letting the two they'd been dispatched to 'deal with' get away and make fools of the city soldiers. The sheriff threatened to contact a general to get Corin demoted for such a stupid mistake.

He took the berating without argument. It'd been rather dumb of him to fall for Jarrod's affection and let him push him in the harbor. Though, he probably deserved it with all he'd put the thief through.

Dismissed for the night to clean up and 'evaluate' his mistakes, Corin made his way to the Hedge on foot. He didn't bother drying off, covering himself with the thick cloak he'd purchased in Mirage to hide his uniform without removing it. Walking with a trail of water at his heels didn't inspire people to think him a city soldier either. The drying saltwater made his skin crusty.

He followed the pattern they'd agreed on to find each other, entering the easternmost tavern and asking their recommendation for an inn.

Corin climbed the rickety stairs, ignoring the look from the innkeeper as another pocket of water inside his armor released when he took the first step. He selfishly hoped his companions had purchased two separate rooms.

Corin rapped three times on the door with a crooked number nine, listening for movement inside.

Boots scuffed against the floor, and the lock turned.

Jarrod jerked the door open, one arm behind his back. His vest hung loose, unfastened at the front, with the long sleeves of his shirt rolled up to his elbows.

"Please tell me you have a bathtub." Corin rested his temple on the doorframe.

Smirking, Jarrod stepped back, silently inviting Corin in before locking the door behind him. Letting his arm relax, he returned the blade he'd been hiding to his belt. "A bath? Now, why would you need a bath?"

Much to Corin's relief, a full tub occupied the center of the room and he moaned softly in joy.

"Probably not so hot anymore. You took longer than I expected."

"Had to get my ass handed to me by the sheriff first." Removing the cloak, he tossed it over the foot of the bed. He stripped off his armor, piling it onto a chair. Everything felt sticky, and he didn't look forward to cleaning the steel to prevent rust.

Jarrod grinned. "Going for a swim wasn't in your orders?"

"I believe that would be called a *recreational activity*. Not exactly allowed while on duty." As he walked towards the tub, his undershirt clinging to his skin, Jarrod caught his wrist and pulled him back.

"No, *this* is recreational." He chuckled, claiming Corin's mouth.

The kiss nearly made the captain forget how gross his body felt, still saturated with seawater. He hummed against Jarrod's lips before pulling back. "While I am rarely one to deny such enjoyable recreation, I'm a tad salty right now." Putting a hand on Jarrod's chest, he pushed.

Jarrod didn't budge. "Takes more than salt to keep me away from you." His gruff tone made Corin's body heat, but the thief loosened his grip. "But I suppose I can concede, while your water is still warm."

"Oh no, now you've got my attention. You're going to scrub my back." Corin smirked.

Jarrod laughed, a rich, warm sound. "Who said I wasn't going to already?"

Corin leaned into him, stealing another kiss. The combination of the seawater dried on his lips with the sweet taste of Jarrod made his heart race. He broke the kiss as he started to untuck his shirt. "Better turn away. I get bashful." He stepped back from Jarrod, drawing the wet shirt over his head and letting it fall to the ground with a flop. Turning his back, he enjoyed imagining what Jarrod's face might look like as he slipped from his breeches and climbed into the bath.

Despite being tepid, the water brought the relief he sought as he leaned his head back and let his eyes close.

He hadn't had time for this kind of luxury in a while, often resorting to sponge-downs and quick, cold bucket showers in the military camps.

Knowing Jarrod watched added a nervous feeling in the pit of his stomach.

"I figured you might be." Jarrod's voice grew closer behind him. "That's why I got you this room all for yourself. Your brother and I will be across the hall." His tone held the vaguest lilt of humor, but if he hadn't been listening for it, he would've missed it.

Opening one eye to peek behind him at Jarrod, Corin sucked in a deep breath that escaped in a long, regretful groan. He grinned at the little shift it caused in Jarrod, a subtle rock on his feet. "That's a shame. I'd hoped for company tonight."

Jarrod left his peripheral vision and a moment later the thief dragged a chair noisily over the floor to come to a stop behind him.

Warm hands touched Corin's shoulders, moving over his bare chest as Jarrod leaned forward from his sitting position to hover his mouth near the captain's ear. "Should I let Damien know you're feeling lonely?"

A buzz rumbled through Corin's body, his head tilting of its own accord to grant Jarrod's breath better access to his skin. The feeling made his brain stumble for an answer, even though he'd started to come up with something properly witty. Instead, the words turned into a breathy whimper, and he ran his wet hand over Jarrod's head, the short hairs on his scalp tickling his palm.

Jarrod scooped water from near Corin's chest over his shoulders. Wetting his hands again, he did the same over his neck and up the back of his head into his hair.

Closing his eyes, Corin allowed the bliss to overtake him. Jarrod's rough hands felt amazing.

Gods, I will miss him.

The realization of their quickly approaching separation had settled in Corin's mind while dripping through the streets of Lazuli.

They had taken Rae to Eralas. Jarrod would pursue her with Damien, but Corin couldn't follow. He didn't want to say it, certain the thief had to be thinking the same thing.

Speaking it will make it real.

Corin caught Jarrod's hand as it slid down his chest and brought it to his mouth, kissing his knuckles.

Jarrod sucked in a breath, turning his hand in Corin's grip to touch his jaw before sliding down his neck again. This time, his grip stopped at his shoulders and rubbed into the back of them.

Tense muscles responded with a satisfying hum of pain as Jarrod worked them. Corin leaned forward from the edge of the tub, water sloshing. "Remind me to return this favor later."

Digging in with his thumbs, Jarrod massaged Corin's neck. "Perhaps while on a ship to Eralas?" Uncertainty laced his tone.

Corin's stomach lurched. He took a slow breath as he tried to sort through all the requirements of his continued service in a hazy rush of thought.

"I was hoping you'd come with us." Jarrod broke the silence that settled. His hands continued massaging down near his shoulder blades.

As his hands worked back up over his shoulders, Corin reached across his chest and closed his fingers over Jarrod's. "I can't." He regretted each syllable as it came out. "I wish it was different, but I *can't*, Jarrod."

Jarrod's hands paused. "Why not?"

Without releasing his hold on Jarrod's hand, Corin turned within the water, wedging his leg beneath him so he could face the thief.

Jarrod's eyes held the same vulnerability as his voice and Corin wanted to kiss him to banish it as quickly as possible. "You know why." Touching his thumb to the scar on Jarrod's chin, he swallowed his hesitation. "I can't leave now, it would endanger too much here."

Jarrod's jaw flexed and his eyes hardened as he nodded once.

"Please say you understand." A pang of guilt stung Corin's chest.

Aren't I doing the right thing?

Jarrod squeezed Corin's hand, but he cringed and shook his head. "I suppose I do. I just thought... What about us?"

"The rebellion needs me here, it's too unstable." He touched Jarrod's jaw. "But with us, nothing is in danger. No matter how much time we have to spend apart, I'll still love you. *That* is indestructible."

Jarrod's dark eyes bored into him, and Corin wondered if the thief felt less certain. But he nodded again, slower. "I wish I could stay here, but..."

"I would never ask that of you. Besides, I need you to look after that idiot brother of mine." He smiled, Jarrod's words making his skin warm despite the cooling water. He slipped his hand around Jarrod's neck, encouraging him to lean forward.

Jarrod slid off the chair, kneeling on the floor next to him, arms over the tub. "And who will look after you?"

Corin pulled Jarrod's mouth to his, meeting it with a needy kiss. He drew away slowly, tracing a slow line down his cheek. "I'll be fine."

Jarrod shook his head. "Keep Liala. That way, if you need to get a message to me, at least you can."

Corin chuckled, withholding his usual witty commentary. He leaned forward, placing a kiss on the underside of Jarrod's jaw. "If you insist. Especially if that means you'll come back?"

"Aye, but not just for my hawk. You must realize I love you."

The words made Corin's body tingle, and he pulled away enough to meet Jarrod's warm eyes. "Suspected, perhaps." He shifted to his knees within the tub so he could lean closer. The cold rim of the tub pressed against his abdomen as he drew Jarrod into him. "But it is nice to hear." His wet hands slipped beneath the layers of Jarrod's tunic, playing with the skin at his waist. He took Jarrod's mouth with a heated kiss, pulling him against his bare chest.

Jarrod returned the kiss with equaled passion, but abruptly broke away. "I think you're clean enough." His gaze wandered down Corin's naked body.

The gruffness in his tone sent ripples of anticipation through Corin. Without further thought, he rose with Jarrod's bidding, eager to enjoy every moment they had left together.

Chapter 23

RAE'S HEART THUDDED AS SHE stepped off the single-sail ship onto the sand-strewn dock. She'd never laid eyes on Eralas before and even in her awe at the beauty of the island, nothing diminished her pain at venturing farther from Damien.

When they'd departed Lazuli, her ear cuff back in place, she'd watched the docks until they'd disappeared from the horizon. For a torturous moment, she thought she'd heard Neco's howl.

No matter how she'd pleaded with Kynis, he'd refused to take her anywhere but Eralas.

Her body no longer ached, having received extensive healing from auer menders while aboard. The process was excruciating but worth every moment of agony. The bottoms of her feet still donned the thin scars from the whip, but she walked comfortably in the simple canvas shoes Kynis provided her.

Yet, no amount of healing could save her from the dark recesses of her mind that surfaced while she slept. Instead, the auer focused on what they could physically fix. One auer took the time to even out the jagged state of her hair and gave her a mirror.

She'd hardly recognized her gaunt appearance and tired eyes. Malnourishment thinned her body, diminishing the muscle, and making her ribs show at her sides. Her hair ended beneath her jaw, naturally wavy. To help her feel like herself before arriving in Eralas, she'd braided one side back in two rows.

The sky above Eralas shone a perfect radiant blue without a cloud in sight. The island grew in a gentle slope of white beaches from the teal tides. The white ended with the roots of banyan trees, growing out like veins from the shadows of the forest. The trees were the largest Rae had ever seen, stretching so far above that she strained to see the tops. Their branches curved in ramps towards the blinking lights of the city nestled high within. Baskets, though that hardly seemed the right word for the woven monstrosities the size of houses, lowered up and down with ease to carry the cargo brought in from the crowded docks.

The trunks of the banyans grew in tangled, but deliberate patterns. From the distance of the harbor, the auer looked like ants crawling up the vines around a tree.

Kynis approached from behind Rae, making his steps louder than they usually would be on the sprawling dock. "Maelei." The Aueric city's name rolled delicately from his lips. "The southern jewel of Eralas. You've never been, correct?"

Rae shook her head. "Never. My father used to tell me stories of his visits before I was born."

"From what I've heard, the stories rarely do it justice." He smiled, stepping around her. "How are you feeling?"

"Like I'm still missing half of my heart," Rae whispered, the same response she always gave his repetitive question.

He frowned, his icy hand patting her shoulder. "Come. Our first stop will aid that pain."

"I don't want to *aid* the pain." Rae couldn't keep the bitterness from her tone. While she felt gratitude for being spared the continued torture of Helgath, this wasn't where she wanted to be. Not without Damien. "I want to see Damien. He's probably in Helgath right now, risking his life for me, and I'm not even there anymore."

"Helgath is no longer a concern of yours." Kynis's tone hardened as it often did when she persisted. "Nor are your old human relationships. There are much greater duties—"

Rae batted his hand off her shoulder. "You might be my cousin, or whatever, but you're not my family. Damien is. Jarrod is. And the Hawks. Until you return my life to me, I am your prisoner, no different from how you found me."

Kynis sighed, rubbing his forehead. "I fear you're right and you'll be a poor student with such distractions." He relaxed, clasping his hands together in front of him. "Please come, Raeynna. I'd rather not force you. It's easier this way." He turned away from her, walking down the dock ahead of her.

Rae closed her eyes, then turned to look back at the western horizon, brilliantly lit by the morning sun. How they'd sailed to Eralas in just two days was beyond her. "Please find me." She rolled her lips together before reluctantly following Kynis.

They walked alone, the rest of the auer staying behind on the ship while they stepped onto the winding pathway across the white sand beach. Birds chattered, playing in the surf and sand. They dove in and out of the trunks of the trees ahead, unaware of Rae's pain.

Instead of turning to the city as she suspected, Kynis headed west towards a grove that looked more foreboding. The squat trees grew wider than they did tall, their bases woven into a tight cross-hatching that prevented the sun from penetrating.

A pair of auer guards stood on opposite sides of a dark entryway which sank in a slope beneath the forest. The sand ended at its entrance, turning to thick patches of moss.

An eerie green glow emanated from the cavern.

Kynis stopped beside one guard, offering a greeting. He pressed his three middle fingers to his forehead, bringing them away to loop down towards his chest. He spoke Aueric. Her father had taught her parts of the language, but she didn't catch all Kynis said in his low tone. The only word she understood was 'expected.'

The guard nodded to a woman with silver hair flowing loose over her shoulders and held in place by a silver circlet. She responded with what sounded like directions.

Kynis looked back at Rae and approached the mouth of the cavern. He stepped aside and made a sweeping gesture for her to go first.

Rae cautiously walked to the precipice of the entryway, peering down a steep set of dark stairs. The glow emanating from somewhere within made each step difficult to see, but the narrow walls brought some comfort as she ran her hands along them, tracing the ivy vines and roots. "Why do I have the distinct feeling you're taking me to my next dungeon?"

"This isn't a dungeon. It's a sacred place. How many times must I assure you we don't wish to imprison you?"

"Then let me leave." Rae tilted her head at him.

"Humor me in this and then after we're done here, I'll let you leave if you still wish to."

Rae's heart leapt, but she forced it not to show on her face. He'd never let her leave, not after everything he'd done to bring her here. A loophole existed in his statement, she just couldn't see it yet. "I'll believe that when it happens." She continued the dark descent.

Kynis didn't respond, as per usual, but followed closely behind.

As she reached the bottom of the stairs, the ceiling curved in an arch, the walls rounded with dirt like a hall carved by a great worm. The green glow came from orbs nestled among the sod in tiny dimples in the walls. She could see no end to the tunnels ahead.

As they walked deeper, more walkways sprouted off the main one, each appearing endless. All were empty, and they continued until they reached a particular hall which as far as she could tell didn't differ from the others.

Kynis stopped and turned, ushering her forward. Another pair of guards stood in this one, their hair lime green in the light, like Kynis's. They barely offered an acknowledgment as Kynis led her past, slipping through another doorway and tunnel.

She couldn't tell which way she was facing anymore when they passed by two more statue-like guards, finally entering a space that offered some reprieve from the strange light. The green took on a subtle tone, tinted blue as the tunnel opened into a circular room. A rectangular stone table stood at the center. It was just wide enough for someone to lie on, with a supporting ridge for a neck near the head of it, suggesting displaying a body was its likely purpose.

Another auer stood in the room, a woman with long, flowing robes.

Rae stopped and shook her head. "I don't like this." She backed away from the ominous stone bed. She collided with

Kynis, who'd crossed to stand behind her and block the doorway.

He closed his hands on her shoulders. "There's nothing to be afraid of."

"When people say that, it's usually very, very untrue." Rae pushed her back against him, planting her feet.

The woman stepped around the bed towards Rae and held out a hand. Her eyes looked dark, nearly black. Her face was young, but something in those eyes spoke of years Rae couldn't fathom. "Child." The woman spoke in the common tongue, her voice like rain. "This will be far easier if you don't fight."

"*What* will be far easier?" Rae kept her hands tucked against her body. Kynis didn't let go, his auer strength keeping her in one place even though she tried to turn and run.

"An ancient tradition of our people." The woman snatched Rae's hand before she could pull it away. Her hands felt just as cold as Kynis's and sent a pulse of something indistinguishable through Rae's body.

All her muscles relaxed at once against her will.

"One that will help you in your training as a Mira'wyld."

Rae shook her head. "I'll pass, if it's all the same to you."

The woman's hand tightened like a vice on her wrist as she dragged Rae towards the center of the room. "You make the assumption this is an optional part of your training. It might have been, once. But we are beyond that point now."

"I'll cooperate." Rae looked at Kynis as the woman pulled her towards the stone bed. "I swear, I'll be a good student." Whatever hellish power the auer kept in this dank underground dungeon wasn't one she wanted to experience.

The woman tugged Rae closer with a jerk and as her hip touched the edge of the stone, something shifted beneath it. Before she could recoil, something wrapped around her waist and yanked her onto the stone. All the air left her lungs in a gush, her head forced to lay on the hard neck rest. Something crunched, like the sound of footsteps in the woods, a pressure curling around her body.

Opening her eyes, she realized the woman had released her and stepped away. She spoke in a low tone with Kynis while roots rolled over Rae's body to trap her on the bed.

Unable to continue her struggle, Rae closed her eyes, repeating her phrase in her mind.

Please find me, please find me.

The creaking of the roots stopped and footsteps echoed somewhere around her head.

"Try to clear your mind. It'll make this faster."

Instead of doing as instructed, Rae flooded her mind with every image of Damien she could think of. Memories of their time together, good and bad, and she let out a quiet sob.

The woman's cold fingers touched her temples. "You won't feel any pain as the Slumber takes hold."

Chapter 24

NEEDING TO HOLE UP AND hide after the close call with the Lazuli guard would've made Jarrod stir crazy without Corin to keep him company. He praised his foresight in purchasing two rooms for the duration of their stay. Saying goodbye to Corin would never be easy, but at least this way they could spend some time alone together first.

Morning came and Jarrod woke to Corin's arms wrapped around him. He'd been with men before but had never stayed past an evening. With Corin, he already craved the next night. He roused Corin with kisses and urged him to get dressed.

"You really don't have to leave Liala with me." Corin walked next to him up the hill outside the city gates. "I'll be fine." He squeezed Jarrod's hand, rocking their interlocked fingers between them.

"If you don't stop complaining, she will get offended." Jarrod tilted his head, even though the hawk circled high in the sky. He turned to look at Corin. "Please take her. For me, if nothing else."

Corin groaned with a playful frown and thumbed Jarrod's chin. "You're so cute when you're worried." His face grew serious, and he pursed his lips. "But all right. If it will make you feel better, I'll keep her with me. You'll have to teach me though. I don't know the first thing about falconry."

"Why do you think we're out here?"

"Scenic views and long walks hand in hand?" Corin kissed Jarrod's knuckles.

Jarrod rolled his eyes and took his hand away, withdrawing the gold chain he'd hidden before and a bone whistle.

Corin eyed the chain, touching where it tangled around Jarrod's finger. "I forgot to ask about this. You hid it so quickly in Mirage."

"I thought a gold necklace might raise questions. Questions I didn't feel like addressing." Jarrod slid the hollow end of the whistle onto the chain before lacing it around the soldier's neck to clasp it in place. When he pulled his head back, Corin's deep brown eyes locked on his.

"Do you still not feel like addressing them?" The captain touched the metal idly with a finger. "Or do I get to know the significance?"

Jarrod smirked. "I stole this when I left my old life. Sold it to get by for a time, before buying it back. Now, I keep it as a reminder of how hard I worked to gain my freedom."

Corin furrowed his brow, and it made him more handsome. "You're sure you want to give it to me?" He took his hand again. "Especially since I've been such an asshole about asking you to remember that past?"

Smiling, Jarrod pulled him closer and kissed him. "You've shown me a different kind of freedom. I think it's especially fitting that you wear it."

Corin smiled as he leaned in to kiss him again. "Thank you."

Lifting the bone whistle, Jarrod nudged Corin to take it. "Three short blasts and lift your left arm."

Corin checked the leather bracer on his left wrist before lifting the whistle to his lips and doing as instructed. Eyeing the sky, he tensed at Liala's screech as she plummeted towards him. He scrunched his eyes closed, but kept his arm up, putting a foot back to brace his stance as the hawk whooshed to a clawed stop on his arm. Peeking through one eye, he heaved out a sigh of relief as Jarrod laughed.

"Was that so terrifying?"

"Yes. I just keep imagining those claws missing and going for my face. I'm too pretty to let that kind of trauma happen. How would I ever keep the attention of such a charming, handsome, young nobleman-turned-thief?" He nervously scratched Liala's chest, like Jarrod had shown him before.

She cooed, cocking her head at Jarrod.

Quirking one eyebrow, the thief stroked his hawk. "Then it's a good thing she has exceptional aim. I'd hate to lose interest." His eyes stayed on the bird while he tapped the whistle on Corin's chest. "Corin."

Liala chirped.

"Corin."

The hawk flapped her wings wide in understanding.

"She'll know to stay with me instead of following you to Eralas?" Corin's tone sounded hollow, like it did every time they talked about the auer island.

Jarrod swallowed. "She knows. But I still wish you'd come."

Corin's jaw tightened. "Jarrod..."

"I know. I understand, I swear. It's just..."

"I know." Corin offered a slight smile. He gripped the thief's upper arm with his free hand. "Me too."

Jarrod sighed and pulled a piece of parchment from his other pocket, trying to refocus his thoughts.

On the paper, he'd written a note to Andi about needing her in Lazuli. A big ask for his privateer friend, even if she'd responded to his last letter with confirmation of sailing in the southern sea.

"Wrap it like this around her leg." Jarrod slid the metal cuff over the parchment. "Then secure it tightly. Even if it rains, her feathers will protect it while she flies. Say the name of who you want her to find and as long as they have one of her charms, she will find them. I'm the only one who doesn't need a charm." He spoke quickly, pushing his worries from his mind.

"How does it work? The Art?"

"In a way. Each hawk has three whistle charms bonded to their metal cuff and they work like a beacon. Her bond to me is embedded in my ink." Jarrod patted the tattoo of the three blades on his tricep. "You're lucky, since this is my last charm."

Corin smirked. "Impressive. That's a bit of information Helgath would kill to know about the Ashen Hawks."

Jarrod frowned.

"I won't tell anyone." Corin rolled his eyes. "Just commenting. Say, does this make me an honorary Hawk now?"

"No."

Corin blew out a breath. "So what's it going to take then? There some kind of exception for lovers of Hawks or anything?"

"Spouses can go through a vetting process to gain privileges to some areas."

"Marriage?"

"Aye. So you're out of luck. I'll have to keep enjoying our underground hot springs by myself." Jarrod grinned.

Corin groaned. "You won't marry me?"

The thief laughed. "Not just so you can sit in pools of hot water with me."

"I could want it for more reasons. Do you really have such little faith in my sincerity?"

"Oh, I have every faith in your sincerity, but you'd fail the vetting process, anyway."

"Fail?" Corin stroked Liala's chest. "Well, then I suppose I'll have to survive with the other benefits of having you as my husband, should you say yes. I'll forgo the obvious perks of being a Hawk and take those of just being yours."

Marriage? Is he joking?

Jarrod's stomach twisted, and he swallowed. "Enough with the teasing and learn how to send the damn hawk."

Corin frowned, looking at the hawk. "What do I do?"

"Tell her to find Andi and send her into the air like you've seen me do."

The captain squared his stance as if it helped him be more authoritative with the hawk. "Andi." He pushed his arm up, heaving her into flight.

Liala took to the air with a flurry of feathers and a quick screech.

Jarrod watched her fly. "She'll come back to you this time. But the next time you send her anywhere, she'll likely return to me, so don't send her unless it's important."

"Can't say I'll have anywhere to send her, but to you." Corin nudged Jarrod's shoulder with his, then leaned his head against him. "I need to go report soon. Remind the sheriff that I technically outrank him and get someone else to scrub my armor of all that saltwater."

Jarrod forced a smile, bitterness lingering in his gut. “Aye,” he muttered, momentarily lost in contemplation. “I’ll see you back at the room, then.”

Corin fiddled with the chain around his neck, twisting it as he nodded, resistant to pull away.

Silence loomed for a moment before he sucked in a sharp breath and stepped away. “See you soon.” He placed a light kiss on Jarrod’s clean-shaven jaw.

Even after Corin left, Jarrod remained. He stared at the southern horizon, but the reminder of his past towered in the distance to his left. Finally turning his gaze, he took in the view of his family’s home.

The castle, made of black bricks offset by bleached stone, reached towards the sky. The contrasting tones separated it from nature, only the ivy daring to climb the walls. The maroon colors of Helgath flitted in the wind above the parapets, declaring House Martox’s loyalty to the king. It looked like a fortress, and his stomach lurched.

I can’t go back there. I can’t reduce my life to those walls again.

Jarrod walked away, towards the Hedge.

Jarrod stood at the inn room’s window overlooking the Hedge, morning sun casting long shadows. He stuffed his hands into the pockets of his breeches, damning his lingering broody mood despite peaceful sleep with Corin beside him.

The soldier crept up from behind, his bare feet making the inn floor squeak as his warm arms encircled Jarrod. Corin's chest touched Jarrod's bare back, and he placed a soft kiss on the thief's shoulder, his fingers tracing over the lines of his wolf tattoo as he'd done the night before.

Will miss that, too.

When he joined the Hawks, Jarrod had memorialized the new life by inking a wolf's face on his back to symbolize his kindred animal. Half its face was covered in fur, the other made of steel plating. The art took up most of his upper back, ending at the middle of his ribs.

"Is it selfish of me to be happy we haven't got you out of the city yet?" Corin whispered in his ear, kissing his lobe.

Jarrod laughed and nodded, pushing away his guilt for being happy. "Aye, it is. But I will take whatever time with you I can get." He turned around, kissing Corin. "Are you sure they're still looking for us, or are you making it up so I have to stay here?"

"While that's a tempting idea." Corin pulled his hips closer. "I'm telling the truth." He hadn't dressed yet, still naked as he pressed against Jarrod, sending a rumble through his body. "Are you tiring of me already?"

Jarrod grinned. "Never."

Corin returned the thief's kiss with a soft hum, running his fingertips up Jarrod's neck and over his hair. The kiss drew to a slow conclusion, and he pulled away without opening his eyes. Leaning his forehead against Jarrod's, he heaved a sigh.

"What is it?" Jarrod whispered, nerves fluttering through his insides.

"It's just..." Corin remained close, refusing to pull away. "Everything. There are no pleasant options."

"What are you talking about?" Jarrod lifted Corin's chin.

His eyes, usually bright with humor, looked dark and shone with an unfamiliar emotion. Hesitating, he pursed his lips. "The rebellion. This country..." He cradled Jarrod's hand in his. "Us."

Jarrod sighed, wondering if they'd ever leave this conversation behind. He lowered his voice. "Would you be with me if I wasn't a Martox?"

"What?" Corin's brow furrowed. "How could you ask that? Of course I would." He squeezed his hand. "I've never cared for someone the way I do for you. And I'm pretty sure that's half the problem."

Jarrod's shoulders relaxed, but he worked his jaw. "What do you mean by that?"

Corin sighed and dropped his hand but didn't pull away. "I'm so shitty at saying these things right... I mean I want you to be happy." He touched his jaw. "And I'm trying to understand my willingness to put your happiness above the survival of the rebellion and everything I've fought for in the last year. I'm trying to say that if you don't want to be the proxiet, I'll support your decision."

Jarrod closed his eyes, breathing deeper than he had in days, and pulled Corin into an embrace. He buried his face into his neck. "Thank you."

Corin's lips formed a kiss on his neck, near his ear. "You know you can talk to me, right? I'm always going to listen and I know you keep a lot bottled up."

Pulling away slowly, Jarrod smirked. "It would be easier to talk to you if you put some pants on." His smile faded. "I've never talked about my old life and why I don't want to return. No one's ever known, so it hasn't been an option."

Corin smiled. "Well, I suppose I'll sacrifice and put some pants on if it'll help you open up about it." He stepped away, not making any effort to hide himself as he crossed the room to where his breeches draped across a chair.

Jarrod watched him, walking towards the bed to sit at the foot of it. "At least if you're wearing something, I'll have a harder time remembering all the things I'd *rather* be doing."

"You always say the most tempting things." Corin grinned, tugging the pants up and buttoning them. "To save future time, I'll forgo the shirt." He knelt on the floor in front of Jarrod and placed a hand on his knee. "But first, tell me. I know you've been keeping a lot of secrets up in that head of yours. But you don't need to with me."

Jarrod sucked in a breath and shook his head. "I don't even know where to start. But one of my earliest memories—I was maybe six—was this serving girl. She spilled a bit of something on my shirt at a banquet and my mother struck her across the face. I think that was the first time I realized I hated what our family stood for. My pride dwindled into shame, but I kept trying. My father always told me that my mother was like that because she held a lot of pain. I don't know what from, but she spread it to others constantly. She never wanted children, either, and made it quite clear that while she loved me as much as required, my bloodline was more important.

"When I was eleven, soon after we bought Titian, actually, they announced my betrothal. I think the horse was a way to placate me into accepting the idea. Her name was Evie, and I hated the idea even though she was my friend. Didn't understand why, at the time, but whenever I told my mother I didn't want to marry her, she told me it didn't matter."

Touching Corin's face with his index finger, Jarrod trailed an invisible line down to his chin. "So I jousted. I think a part of me hoped the sport would kill me. After I landed on my back in Degura and saw your face, I realized why I didn't want to marry Evie, or any girl. I told my mother that night, and she hit me. Not only for coming in second place, but for threatening the family line she worked so hard to sustain. Then she locked me in my room for a month, forbidding any visitors outside herself."

Corin's grip tightened on Jarrod's knee, and he turned to kiss his wrist. "And you ran away instead of being forced to be someone you aren't?"

Jarrod nodded. "I couldn't adapt to the cruelty, and even though I knew who I was, I wanted to change. It's why I started a relationship with Rae after joining the Hawks. A part of me wanted to be who everyone wanted. She was surprisingly understanding when I finally told her the truth."

Corin bit his lower lip and took Jarrod's hand from his face. "I can understand that. Kind of explains why you and my brother get along so well. You both saw evil and turned your backs on it. But that only ends it for you. What if you could fight it and change that reality for a lot more people?"

Jarrod swallowed, resisting his inclination to withdraw. "Fighting it would do no good."

"Why? Don't you want things to change?"

"What I want doesn't matter." Jarrod cringed internally at reaffirming the words his mother constantly said to him. "I'm a thief and that's on my best days. Hardly one to criticize a corrupted monarchy."

"You're wrong, though." Corin scooted closer and took both his hands. "What you want matters. Hells, it's all that matters to me. I want to know what *you* want. And don't we all have the right to fight for a better way?"

Jarrod smiled at Corin's idealism. "What I want is to discharge you from the military and keep you in Mirage with me."

Corin smirked. "I'd make a rotten thief, even if it came with hot springs. And we both know there's only one way to be discharged from the Helgathian military. If I took my brother's route, we'd all be running for the rest of our lives."

"Dannet families can grant discharges," Jarrod muttered.

"They can do a lot more than that. Like make a difference. You'd have to go back."

Weight settled back onto Jarrod's shoulders. "I don't want to return to that life. And what you're asking is complicated. I'd have to lay the name of my house down as a challenge for the throne. Do you know how long it's been since that's been done?"

"One hundred and eighty-six years ago, but it failed."

Jarrod quirked an eyebrow. "Impressive... And if I made such a challenge, the country would fall into chaos. The reigning house would have to either step aside and concede, or force the remaining three houses to choose sides. The other three are heavily invested in King Iedrus and if I pushed the matter harder, a civil war would erupt. Martox may be the richest house next to the monarchy, but to take on the other four..."

"Civil war will come one way or another. The country is already on the precipice of chaos. This has been a long time coming." Corin stood, touching Jarrod's jaw. "You haven't seen what I have on the front lines, amidst the battalions and soldiers. Recruitment for our cause has been easy. Everyone is eager to rebel against a tyrant king who allows his people to starve and suffer." He leaned over and kissed Jarrod on the forehead. "Just think about it?"

Jarrod swallowed the bile rising in his throat. "If I promise to think about it, will you go back to being supportive of how things are?"

"I didn't mean for you to question that support. None of that has changed. I just wanted you to know what was at stake. But I support you, Jarrod, no matter what. I love you."

Jarrod's insides warmed, and he smiled. "And I, you. I appreciate what's at stake, but—" Someone rapped at their door and he sighed. "If that's Damien again..." He rose from the bed.

Corin turned. "I'll take my pants off and answer the door. That will make him go away."

Jarrod laughed, reaching the door and unlatching the lock. He jerked the door open only an inch and peered through. When his eyes met Keryn's, Andi's first mate, his back straightened, and he cleared his throat. "One minute." He shut the door.

Corin lounged against the wall, his pants unbuttoned as if ready to strip at a moment's notice. He offered Jarrod a quizzical eyebrow which almost made Jarrod forgo the promise of only a minute.

"Keep the pants on, Captain." Jarrod forced himself to keep his gaze on Corin's eyes. "I'm afraid the time has come." Dread mixed with excitement in his gut, thrilled at the possibility of continuing their pursuit of Rae, but hating the thought of leaving Corin.

Corin's face turned serious, and he frowned. He buttoned the pants while crossing the room to Jarrod. Before he could say more, Corin pulled him close and claimed his mouth with a hard kiss. He pulled away regretfully. "Don't you dare forget how much I love you," he whispered, touching the scar on Jarrod's chin.

Jarrod clenched his jaw and shook his head. "Never. I'll prove it next time I see you."

Corin smiled and leaned in to kiss him again when a knock came at the door and he grumbled. "Impatient, aren't they?"

Jarrod chuckled. "You're one to talk." Grabbing his tunic on the way to the door, he swung it open before pulling it on and buttoning it up. "Keryn. It's good to see you again."

Keryn didn't wait for an invitation before she strode into the room, a long cloak swishing around her ankles. She wasn't a large woman by any definition, but something in the way she carried her body made it clear no one would want to mess with her. Her ebony skin complimented the rich tone of her purple cloak. Braided in tight cornrows on top of her head, her hair held streaks of grey among the black locks, new since the last time they'd met. Before Keryn became first-mate of the Herald.

Her hard eyes moved from Jarrod to Corin, where they narrowed.

Corin didn't seem to be in any hurry to pull on his shirt, recovered from beneath the bed, unfazed by the incredulous look on her face.

"Well, this explains a lot." Keryn's voice sounded gruff from shouting above the roar of the sea.

Damien appeared in the hallway behind her, his pack over his shoulder.

Neco's big head pushed past him to look inside Jarrod's room, where he'd been strictly forbidden after attempting to claim half their bed the night before.

"You ready?" Damien peered over her shoulder.

Pulling his vest on, but leaving it loose at the front, Jarrod nodded solemnly. He latched his dagger to his belt, a smaller one already in his boot. He left his cloak in his pack, wishing for the cool air to chill his skin.

"I'm looking forward to how you will explain this hunk a' fur and fangs coming on board to the captain." Keryn jutted a thumb towards Neco. "Not to mention a Lanoret... again." She eyed Corin, with a glance over her shoulder at Damien. "Or is it two Lanorets?"

"I'll talk to her. But no, just one Lanoret. This one can't come with us." Slinging his pack over his shoulder, Jarrod looked at Corin. "Stay outta trouble." He wanted to repeat all the things he'd already said, but he held them back.

Corin gave him the boyish smile that Jarrod adored. "You know me."

Lifting a hand, Jarrod touched the scar on his own chin and nodded, exiting the room before he dared to change his mind. Rae needed him and he had to do whatever he could to help her.

Neco thundered down the stairs behind Jarrod, eager to leave the confines of the inn.

Damien brought up the rear after a short while, walking with Keryn.

"Berthed as The Harpy." Keryn watched Jarrod. "Best to go down to the docks separately, but I suppose the mutt should go with me since I clearly ain't a man. The westernmost docks, look for the blue sails. We're Isalican today."

Jarrod nodded, fearing if he spoke, his voice would give away his distraction.

Damien knelt next to Neco, stroking his ruff, likely giving the wolf silent instruction before he stood.

Neco sauntered closer to Keryn, not looking happy about the arrangement.

She eyed him, but extended a hand for him to sniff while she looked at Jarrod, studying him before she jerked her head towards the front door of the inn. "Ladies first."

"I'll go." Jarrod didn't wait for anyone to concur before he left the building, sunlight hitting his face. As he walked away, his boots felt heavy. Pausing, he looked back at the window to the room he'd shared with Corin. Seeing nothing but darkness, he jogged down the street, rounding the corner towards the docks.

Keryn's directions proved necessary, otherwise Jarrod wouldn't have recognized the Herald. The crew had gone to impressive lengths to disguise the wanted privateering vessel, to the detail of adding new filigrees to the banisters. They had modified the alcan figurehead to have wings protruding from her back with a wicked-looking beak.

Surely Lygen's work.

Jarrod didn't recognize the man, dressed decadently with a tricorn hat, who stood at the helm playing the part of the captain. The thief wasn't allowed to remain on deck long, ushered below by one of the crew, and left to wait for the others sitting on a barrel in the crew quarters.

Damien arrived next, with Keryn and Neco not long behind.

Neco's ears pinned back against his head, skittish with all the unfamiliar smells around him and the sway of the docked ship. He padded to Jarrod, who gave him a soothing stroke before the wolf checked on Damien.

"This way." Keryn motioned with her head towards the bow of the ship.

Lygen, the ship's Artisan, rounded the corner in front of them. His gaze flitted down to Neco and he pursed his lips. "I see the beast is joining us this time. Hope he's housebroken."

Jarrod smirked, but couldn't bring himself to make the witty remark hovering at his lips.

Keryn nodded at Lygen. "I will get this rig underway. The pre-departure search shouldn't take long." She tugged a folded white square of cloth from her pocket and shoved it into Jarrod's hand. "Plenty a' time for you to explain to the captain."

She spun on her heels while Jarrod looked down at the handkerchief. Furrowing his brow, he looked at Lygen, who seemed amused. "Let me guess, the hiding quarters are spacious with a delightful view."

Lygen gave an abrupt laugh. "Hate to disappoint." He gestured to the wall directly behind him. It looked like an ordinary bulkhead, the space behind it seemingly part of the sleeping quarters. But with a gesture of Lygen's hand, the wood rippled and splintered apart like it was being broken from the inside.

Neco's hackles rose, but he kept quiet.

Inside, wedged into the back corner with one booted foot up on a narrow bench secured to the curved hull of the ship, Captain Andirindia Trace lounged with a book in her hands. Her dark brown hair, done tightly in her customary braid, trailed over her shoulder.

Jarrod entered first at Lygen's beckon. "Andi." He dipped his chin.

Engrossed in whatever she was reading, it took her a moment to glance up. Jarrod didn't keep her attention before her eyes roved down to Neco, leaning against Damien's leg. She muttered a soft curse.

"Keryn's getting us underway, Captain." Lygen urged Damien and Neco forward.

Damien held the wolf's ruff, as if constantly comforting him, and they climbed into the compact space no larger than a closet.

Jarrod sat on the floor and Neco followed suit, putting his head in the thief's lap.

Andi's eyes never left the wolf.

"He doesn't bite." Jarrod scratched behind Neco's ears.

"It ain't his bite that offends me." Andi leaned forward to snatch the handkerchief before Jarrod could wonder longer what it was for.

Damien settled onto the bench near Andi's foot and the bulkhead behind them crackled as Lygen stitched it back together.

"Damien." Andi said his name as if it constituted a greeting, eyeing him. "I thought I'd made myself clear on the terms of your invitation back on my ship."

Darkness engulfed them as the last board locked into place, but a dim glow radiated from an artificial light source at Andi's neck.

The shell-shaped charm resting against her pale skin illuminated just enough for her to read by.

Damien leaned against the hull. "I wish circumstances were different."

Andi growled. "Not a day off my ship and you utterly failed at every request I made of you. Shouldn't have expected more of a Lanoret, I suppose."

Damien sighed, crossing his arms.

Andi mumbled something in a language Jarrod didn't know. Based on the tone, it sounded like a curse. Her head rocked forward as she sneezed, lifting the handkerchief to her nose. It temporarily blocked the light while she groaned.

Neco whined, and Jarrod smoothed the fur on his neck. "It's all right, boy, she's all bark too."

Andi glared at him as she rubbed her glassy eyes with the clean edge of the handkerchief. "Let's not flower this up any, it isn't *all right*. You got just as much explaining to do as Mister Lanoret over here. Thought you were smarter than to get yourself wrapped up in Helgath business." She shook a hand at him. Her cobalt eyes blazed, the odd curve of her pupil more prominent in the dim light.

Jarrod tilted his head. "Really, Andi? It's Rae we're talking about here. What would you have me do?"

"Rae is the only reason I even considered answering that damn hawk of yours. If I didn't know any better, I'd say you were still hung up on that girl."

"Oh trust me, he's not." Damien rubbed his forehead. It earned him another ugly scowl from Andi.

"He's right. Otherwise, do you think Damien and I would get along? I've met someone else."

Andi might have answered if another sneeze hadn't interrupted her. Her glower turned towards Neco, another explosion of air rocking her body. "*And* you had to bring a damned dog on board. While we're all supposed to keep quiet, I'll have to hold my breath."

Neco opened his maw and barked a string of wolf-chatter at Damien before resting his head back down.

"I think you've offended him." Jarrod looked at Damien for confirmation.

Damien smirked and nodded. "He is insulted. Usually, he's so popular."

The wolf whined again and Jarrod smiled, grateful for the distraction.

"His usual crowd probably doesn't have such an uncomfortable reaction." Andi waved her white handkerchief as if she meant to surrender.

"If you can overlook my family name, I might be able to help with your discomfort."

Andi gave Damien a sideways glance. She sneezed again, then started nodding her head.

Damien scooted down the bench to hover his hand above her knee. Andi rubbed her nose while the light in the space shifted to a more vibrant blue. It flickered from his fingers, then trailed up Andi's body towards her face. She didn't react, keeping herself still as the power faded into her skin, taking the glow with it. She blew her nose a final time, but then her sniffles diminished.

"Thank you." She wiped away the remnants of unbidden tears from the corner of her eyes. "I'm assuming Rae told you the truth about her allegiances, since Jarrod's with you." She tucked the handkerchief away.

"In a way. Though my first meeting with Jarrod was a bit... strained."

Andi gave a knowing smile and looked at the thief. "You said you met someone. Didn't think you'd ever get over Rae. Where's this mystery girl?"

Damien snorted but held his tongue.

Jarrod rolled his eyes as he scratched the back of his neck and cleared his throat. "Well..." He pointed at Damien. "It's actually his brother."

Andi's eyebrows rose before her gaze hardened. "You mean to say, you've got yourself involved with a *Lanoret* as well?"

Jarrod maintained a sheepish smile and shrugged. "It would seem so."

Andi's mouth opened, but the light on her neck pulsed. It drew her attention down, then she lifted a single finger to her lips.

Damien nearly choked, trying to contain the snorts of laughter wanting to escape his lips, and Jarrod punched him in the side of the thigh. Opening his mouth to form a silent 'ow', Damien rubbed his leg, and they settled into a tense silence.

The light continued to pulse, adding a strange series of shadows in the small closet. When Jarrod turned back towards Andi, she glared at him. The air thickened between them and Damien looked more than pleased to have the attention off him.

Andi finally ceased her angry stare and picked her book up.

Eventually, the light resumed its normal glow and Andi slowly closed her book, tucking it under her arm. She looked blankly towards the wall they'd climbed through. "So which port in Eralas?"

"Ny'Thalus."

Corin had found the documentation granting the auer ship passage from Lazuli, which marked the western port as their destination.

When Andi frowned, Damien exchanged a look with Jarrod. "Is that bad?"

She gave an indistinct shrug. "It's the largest port on the island. Means they'll be organized enough to give us the runaround if they want to. While the auer aren't my enemies, they aren't my friends, either."

Jarrod scowled. "You could drop us near the port. We could take a dinghy to shore."

"You've never been to Ny'Thalus, have you? Ain't no shore to row to like that. We will have to play their games."

"Means more delays." Damien groaned, dropping his head towards his knees.

Jarrod closed his eyes and let his head fall back, hitting the wall with a thunk. "Fantastic."

"WAKE UP, RAEYNNA."

Opening her eyes, she stared at the dirt ceiling above her. The back of her head ached, and she rubbed it as someone helped her sit up. "Where am I?"

"Home." The figure the voice belonged to crossed into her vision. "Eralas. But you've forgotten many things, Child." Her eyes were a fathomless black, and she motioned to another person in the room.

A tall Aueric man came forward and helped Raeynna to her feet.

"This is Kynis'cairn, he'll teach you what you should know."

Raeynna met Kynis's topaz gaze and nodded, her feet unsteady beneath her. She grasped the stone bed for balance as a headache touched her temples. "What happened to me?"

How did I get here?

"You are a Mira'wyld." Kynis sounded gentle, despite his stern appearance. "And were captured by Helgath who sought to abuse your power, but your people have brought you home to teach you how to properly use it."

"Mira'wyld..."

Why haven't I heard that term before?

Kynis reached into a pocket on the side of his tunic and withdrew a slim tome. He placed the hardbound leather into her hands. "This is a loq'nali phén, a journal of sorts that belongs to our family. I'm a Moro'wyld and I'll teach you. As will this." He closed her hand on the binding. On the front was scrawled text in a language she didn't understand.

"I can't read this." Raeynna ran her hand over the indecipherable letters.

"I'll teach you, cousin. If you come, we can get back under the sky. I'll take you home to rest and recover." Kynis motioned to the door.

Sleeping off this headache sounds good.

Raeynna nodded. "Is it far?"

"No." He placed a hand on her shoulder, steering her towards the exit. "And it is peaceful there, far more than you've known before."

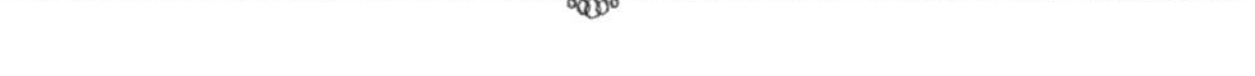

The days blended together in a blur of leisurely activity.

Kynis hardly left Raeynna's side, having her join him for walks through the forest and teaching her their language. Something about the letters and words seemed familiar, but whenever she tried to remember anything specific, her mind remained profoundly blank.

They enjoyed picnic lunches in the warm sun and, after only a few days, Kynis refused to speak anything but Aueric to her, prompting her to learn faster. The history lessons began soon after, a spiderweb of lineages that traced the blood of the Mira'wylds, unique to their family line.

Raeynna learned more about what she was. An auer blessed with an innate connection to the elements.

Despite her rapid progress in the language, her training had yet to begin. Kynis implied her human blood could hinder her and wanted to be sure she had the fundamentals in place prior to removing her earring. It kept her power dormant until she gained the knowledge necessary to control it.

They provided her attire, a mix of pale-colored dresses and flat canvas shoes. In the warm weather, she found the dresses comfortable, the fabric flowing airily around her knees. Thin straps kept them in place while letting the sun kiss her olive skin.

"If it's too much, I can replace it, but I think you're ready."

Kynis lifted the gear-shaped key towards her.

They stood together in the garden behind the little structure she called home. The leaves rustled in the wind as if whispering reassurances for the twisting nerves in her stomach.

She nodded, and Kynis stepped closer.

A click echoed in her eardrum as he released the lock, and it fell into his palm. He transferred it to her hand, the tiny key still turned inside the mechanism. An odd sensation passed through her limbs like creeping cold.

"Where would you like to start?"

Raeynna rolled her lips and thought about it. "Can I make it rain?"

Kynis chuckled. "On such a pleasant day?"

She laughed. "Well, if it wasn't such a pleasant day, it'd be less of a feat."

"You have a valid point. But it will be far more challenging to form the clouds with so little moisture in the air. It might not be the best place to start."

Raeynna frowned but nodded. "All right, well... maybe I can make something grow?"

"A far more fitting beginning."

She smiled with his approval, looking at her home.

The mile-wide compound hardly felt like what its name suggested. Trees grew in a solid wall at its border, their trunks butting up together. One gate provided an entrance, but Raeynna saw no reason to worry about what was beyond it.

Everything she needed was within the walls.

Smaller trees grew together, shaped by the Art, to form the collection of houses at the center of the compound. One for herself, one for Kynis, and a third she'd been told not to enter. The resident, a man deep in study, preferred to be undisturbed. She'd acquiesced to the rule, but her curiosity grew each day, as she saw no one enter or leave the house.

The forest flourished within the compound and a family of deer even called it home. The gardens stretched behind the houses towards a gurgling stream that cut the compound in half.

Kynis approached a rose bush in one of her side gardens. He wove his fingers in front of him and the bloom responded to each gesture, reaching towards him. Its petals fell away to expose the swollen rose hip.

He plucked it, splitting the casing with his nail, then took a single seed and held it out to Raeynna. "Let's see what you can create from this." He dropped the seed into her waiting palm.

A challenge.

Walking a few yards away, she settled into the grass. Her power swirled in her veins and she did her best to recall what he'd taught her about how to manipulate it.

Trying to join theory with practice, she focused on the seed.

It responded to the energy she fed it, sprouting, and her breath caught. A vine uncurled from within the seed, reaching towards the sky.

She imagined what she wanted it to do and leaves protruded from its stem along with razor thorns. Roots tangled around her fingers, reaching to the grass. Unhindered by the typical needs of a plant, the stem thickened, splitting into more and climbing taller as it formed a new bud on its tallest tip.

Raeynna stared at it, tilting her head and pushing more into the growing bud. It colored to a rosy pink before petals unfurled into a full blossom.

Her gaze lifted to Kynis.

"Are you happy with it?"

Raeynna shook her head and placed the plant on the ground next to her house. With continued focus, the first blossoms shriveled, cascading more seeds into the dirt. Roots burrowed and spread over a barren mound of soil. She stepped back as vines climbed over the outer wall of her domicile, thorns and buds abundant.

Surging more energy into it, the plants overtook the wall, and each bud blossomed into variations of color.

Taking a deep breath, she stopped to admire what she'd accomplished, lethargy passing through her mind. From what she understood, using the Art to grow a rosebush was far from an impressive feat for an auer, but she couldn't help feeling proud.

The smile on Kynis's face only increased the feeling. "Beautiful." He stood beside her to admire her work. "A wonderful start. Shall we move on to water?" He took a step back and gestured with an open hand towards the stream.

As she nodded, her gaze wandered to the forbidden third house. Someone stood at the window watching them. She straightened her spine under the unknown scrutiny, unable to see the man's face. As if responding to her recognition, his shadow backed away from the window and a mossy curtain fell into place.

Kynis pushed her through a series of intense exercises that filled the rest of the day. Progressing through all the elements that she could control as a Mira'wyld. The hardest among them was fire, which raged with its own desire to destroy, but she felt satisfied when she successfully quenched the flame.

At the end of the day, Kynis bid her goodnight, and she started towards her front door.

Crossing the short porch, she touched the door handle, a headache at the front of her skull. She furrowed her brow, twisting the knob as a crash echoed from the forbidden home. Her heart jumped, but she hesitated.

Kynis had specifically told her not to bother the man living there.

But he could be hurt and need help.

Ignoring Kynis's demand, she jogged over and knocked.

Listening for a reply, she got none other than the breathy sound of the man cursing in Aueric.

Cringing, she twisted the handle and slowly opened the lockless front door. "Hello? Are you all right?"

The cursing stopped and the light in the room beyond, likely the kitchen if the layout was the same as hers, shifted. The man emerged in the doorway, holding his hands in front of him with one wrapped in a crimson-stained linen towel.

Raeynna cringed again, looking at the ground. "I'm sorry. I know I'm not to disturb you. I heard a crash, and I didn't know—" The words, still new to her in the Aueric tongue, sounded clumsy.

"No need to apologize." The man's voice had a deep, sweet tone.

She looked up to see him smiling at her. His unbuttoned shirt hung open to his abdomen, displaying his rich, dark-umber skin. Light grey hair, cut to frame his handsome face, brought attention to the stunning amethyst shade of his eyes.

Raeynna looked away again, warmth rising to her cheeks. Something about his voice made her doubt he was in any distress, but he hadn't given her an answer.

"Are you all right?" Finding the nerve, she returned her gaze to him. She couldn't help feeling like she was venturing somewhere she shouldn't.

Guilt for disobeying Kynis, perhaps.

"I broke a dish and cut myself." He looked sheepishly at his hands. The red stain seemed too prominent for a minor cut and he lifted the cloth to glance at it. He winced. "Though it's a little deeper than I first suspected."

Raeynna kept her feet on his doorstep. "Do you need help?" Half of her wanted to back up and go home to sleep, while the other felt compelled to enter.

"Oh, I'm sorry." He blinked at her as if just realizing she stood outside. "Please, come in. I'd be a fool not to accept help."

She still hesitated, glancing at her cousin's house. "Kynis told me not to bother you."

"Is that why you haven't come to introduce yourself?" The man smiled, and she nodded. "I'd wondered if I'd accidentally offended you. Kynis can be rather stuffy about these things. I can stand to be interrupted from time to time and I doubt you'd be a bother."

Taking a breath, Raeynna stepped inside. "I suppose Kynis can be *stuffy*." She repeated the new word she assumed from context. "I thought you... liked to be alone." Finding her confidence, she strode over to him and reached for his injured hand. "May I?"

Though I don't know a thing about healing.

He didn't question her request, offering his hand.

Taking it, Raeynna lifted the cloth to inspect the deep wound. "I thought auer were supposed to be graceful?" she teased, which earned her a warm smile. The expression suited him, and Raeynna returned it.

"A common misconception. I'm actually quite clumsy, to my embarrassment. I'm Maithalik."

Re-wrapping his hand, she smirked. "I'm Raeynna. It's a pleasure to meet you. And to *my* embarrassment, I can't heal, but I could find someone?"

"No need, it's already feeling better. Perhaps the attention of an enchanting young neighbor."

Her cheeks burned, and she let go of his hand. "I doubt attention alone will fix it. I could probably..." Her voice trailed off as she tried to recall the word for 'stitch'. "I'm sorry, my Aueric is still... imperfect. I could sew it?"

He smiled and eloquently spoke the correct word for her. "Aueric is a tough language, we have far too many words for the same thing in the common tongue."

Raeynna nodded with a sheepish smile. "Would you like me to *stitch* it?"

"I'd be grateful." He gestured for her to enter the kitchen. "I have the supplies."

The sun disappeared soon after they took a seat at his kitchen table made of intricately woven roots. After she'd finished tending to his hand and re-wrapping it, he poured them each a glass of wine and they talked long into the night. He hardly asked much of her life, for which she was grateful since she still couldn't recall anything prior to awakening on the stone bed.

Maithalik made her laugh more than she had since waking.

The need to rest came with heavy eyelids, but she regretted the need to leave. She stifled a yawn as she bid farewell.

"Please, I hope you'll visit again." Maithalik stood in his doorway as Raeynna turned to say a final goodnight. "I enjoyed the company."

"I did too." She opened her door, looking at him. "Don't be a stranger. Kynis runs a tight schedule, but you're welcome anytime."

"I appreciate the invitation." He leaned against the doorframe in a way she'd never seen Kynis do. "Though my days are usually filled with study... I hope we can make a habit of these evening visits. It disrupts the tedium."

"Then I'll see you tomorrow night."

The following week kept Raeynna busier than she expected. Kynis trained her from dawn until dusk, pushing her limits and abilities as far as he could. She'd thought the auer moved slowly in all things, but her training seemed to be an exception.

When Kynis found out she'd met Maithalik, due to her incessant yawning one morning after staying up too late talking, he didn't mind. Much to her surprise, he encouraged their friendship as long as it didn't interfere with her training or Maithalik's studies.

She visited Maithalik, who insisted she call him Maith, every evening. They shared food and wine well into the night. The interaction granted her reprieve from the intensity of her days, while also giving her a chance to practice her Aueric. He helped her, showing infinite patience.

That evening, Raeynna sighed as she rose from Maith's chair by his hearth. The night grew late and after the particularly grueling day she'd had, nothing sounded better than sleep. Placing her empty wineglass on the table, she smiled at him. "I should turn in. Kynis didn't go easy on me today and if I don't go now, I'll fall asleep right here."

Maith frowned, placing his glass beside hers and stood. "He pushes you too hard." He touched her upper arm, sending a shiver down her spine.

Raeynna looked at his hand and smiled, returning her gaze to his charming face. "He just wants me to be stronger." She turned, walking to his front door.

He followed and sped his steps so he reached it first to open it for her. "Raeynna," he whispered her name as she stepped past him, but his hand caught hers.

The touch made her stop, looking back at him.

"I have a confession, that I hope won't be too forward."

Raeynna tilted her head.

"I greatly enjoy the time we spend together and my affection for you has surpassed friendship. I hope you may be amenable to allowing me to pursue these emotions, and ask if you might feel the same?"

Staring at him, her breath caught. "I..."

How do I feel?

Raeynna nodded, but a strange sensation twisted in her gut. She couldn't remember ever feeling this way with another.

Maith smiled, his hand tightening on hers as he stepped closer. His other hand lifted her chin in a tender motion. Time drew out as he waited, but she remained frozen in place.

When his lips met hers, they were cool and gentle, like an autumn breeze.

Her body responded without her fully understanding, returning the kiss for a breath before she pressed her hands to his chest. Head spinning, she met his rich purple eyes as he released her.

"Good night, Raeynna." Maith stepped back into his doorway, his hand on her jaw the last to part from her. "I'll see you tomorrow?"

Raeynna nodded, struggling to comprehend her feelings as she stepped from his porch and walked to her own.

What do I want?

Chapter 26

IT TOOK AN ENTIRE DAY to get clearance from the auer to dock.

The air around Eralas, even at sea, weighed suffocatingly thick. It wasn't the weather, but the plethora of voices Damien's ká had to sort through. His heightened emotions made maintaining his barrier against the complex energies more difficult. Everything in the auer lands held a tight bond with the Art and thus, their ká.

While he kept the headaches at bay most of the time, they bubbled up at inopportune moments. Too many of the crew saw him talking to himself and began taking a wide berth. It did little for his mood and reputation on the ship.

Meditation became a constant need to aid in cleansing his ká.

We're so close.

He'd concluded his morning routine and slung his pack over his shoulder in anticipation of departing the ship when Rae's energy set off the alarm he'd prepared in his mind. It coalesced into a headache, opening the gates for a tidal wave of extra energy from the island.

Cursing, he grabbed his forehead and closed his eyes as they flashed white.

Neco's ears pricked, and he whined.

Damien ignored him as he traced the thread of her power to her location. It faded as he grew closer, restricting him from following the tether too far. He could only decipher one piece of information.

We're on the wrong side of the island.

"What's wrong?" Jarrod stood behind him, prompting Damien's eyes to open.

"They finally removed whatever was blocking Rae from my senses. But she's not here in Ny'Thalus. She's farther south."

"You've got to be kidding me." Andi groaned, the click of her boots signaling her arrival as much as her aggravated tone.

Jarrod sighed and ran his hands over his hair.

Andi whipped her hair back over her shoulder and turned to Keryn. "Turn us around."

The first mate frowned. "Not that easy anymore, Captain. I'll get us back to sea as quickly as I can."

The auer had a talent for dragging out the most mundane tasks, likely due to their ambivalence regarding short human life spans. Each time Damien asked for the progress, Keryn would roll her eyes and say, "Any time now."

Then another half day would pass.

When they finally arrived in Maelei, it felt like months since they'd reached Eralas, but it'd only been days. Damien's short temper grew shorter, encouraging even Neco and Jarrod to avoid him.

Jarrod's incessant pouting had worsened, and it grated Damien's nerves. He'd done his best to maintain his cool around the thief instead of showing his annoyance.

While Keryn negotiated with the dock masters of Maelei, Damien glared at the pacing thief. He wanted to tear Jarrod's head off with his bare hands. The waves the thief's ká radiated when he looked at the horizon drove him mad. Each time Jarrod saw no sign of a hawk, he'd stomp away and start the process over again.

"Gods, will you stop that?" Damien threw his hands up, knuckles sore from gripping the banister.

"What?" Jarrod narrowed his eyes.

"I get that you're worried about him, but Corin isn't important right now. Don't make me punch some sense into that head of yours."

Jarrod scowled, stalking closer to Damien. "Really? I'll put you on your back, Lanoret, but I'll let you have the first swing to make it fair."

The lingering pain in the front of Damien's head spurred his anger. He shoved Jarrod's chest. "I'm not above making you eat those words, Martox or not."

Jarrod cast a wary glance around before spinning to glare at Damien. "You've got a dangerous habit of having a loose tongue, asshole." He grabbed Damien by the collar and yanked him closer. "You best check yourself."

A little voice in Damien's head screamed that he was being foolish, but his rage blinded him. Jarrod's pull made slipping his foot behind the thief's ankle easy. He tugged it to the side as his hands came up to break Jarrod's grip on his shirt so he staggered back.

"Better a loose tongue than a lack of honor."

Jarrod's jaw flexed. "I know you're upset. I am too, so I'm gonna give you one more chance to walk away." His hands balled into fists at his sides, and he held his ground.

Damien stomped forward, ignoring the warning. Fueled by the blood pumping in his veins, he didn't see Jarrod's fist before the sudden impact on his jaw rattled his skull. It threw his head to the side, stars filling his vision. The coppery taste of blood touched his tongue.

The pain brought a fresh wave of red in his vision as he settled on the best course to express his anguish.

Rotating his jaw, Damien turned back to Jarrod, wanting nothing more than to see his face bloody. He lunged, grappling Jarrod's waist and tackling him to the ground. They slammed into the deck with a loud thud and huff of breath.

Neco barked wildly but Damien ignored him.

Jarrod got the Rahn'ka in a headlock as they both rolled to the side. "As much..." Jarrod grunted with the effort. "...As I'd like to be rolling around with a Lanoret right now..." He coughed. "This is *not* what I had in mind."

Damien threw an elbow into Jarrod's abdomen, which loosened his hold enough to let him wiggle free. He pinned the thief on the deck with his knees and got a solid punch in on Jarrod's jaw before the thief caught his wrist and twisted. The pressure forced Damien to turn, and Jarrod followed the motion to flip Damien onto his back again.

Forcing Damien's arm straight, Jarrod pinned him with his legs constricting his chest and throat.

Damien choked and bucked, unable to breathe, but Jarrod's hold was unrelenting. Neco danced like a blur in the edge of his vision as his body weakened and, with it, his logic returned.

Where he'd attempted to wrap his bicep around Jarrod's thigh, he let go and started tapping on the thief's leg.

Jarrod relaxed and let go.

Sucking in a grateful breath, Damien slumped against the deck and looked up at the sky, finding the captain hovering over him.

Andi held a bucket at her side, her other hand on her hip. "You boys done?"

Jarrod sat up and touched his split lip. "Aye." He grunted, kicking Damien. "Right?"

"Right." Damien propped himself up on an elbow.

"Good." Andi gave a curt nod and lifted the bucket. With a jerk, she threw its cold contents all over the pair of them.

Damien sputtered as the water hit him in the face. He jolted into a sitting position and wiped his eyes, the saltwater burning the abrasions on his chin. "Gods, I said we were done."

"Didn't want to waste a good bucket." She shrugged and sauntered off.

Jarrod pushed the water back out of his hair, looking at Damien. Blood tainted the streams flowing from his face. His stern expression softened, and he started chuckling.

A laugh bubbled from Damien even though his mouth hurt. He touched his jaw where Jarrod's first punch had caught him. It'd already started to swell, but that made it funnier.

"You split my lip." Jarrod laughed, pressing the back of his hand to where it still bled

"And you almost broke my jaw." Damien pushed himself up to his feet. He held out a hand to Jarrod, his sleeves dripping.

Jarrod eyed the offer suspiciously before accepting it. "At least we know who'd win now."

"Yeah, but I put you on your ass first."

Laughing, Jarrod gave a nod. "I'll give you that, but you tapped out on your back, just like I said."

Damien shrugged. "I'm sure you'd like a different Lanoret on his back much better than me."

Jarrod huffed. "Obviously... Rae would be so proud of us."

Her name made Damien's mind buzz, a stone sinking in his stomach as the laughter faded. "She'd kick both our asses."

"Probably. At least, either way, you can tell her all about it soon."

I hope so.

He nodded and glanced at the gangplank, being brought out by the crew. Keryn must have come to some agreement, and they were finally allowed off the ship.

Neco, no longer concerned with Jarrod and Damien, stood next to Andi who scratched his ears. The wolf leapt before the plank was fully in place, causing startled yelps from the dockhands. He bolted down the docks, headed towards the trees beyond the white beaches of Maelei.

"At least we're more subtle about wanting off this ship." Damien gestured at the wolf darting across the beach.

"The locals think we just released a rabid beast onto the island." Andi looked over her shoulder at them. "That'll be fun to explain."

"I'm sure you'll do a marvelous job." Jarrod smiled as he jogged down the gangplank.

Damien paused, focusing his ká despite the rumble of anxiety. It surfaced, heating his skin and drying his clothes. Touching the collar of his shirt to straighten it, Damien locked his power beneath the barrier and an aura of hiding Yondé had taught him.

When he stepped onto the dock next to Jarrod, who still dripped, he smirked. "You planning on going into town looking like that? We're supposed to look respectable."

Jarrod looked down at himself, furrowed his brow, then looked at Damien and his shoulders drooped. "You cheated. Dry me?"

Damien rolled his eyes as if the request was ridiculous. With a gesture of his hand, he pressed enough power into Jarrod's ká to elicit the necessary reaction.

Eyeing Jarrod to make sure he looked ready to go, Damien nearly jumped when he heard someone clear their throat behind him. He spun, instinct readying his power as Jarrod's hand subtly slipped to his side where he kept his dagger.

Before them stood two female auer, who looked unimpressed and possibly bored.

"Damien Lanoret?" Her pale pink eyes stood out against her dark skin. Onyx hair, tied back in braids and loops, flowed past her exposed shoulders.

Both women wore long flowing gowns made of a pale gold material which left little to the imagination.

"It depends on who's asking." Damien locked his gaze with hers.

"That's doubtful." The second woman's shale hair was cut short to her scalp. "But all the confirmation we need. The Elder Council would like to speak with you."

Damien furrowed his brow.

More delays, though this one is more impressive than being dragged along at port.

As a Helgathian soldier, he'd learned the basics of auer government, including the structure of their primary leadership. The nine elders were a combination of elected officials and those born into particular bloodlines. They served as the final word of law for all auer, surveying from their aptly named sanctum.

"And you are Jarrod Martox, are you not?" The first woman turned towards the thief, ignoring Damien's quizzical expression.

Jarrod shot Damien a look and clenched his jaw. "Aye."

"You are also summoned. Transportation awaits. Follow, please." She turned without waiting for an answer, walking away.

The second woman waited, her lilac eyes locked on Damien.

It made him uneasy, and he rolled his shoulders, lowering his voice. "What do you think?"

Jarrod grunted. "I think we're getting closer to her and it makes them unhappy. But they can delay all they want, it won't change the outcome."

His certainty sent a ripple of relief through Damien. He nodded, following the first auer with Jarrod behind him.

At the edge of the city, a pair of elaborate horse-drawn carriages waited. The women reunited after one had followed behind, as if Jarrod and Damien might flee. They whispered to each other in rushed Aueric, and Damien strained to listen. Yondé had schooled him hard during his months of training on not only learning the power of the Rahn'ka, but also the language of their enemies.

He and Jarrod rode alone in the second carriage, which hardly bounced as they made their way towards Quel'Nian.

Damien stretched out his legs while looking at Jarrod. "They know your real name." He tried to keep his tone even so Jarrod wouldn't feel like he was prying. "How do you think that is?"

Jarrod shook his head. "I don't know. It's been nearly a decade since I've used it and Rae couldn't have told them. She doesn't even know."

"Decade's awful short to an auer. All the same, it makes me uneasy."

"You're not the only one."

Damien didn't like yet another purposeful distraction from finding Rae. He tried to convince himself that some good might come from going straight to the source of his problem, the council.

Or they'll sell me to Helgath.

The trip took two days with the carriages continuing through the night and meals at their leisurely speed. They stopped sparingly, letting Damien and Jarrod sleep on the cushioned seats.

Settling into a meditative state, Damien rocked back into awareness when the carriage lurched to a stop. He and Jarrod exchanged a glance before he opened the door and stepped out.

Several steps led to the Sanctum of Law, with two guards on either side of the entrance. The structure curved outward and, belatedly, Damien realized it was the trunk of a tree. The massive roots dug deep into the surrounding soil, the wood manipulated into grandiose exterior walls covered with tapestries of flowers. The trunk rose for fifty feet before it ended. Jagged splinters of branches supported the crystal-spired roof, draped with more greenery. The glass glittered in the dimming sunlight that penetrated the canopy above, a gaping hole between the trees where the monstrous oak-turned-sanctum had once towered.

Jarrod let out a low whistle behind Damien as they both looked up.

The auer women approached. "It's late, and the council has retired for the evening. I'll show you to your accommodations. You will meet with them in the morning."

"Oh, hell no." Damien's frustration boiled. "You just carted us along for two days without us asking any questions. I think the council can stay up a little later to explain why they're jerking us around."

Jarrod crossed his arms next to him, frowning at the auer.

The first woman pursed her lips, anger flitting in her pink eyes, but her companion placed a hand on her arm and whispered the Aueric word for patience.

"You'll find that aggression won't get you far in Eralas. But I will inquire for you, if you wish."

"Please. We'll wait here."

Once the women left, Jarrod turned to Damien. "Can you still feel her at least?"

During the ride, Damien erected a tight lock between him and the ká around him, granting him peace. Unfortunately, it had been necessary to include his awareness of Rae's ká or risk his sanity.

He closed his eyes to rediscover the tether and nodded. "She's somewhere south, the direction we came from. They rode us right past her. Whatever's blocking me from tracking her isn't the island itself. I can find Neco without a problem."

Jarrod took a deep breath. "And where is our large furry friend?"

"Still near Maelei. He's entertaining himself by hunting prey that's never seen a wolf before." The thought made him smile. He couldn't imagine the auer would be pleased with a new apex predator stalking their wildlife.

Damien stood waiting with Jarrod for what felt like far longer than necessary before the auer returned. He opened his mouth to speak, but the pink-eyed auer beat him to it.

"They have retired for the evening. We will show you to your accommodations."

He had half a mind to shove right past the smug woman and introduce himself regardless, but threw his hands up in the air instead. "I don't have your infinite auer patience. So this *human* will walk back to Maelei. I'll find her myself." He didn't say her name, but there was no way they didn't know why he was there.

He backed up, preparing to turn if the auer didn't have another word to say to stop him. But Jarrod grabbed him by the shoulder and halted his steps. He glared at the thief, who gestured with his eyes behind him.

Damien spun, suddenly grateful Jarrod had stopped him.

Spears held parallel to the ground pointed directly at his gut, held in place by a pair of male auer he hadn't seen standing there before. They wore silver armor, shaped specifically for their lean bodies, a thin mesh material at the joints. They wore no helmets, which gave Damien a clear vision of their menacing jeweled eyes.

One of the women cleared her throat. "We were merely being polite. It isn't a request. You will await your scheduled council with our elders in the morning. It's preferred you don't force us to draw blood."

Damien's chest vibrated in a low growl. He contemplated reaching into his power and showing the auer how little control they had over him. Tearing their souls in half in the blink of an eye sounded like a satisfactory release of his anger.

Jarrod squeezed his shoulder. "Not a good idea," he whispered. "It's just one more night."

With a huff, Damien conceded.

True to their word, the next morning, they were escorted to the Sanctum of Law by the same auer who'd met them at the docks.

They separated Jarrod and Damien, leading Jarrod ahead into a round room before closing the doors between them. When the doors reopened, Jarrod no longer stood there and the guards who had shoved spears at his back the day before encouraged Damien forward.

The ground grew in a swirl of roots, a transparent floor guarding the pattern. Looking down made Damien dizzy, as if he'd trip over the uneven surface. An extended hand urged him to stop at the center, and he swallowed.

The tug knocked the breath out of him. Something

invisible tore up through the floor and grasped his ká before he could build a barrier to stop it. The flickering motes above his head trembled, pulsing with new brightness. With a sharp breath, Damien isolated the origin of the theft and lopped off the section of his power, prohibiting the chamber from draining the rest of him.

His chest tightened as he realized the purpose of the room. As a Rahn'ka, he had unique control over how his energy could be spent, but if he'd been anything else, the chamber would have depleted everything he had.

When the doors in front of him opened, Damien took a weary step forward, portraying the exhaustion they probably thought he'd feel.

The Sanctum of Law glowed with morning sunlight trickling through its crystal ceiling, refracting little specks across the oaken floor. Shaped like a giant crescent moon, the chamber felt ceiling-less with the blue sky glittering through the buttresses shaped from the tree's branches. On the ground level, the floor followed a similar pattern to the one inside the previous room, a pattern of roots spiraling towards the middle. They merged into a maelstrom at the center, forming a circle of vines Jarrod stood within. Just beside it was a ring of gold inlaid in the wood, which served a purpose Damien didn't know.

Jarrod stood with his back to the Rahn'ka. He glanced over his shoulder at the sound of Damien's boots scraping across the floor.

"I miss anything?" Damien eyed the nine imposing figures seated on a curved platform.

Steps led up the sides to the nine thrones, each occupied by an elder of the council. Their appearances ranged from youthful to old enough that he could see the curve of age in one auer's posture.

Gods, some of these auer were probably born before the Sundering.

The ancient cataclysmic event was to blame for the end of the Rahn'ka, which meant someone in the room might recognize his power if they had the opportunity.

The two auer who'd escorted them from Maelei approached the platform but didn't step onto it. They clasped their hands in front of their hips, playing the part of statues.

Jarrod shook his head. "Just a lot of intense staring so far."

"Damien Lanoret." The elder at the center stood, interrupting Damien before he could get out a witty retort. "You're not welcome on our lands and will depart at once."

They brought me all the way here just to say that?

Damien fought the urge to roll his eyes at the man with long black hair, a woven crown of oak on his head. He contemplated how diplomatic he wanted to be. "Well, I think that's a little unfair." He took a step towards the stairs that led to the elders' chairs. "You owe me an explanation."

"We owe you nothing." An elder to the right of the center stood, her pine crown blending in with her silver hair. "And you are fortunate this meeting is informal, or you'd be severely punished for speaking so to the Arch Judgment."

Memories of his auer cultural lessons returned. So far he was just thankful he wasn't having to test his knowledge of Aueric. "Quite the contrary, I have been infinitely patient, all things considered. I'd be happy to leave your lands at my earliest convenience as long as Rae comes with me."

The elders paused, exchanging glances.

Jarrod quirked an eyebrow at Damien.

Damien clenched his jaw. "Please don't insult me by pretending to be ignorant of her. I know she's on this island and one of your people dealt with Helgath to take her from Lazuli. But Helgath had no right to have her."

"Are you implying that your country doesn't have the right to exact punishment on you? One of her soldiers who betrayed their oath?" An elder near the far left side rolled his shoulders. His light amethyst eyes looked amused more than anything else. "Did you not desert? Did you not know there would be punishment?"

"But Rae doesn't deserve that punishment. And I understand you may have reasons for keeping her here, but I must see her. You don't know what I... what *we* have been through to get here."

"Inconsequential." The Arch Judgment waved his hand in dismissal. Honey eyes, which might be kind to others, looked hard and cruel.

Apparently out of patience, Jarrod spoke up. "Where *is* Rae?"

The hall quieted, the jeweled and black eyes of the elders turning to Jarrod.

"Our interest in you, Lord Martox, is a coming topic. You need not involve yourself in this matter."

Hearing the formal title applied to his friend, Damien straightened.

Jarrod seemed unfazed. "Apparently I do, otherwise I'd be waiting my turn somewhere else. You've given us delays for days and now you have the nerve to jerk us around now that we're finally here. You have taken our friend against her will and we'd like her back with no more bullshit."

"Raeynna is not being held against her will." The woman to the right tilted her head, sweeping a hand in front of herself. "And it is not within the right of any human to demand access to her like a jilted lover. Raeynna is betrothed to another, and it's best for all involved to forgo any further attempts at interrupting her training."

Jarrod shot Damien a look, falling silent.

Betrothed?

Damien felt as if someone had clubbed him in the head with a rock. His throat tightened. "What?"

"We'll allow you to remain in Eralas until your ship is ready to make way once more as a gesture of goodwill. But then you will depart. Unless we can make another compromise." Her eyes ventured to Jarrod, and Damien didn't like the greed within them.

"You are dismissed, Damien Lanoret. We'd like a word with Lord Martox alone."

Confusion for what the council suggested turned to a rumbling worry as Damien looked at Jarrod, silently asking his friend if he would oblige their request.

Jarrod contemplated for a minute before letting out a breath and nodding. He looked at Damien. "Perhaps some good can come of it. It's all right. Go."

The Rahn'ka hesitated, regardless of the surety on Jarrod's face.

Their escorts stepped forward, waiting for Damien to exit.

With a nod, Damien turned. Leaving Jarrod behind, he hoped the thief could work a miracle.

Chapter 27

SILENCE SETTLED OVER THE SANCTUM for several minutes even after the doors shut with Damien's departure.

Jarrod crossed his arms and waited for an elder to speak. A rock in his gut told him it had to do with his family name.

The woman who had declared the status of Rae's betrothal still stood, studying him.

Finally, the Arch Judgment broke the silence. "Sit, Elder Paivesh."

She glanced over her shoulder, then obeyed.

"Tell us, Lord Martox. With the knowledge of Raeynna's training and the family's intention to marry her to another, what is your purpose here?"

"While the final outcome will be whatever Rae wants, for now, we wish to see and speak to her. If it is as you say and she wishes to remain here, then I'll accept that, but only from her lips."

Some elders leaned over the arms of their chairs to whisper to each other.

"An acceptable request." The Arch Judgment's voice silenced the rest of the elders in the chamber. "Though extenuating circumstances make it impossible to accommodate. Too much would be at risk should we interrupt the delicate process Raeynna undergoes."

The delicate process of manipulation.

Jarrod ground his teeth, keeping his tongue in check. "You implied that we might reach a compromise, so I'm assuming you have more to say."

"We do." The Arch Judgment turned to his right, acknowledging the man on the end with a nod.

The auer stood at the offering from the leader of the council. His eyes were dark and faint creases hinted at his advanced age. Stoney grey hair, cut close to his scalp, was accented with a braided band of green foliage. "I speak for the council on this matter as I am the most familiar. It is my duty to monitor the kingdom of Helgath. We know of the *rebellion* beginning due, in part, to the desertion of Damien Lanoret. We acknowledge the pivotal role this may play in reshaping an otherwise *tyrannical* nation." He paused as if waiting for Jarrod to speak.

Oh, if only Corin could hear this.

"And?" Jarrod lifted his hands then dropped them.

The elder glowered. "We also know of your unique opportunity to play a crucial role in the reformation."

Jarrod raised an eyebrow. "Did Corin put you up to this?" He smiled at his own joke.

The elder frowned. "I don't know who Corin is. I speak only in the interest of the council."

Sighing, Jarrod refrained from rolling his eyes. "What exactly are you proposing, then, *interest of the council*?"

"Our aid." The auer clipped his words. "The support of Eralas and her armies in claiming the throne of Helgath for House Martox."

Jarrod's stomach plummeted as they confirmed that he wouldn't like whatever they had to say. This went beyond what he'd imagined they'd suggest. Far beyond.

Why does everyone keep pushing me towards the same thing?

The auer wanted in on the conflict and they had warriors with thousands of years of training.

Victory would be possible. No... it would be practically guaranteed.

Instead of outright refusing like he wanted to, he took a calming breath and found the dormant formality of his past. "Under what terms?"

"Ones we believe to be generous. When you consider this will be the first time the Aueric people have chosen a side during a human civil war. Our only terms are that you consider brokering a long-term treaty with Eralas and name one of our people as Chief Vizier."

Even considering taking the throne of Helgath made Jarrod's heart race with anxiety. He never wanted to rule, but Corin had made several valid points on the matter. Yet, his gut told him to distrust the offer.

"I'll consider your proposal." Jarrod forced the words out. "Only if you give me Rae's location and a time for us to visit her."

The elder looked to the center of the council and the woman to the right of the Arch Judgment leaned forward in her chair.

"She is in the Mira'wyld compound on the north-eastern border of Maelei, where she undergoes extensive training in her Art. I'll arrange a time to visit, but you must be patient as I do so. It may take days, as such things must be carefully planned so as not to disrupt her progress. And be warned, she is no longer the friend you once knew."

Jarrod nodded. What she possibly meant about Rae not being the same stirred dread within him. "After I've had the chance to speak with her, we can discuss the matter of Helgath further."

"And what of Damien Lanoret?" The Arch Judgment crossed his arms.

"Damien will see Rae. If only one of us is permitted, it'll be him."

The statement caused the council to chatter quietly among each other again, to be silenced by a wave of the Arch Judgment's hand.

"Then I suggest you return to your ship and await word of your appointment. You are dismissed from our sanctum, King Martox."

The title sent a shiver down his spine and he turned, exiting the same way he'd entered.

Damien waited near the single carriage, and Jarrod motioned for him to get in, following.

"Well?" Damien settled in the seat across from him.

The carriage bounced into motion.

"We're going back to the Herald for now." Taking a moment to compose his thoughts, Jarrod relayed all the information he'd gained, leaving nothing out. Even without Corin, having Damien to confide in lessened the weight on his shoulders.

When he finished, Damien whistled. "That's unexpected. Eralas wants to get involved?"

"Apparently. Maybe you can shine some light on why everyone around me seems to think I should be king?"

"Better you than me." Damien shrugged. "But maybe everyone else is seeing something you can't?"

Jarrod sighed. "Either that or they're all insane."

"So what are you going to do? Though, I guess it doesn't matter since we get to see Rae either way?"

Jarrod shook his head. "I don't know what I will do, but I won't worry about it until after one of us sees her. I don't know what they meant about her being different, but you'll have to keep that in mind if you're the only one who gets to visit. Perhaps the treatment she received from Helgath changed her."

Damien's gaze drifted out the carriage window to the dense trees rushing by. "I don't know how it wouldn't. Gods, I wish I could take it all away."

Jarrod nodded solemnly, imagining his excitement to see her likely couldn't hold a candle to how Damien felt. "Aye. No matter how she's changed, she'll be ecstatic to see you."

"I hope so. Even though she's betrothed to another now, apparently."

There's no way that's true. Rae wouldn't have agreed to marry anyone, let alone someone she just met.

"They said it was her family's intention. Perhaps Rae doesn't want to? She hates the idea of marriage."

"I know. And I feel like an ass for being jealous. I should just be relieved that she's alive, and I'll be able to see her. But if I can't hold her like I used to... Kiss her..."

Lifting his gaze, Jarrod narrowed his eyes. "Would you still try to talk her into marrying you?"

"Without a second thought. I'd marry her right now, right this moment if I could. I didn't realize how strongly I felt about it until that auer said she was promised to another. But it's all I can think about now."

Jarrod's mind wandered to Corin, and he wondered if time and distance would change their relationship too. They had made promises, promises that Jarrod had every intention of keeping, but if Rae could have a change of heart, couldn't Corin?

I'm projecting.

"Don't assume that the auer are telling us the whole truth about anything, Dame. You know they're manipulative. I'm sure there are some vital pieces of information they've purposely left out."

"You're probably right." Damien sighed. He leaned his head against the carriage wall, staring at the window.

Jarrod watched him and bit his lip. "Tell me the truth. Do you think I'd make a good king?"

Damien blinked, returning his gaze, and smirked as he opened his mouth. But before he said something Jarrod was certain would have been sarcastic, he closed it again briefly. "I don't know. I don't know how anyone can know until they're doing it, especially with something like that. But..." He rolled his lips together. "From what I've seen, you're level-headed under pressure, even if I don't always agree with your tactics. And I think with the right people at your side... Yes, you could be a great king."

Jarrod turned his gaze out the window, leaning his head on the side of the carriage. "If I have to sit on that throne one day, I can already name the people I'd want with me."

Damien snorted. "Now, if you're thinking who I think you are, that's a terrible idea. I take it all back, you'd be an awful king."

Jarrod laughed and shook his head, looking at his friend. "Does that mean you wouldn't want the job?"

Damien quirked an eyebrow. "Me? That's an even worse idea than Corin and a few Hawks like I thought you meant."

Jarrod shrugged. "If I get roped into this mess, you'd better bet I'm dragging you, Rae, and that brother of yours with me."

Rubbing his chin, Damien looked at the ceiling of the carriage. He let out a slow sigh. "Gods, I never thought about something like this. I mean, especially after I deserted."

"At least we both have things to think about now," Jarrod muttered. His eyelids weighed, and he let them shut.

"You're so generous."

"Sleep on it." Jarrod put his feet up on the bench seat beside Damien.

The Rahn'ka replied with unintelligible mumbles, the carriage rocking as he shifted his weight around to find a comfortable position. He started snoring before Jarrod could beat him to it.

The monotony of the Eralasian forest continued through the next morning and Damien took to long periods of meditation again, leaving Jarrod with nothing to do.

He plucked a small blade out from the inner sheaths in his vest, sitting with his feet up on the opposite bench. Quirking an eyebrow, he flipped the knife through the air, letting it thunk into the wall above his feet. Looking sideways at Damien, he searched for a reaction, but found none.

Pulling another blade, he tossed it a few times in the air. Catching the tip of the blade, he whipped the next one closer to Damien. It protruded from the wall, a foot over from his first knife.

Still no reaction.

Smirking, Jarrod drew another, leaving half his vest empty. He twisted it before launching it. It sank into the wooden wall only inches from Damien's head and Jarrod held his breath.

Nothing.

Is he asleep?

Jarrod pulled a fourth, tossing it up.

"No, I'm not." Damien's voice startled Jarrod enough that the knife clattered to the bottom of the carriage when he missed the catch. He opened one eye and peeked at him with a slight smile.

"Jeez." Jarrod exhaled, picking up the fallen knife. "What if I'd been mid-throw?"

Damien shrugged, closing his eyes again. "It'd miss."

Jarrod laughed. "Right."

"Do it if you don't believe me."

"I'm not throwing a knife at you."

"What? Is his Highness scared?"

Jarrod flicked the blade, sending it flying towards Damien's shoulder.

The Rahn'ka jerked to the side without opening his eyes, twisting his torso the fraction of an inch it needed for the dagger to sail past him and sink into the wall behind.

Jarrod frowned.

"Told you." Damien smirked, stretching his shoulders.

"However does Rae keep her hands off you?" Jarrod rolled his eyes.

Damien chuckled and leaned back, opening his eyes. He grabbed the knife out of the wall beside him, swiveling it. "Boredom is unbecoming of you, my liege."

Jarrod sighed and leaned forward, retrieving his blades to replace in his vest. "Not all of us have voices in our heads to talk to."

Damien rubbed his forehead as if he was getting another headache, but smiled. "Can you tell the carriage to stop? Neco's found us and wants a ride."

Jarrod shook his head, lowering his feet. He stuck his arm through the open window to bang on the carriage next to the driver.

The carriage lurched to a stop, and Damien swung the door open with his foot.

Neco bounded full speed out of the forest, lunging into the carriage with enough momentum that it rocked when he slammed against the opposite door. He panted hard, but started licking Damien's fingers as he pulled the door shut, then promptly turned his attention to Jarrod.

The driver called out, "Is there a problem?"

Jarrod scratched Neco's ears. "No, carry on." Turning his attention back to the wolf, he cupped the animal's face. "Where you been, boy?"

Neco climbed onto the bench seat with Jarrod, pushing against his chest to climb into his lap. He let out a quiet howl, undulating his wolf-speech in excitement.

"Whoa. Slow down, bud." Damien furrowed his brow. His face looked pensive before it cracked. He burst into laughter, leaning back and crossing his arms. "Seriously, Neco? That poor shepherd."

Jarrod shuffled his feet like an impatient child. "Whaaat? What'd he do?"

Damien tried to stifle another laugh as Neco butted his head up under Jarrod's chin, chuffing in the Rahn'ka's direction. "I don't know if I can properly explain it." He lifted a finger to wipe a tear from the corner of his eye. "It's hard because he doesn't speak Common. It's a mix of words and pictures. I don't know if it'd be the same when I repeat it."

Jarrod pouted, scratching the wolf's ruff and letting him lick his chin. "I wish I could hear you too, bud."

"Long and short of it, Neco found himself a herd of sheep who'd never seen a wolf before, let alone have the good sense to run from one. He taught them pretty fast, and the shepherd didn't take kindly to it and chased Neco off, but not before Neco left the shepherd a present on his porch. And he's rather proud of himself for it."

Jarrod scowled playfully. "That's not very royal of you, boy. But I still approve."

"Now the wolf's royal too? We really need to work on your standards."

Jarrod laughed. "Oh, you thought somehow you were *above* Neco in the line of succession?"

"Seriously?" Damien rolled his eyes and plopped his feet up on the bench next to Jarrod, making the wolf crawl further into the thief's lap. "Then I'm going back to sleep since you clearly don't need me."

Neco slept soundly for the last few hours, content on the floor between Jarrod and Damien.

By the time they arrived at the Herald, the sun had disappeared below the horizon again. The Herald was looking like her old self, her crew working on restoring her usual appearance, including the alcan figurehead.

The wolf's ears pricked when the carriage halted and he stretched his front legs, his toes spreading. Shaking out his ruff as he stood, he waited patiently for Damien to open the door to hop out. He turned back, his tongue lolling out while he looked at the Rahn'ka.

Damien's brow furrowed and Neco yipped as the two of them communicated.

Neco barreled into Jarrod just as the thief finished climbing out of the carriage, rubbing up against his legs and nipping at his fingers.

"Whoa, boy. Take it easy, you weigh almost as much as I do." Jarrod stroked the wolf's side.

Neco must have taken the affection as an invitation. As the carriage moved away, he pushed harder against Jarrod, hopping up on his hind legs. Upright, the wolf was as tall as him and pushed him backward onto the ground.

"That's..." Jarrod tried to get words out as Neco licked his face. "Not... What. Easy... Means." Using his hands to combat the wolf's affection, he growled as slobber covered his fingers.

"I told you, he doesn't speak Common." Damien stepped back from their roughhousing, crossing his arms. "But I believe he's trying to convey something like... He wants to play."

Finally pushing the heavy wolf off, Jarrod glared at Damien. "Aye, I think I got that."

"He also wants to tell you about the deer he chased yesterday and the way the banyan trees smelled right after a cloudburst hit the coast this afternoon. Oh, and something about a crab." Damien shook his head. "It's exhausting keeping up with him. He's learning to compartmentalize his thoughts so I can understand them easier and keeps asking me to convey the meanings and messages to you. He's too damn smart."

Jarrod smirked, imagining Neco meeting a crab. "Maybe he's just smart enough." He scratched the wolf's head again as he sat up. "I love hearing all his stories."

"Well, it's interesting you should say that, actually. Because Neco asked me something just now and you've conveyed a similar interest."

The wolf barked, turning towards Damien as if he somehow understood what was coming next. Then his giant head spun around and he shoved it against Jarrod's chest.

"What's he asking?" Jarrod pushed back against Neco to keep himself sitting upright.

"It seems he's almost as annoyed as I am with me needing to be the middleman. He's decided that your reactions are rarely how he expects and blames me for a poor translation. So he asked me why he isn't able to talk to you directly. When I explained how I could understand, but you were not, he promptly questioned why I couldn't fix you."

Jarrod shrugged at the wolf. "I don't think it works that way."

"Actually, it could."

"How?"

Damien sighed, crouching beside them and reaching out to give Neco some scratches. "The ancient Rahn'ka used to bond their spirits with those of animals, turning them into half-man, half-beast amalgamations. Over time, they realized they could pair the ká of other creatures, creating new species. There are many ways to tether ká together and with varying results in what it changes. Strength, speed, reflex. But at the very surface of all this is our minds. Instead of bonding you to Neco in a way that might change you physically, I could do it in a subtle way to link only your minds. So you could speak to each other."

Jarrod's insides fluttered, and he narrowed his eyes. "You can bond me to Neco? With no physical changes?"

"Sure. I just have to be careful about the way I construct the bond." He sounded too casual. "You worried that I might change you in a way that Corin won't find attractive?"

Jarrod frowned. "Just don't want to end up looking like a grygurr... Plus, you *are* talking about messing around with my soul."

"Your ká. It's more complex than your soul."

"And that's supposed to make me feel better?"

Damien shrugged. "I won't make you a grygurr. You'd have to be Rahn'ka yourself to let it go that far. Maybe you'd grow a little extra chest hair..."

Jarrod laughed. "You've seen the tattoo on my back, so your offer is rather... ironic."

Damien smirked. "Wasn't my idea." He gestured to the wolf who'd rolled onto his back, wriggling his whole body back and forth in the sand.

"Might not be a terrible one."

Neco looked at Jarrod with an expectant yip before rolling over and lowering the front of his body, lifting his haunches.

Damien huffed. "He wants to know your answer. The auer who think we humans have no patience have clearly never met a wolf."

"Clearly. I'm game."

After a short pause, Neco bounded at Jarrod, tackling him with joyous growls and licks to his face.

"I don't think that needs translation. I can get started tonight, if you'd like. I don't think I'll be able to sleep for a while anyway. And Neco probably won't let us wait either."

Jarrod shoved the wolf off of him. "Probably best once he calms down, I'm sure." He wrestled the wolf onto his back. "Don't know why he's so worked up. Think he knows Rae is nearby?"

At her name, Neco hopped to his feet and perked his ears, looking from Jarrod to Damien. He gave Jarrod's chin a quick lick as if affirming everything.

"He knows. It's why he took off so quickly from the ship. He picked up what remains of her scent out here."

The elders made it clear that they were to wait for an appointment to visit Rae, but Jarrod couldn't deny the temptation to see if they could locate the compound and use Neco to find her within it. "He can probably track her better than you can right now."

"Just more reason for us to get started on linking the two of you to distract me from the temptation to go find her now." Damien rose to his feet. "Let's get back to the ship. I'm hungry."

After boarding the Herald and filling their bellies in the galley, the three of them returned to the guest quarters. Damien insisted on taking the cot on the floor, leaving the bed for Jarrod and Neco.

Neco invited himself onto it as soon as they entered the room, circling before he settled into a comfortable position.

"So how does this work?"

Damien secured the door behind them. "Well, considering I've never done this before..."

Jarrod's shoulders slumped. "You won't give me fangs, right?"

"I'll do my best?"

"Really testing my trust in you, Lanoret," Jarrod grumbled, but a smirk played on his face.

"Rest assured, if I mess up your pretty face, my brother will beat the shit out of me. That's motivation enough. I know how hard he punches."

Jarrod laughed. "At least that works in my favor."

Damien settled on his cot to take off his boots. "Floor will be easiest for us to sit on, despite how comfortable Neco looks. And take off your shirt."

The wolf whined, but scooted to the side of the bed and hopped off.

Jarrod raised an eyebrow, removing his vest and shirt. He threw them onto the bed before returning to sit near Damien.

Damien gave a thoughtful hum. "That tattoo *is* rather ironic. Why did you get it?"

"The Hawks gave me the name wolf and the plating on half his face symbolizes the armor I used to wear."

"Or is it the armor you've put on to hide behind as a thief?"

Pausing, Jarrod narrowed his eyes. "Reading my thoughts or taking a guess?"

"Either way, apparently I'm right."

"Never said it only had one meaning..."

Damien grunted in understanding and eyed Neco. He crossed barefoot towards the wolf, kneeling to scratch behind his ears. "You both sure about this? I don't think I'll be able to reverse it if you change your mind. You shouldn't have any doubts."

Jarrod nodded without hesitation. "It sounds *fun*. Besides, I trust you. Communicating with him could be useful, joking aside."

"All right. I need you to line your ká up with Neco's as best you can. So... glad you two have already practiced cuddling at night."

Jarrod assumed that meant he needed to lie down and the wooden floor cooled his skin as he did. Patting the spot in front of him, he called Neco over to join him. "At least I get puppy snuggles." He pulled the big wolf closer.

Neco groaned as he was dragged across the floor, but seemed content to lay with Jarrod's arm draped over him.

"Just a reminder before I do this. Neco's been getting better at compartmentalizing, but it's still not like regular speech. It might be confusing at first. So take it easy on him, Neco." He knelt on the floor near the top of their heads.

Jarrod wasn't sure how to tell if Damien was even doing anything, but kept his mouth shut to avoid distracting him. He glanced up once to see that Damien had closed his eyes, his hands hovering above him and Neco.

In the streets of Lazuli, Jarrod had shared his energy with Damien. He remembered the shock as he abruptly felt like he'd run for half a day. But the sensation he gradually became aware of was something different.

A heat started at the back of his head, then turned to a distinct vibration. He tried to keep his eyes open, but when streaks of white and pale blue blocked everything, he closed them tight.

Instead, he focused on his breathing.

Each breath slowed as the heat reduced to bitter cold. As the back of his eyelids brightened to a brilliant white, Neco let out a low whine.

In a blaze of light, colors swirled into the shapes and figures rushing towards him and he suddenly wondered why he'd agreed to this. A voice hummed, whispering to him in syllables that made little sense. The figures circled him, lunging towards his chest. He wanted to block it, but couldn't move his limbs.

He tried to decipher the voice's whispers, and when Damien spoke, it nearly deafened him.

"Nearly done."

The white faded, and he dared to open his eyes.

A rush of pale-blue light raced across his vision, then vanished. The voice hummed in his mind, but said nothing specific. It merely made its presence known, though anxiety touched its tone. An anxiousness for something to be done. And a complaint about a smell.

Damien sat on his heels and let out a loud exhale. He rubbed the back of his neck as he opened his eyes. "Should be done. Can you hear him?"

Jarrod's breath came fast, his heart pounding, but it didn't strain him. As he released Neco and sat up, he tilted his head at the wolf. Furrowing his brow, he looked at Damien. "Neco thinks you need a bath."

Damien frowned and looked at Neco. "He says that every day. How about a little gratitude..."

Damien might have kept talking, but Jarrod couldn't make it out as the voice in his mind overwhelmed him, shouting. He covered his ears, but it did nothing to diminish the noise. "Damn it, Neco." He curled over onto himself as a headache ignited at his temples.

Neco whined and the voice in his mind conveyed a similar sentiment, apologetic in tone. But then clarified it with excitement. Neco rolled onto his paws, doing an awkward crawl towards Jarrod. Whatever came next was questions, but he couldn't make them out.

Lifting his head, Jarrod met Neco's gaze, then looked at Damien. "Please tell me I'll get used to this."

"You get used to it. Now imagine what you're getting and multiply it by every living thing within one hundred yards and you might have some sympathy for me."

Jarrod scoffed. "How did you survive that again?"

"Rae."

Chapter 28

AIDING JARROD IN NAVIGATING HIS new connection with Neco proved a worthy distraction while Damien waited for the auer to send word of their appointment to see Rae. He resisted allowing Neco to lead him to where the wolf insisted her scent led.

We need to maintain a modicum of good standing, just in case.

The same two auer who'd escorted them to the council arrived at the docks several days later. The one with short hair and lilac eyes did all the talking this time, while the other glared as if dealing with humans was beneath her.

Their news made Damien's blood boil. "Summer? It's barely spring. You're saying we can't see Rae for three months?"

"It's a reasonable compromise." The auer pursed her lips. "Especially considering the council will extend your welcome on our island to encompass that time. Pending your cooperation, of course."

Damien bit the side of his tongue to stop himself from telling her exactly what he thought about the council and cooperation.

"I trust you'll pass the word on to Lord Martox?"

Jarrod had been gone most of the afternoon, on a walk with Neco to practice their communication.

Damien nodded, not masking his furious tone. "Then I guess we'll see you again in three months?"

The pink-eyed auer gave a dry smile. "Appointments such as this rarely get rescheduled, though I hope they will give another the task of conversing with you next time."

"Was there anything else, or are you merely standing around so I can marvel at the depth of auer hospitality?"

It received the reaction he hoped for and the pink-eyed auer spun on her heels and walked away.

The other took her time, not as affected by Damien's sarcasm. "You should be grateful, Mister Lanoret. By the graciousness of my people, we offer you a place where you need not flee from your kinsmen, at least for a time. We have been extremely hospitable. And I caution you not to give us reason to retract such courtesies."

Damien watched her depart without further conversation.

No wonder Yondé hates auer so much.

They were too fake for Damien to find any good in them. Rather, he distrusted every auer he met. Lygen proved to be the only one he could tolerate for an extended period of time.

Rae doesn't count.

The awareness of his power made him sensitive to how secretive they all felt. Even the few he passed on the ground-level streets outside Maelei would glance at him and step away as if he wouldn't notice. They'd smile, but something sinister lurked beneath it. Something untrusting and cruel.

Looking down the length of the beach, he answered the distant call from Neco in his mind as the pair rounded a grove of trees beside the sand.

Jarrod ran beside the valley wolf, keeping an impressive pace even in the sand. His shirt clung to his skin from sweat and he slowed to a stop a few yards away.

"Those two auer women were here." Jarrod looked in the direction the carriage had gone. "Neco caught their scent. Got here as quick as I could. When is the appointment?" In the time it took him to ask, his breathing normalized.

Scratching behind Neco's ears, Damien tried to ease the frustration from his voice. "Three months. And they act like that's generous."

Jarrod gaped at him. "Three months?" Hearing it aloud again made the angry knot in Damien's stomach clench. "They're just using the time to brainwash her. I bet they're trying to convince her to stay because I said that if she wanted to, I'd respect that."

Damien tensed, and his power ebbed to the brink in his anxiety. He'd kept it a secret from the auer and that would have to continue. But he refused to be jerked around by the council any longer. The constant anxiety of the wait only made it more difficult to maintain his hiding aura. "And that's exactly why I'm done waiting. I've played patient and I'm done."

"What's your plan?" Jarrod pulled off his shirt and used it to dry his brow.

Neco chimed in before Damien could speak, and both he and Jarrod grinned. It earned Neco an extra scratch on the chin from Damien.

"I like that idea, buddy. But I think we'll need to be more cautious than just running in."

Jarrod nodded. "And I'd suggest only one of us goes. Would be harder to sneak in with all of us."

"Agreed. And you already know it will be me, right?"

Smirking, Jarrod scratched Neco's ears. "Wouldn't dare argue with it, either."

"You ready to lead us to her, bud?"

Neco barked his excitement and took off down the road.

"Tell him to be quiet about it." Damien mentally prepared himself for the run through the woods and the onslaught of pressure to his barrier.

"Can't you tell him yourself?" Jarrod pulled his shirt over his head.

"You need the practice. And I enjoy making you play messenger for a change." He didn't wait for Jarrod before he raced across the beach to pursue Neco.

When Neco stopped, Damien panted and leaned against a tree to catch his breath. No matter how in shape he felt, the precarious run through the forest exhausted every part of him. He sorely missed the advantage his power gave him.

Ironic when considering how much I didn't want it.

Jarrod came to a stop beside him, looking up at the dense wall of trees. "In there?"

The wolf gave a yip of confirmation, pushing a flurry of images into the men's heads.

Jarrod tilted his head. "There's a gate to the north, I think."

"That's a little too obvious for my taste." Damien looked up at the top of the wall.

"Feel like climbing? They might have alarms in place, but maybe you'll get lucky."

Damien eyed one tree, pressing his palm to the bark. He cleared his mind to sort through the voices to find the beech's voice. It was far younger than the others and happy to talk with someone interested in hearing its concerns rather than just continually making it change shape. Through the tree, Damien found answers to his questions.

"There's a ward in place, but if I climb high enough I can jump right over it to the other side. Shouldn't be a problem."

Jarrod shrugged. "If you say so. You want us to stick around?"

Damien's chest tightened as he looked up at the sky, barely visible through the canopy far above. By the time he could reach the height he needed, night would set in. The darkness wouldn't affect him if he loosened his barrier and allowed his senses to see for him. It meant he might get a headache, but it'd be a small price to pay to find Rae.

The forest was empty enough for him to risk loosening his hold on his power to use it again.

"Yes. Just in case." Damien hoped the wards the tree told him about were also what blocked him from sensing Rae. Otherwise, she could be anywhere within the compound.

He leaned on the beech's trunk, unlacing his boots so he could hand them off to Jarrod. The direct contact with the tree would aid the continued communication and his climbing skill.

"Good luck." Jarrod took the boots and stepped off the worn path. "We won't be far."

"Thank you." Damien tried to push all his appreciation for the man into the words. As he turned back to the tree, carefully putting his hands where it instructed, he began the precarious climb.

His heart lodged in his throat as he realized how close he was. He wouldn't miss her this time.

I'm coming, Rae.

He'd been correct about how dark it would be by the time he reached the height he needed. The distance to the ground almost made him dizzy, but he'd survive the drop if he planned it right. Balancing on a branch, he stepped one foot in front of the other until he was five yards away from the trunk of the tree and eyed the ground.

Thank all the ancient spirits of the Rahn'ka I'm more than human.

He sucked in a breath to make a leap all his instincts said would kill him. He held his breath the full thirty yards of the descent, pushing power into his knees and legs. He struck the ground hard enough that it knocked all the air out of him, but his bones didn't break as he fell forward into a roll and back to his feet.

It was too dark for him to make out anything without allowing the ká around him to manifest in his vision. He isolated the feeling of Rae, and her energy glowed like a beacon in his consciousness as he cautiously made his way towards the homes at the center of the compound.

Keeping his knees bent and body low to the ground, Damien stuck to the shadows as best as he could. His bare feet traversed in perfect silence. Looking at the homes, the faint outline of a second ká within confirmed she wasn't alone.

Another ká lay isolated away from the two in the farthest structure, already asleep, which helped to narrow which of the three residences belonged to Rae.

No guards patrolled as he'd expected.

Is she really staying here willingly?

As he crept into the shadows of the empty home's garden, two figures emerged from the neighboring house.

Rae's laughter carried over the wind.

The excitement nearly made him leap from his hiding place, but he forced himself to take a steadying breath. He didn't know who this other person was but, based on his recent exposure to their secretive auras, he certainly recognized him as auer.

Damien took slow steps towards the porch of the center home, which radiated with pieces of Rae's ká now that he was close enough to feel it, confirming it was her dwelling. But she'd been visiting her neighbor, who stood close to her in his doorway.

In the dim candlelight, shining from inside his home, the auer stroked Rae's cheek.

A boil of questions surfaced, but the Rahn'ka swallowed them.

All show. She's pretending because of her situation.

How he longed for her smile to be directed towards him again.

An eternity passed before the pair parted and the man

disappeared back into his home, closing the door behind him.

Rae ran a hand through her hair, cut above her shoulders and unbraided. She wore a knee-length white dress, which drifted in the night breeze as she made her way to her house.

Damien's heart thundered as she stepped closer to him, finally alone. She looked so much better than when he visited her in the Lazuli prison. Radiant and full of the life he admired her for. It brought some comfort to know the auer treated her well.

"Dice," Damien whispered once she was within earshot. He waited for her to turn towards him before he rose, his entire body shaking.

Her eyes met his, one of her irises green, the other yellow. They narrowed and then widened, her feet stilling a few yards from her front door. Something other than the excitement he expected tainted the shock in her expression, but he couldn't tell what caused it.

He took a wary step and lifted his hand out to her. "No time for questions. We need to get out of here."

Rae stepped back, looking behind her at the house she'd just exited.

Breathing became difficult. "Rae? Rae, what's wrong?"

She met his gaze again. "Who are you? How do you know my name?"

The world around Damien collapsed inward and his eyes widened. "It's me, Damien. I promised I'd come for you. I know the beard's a little thicker, but it's me. I swear."

Rae shook her head. "I don't know you." The words pierced his heart like shards of glass. "You should leave." Her feet took her backward, and she glanced once more at her neighbor's house.

"No, no, wait." Damien advanced, holding his hands out to her, palms flat so she'd understand he wasn't a threat. His mind rushed. In desperation, he sought to examine her ká, looking for answers. Something was different about it that he hadn't noticed before. An artificial gap between two pieces of it. "The auer. They must have erased your memories somehow. But Rae, I swear to the gods you can trust me."

Rae blinked slowly. "They wouldn't have done that. They're my family." She'd stopped again, but fear lingered on her face. "Please leave, I don't want to yell for Kynis or Maith, but I will."

Cold built inside Damien as he fought wanting to take Rae into his arms and kiss her until she remembered everything. She stood so close to him, yet still miles away. "Please." He failed at controlling his emotions. A headache rumbled, but he swallowed the pain. "Don't. Jarrod and Neco, they're right outside the walls waiting for us. They've missed you so much. I've missed you." Hot tears welled in his eyes despite trying to fight them. "Dice, please. It's me."

Rae seemed to debate his words for a breath before turning and jogging back towards the house she'd exited. Once she reached it, her fist rose, and she rapped on the door while glancing back at Damien.

Damien crouched back into shadow. Chasing would only make it worse. His heart crumbled, chest growing impossibly heavy as he heard the door open.

"Maith..."

He didn't wait for the rest of what she might say, ducking behind the corner of the house. He leaned against the cold surface of the exterior wall and found what comfort he could in banging the back of his head against it. To his surprise, no one came looking for him, but the door clicked shut with Rae inside.

How can this be happening?

He groaned as more emotion swelled in his eyes, making them hot and blurry. He rubbed them as he tried to remember how to breathe.

Inside him, the currents of his ká swam erratically and no matter how much he tried to calm it, nothing worked. The barrier he'd reinforced since coming to Eralas fell apart. The voices came tumbling into his consciousness, and a grunt of pain escaped his lips. It started at the front of his skull and passed mercilessly to the back, bringing a fresh wave of tears as he stumbled away from the house towards the outer wall of the compound.

Chapter 29

RAEYNNA COULDN'T BRING HERSELF TO tell Maith that she'd seen a man outside her home. A human who'd known her name. She'd made up an excuse about forgetting to tell him an unimportant thing Kynis had told her and then promptly returned to her own house. The man was gone, and she couldn't decide whether to feel relief or disappointment.

Something about him demanded she not forget him.

Damien.

The name meant nothing to her, yet it made her heart thud. The surprise of being confronted by a stranger within the compound surely encouraged the reaction, but she struggled to accept it as the complete reason.

Pacing her house, she tried to calm her nerves, but they kept screaming at her. After what felt like hours of indecision, she sighed and opened her front door. Kynis and Maith's homes were dark, the surrounding woods rich with nighttime chirps and creaks. She stepped outside and quietly shut her door behind her.

Raeynna rounded her house. She stared at the bare footprints in the dirt of her garden.

He wasn't my imagination.

The need to catch him before he left forever overwhelmed her. She stared into the darkness, considering only a moment longer before she sprinted off in the direction his tracks led. Her bare feet carried her noiselessly. She wove through the trees and paths she'd already memorized during her training within the forest.

As she drew closer to the wall surrounding the compound, something tickled the edge of her senses and she slowed. Creeping through the grass, she stopped behind a wide beech trunk. Her gaze fell on the man, facing away from her, and her pulse pounded in her ears.

He sat perfectly still among a patch of ferns, his legs crossed beneath him. His hair hung shaggy at the back of his neck, a rich golden blond she'd never see on an auer. The moon broke through the canopy to cast its beams across his densely muscled body covered in a simple tan shirt and open leather vest.

Everything around him seemed to glow with a pale light, like a faint haze in her vision.

This is crazy.

With a quiet, steady breath, Raeynna tentatively approached. “Damien?”

He jumped, his entire body tensing as he twisted to face her. His wide, bloodshot eyes locked on her as she froze. He blinked, cringing as he lifted a hand to his temple. “Rae.”

“No one calls me that. My name is Raeynna.”

The slightest smile crossed his lips. “It is, but I’ve always called you Rae. Or Dice.” He shook his head and winced, closing his eyes.

“Dice?” She tilted her head.

“It’s a nickname I gave you. You like dice games and putting dice in my pockets when you...” He shifted, turning on his knees towards her.

Nerves jumped in her belly and Raeynna glanced back the direction she came. Curiosity thrummed within her, and she tilted her head at Damien. “Why are you here?”

He sat and crossed his legs, his chest swelling with a slow breath. Opening his eyes, he met hers. “I came for you. I promised you I would when I visited you in Lazuli. But I suppose you’ve forgotten that?”

Raeynna looked down, focusing as hard as she could on whatever might have happened in Helgath, but her mind returned blank, yet again. “I don’t remember. Why would you need to come for me? I’m safe here.” So many pieces were missing, she had an arduous time deciding where to start.

If Kynis knew I was outside, talking to a stranger in the middle of the night...

She shook her head. "I don't think I should be here."

He shifted, looking as if he meant to lean forward, but then composed himself. "Please, stay?"

Her mind warred against her instincts, but she reluctantly nodded.

"What is the earliest memory you have?"

Raeynna rubbed the back of her head. "Waking up. On a stone bed a few weeks ago. They told me something happened, and I needed to start over."

Damien's eyes lowered to the ground. The corners of his eyes wrinkled as he closed them tightly.

Raeynna took a step towards him. "Prove it. Prove you know me beyond my name."

He paused a moment, but then tapped his left ribs. "You have a tattoo here. A fox and sparrow. And another on the bottom of your neck of an arrow with a feather wrapped around it."

Raeynna touched her left side and furrowed her brow. The thin material of her dress did little to conceal the ink on her skin there, but he couldn't have been able to tell what the image was. Her jaw worked, and she took another step forward. "Something else." If he could banish the doubt lingering in her mind, she wanted him to.

His jaw tightened. "I don't know if they've healed more, but there were scars on your right side. A grygurr nearly killed you." He traced a pattern on his right side that mirrored the thin white lines on hers. "And... your feet. The auer are good healers, but they wouldn't have been able to erase everything Helgath did to you."

Helgath.

Kynis had mentioned something about what had happened in Helgath, but he'd refrained from answering her questions.

Fear diminished, turning into an odd sense of calm.

Raeynna walked the rest of the way to Damien, kneeling in front of him. "Why did Helgath hurt me?"

He grimaced and looked away. Running his hand into his hair, she wondered what it would feel like to touch him.

I shouldn't think such things. I'm committed to Maith.

"If you've really forgotten..." His voice was so low she almost couldn't hear it. "That might be better than knowing all they did. There are no words to describe the atrocities. And they did it because of me."

A rock formed in her stomach. "You told them to?" Finding her feet, she moved to stand again.

"No, of course not." Damien caught her hand. His skin was remarkably warm, nothing like Maith's. "I never wanted them to take you. They thought they could use you to get to me."

Raeynna sank back to her knees, wishing she could make sense of what he told her. "You didn't answer me when I asked why you're here. You said you promised you'd come for me, but why?"

"Because I can't imagine living without you. Because I love you."

Her world shook, and she let go of his hand. "No. I'm promised to another. Kynis wouldn't have supported it if I had someone else already."

Damien's brow furrowed, and it somehow made his face more handsome. He didn't reach to take her hand again, bringing his back into his lap. "I know you have no reason to trust me, but the auer aren't as honest as you believe. They want to keep you here, and they'll do anything to accomplish it. Along with making you forget me."

"Are we married?"

His cheeks flushed a charming rosy color. "No. You told me you hate the idea of marriage, so I haven't had the courage to ask."

Raeynna swallowed, but shook her head again. "This is my home, my family. I'm happy here."

"You have other family. The Hawks in Mirage, which is your real home. Sarth. Jarrod. Me."

Sighing, Raeynna sat in the grass, a strap of her dress slipping off her shoulder. "I know you want me to remember, but I don't." She played with a piece of grass between them.

A comfortable silence settled, broken by Damien. "I might be able to help, if you'll let me?" Whatever pain he'd been in before seemed to have faded.

"How?"

"I have a unique connection to the Art. I don't know if I'll be able to do anything, but I could try?"

Her pulse escalated at the glimmer in his eyes. Kynis would be furious, and Maith would be hurt.

But how can I pass up the opportunity to know myself again?

Raeynna nodded, despite the voice in her head screaming at her not to. "I want to trust you."

Damien offered his hand to her, and she took a breath before accepting it. "I've never read about this in Yondé's books. I don't know what caused your memories to vanish. So this might take a little while for me to piece together." He smiled as he drew her hand closer to him, cradling it in both of his, and her heart skipped a beat.

"Will it hurt?"

"I don't know. I suspect it will, considering what you'll remember." He looked remorseful. "It feels selfish to even offer this to you. Perhaps you're better off forgetting me if it means you don't have to remember the last few months."

Raeynna's shoulders slumped, and she squeezed his hand. "If I'm living a life I never wanted, then I want to know. If all of this is a lie, then I *need* to know. I don't want to forever wonder who I was. Who you are."

He nodded, touching her cheek with his palm against her jaw. “Close your eyes and try to clear your mind. I don’t know what this will feel like.”

Clenching her jaw, she did as instructed, but found it difficult with a stranger touching her face. Centering herself, like Kynis had instructed when using the Art, she let go of her doubts and relaxed.

Where his hands touched, her skin heated. It spread to her entire body until she felt submerged in a hot spring. A tingling sensation passed through her, followed by a distinct shiver and she gasped.

Something else came, a pressure on her skin like wool blankets layered over her on a frigid night. It altered to an inferno of heat, the smell of smoke, and her eyes burned. Screams echoed in her ears, the flicker of amber piercing through her eyelids. Images and feelings scorched through her. Arms encircled her in a moment of peace before her vision flipped to watching a friend hang in the city streets.

Raeynna wanted to scream, but no sound came out as she plunged into water. Breath became impossible. Pieces of debris sank around her, but she couldn’t swim.

Damien’s face appeared frequently among the visions, so much that she couldn’t properly sort the emotions tangled with it. It changed so often she struggled to keep up, but feeling his body pressed against hers with the incessant ringing of a bell somewhere in the distance solidified a deep connection.

She watched Jarrod die, blood splattering as a knife drove beneath his ribs. She sobbed as the cart that carried her bounced away from his body.

Darkness commenced.

Beatings, threats, and someone choking her. Whipping her feet and kicking her. Bellamy's voice, echoing through stone behind her.

All the pain seared her body until the moment Kynis and the auer woman took her to the chamber beneath the ground.

Old memories joined her new ones, colliding in a wave of impossible strength. Maithalik, Kynis, and the rest of it ground to a halt when it merged with the present. Tears raced down her cheeks, dripping from her chin as her body ached at the cruel reenactment of all she'd endured.

With a jolting quiver, her eyes flickered open. "Damien," she whispered, her body shaking.

Tears filled his hazel eyes, and he touched her cheek, running his fingers down her jaw. "It's me. It's really me this time."

Rae choked on a sob and threw herself into him, his arms encircling her in a tight embrace.

He wept in her ear, burying his face in her hair as she closed her arms around him. "Gods, Rae." He kissed her temple. His hot tears mingled with hers. "I'm so sorry."

Rae pulled away, but remained in his lap as she inspected his face. The face she hadn't been able to see or touch for months. She could hardly believe he was here, but no one was around to verify his presence. Running her hands through his hair and down the back of his neck, her fingers tangled with a necklace she didn't remember him having.

Tugging on it, she withdrew the crystal shard from beneath his shirt. Shaking her head, she swallowed hard. "You came." She touched his face again. "You're here."

He smiled, but it came with another half sob, urging her to hold him tighter. They pressed their foreheads together. "I'm here."

Rae met his mouth in a desperate kiss. It deepened as he returned it.

His arms tightened around her as his lips moved against hers in a constant renewal of passion, fingers tangling with the roots of her hair. He hummed against her lips.

Inhaling sharply, Rae forced her mouth from his. "I love you. I'm never letting you go again." Without waiting for a response, her mouth claimed his. Desire seared through her veins.

His warm hands ran up her legs, slipping beneath her dress to send fevered waves up her spine. Nails dragged over her skin, teasing her with forgotten sensations only encouraged by his mouth. Savoring her lower lip, Damien pulled away to shift his kisses to her neck.

Her hands returned to his hair, and she closed her eyes, losing herself to each touch of his lips.

Leaving fiery trails along her neck, he ran his hand up her bare side beneath the dress.

Rae rocked her hips, encouraging the soft moan that escaped him and tickled her neck. She tugged his hair to guide his face from her skin so she could look at him. "I want you." She could barely hear herself over her pounding heart.

Damien leaned in and kissed her hard, a heavy breath coming in with it before he pulled away and took hold of her hips. He lifted her from where she sat and encouraged her back onto the grass, lowering himself over her. One hand shifted low, running along her thigh and playing teasingly close between her legs.

With agonizingly slow movements, he pulled his hips back from hers, reaching to unfasten his pants. When he finished, he leaned over her for another sultry kiss. He pulled back to nuzzle close to her ear, his tongue playing on her skin. "I am yours."

His hand teased her, playing along the creases of her womanhood before he shifted his hips and pressed into her. Slipping deep, her breath caught in tandem with his, her hips rising as a moan of pleasure buzzed from his lips.

Rae gasped as he rocked forward again, and she wrapped her legs around him. Bringing his mouth back to hers, she kissed him, never wanting to stop.

Their souls and bodies merged, a vibration passing through her entire being with each movement of his. Each pulse of pleasure struck harder and her body flooded with bliss.

Damien gasped in her mouth, forced to pull away for a deep inhale of breath as he thrust deeper. Her moans mingled perfectly with his as his body shuddered. Ecstasy found her and she arched her back, her nails biting into him as she held him close.

They rocked together as she heard his release a moment later, a long and pleasant exhale after shaky breath. He trembled in her arms as he took her mouth again, allowing her to savor him as their bodies and breath slowed.

Rae buried her hands beneath the bottom of his shirt, relishing in the warmth of his skin as she kissed him. Her world finally felt complete after all the chaos and agony she'd gone through. Tears rolled from the corners of her eyes and she wrapped her arms around him again to hold him closer.

Damien obliged, leaning to the side so he could support his body with one elbow on the grass. He drew away from their kiss, his hand brushing through her hair, tickling her temple with his fingertips. He had a smile on his face, his eyes far less burdened. Without saying a word, he remained, watching and studying her as his hand caressed the tears from her face.

"I can't believe you considered leaving me in the dark." Rae stroked a hand over his jaw and behind his ear.

"I'd do anything for you. Especially if it meant you'd be happy. No matter the cost. Though, I am selfishly pleased with this outcome."

A grin spread over Rae's face and she shook her head, fighting the flow of tears to her eyes.

He continued to wipe them away.

"Nothing would ever be worse than forgetting you," she murmured, tracing a finger over the features of his face. "Nothing. Even if it meant Helgath never happened. My life without you isn't a life at all."

Damien's eyes sparkled in the dim moonlight, the gleam of his tears reflecting the pale glow. Leaning close, he kissed her. "I know what you mean."

They laid in silence for a blissful amount of time, just touching.

"The auer will be pissed when they find out I snuck in here," Damien whispered, breaking the spell Rae was under. "But I couldn't wait any longer."

The auer.

Rae cringed. "Damien... I forgot you... I met this auer, Maithalik, and we..." She swallowed.

His fingers glided over her lips in a reassuring touch. "It's all right. Honestly, it makes a lot more sense now. They warned me you were betrothed to someone else and I guess it's Maith?" He looked remarkably calm. "You don't need to explain anything to me. None of it matters. What matters is where we go from here."

Relief washed over her, but the memory of Maith kissing her haunted her like a bad dream. "Yes, Maith. He kissed me. I remember feeling uneasy about it, but I didn't know why. I think my body remembered you, even if my mind didn't."

Damien gave her one of his soft half-smiles that made her feel like she was melting. "I think our past and present far outshines one kiss, especially when I'd like to assume it won't happen again. The kiss... not the, you know..."

"Never." Rae kissed Damien again before grinning. "The kiss... Not the, you know." She paused. "You knew I was betrothed to another? And you still came?" Closing her eyes, she buried her face in his neck. "I don't deserve you."

Damien's hand tangled in her hair, guiding her away so he could look at her again. "What part of *I love you* did you not fully understand? And you deserve everything, my love. And I'll keep striving to give it all to you."

Rae's entire body warmed, never having felt so lucky in her life as she gazed into his eyes. "Have I mentioned that I love you too? Because gods, Damien, I do."

"You have. But that doesn't mean I don't mind hearing it over and over again. How about tomorrow? And every day after that?"

Rae nodded. "I can do that. Every day. I promise."

"I will hold you to that." When he pulled away after one more kiss, he shifted with his entire body, tugging his pants back into place. "We better go though, Jarrod's probably getting worried."

Rae's heart constricted and her eyes heated again as she sat up. "Where is he?"

"He and Neco are waiting for us just outside the wall." He stood and offered a hand out to her. "I was sitting here trying to come up with a plan on how to get out without setting off the wards when you surprised me." He cast a playful glance down her body. "Not that I'm complaining."

Rae smirked, taking his hand. "I can get us out."

Chapter 30

DAMIEN JOGGED TO CATCH UP as she walked towards the wall. Any distance between them felt like too much and he caught her hand. "You didn't remember who I was, and you still came after me?"

Rae looked at their hands and smiled. "I had a feeling. I can't explain it. I went back to my house and I couldn't get your face out of my head. I knew you had to be from before I lost my memory and I thought you might have answers." She pulled him closer and wrapped her arms around his shoulders. "Best decision I ever made, aside from breaking you out of that prison in Jacoby."

She fit perfectly in his arms. He'd missed it and having her there felt so wonderful he doubted his ability to let her go. "Not going to hear me complain, on either count."

Rae slid her hands down his chest to his waist and held him tight. Her yellow and green eyes flashed in the moonlight, and she smirked. "Enlighten me on how you and *Jarrod* got along all this time, considering." Wind whipped her short hair to the side.

"Oh, I have it on good authority that Jarrod is over you."

A distant tickle of Rae's power surged up through the air, rustling the loose hem of his shirt.

She raised an eyebrow. "Over me? Has he met someone?"

Damien gave her a wicked smile. "You could say that. I have a lot to catch you up on."

Rae laughed and glanced down.

He followed her gaze, only to find his feet no longer touching the ground. Air circled beneath them, lifting them higher. The currents of power felt far more refined than he'd known her to control before.

Rae uncurled one arm from his waist and lifted it, meeting the downward reach of a leafy vine. It slithered around her arm down to her shoulder and helped pull the two of them up high enough to clear the wards of the wall and then the wall itself. With the help of the wind, the extension of the tree lowered them to the ground on the other side.

"They should have taught me slower," Rae whispered as the vine retracted back into the canopies of the trees. She sucked in a deeper breath and he could feel her pulse pounding from the exertion.

"I'll say." Damien looked up the expanse of the wall. "You'll have to show me more of the tricks they taught you later. At least something good can come of this."

The barrier blocking the forest's voices fell firmly back into place as his emotions stabilized. His face still felt hot from the tears he shed, but he wasn't ashamed. Instead, the confidence of being able to express them finally left him in control. He looked at Rae's bloodshot eyes, and his heart hammered.

The forest's voices pressed against his awareness, trumpeting Neco's swift approach. Jarrod hung back, letting the wolf barrel towards them on his own.

"Better brace yourself," Damien whispered, forcing himself to let go of her.

She gave him a quizzical glance as he stepped away.

Snapping twigs and brush filled his ears and Rae turned just in time for Neco to hurl himself out of the forest and tackle her onto her back.

Rae laughed, squirming and trying to breathe in between Neco's damp affection as he licked her face.

The giant wolf didn't let up for several minutes, Rae giggling and struggling beneath him. Abruptly, his ears pricked up, and he swung his head around to look at the thief standing six yards away.

Rae struggled to her feet, patting Neco. She didn't notice Jarrod until she lifted her gaze from the wolf. When their eyes met, she stood perfectly still before bolting towards him.

Jarrod's glassy eyes stayed on her as she jumped into his arms. He caught her and spun around once with the momentum before standing still again with her legs wrapped around his waist. With her face buried in his neck, he closed his eyes and whispered to her.

Damien walked to Neco, crouching to scratch his neck, happy to serve as a temporary distraction so Jarrod and Rae could properly greet each other.

When Jarrod finally set her down on her feet, both their faces were wet with tears. He hugged her again, nodding to Damien before releasing her.

Damien couldn't hear most of what they'd said to each other, but Rae's next words were louder.

"I hear you met someone."

Jarrod laughed. "And you'll likely find it just as hilarious as Andi." He led her away from the wall.

"Andi's here?" Rae looked at Damien. "You left that out."

"I had other priorities." Damien shrugged, unable to stop the smile as he followed them. He never thought he'd look forward to getting back to the ship.

Rae reached for Damien's hand and their fingers laced together. "Understandable, I suppose." She leaned against him, and he happily accepted her back into his arms. He kissed her temple, savoring the sweet scent of her hair.

Jarrod rolled his eyes. "I guess after enduring your brother and me, you've earned a little leeway." He coughed. "And possibly the guest quarters all to yourself."

"Your *brother*?" Rae all but shouted. "Wait." She stopped. "You." She pointed at Jarrod. "Are involved with..." She pointed at Damien. "*His* brother?"

Damien grinned. "Well, I was already taken, so he had to go for the next best Lanoret, I suppose."

"Also, the more handsome of the two." Jarrod crossed his arms. "Turns out Hawks get along with Lanorets."

Rae's eyebrows turned up in the middle, and she squeezed Damien's hand. "Oh, how much I've missed."

"And that's just the beginning." Damien returned the pressure on her hand. "But it can wait until we figure out how to get out of here. Might be easier to leave before the auer notice you're gone." It was the middle of the night and the Herald could slip away before the dock masters ever realized what was happening.

Rae's pace slowed, and her eyes lingered on him. "I can't do that."

A cold shiver passed through Damien. "You want to stay?"

"No. Not for long, anyway. But Kynis, as infuriating as he is, is my cousin. And he's like me. He's training me and, even though I disagree with their methods of making me cooperate, I need instruction from someone who understands." She stopped walking, moonlight reflecting off her gaze.

Jarrod remained remarkably silent, patting Neco.

"What were their methods?" Damien pulled away from her. "How did they make you forget?"

"At first they had a cuff in my ear to keep my Art subdued and then they forced me onto this stone bed. They called it Slumber and, when I woke up, I remembered nothing." Sighing, she ran a hand through her uncharacteristically straight hair. "I wasn't exactly being cooperative."

Damien narrowed his eyes. He'd never heard of Slumber before and doubted the council would be forthcoming with information about it. "The auer will probably be furious about me returning your memories and they were already threatening to kick me off the island." He'd be a hypocrite to deny Rae her opportunity to train after abandoning her to learn from Yondé. He paused and glanced at Jarrod, watching the thief's jaw flex. "I wonder if we could reach some kind of compromise. With your answer to their request."

Rae lifted an eyebrow and looked at Jarrod, who frowned.

"Pretty sure my credibility might be in danger. We weren't supposed to go near her. I can see if they'll listen, but I don't have a lot of hope unless I outright agree with their terms."

"Terms?" Rae looked back and forth between the men. "What are you talking about? What do the auer want from a Hawk?"

Damien pursed his lips and met Jarrod's gaze. It wasn't his story to tell.

They resumed walking, and the thief filled Rae in on the rebellion, Corin's role, and Sarth's stance on guild support. He steered around his own precarious position with the rebellion, never mentioning who he was.

He's stalling.

Damien grimaced when Jarrod mentioned Corin's suggestion that he'd been an unintentional inspiration and assumed status as the leader of the rebels. "I'm not meant to be a leader, though. I'd make a mess of it like I do anything. And really, for the rebellion to be successful, it needs the backing of one of the Dannet families. They need a proxiet."

"The rebellion won't get one." Rae shook her head. "Of the four non-ruling Dannet families, only two have possible proxiets since the Martox heir died and the Cortise family never produced one. But the one from House Balarast is too young, and the brothers of House Oraphin are just as corrupt as House Iedrus."

Jarrod raised an eyebrow and exchanged a glance with Damien.

"Didn't know you paid that much attention to Helgathian politics."

Rae shrugged. "Helgath is a tyrannical nation. It's part of the reason I joined the Hawks. Sarth and I had plenty of talks about where the country could do better and where it did the worst. House Iedrus is a blight, and we always talked about what would happen if one of the other Dannet families stepped up. The things Helgath has been doing... You wouldn't believe the stories Sarth has told me. From before she took over the Hawks."

Damien paused, studying her. "Someone else led the Hawks before?"

"Her brother founded them in Veralian."

"Part of your political knowledge is incorrect, though. Sarth doesn't have all the information." Jarrod bumped her shoulder. "The Martox Proxiet isn't dead, and he certainly isn't corrupt."

Rae stopped walking again. "Then there's hope. If Corin is leading the rebellion internally, then he has to recruit the proxiet. Why didn't you start with this?"

Damien snorted before he could hold it in.

Rae glared at Damien and whined. "Tell me what I'm missing."

Damien swallowed the next laugh and looked at Jarrod.

Just tell her.

Jarrod groaned. "I don't *want* to be king."

Rae's mouth fell open. "What?" She looked at Damien, who shrugged.

Gritting his jaw, Jarrod flinched at Rae's expression. "Just try—"

"You're not... You're a Martox?" Her expression turned furious as she stepped towards him. "And you never *told* me?" She punched him hard in the arm.

“Ow!” Jarrod pulled away and rubbed his shoulder while smiling.

Damien smirked. “You deserved that.”

Rae just stared. “You’re going to be king!”

Jarrod rolled his eyes.

“And to think, you could’ve been his queen,” Damien teased.

Rae laughed. “Sounds like he found a new queen.” Her face turned grim. “But what do the auer want with you?”

Jarrod grumbled and begrudgingly filled her in on their desires and terms for the agreement as they resumed walking.

Rae scowled. “Everything will change.”

“Hopefully for the better.” Damien eyed Jarrod. “Assuming the right people back this rebellion. Otherwise, it will fail like all the others. As much as I hate to admit it, the only thing keeping this one going is that they haven’t found me yet and the rebels are keeping things relatively quiet. But Iedrus knows something is going on. They’re already seeking *traitors* in the military and finding them.”

Neco’s ears perked up, and he spun his head back the way they’d come.

“Someone’s coming.” Jarrod held up a hand. “Neco says it’s two auer.”

“Neco says?” Rae wrinkled her nose at Jarrod. “I expect that shit from Damien, but why do you—”

Damien sighed. “Because I—”

"It doesn't matter," Jarrod interrupted. "It's probably your cousin looking for you. Are you sure you don't want to make a run for it?"

"I'm sure." Rae grabbed Damien's hand. "I can talk to them."

Lifting her hand, Damien kissed her knuckles despite the knot in his stomach insisting they should be running. "I trust you."

Rae smiled, but it looked half-hearted. She let go of his hand and turned, jogging off in the direction Neco's ears pointed.

The wolf whined.

"I don't like this." Jarrod sighed.

"Me neither. But we should follow her lead." Damien gestured with a tilt of his head in the direction Rae had gone.

As they approached, voices carried over the breeze.

"What are you doing outside the compound?" A man with white hair spoke to her in Aueric. "It's not safe for you out here."

"I know, I'm sorry." Rae used the same language.

Two male auer stood in front of her. An orb of orange fire swayed in the air above the man who'd spoken, making his vibrant eyes glow. His long tunic hung crooked, like it'd been pulled on quickly.

The second man touched Rae's shoulder, purple eyes intent on her face. "I was worried about you."

Rae shied away from him. "I…"

"What's wrong?" His head shot up at the sound of the undergrowth rustling, eyes finding Damien and Jarrod. He grabbed Rae by the arm and tugged her behind him.

Damien lifted his hands, exposing his empty palms. Locking down his senses, he denied his instinct to use his Art to discover more about their intentions.

"Who are you?" The man sheltering Rae spoke in broken Common.

"Damien Lanoret and Jarrod Martox." He gestured behind him to where Jarrod and Neco had stopped.

Rae put a hand on the auer's shoulder, walking around him. "Maith, it's all right."

Maith turned to who Damien suspected was Kynis and locked eyes with him.

Damien examined the auer betrothed to Rae with narrowed eyes. The man's frame was smaller than Damien's, despite his taller height. His sleeveless tunic exposed lean, muscled arms. Fine, light-grey hair clung to his umber cheeks, sticking to the perspiration from his run in the forest. Even without getting a read on Maithalik's intentions, Damien distrusted him.

"Raeynna." Kynis forced Damien to switch to comprehend Aueric. "You shouldn't be—"

"Please, don't." Rae's tone hardened. "I remember everything."

Kynis's brow furrowed. "How?" He looked at Damien again.

"It doesn't matter. They mean me no harm and I'd like to tell them the same of you."

Jarrod came to stand next to Damien, Neco at his heels.

"We would never hurt you." Maith shook his head. "But are you sure you're feeling well? If your memories have return—"

"It complicates matters." Kynis frowned at Damien. He switched to common effortlessly, speaking it for the first time. "You were told to stay away."

"And I did pretty good with it for a long time. I got impatient. Sorry, I'm only human."

"You knew they were here?" Rae eyed Kynis, also changing her speech to Common. "After everything I told you on the way here, you knew Damien was here and you didn't tell me?" Her voice raised an octave, and it was Maith's turn to frown.

"Raeynna, who is Damien to you?" Maith didn't make the shift, remaining in Aueric, and Damien's mind reeled to keep up. The auer stepped towards her with his hands extended, eyes kind and concerned.

"Please call me Rae."

His hands came to rest on her upper arms.

Damien battled the knot of discomfort tightening in his stomach as Maith touched her.

Taking both Maith's hands, Rae lowered them. "He's..." Her voice trailed off as she looked at Damien, her lips twitching in a smile. "He's the man I love."

Maith's hands withdrew from her and he exchanged a look with Kynis before swallowing and meeting Damien's gaze.

Kynis remained speaking Common, clearly fluent. "Raeynna, you need to come with us back to the compound. The council—"

"We'd actually like to speak with them," Damien interrupted. "There are extenuating circumstances that make it necessary for us to leave Eralas. And I'm sure you understand our desire for Rae to accompany us."

"Impossible." The sphere of flame flickered above Kynis. "They'd never—"

"You don't know what we have to offer." Jarrod spoke for the first time. "We're willing to compromise."

Kynis frowned and looked at Rae. "Shall I assume you also want what they propose?"

Rae nodded. "But we can reach a middle ground now. We need to speak to the council, but until we do, I'd like to continue training *and* be able to see my friends."

"While living at the compound, separate from them." Her cousin angled his chin down.

Damien opened his mouth to protest, but didn't get it out in time.

"While living at the compound." Rae nodded again, and Damien gaped.

Maith kept watching Damien, but added nothing to the conversation.

Kynis looked up, gritting his jaw. "Once a week. For half a day, but never at night."

What is he, her mother? Never at night, she'll never agree—

"Three times."

Kynis scowled. "Twice."

"Fine."

"Wait." Damien took a step forward. "*What* just happened?"

Rae walked away from the auer and they both tensed. She placed her hands on Damien's chest, tilting her chin up. "Compromise. We're lucky to get this much. I can see you for half a day, twice a week, but I need to return to the compound each night."

"For how long?" Damien's chest felt heavy despite the good news. He'd searched for her for months and his glee at reuniting with her dimmed with the regulations.

"Until we can see the council and find a solution." She kept her voice low. "Please." She tilted her head and mouthed the words 'I love you.'

Damien touched her cheek, tracing her jaw. He desperately wanted to ask for more, beg for it. But he nodded. "All right," he whispered, touching his forehead to hers. "But I hate this idea."

Rae smiled and kissed him, her hands sliding up to his neck.

He sank into the affection, ignoring the eyes watching them as he pushed every ounce of his love into the kiss.

Running a hand through his hair, she parted from him, her eyes glassy. "I'll see you tomorrow, all right?"

Damien nodded. "Wait." Slipping the crystal necklace over his head, he lowered it over Rae's. It hung lower than it had on her before, the new chain necessary after he'd found it by the river in Helgath. Covering the crystal where it lay against her sternum, he kissed her forehead. "I'm glad I finally found you."

Rae squeezed his sides. "Thank you for not giving up," she whispered back, her chin quivering for a moment. "I'll see you soon."

He closed his eyes as he took a step back. "Tomorrow."

"Afternoon," Kynis interjected. "I'll see to sending a request to the council, but it might take some time." He met Damien's eyes as he opened them. "And while you are human, as you put it, I recommend you remain patient this time and *wait*."

Neco whined, and Jarrod patted his head. The thief put a hand on Damien's shoulder, which reminded him to breathe.

Rae walked away from them, holding her arms around herself. When Maith draped an arm over her shoulders to lead her to the compound, she looked back at Damien.

Chapter 31

Summer, 2610 R.T.

JARROD PACED IN FRONT OF the porches of the structures provided to house them away from the compound.

Damien stood remarkably still.

"Are you sure it's today?"

How has he stayed so calm after two months of abiding by their damn rules?

Neco watched each change of direction, quirking his head as he sent a flurry of thoughts into Jarrod's mind.

"I'd love to hunt with you, boy, but we're kind of busy today. Later?"

Neco whined and thumped down onto the porch, huffing out a breath that sent a cloud of dust into the air.

The auer had provided each of them a small dwelling outside of the tree-city of Maelei, trying to coax them into submission with soft throw pillows and hand-delivered meals. Regardless, nothing would deter them from taking Rae from the island.

Jarrod would have preferred staying aboard the Herald, but once Andi realized how long they'd need to stay in Eralas, she regretfully informed them she needed to get back to the sea. Summer was a vital season for a trade vessel like the Herald, and she'd already lost too much profit during Eralas's docking games.

"Will you stand still?" Damien held up a hand. "You're going to make me anxious and I need my focus to stop more than just your ká from disrupting mine."

Jarrod stilled his feet, his worry for Corin merging with his nerves about meeting with an elder. Along with Kynis and Maith. "Sorry."

"Corin's fine."

The closer they grew, the more in tune Damien seemed to be with Jarrod's mind. They'd also discovered a clever ability to speak to each other through thoughts, now that Jarrod's mind had been granted a new level of awareness through his connection to Neco.

"Looking forward to seeing Maith again?"

"Gods, I wish I could just punch him in that smug face of his." Damien's jaw flexed. "I don't see why he has to be part of this meeting."

Jarrod pursed his lips. "Me neither. Did Rae mention if she still sees him?"

"He actively pursues the *friendship*, apparently. Plus, he lives next to her. But that's not her fault and I don't blame her for not isolating herself." Damien pushed off the porch railing and stepped into the garden in front of their accommodations.

Little else surrounded the properties far outside the city, limiting the number of stares the two humans received. They remained isolated in the forest, forced to entertain themselves. Damien had morphed a section of the garden into an exercise arena of sorts and Jarrod enjoyed it immensely.

The thief took his frustration out on his body, and they pushed each other's limits. The two men sparred most days of the week, but their relationship flourished beneath the surface. Jarrod confided all his fears in Damien, including the information he'd shared with Corin about his upbringing. No one knew him better than the Rahn'ka, his knowledge rivaling even Rae's.

"The part I don't get..." Damien walked towards the roadway. "Is why we're not meeting at the Sanctum of Law. From what Kynis said, it sounds like this will be too casual for what we're discussing."

Jarrod followed. "Probably means it isn't the final *discussion*."

Damien sighed. "Damn auer. They have to drag everything out."

Jarrod put a hand on his friend's shoulder. "I know you're annoyed with having so little time with her these days, but it will get better. It already has. At least she's safe and remembers who the hells she is."

"And she's probably more stir crazy than me."

"Probably. But she's also learning a lot, right? I wish I could see her in action. I still can't believe this is the same Rae from years ago."

"She's changed in a lot of ways. But she's still the same in a lot more." Damien glanced down the road. "You know she still takes things from me when I'm not paying attention? Sometimes she slips things into my pockets too, for me to find later."

Jarrod laughed. "Sounds like her."

"Have you decided if you'll accept the auer's offer to support your claim to the throne?" Damien broached the question Jarrod had debated many sleepless nights.

"I want to do everything I can to get Rae back, but it can't be entirely about her. This is so much bigger than one person and I have to look at it realistically. It depends on the timeline they want."

Damien nodded. "Sounds like you're considering it, though. Actually challenging Iedrus for the throne."

Jarrod's stomach flopped, and he stared at his damaged signet ring. "I can't keep avoiding it. Corin made a lot of valid points and what kind of man am I to turn my back on my country when it needs me? Especially with the support the auer are offering."

Twigs snapped around the bend and Jarrod lifted his gaze as a carriage rolled around the corner.

"About time," Jarrod muttered as it came to a stop.

The driver hopped down, opening the door for them to step inside, forced to leave the wolf behind.

The trip to the compound took less than an hour and Jarrod watched Damien's nerves escalate to finger tapping on his knee.

After abandoning them alone at the entrance, the carriage continued down the road. Before Jarrod could make a sarcastic remark, the gate of thin beech trees creaked and parted.

"Why do I feel like we'll be lucky to leave here in one piece?" Jarrod stepped forward.

"Because you're intelligent."

The gravel path led directly towards the three structures within, a glittering pond nestled in front of them. Woven foliage grew across the water, twisting together into a decorative tiered fountain at the center. The water bubbled unnaturally in orbs, gurgling out from them to be refilled by invisible threads of the Art.

Kynis waited on the other side, waving his hand to close the entrance after they'd passed through. "It's comforting to see you abide by rules after all. Wasn't sure it was possible."

Damien forced a grin. "I'm full of surprises."

Neither man offered a hand in greeting.

"If you care for Raeynna so much, I would've thought you'd be more amicable to the one who halted her torture in Helgath and brought her somewhere safe. I feel the need to remind you that her interests will always be held in higher regard than yours."

"Forgive me." Damien frowned. "I may have been more understanding if you hadn't erased her memories against her will and betrothed her to another man. But I can see how I'm being the unreasonable one."

Kynis's lips twitched in a shallow smile as he turned to lead them further into the compound. "Her life will be long. The memories we erased were merely a drop in her lifetime. Betrothing her to one whom she won't be forced to watch wither… was something she agreed to. Nothing was forced on her. I hear they still enjoy wine in the evenings."

Damien growled, his shoulders tensing.

Jarrod put a hand on him. "Where is this meeting happening? Are we waiting for others to arrive?"

"You're the last." Kynis led them down stairs made of curved roots.

As they passed under a canopy of branches, Jarrod's gaze landed on a wide-grown table at the center of a garden, surrounded by chairs. The round table seated seven, with four places already occupied.

Rae sat between Maith and the female elder, Paivesh. Next to Maith sat the elder who'd spoken to Jarrod about the proposed arrangement for his kingship.

Kynis took the seat next to Elder Paivesh, gesturing with an open hand to the other seats.

Jarrod sighed and sat next to Kynis, eyeing Rae. Her hair had grown longer, touching her shoulders on one side. She'd braided the other side flat against her head.

She smiled at him before looking at Damien and smoothing the pink fabric of her dress before resting her arms on the table.

Gods, she's beautiful. Jarrod heard the thought in his mind, but it wasn't his own. He glanced at Damien, who watched Rae as he settled into the last chair.

"How are you?" Rae's gentle tone broke the silence.

Jarrod offered her a smile. "All good. Don't you worry about us."

Damien opened his mouth, but Kynis interrupted.

"We best get this discussion started." He wrote on a piece of parchment. "Elders Paivesh and Qualtavik have graciously joined us to serve as the governing voice of any decisions made here today. I've briefed Maithalik on everyone's wishes and I encourage all to remain respectful as we try to reach a mutually beneficial solution."

Damien snorted, but it was quiet enough that probably only Jarrod heard it. *Yeah, right.*

Jarrod centered his thoughts the way they'd practiced, sending Damien a message. *Behave, Lanoret. They hold most of the power here.*

Damien tensed, but pursed his lips and nodded to Kynis.

Elder Paivesh spoke. "Raeynna's training is going well. I believe our original timeline is ahead of schedule and she will be able to leave, quite possibly, sooner than expected."

"And how soon is that, exactly?" Damien sounded hesitantly hopeful.

"About a year."

Rae's eyes widened. "A year?" She opened her mouth to continue, but Maithalik put a hand on hers and whispered something Jarrod couldn't hear. She fell silent, her jaw flexing.

"Proxiet Martox." Elder Qualtavik looked at him. "Have you come to a decision about our offer? Perhaps a compromise can be reached with Elder Paivesh if your choices align with ours."

Choices. A perversion of the word.

"Though, please keep in mind that Raeynna is at a delicate time in her training and compromises can only go so far. Regardless of what decision is made today, her training will need to continue for years to come."

Jarrod took a steadying breath. "If I agree, how long until she can leave with us?"

Kynis cleared his throat. "I have to question your objectives in taking Raeynna with you to the mainland. It's hardly safe for her there, which was already proven by her imprisonment in Helgath."

"I think where I go is my decision." Rae stared at Kynis. "So destinations are irrelevant to this discussion."

Kynis turned to Rae, speaking in Aueric, and Jarrod shot Damien a glance. The Rahn'ka translated, sending the words with only a slight delay into Jarrod's mind in Common.

"You would need an escort. We've discussed this."

Rae's jaw worked, but she kept to Aueric. "I understand the need for an escort. Send him with me if you must, but I have a choice in when and where I go. I am not yours to command."

Kynis took a deep, slow inhale and Rae's eyes narrowed. "Fine. But we still need more time with you and your friend must agree to the council's terms."

Rae looked at Jarrod, and the thief tilted his head as if he didn't understand.

"Humbly," Damien said in Common. "I'd appreciate it if we stuck to a language we all speak. I believe it might be considered rude, otherwise."

Qualtavik nodded, glancing towards the others, while Paivesh looked annoyed.

"Apologies." Kynis's tone sounded less than genuine. "Speaking Aueric may become necessary at times, however, as Maithalik is not fluent in Common. I hope you might forgive future clarifications on his behalf."

"Fine, but can we get back to business?"

"We are prepared to allow Raeynna to leave Eralas after six more months of training, provided Proxiet Martox agrees to our terms. It is the shortest time frame allowable."

"Care to reiterate those terms, so we're clear?" Jarrod leaned back in his seat.

Elder Qualtavik reached into his robes and produced several sheets of parchment. He slid them over the table.

Jarrod's heart thundered in his ears as he looked over the agreement. All fell silent as he read, with the occasional whispering between Maith, Kynis and Rae in Aueric which Damien didn't translate.

The documents dictated what the council had proposed previously, but in greater detail, to the point of designating the exact numbers of troops available. Jarrod would formally challenge House Iedrus for the throne, sometime in the next ten years, and Eralas would send the armies available. House Martox would take control of Helgath and appoint an auer of the council's choosing as Chief Vizier. It also included the details of a longstanding treaty between the two countries, which put Helgath in debt to the people of Eralas, enabling the island country to call for aid.

Ten years doesn't seem so bad. Lots can change in a decade.

As Jarrod finished reading, Elder Qualtavik slid a quill towards him and a small, empty well with a silver knife laid across its rim.

"No pressure, huh?" Jarrod mumbled, looking at Damien.

The Rahn'ka nodded. "Before this compromise can move forward, we need to discuss details about what the next six months might look like. As you said yourself, Kynis. I have been extraordinarily patient."

Kynis eyed Damien. "The visitation schedule may continue, provided Raeynna keeps up her end of the deal."

"Deal?"

Rae brought her hands together before tucking them under the table. She opened her mouth, but Kynis explained first.

"Raeynna can't make an educated decision about her future without knowing all possibilities. It is why her betrothed continues to court her. For her to only spend time with you would be unfair. In allowing you the opportunity to see her, we must also give Maithalik the same courtesy."

Damien's body tightened, and his knuckles popped under the table. "Seriously?" His tone darkened. "If that's the case, the time split between us seems hardly equitable. She sees Maith every day."

"Damien..."

Kynis raised a hand, cutting Rae off and she gritted her teeth. "Those points are not yours to argue. Raeynna agreed and I—"

"Could I *please* speak for myself?" Rae's suddenly sharp tone made Jarrod quirk an eyebrow.

The elders exchanged a glance, and Maith's frown deepened.

"I think Damien makes a valid point with the unequal share of time. I am happy to continue our arrangement, but I want to see Damien more than twice a week."

Maithalik whispered something into Rae's ear and she nodded.

Kynis huffed a breath. "Seeing as it hasn't hindered your progress, I am willing to increase frequency. How does an entire day, plus three half-days per week sound?"

Paivesh quirked an eyebrow. "That seems overly generous to me. If we agree on such lenient terms, I insist on a probationary period to ensure Raeynna's training does not suffer."

Rae nodded and looked at Damien. "Damien?" She rolled her lips together.

Jarrod's heart squeezed, and he sent a message to his friend. *She's worried you'll leave.*

Damien glanced sideways at him, chewing his bottom lip. *She's crazy. I'm just tired of all this auer bullshit.* With a deep inhale, Damien gave a slow nod. "Agreed."

Rae smiled, clutching the crystal pendant around her neck.

"Have we reached an accord, then?" Elder Qualtavik looked from Rae to Damien and finally to Jarrod.

What do you think? Jarrod flipped back through the pages as if still contemplating them while he spoke silently to his friend.

I think the auer have us exactly where they want us. But this is your decision. Like you said, this is way bigger than Rae and me.

Jarrod sighed, lifting his gaze and meeting Rae's hard stare.

She shook her head. "Don't do it just for me. Six months is nothing."

Kynis cast a sideways look at Rae, but she didn't return it.

Jarrod had talked in depth with Damien about the future and what it could look like for them. Ten years gave him a lot of time to consider his options. Take his time making sure everything lined up the way he needed it to for minimal conflict. Particularly with his family.

He thought of Corin and imagined the captain at his side through all of it.

If he waits another half a year for me.

Picking up the provided blade, he cut down his left forearm without flinching. Picking up the empty inkwell, he held it against his skin as his blood dribbled into it.

Maithalik offered him a handkerchief which he wrapped once around his arm.

Dipping the quill into his blood, he signed his name at the end of the document.

"Excellent." Qualtavik reached across Damien to gather up the documents.

Jarrod watched the parchment disappear beneath the table, and his chest weighed heavily.

Ten years.

Plenty of time to get used to the idea.

Paivesh smiled. "As a gesture of goodwill, Raeynna is welcome to return with you to your provided dwellings for the rest of the day. Her training can resume tomorrow."

Kynis frowned, clearly not having been consulted, and turned towards Rae, who smiled. "I'm assuming you'd like that?"

Maith muttered something in Aueric.

Rae nodded at Kynis. "I'll make up for it tomorrow."

Chapter 32

Rae laughed, and it made Damien's heart lighten. She pushed her bare toes into the white sand, waves licking the beach near her feet. "I'm surprised it took you so long to notice it was missing."

"It's not like I check my pockets obsessively. I naively assume that things I put there will stay there."

"Naive is right." Rae leaned on his shoulder. Her hair reached past her shoulders now, giving her more to braid. "That's what you get for being with a thief."

Damien lifted her hand to his lips, kissing her warm skin. "A thief being courted by two men."

Rae scoffed, draping her legs over his lap. "Maith is only a friend. And I'm pretty sure you have the sweeter end of the deal. Can you imagine how frustrating it might be, competing with you? Plus, I don't steal from him, and that should tell you everything you need to know."

He snorted and pulled her closer. "Is it because he's not as handsome as me?"

Rae chuckled. "Although it's true, it's not the most important factor when *considering a future husband*." She mocked Kynis's tone.

Damien's heart pounded at the words, his mind jumping to places he'd tried to control. In a strange way, being apart from Rae made him love her more. Each moment together far sweeter than the last.

"So, what is the most important factor?" He nuzzled the side of her head and lowered his voice. "Am I husband material yet?"

Rae tilted her chin up and kissed his neck. "Closest I've seen."

Damien raised an eyebrow, the pit of his stomach whirling. "Having a change of heart about marriage? I've been wanting to—"

Rae lifted a finger to his lips. "Not really. Not yet, anyway. But it doesn't mean I don't love you. It's just not something I've considered for myself."

A little stab of what felt like physical pain manifested in his gut, but he smiled instead of letting it show. "I know. And it's all right. I love you, too, no matter what. I just hope someone else doesn't come along and change your mind before I can."

Rae met his gaze and grinned. "Sounds like an impossible feat, but maybe the auer can find me more suitors."

He whined playfully, grasping the opportunity to change the subject. "I don't think I could stand to share you any more than I already do. It's already hard enough waking up alone each morning. Neco doesn't even cuddle with me anymore. He likes Jarrod better."

Rae laughed, touching his chest. "You don't share me as it is. They just want you to think that. Only four more months and then you can wake up next to me every morning."

"Until you have to return for more training."

"That's only every five years, for a few months. We'll survive, won't we?" She looked up at him, uncertainty touching her tone.

"Of course." Sudden guilt made him regret the teasing. "With everything that's happened, *we* can survive anything." He brushed his lips against hers in a slow, tender kiss.

Rae returned the affection and pushed him back into the sand. Her necklace trailed over his chest as she kissed him. When she pulled away, her hand teased near the top of his pants.

Damien's pulse quickened.

"Could you two get a damned room?" Jarrod called from down the beach, Neco racing ahead of the thief.

Still laughing, Rae buried her face in Damien's chest just in time for the wolf to kick up sand around them.

Damien tried to protect his face in her hair as Neco assaulted them with licks.

The wolf paused, ears perking up before he darted back towards Jarrod.

Rae sat up on Damien's hips and he dared to open his eyes. The way she sat threatened all sense of self-control, despite the unexpected company.

"Do you mind?" Damien looked at Jarrod, pushing himself up on his elbows, but making no move to displace Rae. "We're enjoying ourselves here."

"Oh, I can see that. And I'm enjoying my walk. Or at least, I was."

"So walk the other way. You're not king yet."

Jarrod laughed, passing by them with Neco at his heels. "Lucky for you. Wait until I'm out of earshot at least."

Rae grinned mischievously and rocked her hips.

Damien's body reacted instantly, and he choked trying to hold in the gasp on his lips.

"Not out of earshot yet!"

Rae giggled.

"You're awful," Damien whispered with a grin, reaching out to play against her waist. He sat up and pulled her into him, kissing along her neck. When the call of a hawk echoed down the beach, his first instinct was to ignore it, until it came again.

Rae sat up, gazing at Jarrod with a blank expression.

Damien followed her line of sight, and when Rae stood, he did too.

Jarrod stood stone still, watching the hawk approach him.

Tension rose in the air, and Damien gulped, squeezing Rae's hand. "Is that Liala?"

Chapter 33

Four days prior...

CORIN HATED HIS REQUIRED DUTIES in Lazuli the first time he served there and this time was no exception. The beginning of his disillusionment with Helgathian military practices started when he was stationed in the prison at nineteen and, if anything, the conditions had grown worse.

He maintained the bare minimum of what they expected of him, often using his rank to escape the mundane. As he always did, he evaluated the local troops, pinpointing those who shared in his distaste for the monarchy. The old routine of seeding the rebellion among the soldiers came back to him quickly, even though he constantly thought about Jarrod. He felt like a boy again, haunted by memories of the handsome face of the Martox proxiet.

Jarrod had been gone for months before Corin felt confident in the men and women he'd propositioned with promises the rebellion could fulfill. The lure of genuine freedom like Damien's infected the ranks, but didn't eliminate the need for vetting new recruits.

He taught only Breta, the young woman he'd recruited first, the method the rebellion used for sending messages between military outposts. A secret pattern within general disturbance reports widely distributed among the military.

Corin didn't mention Jarrod or Damien to any of them. The rumor of a proxiet joining the rebellion had already spread fast enough through Ermel, who couldn't keep his big trap shut. It was only a matter of time before someone of consequence heard about it. Fortunately, while Ermel was talkative with those he believed his allies... if he was arrested, they'd never get a thing out of him.

Waiting for the arrival of the fresh recruits for a secret rendezvous had Corin's nerves on edge. He couldn't explain the uneasy curl in his stomach. Trying to find what comfort he could, he showered Liala with the attention he wished he could give Jarrod.

She cooed, gobbling down the strip of rabbit meat he'd given her. Normally Corin wouldn't keep her so close, but his paranoia prompted the desire. As his mind wandered, the hawk nipped his fingers.

"Ow." Corin chuckled, shaking his hand as Liala tilted her head back to consume her prize. "Glad I'm not as impatient as you. Otherwise, I would've already sailed to Eralas weeks ago."

The hawk tilted her head, clicking her beak.

"And now I'm talking to a bird." Corin sighed, dropping his chin into his hands. "Gods, Jarrod would think I've completely lost it."

Liala fluttered her wings at the name, sidestepping on the log.

"What do you suppose is taking him so long?" Corin's imagination treated him to visions of Helgath sinking Captain Trace's ship. Or worse, capturing his brother and lover in one fell swoop. "But I would've heard about something like that happening."

However, if the auer had something to do with their disappearance, he'd never hear about it, left to wonder what happened for the rest of eternity.

Well, now I'm just being dramatic.

The only thing that kept him from sending Liala to Jarrod just for peace of mind was the impending danger he was in. He hadn't stayed in one place for so long since the rebellion started gaining ground.

Looking at the western horizon, the daunting silhouette of the prison loomed against the darkening sky.

The heat of late summer made his armor stick to his skin, and he stood from where he'd sat on a fallen tree. Maybe moving would help to calm his nerves. If the feeling continued to build, he considered turning and walking away.

I could find a ship and be halfway to Eralas before anyone realizes I'm gone. But what would that do to the rebellion?

The forest fell into night, surrounding him with the jubilant chirps of crickets, and he felt remarkably isolated. Surrounding the small pine clearing he'd chosen for the meeting, the dark shapes of the trees stretched towards the sky. The moon cast enough light to see by, which was fortunate because he refused to risk a fire.

In front of him, the needles crunched under an approaching boot, and Corin drew his sword.

"Whoa, Cap." Breta outstretched her hands, palms out. "Just me."

Corin sighed and lowered his sword, but didn't sheath it. "Sorry. I'm a little jumpy tonight."

"Jumpier than a field mouse?" She gave him a cheeky smile at mimicking the phrase he used too often. "That's understandable, all things considered. When are the others supposed to arrive?"

"Soon." Corin eyed the darkness behind her. The continued commotion of the crickets to the east of the clearing brought some comfort. All recruits would arrive from the same direction Breta had.

Breta's gaze glided behind him to Liala, who happily ate the rest of her dinner.

The sound of the rabbit's flesh tearing filled the air between them instead of words.

Frez and Yeoman arrived together but assured Corin it had been accidental when they met at the second marker in the woods. Both as young as he was when he joined the military, the guilt of recruiting a pair of sixteen-year-olds weighed heavily on his conscience.

Though the rebellion could hardly afford to be picky.

"What's with the bird?" Frez jutted his chin behind Corin.

"She's mine. Don't worry about it."

"I didn't realize the rebellion used hawks. Ain't that a criminal guild in Mirage?" Yeoman raised his eyebrows. "Say, they'd probably be pretty good allies, wouldn't they?"

Corin tried not to roll his eyes, keeping his face stern. "Don't get ahead of yourself, kid. Other things you should worry about first."

Yeoman frowned and quiet settled again before the last of the recruits showed up.

Landen lumbered into the clearing, wiping sweat from his brow and cursing. He wasn't the most ideal recruit, being older and chubbier than most soldiers, but Corin thought his general grumbling about his postings meant he'd be sympathetic.

"All here then? Sorry I'm late."

"Fine." Now that they'd all arrived, Corin hoped the feeling of anxiety would leave, but it remained strong. "Let's get to business. You know each other now, but don't get too friendly. I'll be arranging your transfers in the morning."

"Transfers?" Frez frowned.

"Best way to spread word of the rebellion. Plus, being out of your comfort zone will make you appropriately vigilant."

"So how are we's supposed to recognize other rebels?" Landen coughed.

"You don't. You use your instincts to find them. If you're wrong, you don't take anyone down with you. Prove your loyalty by spreading rumors and word to the public. Find support and those sympathetic, they might save your life later. A rebel leader will find you, if you do the job right, and make the next move clear."

"What is the next move?" Yeoman crossed his arms.

Corin narrowed his eyes, and the rest of the recruits looked at the red-headed teenager.

He shifted under the gaze. "I mean, I ain't the only one thinking it, how's this whole rebellion supposed to play out?"

"You're thinkin' too much." Breta smacked him in the chest with the back of her armored hand. "No time for that with what's at stake. We just fight until it's over."

Corin locked away his smile, happy he'd trusted her the most. She understood the cause far deeper than the others. Her family had suffered greatly at the hands of the monarchy already.

"I don't think so." Frez frowned at Breta as the crickets behind them stopped chirping. "I think it's a completely..."

"Shhh." Corin pushed authority into the sound. The soldiers immediately obeyed and looked at him.

The darkness surrounding them hung silently in the night, with only the wind brushing through the trees. Looming shadows made it impossible to see more than a few yards into the forest.

Corin opened his mouth, prepared to tell the recruits to leave when Landen threw himself to the ground with a heavy exhale.

The captain's hand tightened on the hilt of his sword, but before he could raise it from the relaxed position, his shoulder jolted back with searing pain.

He dropped his blade.

His eyes fell on an arrow shaft protruding from the opening between the armor on his right shoulder. Gritting his jaw, he cursed and fumbled with his left arm to recover his sword.

Liala squawked, feathers ruffling as she spread her wings wide.

Blood oozed down Corin's arm, adding a new stickiness between his skin and armor. Shouts rumbled from the woods.

The other recruits drew their swords as the shadows of the trees turned to those of men.

Corin spun towards the scuffling hawk, reaching with his injured arm. Blood flecked from his fingertips, marring the hawk's clean feathers. His shoulder screamed as he lifted Liala.

"Jarrod. Go to Jarrod." With no time to write a note, Corin had to hope sending her would be word enough.

Frantic in the descending chaos, Liala beat her wings and took to the sky as Corin lifted his arm. She screeched as she rose above the trees, an arrow whizzing past her, barely missing.

Corin yelled as his muscles gave out, the useless arm collapsed against his side.

Turning, he witnessed Frez hit the ground, tackled by several Helgathian soldiers, while Breta fought off another pair on her own. Yeoman had vanished, and Landen still lay on the ground with his hands covering his neck.

With a growl, Corin lunged towards the soldier who'd betrayed him. He didn't reach Landen before being pulled off his feet from behind. He swung his sword over his head with his left hand but it clanked against metal instead of finding flesh. Then it was torn from his grip.

His vision flashed white as something solid struck his head.

Blackness promptly followed.

The story continues with...

www. Pantracia.com

JARROD WANTED A CONNECTION TO HIS WOLF, BUT THE WOLF WANTED MORE.

After Corin is arrested for treason, Jarrod rushes to the mainland hoping to save his beloved from the inevitable noose. He returns to Mirage, seeking help from the Ashen Hawks. But it may not be enough, and his true power lies much deeper within himself.

Back in the Ashen Hawks' headquarters, Damien notices the bond he created between Jarrod and their wolf companion could be mutating. While trying to find his brother, he faces the consequences of his desertion, which reach farther than he thought.

Holding dire news from Mirage, Rae sets off on her own journey, intent on sparing Damien's parents from an undeserved fate.

The future of Helgath hangs in the balance, civil war erupting under a corrupt king. Bonds stretch to their limits, and when they fail, blood will spill.

Heart of the Wolf is Part 3 of *A Rebel's Crucible* and Book 6 in the *Pantracia Chronicles.*

Made in the USA
Monee, IL
12 March 2024

54373226R00260